# THE DOCTOR'S SECRET BRIDE

ANA E ROSS

Edited by Jane Haertel
Cover Design by Niina Cord
Formatted by Ironhorse Formatting

ISBN: 0-9883679-1-2
ISBN-13: 978-0-9883679-1-3

# DEDICATION

To my lovely daughter, *Nicoya*, whose childhood
precociousness and beauty inspired the creation of the charact
Precious.  May you forever remain sweet as honey.

# PROLOGUE

Michelle placed her order at the counter and was just about to sit down at a corner table in Mama Lola's, her favorite diner on Elm Street, when she heard someone call her name.

"Michelle," the familiar voice said again.

Michelle looked around and immediately burst into a wide grin when she saw the aged, but easily recognizable face smiling back at her. "Mrs. Hayes." She took the few steps toward the booth the woman occupied. "Oh my gosh," she cried, bending down to give her a big hug and kisses on both cheeks. "I haven't seen you in ages."

"Not since you and Robert moved out of the neighborhood—say about twelve years ago? But I would recognize you anywhere, my child. You look just like your mother. She was a beautiful woman."

Michelle smiled at the mention of her mother. "Lucky me, huh? So how have you been?" she asked as pleasant memories of Mrs. Hayes rose to the surface of her mind.

"The Lord has been good to me. I can't complain. I've already eaten, but I'd love it if you'd sit with me while you eat." Mrs. Hayes pointed to the seat on the opposite side of the table.

Michelle glanced warily at the newspaper tucked under her arm. It was her lunch hour from the temp job she was currently working, and she'd intended to browse through the Want Ads over her favorite turkey sandwich. She usually packed her lunch to save money, but the battery in her alarm clock died during the night, and by the time she rolled out of bed, she barely had enough time to make the bus this morning. Since Mama Lola's was in her old neighborhood and in walking distance from her job, she'd decided to eat here, just for old times sake.

"You in a hurry?" Mrs. Hayes asked at her hesitance.

Michelle stared into the gentle brown eyes. How could she refuse this kind old lady who'd taken such good care of her since she was a baby? Mrs. Hayes had kept her and Robert fed and warm many winter nights when their father was nowhere to be found. "No. I'm in no hurry." She scooted onto the vinyl seat, dropped her bag and newspaper down beside her, and placed her bottle of water on the table.

Mrs. Hayes' face relaxed and she leaned back into the seat.

"What are you doing in Manchester?" Michelle asked. "Last I heard you'd sold your house and moved out of town."

Mrs. Hayes took a sip of her iced tea. "I'm visiting a sick friend. You remember Thelma Parson? She lived in the apartment house behind mine."

Michelle thought for a moment. "Oh yeah. She had that stupid dog that wouldn't stop barking, and a bunch of cats that kept having kittens."

Mrs. Hayes laughed. "Yes. *That* Thelma. She had a hip replacement recently, so I stopped by to spend some time with her. Poor thing; she has no one to help her out. Since I was already in the neighborhood, I decided to stop by to see Lola, but she's away on vacation." Her eyes lit up with curiosity. "So what have you been up to since the last time I saw you?" She glanced at Michelle's left hand lying on the table. "I see you haven't been snatched up by some lucky young man, yet."

Michelle chuckled. "No, not yet. I guess I'm too picky. I'll probably end up as sad and alone as Thelma and hope that some dear friend comes by to pay me a visit in my old age."

"I doubt that very much. Besides, there's nothing wrong with being picky. You should never settle. When you make that kind of commitment, you want to make sure it has a chance to last forever."

Forever was one thing Michelle didn't want to think about. It was hard enough making it from one day to the next, or more specifically from morning to night.

The waitress brought over her sandwich, and Michelle immediately bit into it. She didn't have much time before she had to be back behind her desk at Reagan Electronics.

"How is Robert?" Mrs. Hayes asked when Michelle put down her half-eaten sandwich to take a sip from her water bottle.

"He's well. He has a dental practice in Boston, and it's really flourishing," she said with pride bubbling in her heart for her big brother.

"Good for him. I always knew he'd make something grand of himself. What about you, Michelle? What have you done with your life?"

Michelle took a deep breath. She'd done something well with her life, too, but it had been ripped away from her. *Stolen.* "I'm doing okay," she lied. No need to burden the old woman with her sad life's story.

"What is okay?" Mrs. Hayes reached across the table and covered Michelle's hand with hers.

Michelle glanced at the pale freckled hand against her darker one. Mrs. Hayes had known her from the moment she was pulled from her mother's womb. The woman knew her, maybe better than she knew herself. "*Okay* means I'm not doing as well as I should be. I finished college, landed a great job, but lost it due to the failing economy. I haven't been able to find another one. I've been temping ever since."

"Oh dear," Mrs. Hayes mumbled, patting her hand. "What kind of job are you looking for?"

"I'm trained in Human Resources, but anything permanent would do. What?" she added, eying her friend with hope. "Do you know somebody who's hiring? You used to have a lot of clout back in the day when you operated your cleaning business. You got a lot of kids in our neighborhood summer jobs with some of the most prominent companies in Manchester. Some of them still work for those companies."

Mrs. Hayes shook her head sadly. "I'm afraid I've lost my clout, my dear. With takeovers, sellouts, buyouts, and the likes, I don't know who owns what anymore."

Michelle tried to smile through her disappointment. She should know better than to hope. Hope had ceased being her friend since that fateful night, two years ago. Or maybe she'd never met Hope. After all, her mother had died giving birth to her. Seems like she'd been cursed since the day she was born.

"Cheer up, my child," Mrs. Hayes said, placing her hand against Michelle's cheek. "The Lord isn't done with you. Maybe He hasn't even begun working on you, yet. Who knows?"

# CHAPTER ONE

*One month later:*

Erik frowned as a young woman hopped out of the cab that had just pulled into his driveway. His frown deepened when she hauled a suitcase out behind her, raised her hand to shade her eyes against the noonday sun, and gazed speculatively up at his house.

"They've got to be kidding me," he muttered. He'd distinctly requested an older woman—no younger than fifty, who had experience taking care of young children.

Someone from the agency had called to say that the scheduled candidate had canceled due to a family emergency, and that a Michelle Carter would be coming instead. Was it okay if she brought her credentials with her?

Although the agencies conducted investigations, Erik ran his own background checks before interviewing potential employees. He could never be too careful when it came to the welfare of his only child. Today, he'd trusted Ready Nanny Agency because there was no time to check, and look what they sent him—a girl barely out of her teens.

Her hair was cut too short for a woman. She was too skinny and too tall. Her jeans were too tight, and the seductive sway of her hips was unequivocally too provocative. Despite his objections, and the fact that he handled women's naked bodies on a daily basis, Erik felt a poignant stir in his loins.

After ten years as a gynecologist, he'd learned to channel his sexual energy elsewhere when he walked into an examination room to see a patient. It was all professional. The woman walking up his driveway wasn't his patient, and the images running through his head were anything but professional. They involved tangled sheets, soft sighs, harsh moans, and musky odor rising from damp smooth skin...

Shaking the libidinous thoughts from his head, Erik tightened his jaws and moved away from the window. He'd been without a woman for too long. Yes, that was definitely his problem. It had been two years since his wife's death, and since that fateful night, he hadn't looked at any woman twice, much less bedded one.

At the chime of the doorbell, Erik stepped into the hallway and caught up with his housekeeper. "Mrs. Hayes, tell the young lady that I was called to the hospital, and—um—that I will contact the agency with a new date for an interview."

"Yes, Doctor." Mrs. Hayes threw him a speculative stare at the blatant lie.

Erik marched down the hall to his study. He closed the door, dropped into the chair behind his desk, and stared at the painting of his wife hanging above the fireplace.

As usual, he tried to shift his sexual interest in other women to memories of lovemaking with her, but as hard as he tried, there was no shifting for him today. As he stared into his wife's brown eyes, the only images Erik saw were those of the young girl sashaying up his driveway.

"Come in," he responded to the knock on the door. "Is she gone?" he asked when it opened behind him.

"No. *She* isn't gone. *She's* still here."

Erik swiveled around at the sultry voice. His heart did a triple take, and lust like he'd never experienced crawled through his belly and settled into his groin. At a loss for words, he took a hard, close-up look at the vibrant embodiment of temptation heading his way.

Her facial bones were delicately carved under her dark brown velvety skin. Her short crop of raven hair glittered like strands of black silk in the slivers of afternoon sun streaming through the glass door. Long lashes accentuated a pair of fiery, obsidian eyes, and her lips, full and provocative under a thin layer of gloss, looked as if they'd just been thoroughly kissed.

She was the most enchanting woman Erik had ever seen.

Unwittingly, his gaze fell to the ripe swell of her breasts pushing against the stretchy material of her blouse. Was she even wearing a bra? His gut wrenched at the thought.

"You must be Dr. LaCrosse," she said, breaking the silence and offering him a tantalizing smile.

Her unfamiliar, yet highly stimulating perfume wrapped around him. He grew harder. Restless.

She was probably about five feet, ten inches tall, he thought, suddenly feeling uncomfortable sitting in her presence. But if he dared stand up, she would have a full view of his unsolicited arousal. He cleared his throat. "Yes, I'm Dr. LaCrosse, and you are—"

"Michelle. Michelle Carter." She held out her hand.

Her wrist was delicate, her fingers long and slender, the nails red. *Channel. Channel your thoughts.* Erik's hands curled around the arms of his chair. "Apparently my housekeeper neglected to relay my message to you, Ms. Carter."

She dropped her hand. "Actually, she did relay your message, but I'd already seen you through the window when my cab pulled up."

He held her gaze, not knowing whether to smile or scowl at her pursed lips. It obviously gave her great satisfaction to have caught him in a lie. "Ms. Carter," he began in an attempt to repair the self-inflicted damage to his character, "the minute I saw you step out of the cab, I knew you were wrong for the job. For one thing, you're far too young. I specifically requested someone older who has experience taking care of young children."

Feeling the tension in his groin loosen a bit, Erik stood up and stepped from behind the desk. He stared down at her, still appalled that she'd come to an interview dressed so unprofessionally. "You," he continued, "definitely do not fit that description."

With considerable effort, Michelle suppressed the sensual jitters the deep sexy voice of the extremely tall man was causing inside her. Dressed in no smaller than size fifteen loafers, tan slacks, and a white Polo shirt, his olive-toned body was lean, hard, and athletic. He was classically handsome, with a nice straight nose and a rich crop of curly dark-brown hair. His smoky grey eyes, speckled with an array of golden hues, were as sharp as they were eccentric.

*McDreamy* and *McSteamy* rolled up into one. Move over boys. This doctor was so fine, he made her leak.

Michelle licked her lips as an inexplicable sense of fear washed over her. She'd had to deal with a few arrogant men in her past, but this one made her feel quite susceptible. If she were smart, she would walk out of this room, out of this cold luxurious country mansion and whistle her cab back to Manchester.

But she wasn't smart. She was desperate. She needed this job. She needed a roof over her head and a fresh start.

"Well, have you nothing to say, Ms. Carter? You barged into my study after you were asked to leave. I explain why you don't qualify for the job, and all you can do is stand there gawking at me?"

From the way he assessed her with his eyes, Michelle knew he disapproved of her attire as much as her age. Ready Nanny Agency had warned her that the fastidious widower had requested someone much older. Since they were fresh out of antiquated nannies and would probably lose him as a client anyway, they wanted to know if she was up to trying her luck.

*Heck, yes.* She had nothing to lose.

Michelle took a deep breath. When the agency had called her as a backup, she was in a laundromat in downtown Manchester. With a ninety-minute window of time, she barely had enough to finish the last wash, pull the half-dried load from the dryer, catch the city bus back to her apartment, throw her clothes and a few other personal items into a suitcase—since she was determined to land this job and move in tonight—and catch a cab to 204 Jefferson Drive in the upscale town of Amherst, New Hampshire.

If she told him all that, he would know she was desperate. That wasn't happening. Not today, and definitely not after the way he was looking down his nose at her. She clutched the folder with her credentials to her chest. "Dr. LaCrosse, if I were you and saw me walking up my driveway dressed like this to interview for a nanny position for my seven-year-old daughter, I would have the same reaction."

"Is that so, Ms. Carter? Then perhaps you can explain your attire?" His eyes lingered on her chest then wandered down to her waistline before he looked away.

Michelle didn't miss the faint twitch of his jaws or the quick sparkle of interest in his eyes. Beneath that grim exterior, when all was said and done, he was after all, just a man. He found her attractive, maybe even sexy, but Dr. Rich Boy would shoot himself in the groin before admitting he wanted her, a girl from the wrong side of the river.

The moment she walked into the room, Michelle had figured out his type from the painting of the curvy, longhaired redhead over the marble fireplace.

Truth is, she intended to wear her white cotton jacket over her blouse, but in her haste to get here, she'd forgotten it hanging on her bedroom door. Everything else in her suitcase was wrinkled or damp. This was the best she could do.

She had twelve dollars and a penny in her pocket, and she could really use a home-cooked meal tonight. From the aromas coming from the kitchen when she walked through the elaborate foyer, she predicted it would be delicious.

But as desperate as she was, his arrogance was ticking her off. Since he'd blatantly lied about being at home for the interview, Michelle didn't think he deserved the truth.

"Ms. Carter." The impatient edge in his voice pulled her back on track.

"Dr. LaCrosse, I'll assume you were expecting a model of

Mrs. Doubtfire or Nanny McPhee, but quite seriously, sir, those kinds of nannies don't exist anymore. They are long defunct. Like... gone," she said with a flourishing swipe of her wrist. "I could have arrived, dressed like a matron from the middle ages just to appease your visual palate, but tomorrow morning, I would have rolled out of bed, pulled on my jeans and tank top then we'd be right back to square one."

He grimaced. "Just as I predicted, Ms. Carter. You're young, inexperienced, and unmistakably uncouth."

"Just because I'm young doesn't mean I'm inexperienced, Doctor." She wasn't touching uncouth. "I assure you, I am highly qualified for the job. I may not be as old as you wish, but I have lots of experience with young children. My credentials will attest to that." She held the folder out to him.

His eyes narrowed to amber slits as he continued to stare her down, obviously trying to intimidate her. But Michelle wasn't easily intimidated. She'd grown up in the toughest part of Manchester. She had to learn to hold her ground at an early age, and so she held his gaze and the folder out until he took it from her.

He walked to the sliders and stood with his back to her. As he flipped through the pages, Michelle took the opportunity to admire his broad shoulders, narrow waistline and trim hips. She salivated at the thought of running her fingers down his naked body, cupping his delectable buns in her hands...

Michelle gave herself a mental slap in the head. She and the doctor were from two different worlds, and she doubted he'd ever cross that social line. The man had refused to shake her hand. *And he'd called her uncouth.* Besides, a man as handsome and sexy as Dr. Erik LaCrosse wouldn't be unattached. She was sure he had some lucky *couth* babe to slake his noble passion. Anyway, she wasn't his type, and *he* certainly wasn't hers. *Uh-uh. Too uptight.*

He turned. "You've done a lot of babysitting, Ms. Carter, and your current involvement with the youth center in Manchester is quite impressive. But caring for children on a full-time basis is very different from spending a few hours at a time with them.

It's a huge responsibility. You're always on call."

*Was that a maybe?* "I understand." Michelle spoke hastily, hoping to eradicate all his doubts about her capabilities to take care of his daughter. "I love kids, Dr. LaCrosse. Mostly what they need is love. I give them all I have, and for some reason they love me back," she added humbly, thinking of the kids who flock to her when she walked through the doors of the youth center. "If you give me a chance, I bet you that black shiny Jaguar in the driveway I'd be the best thing that ever happened to your daughter."

He tilted his head and continued to stare at her, his expression shrouded, unreadable. Finally, he strolled to his desk and set the folder down. "Excuse my manners. Please have a seat." He gestured toward the sofa behind her. His face still gave no clue as to whether she was in or out.

Eyeing him skeptically, Michelle slid unto the smooth leather sofa.

"Make yourself comfortable, Ms. Carter. I will be back momentarily."

Erik headed for the kitchen. Mrs. Hayes always carried out his requests, as dubious as they may seem to her. She was loyal, dependable, and more like a member of the family than a housekeeper. Nobody got past her without permission. So why had she let Michelle Carter into the house when he'd asked her to send her away?

She was standing at the island in the kitchen, rolling dough for the bread she would be serving with a beef stew for dinner. "I though I asked you to get rid of her, Mrs. Hayes," he said in a diplomatic tone he knew was wasted on her.

Mrs. Hayes didn't even look up from her kneading. "Oh, Dr., Michelle's as harmless as—"

"You know her?"

"Since the day she was born."

"You know her." This was more a confirmation than a question.

Mrs. Hayes set down her rolling pin and peeked up at him, an affectionate smile on her face. "We lived on the same street in Manchester. Michelle's mother died while giving birth to her. Life hadn't been too good for her and her older brother when they were little, but according to Michelle, Robert now has a successful orthodontist practice." Mrs. Hayes shook her head and sighed. "I reckon Michelle is here because she hasn't quite found her way yet. Who knows, maybe she'll find it in this big lonely house."

"Did you know she was coming for the interview today?" he asked, holding her gaze.

She hesitated before answering. "No. I did not know Michelle was coming for the interview today." She took a pinch of salt from a bowl and sprinkled it over the dough before resuming her kneading.

Erik leaned against the island. The fact that Michelle had grown up without a mother gave her something in common with Precious. She might be able to connect with his daughter in a way Holly hadn't, he speculated, seeing Michelle in a different light now that Mrs. Hayes, his trusted housekeeper, actually knew her and had vouched for her.

In his book, a personal recommendation outweighed an impressive resume any day. Michelle had both. She'd earned a four-year degree in three years with a double major in Human Resources and Business Administration. She'd worked in customer relations until she lost her job due to the downturn in the economy. According to her resume, she'd moved to South Carolina where she worked as a temp for about a year before returning to the area.

Times were tough. She quite clearly needed a break as Mrs. Hayes had pointed out. The girl was desperate, but even so, she had managed to preserve her dignity when faced with his arrogance and skepticism. He liked her tenacity. It showed character.

"But she's so young," he voiced his thoughts aloud. "Too young."

Mrs. Hayes rolled up the dough and placed it into a greased bowl. She turned the ball of dough once then covered it with a piece of plastic wrap. Her task complete, she gazed up at him. "If you'll pardon my frankness, Sir, Michelle is just what that sweet child needs to perk up her little spirit. Little Precious doesn't need an old woman huffing and puffing over her. She needs a young girl with life in her bones. Don't make them pay for Holly's happiness." She reached up and touched a cool hand to Erik's cheek. "Give Michelle a chance. If she doesn't work out, I'll give her the boot, myself." She walked over to the stove and began stirring her pot of stew.

Erik raked his fingers through his hair. He was either a glutton for punishment or he was simply insane to consider hiring Michelle Carter. She wasn't the kind of woman a man could easily ignore. He'd spent a mere fifteen minutes with the girl and she was already wreaking havoc on his world. No woman had ever had that kind of effect on him. Not even his wife.

But, he had to consider his daughter's wellbeing.

Her former nanny had been wonderful in helping Precious cope with her mother's death for the past fifteen months. Then a month ago, Holly married and moved away to start her own family, taking Precious' smile and spirit with her.

Erik longed to see his daughter's eyes light up with laughter again. He longed to hear her squeals of delight ringing through the house and her feet clambering up and down the stairs. All she'd been doing lately was sulking in her room as if she'd lost her mother all over again. He was tired of the endless barrage of applicants coming to his house, only to be disappointed when Precious gave them the cold shoulder, time and time again.

Mrs. Hayes thought Michelle would make an excellent replacement. Perhaps he should listen to the old lady and give the girl a chance. If Michelle could work a miracle in his daughter's life, he would be eternally grateful to her. She had a sparkling candidness that he liked—even admired in a surprising sort of way, he thought, recalling the satisfaction in her black eyes when she'd pointed out his lie.

"Very well then," he said as Mrs. Hayes covered her pot of stew. "I'll give her a chance since you insist."

Mrs. Hayes smiled at him. "That's all anyone can ask for, Dr."

# CHAPTER TWO

Michelle stared at a collection of Monet landscapes lining one wall of the study. A smile ruffled her lips at the idea that she and the stiff-shirt doctor had something in common. He'd probably choke on that bit of info, she thought, her smile spreading to her eyes. *What, a girl from the other side of the river with an acquired appreciation for fine art?*

See, that's the trouble with people, she thought. You think you know them until they surprise the heck out of you by doing something totally unimaginable.

Take her father for instance. He'd been a rotten parent throughout her childhood. In spite of his neglect and abuse, she'd earned a four-year college degree in three years by working two jobs and attending night and summer school. She'd landed a great job as Manager of Customer Operations at a well-established company, and moved into a nice apartment on Elm Street. She had a new car and a so-so boyfriend. Since she had no college loans to pay back, she was able to save a substantial amount of her salary.

Then it was all blown to smithereens one night when her father knocked on her door. He'd knocked on her door before, and she'd offered him a little food here and there—never money, because she knew it would end up in the cash register of the nearest liquor store. Once in a while, if she were in a good mood, she would let him take a shower and sleep off his intoxication on her sofa.

Michelle wiped her hands down her face. She wished she'd been in a bad mood that night. If she hadn't been so nice to her father, when she was unexpectedly laid off a few months later, she would not have found herself penniless, homeless, and free-loading off her best friend, Yasmine, until she got back on her feet.

Michelle didn't even know if she still had feet to stand on. What she did know was that she hated taking charity from anybody, even from her brother who'd been sending her regular checks to help her out. She didn't want Robert's money. She didn't want Yasmine's pity. She just wanted her life back.

A nanny position was just the kind of job that could give her back some control on her life. She would have a roof over her head, home-cooked meals every night, and time to plan out her future. She wouldn't need to depend on anyone's financial support or live in anyone else's house—well only as an employee.

Michelle's heart fluttered around in her chest when the door of the study opened and the doctor appeared in the threshold. She didn't know if it was his presence or the uncertainty of her future that was affecting her ability to breathe.

His expression was still masked as he came further into the room. "Mrs. Hayes assured me that you are harmless," he said directly.

Michelle wondered what else Mrs. Hayes had told him. She was sure she'd mentioned their acquaintance, and she was doubly sure it was the only reason Erik hadn't marched back in here and ordered her to leave.

"So I've decided to give you the chance to prove yourself."

Michelle buried the urge to jump up and throw her arms around his neck. "Thank you," she said, rising to her feet. "Thank you."

"Don't be so quick to thank me," he warned. He glanced quickly back at the half-opened door before continuing in a lowered voice. "My daughter has been in a somber mood since her nanny left. If you can bring a smile to her face, the job is yours."

"You're putting me on the spot, Dr. LaCrosse? You advertised for a nanny, not a shrink."

"Are you saying you're not up to the challenge, Ms. Carter? You told me you'd be the best thing that ever happened to my daughter. Well, here's your chance to put your money where your mouth is. Or should I say, my money," he added with mock severity.

Michelle growled inside as she faced the challenge in his amber-grey eyes. *Cad*. He'd called her bluff. "Okay. I'll make your daughter laugh."

He turned and peeped around the doorframe. "Come here, darling."

Michelle braced herself.

"Come on, Muffin," he coaxed when no one appeared.

*Muffin?* Michelle's eyes widened. Well, celebrities were known to give their daughters names like Apple, Scout, and Rumer. But Muffin? A child with such a ludicrous name would be the butt and butter of baking jokes in her neighborhood.

When his daughter still refused to come, the doctor stepped into the hallway. Michelle heard a series of childish "Nos" in response to his gentle pleas. She was about to go get the little muffin herself when he reappeared at the door, dragging Muffin who was clutching to one of his long legs like a chimp to its mother.

"Ms. Carter, this is my daughter, Precious."

*Precious.* Now that was more like it, Michelle thought, her heart melting at the sight of the little girl with long dark brown pony tails falling on either side of her little heart-shaped face. She was no muffin. She was *precious*.

"Hi, Precious," Michelle said in a buoyant voice, coming closer to the tangled pair.

Precious glared at her through a pair of wide cinnamon-brown eyes. There was no doubt this little precious muffin didn't like her. Well, neither did her father. So... "My name is Michelle, and I'm hoping to be your new—"

"I don't need a nanny."

"You're so right, Precious." Michelle fell to her knees and sat back on her haunches. "Just for the record, I wasn't going to say *nanny*. I hope to be your new friend."

"I don't need any new friends. I don't like you." Her scowl deepened.

Ignoring her father's swift intake of air, Michelle pointed to the rag doll tucked under Precious' arm. "Who's that? I bet she could use a new friend." She smiled with hope in her heart. She needed this job and was willing to do anything to win this kid over.

But Precious just stared her down.

Michelle understood her unfriendliness. Her mother was gone, and according to Mrs. Hayes, her nanny recently left to start her own family with her new husband. Precious felt abandoned. She was tired of people leaving her. She was protecting her little heart in the only way she knew how. If she didn't become attached, she could never be abandoned. It was a hard lesson for someone to learn at such an early age. Michelle empathized. She never knew her own mother, and her father may as well be dead. *It hurts like hell when people you depend on abandon you.*

Michelle longed to tell Precious that it was okay to need and to love, and that when people left, it was their loss, as Robert had often told her. But in order to do that, she had to make her laugh first.

Michelle stared into the cinnamon-brown eyes staring back at her, and took a deep breath. "Okay, little one. Here's the deal. We'll stare each other down and make funny faces and the first one to crack a smile, loses. If I win, you're stuck with me." Michelle had no doubt she would win this game. It was how she and Yasmine settled disputes when they were children. Heck, they still did. "Ready?" she asked Precious. "Okay, here goes. We start on three. One... Two..."

"Wait," Precious yelled, pulling her arm from around her father's leg and handing him her doll. "What happens if I win?"

*You won't.* "I'll walk out of the house and you'll never see me again."

Precious' brows puckered into a frown. "Okay." She planted her feet apart and folded her arms across her chest.

Michelle veiled her smile of impending victory. The kid had no idea who she was up against. It would be over in thirty seconds. She settled her buttocks against her heels. "Alright, on three. You can go first. One... two... three."

Precious made a fish face, stuck her thumbs in her ears, and waved her fingers around.

Cute, but no effect. Michelle shrugged, made a monkey face, and began to sway back and forth on her haunches.

Precious rolled her eyes in boredom.

*Darn*, the kid was tougher than she thought.

"Your turn, Precious," her father chimed, clearly amused at the game.

Michelle wondered if he was rooting for Precious.

Precious pulled apart her eyelids and let her tongue hang out of her mouth.

Unimpressed, Michelle decided to pull out the big guns—her unconquerable pig face.

She placed a finger in the space between her nostrils and pulled her nose upward. When she saw the slight hint of a smile flash across Precious' face, she knew it was over. She rolled her eyes back into their sockets until she was certain that only the whites were visible, pursed her lips, and began making slurping noises like a pig at the trough.

"Hee, hee, hee, hee.... You're silly."

"And you're precious. Come here." Michelle held her arms wide. It was a huge risk, but she let out a long sigh when Precious wrapped her arms around her neck. The feel of those skinny arms about her pushed Michelle over the edge and tears flowed down her cheeks.

Precious was no different from Jessica, Malcolm, Tessa, Ashley, Parker, or any other kid who hung out at the youth center where she volunteered on a regular basis. She may have a lot more toys, nicer clothes, and eat more food in a day than they had in a week, but at the end of the day, all kids needed was love, and to know that somebody cared enough to fight for them, laugh with them, and tell them they were special.

Michelle looked up to find Erik staring at her. There was relief and gratitude in his eyes because his daughter had laughed, but there was something else shrouded in their depth. Something she didn't understand.

"This is Bradie." Precious pulled her doll from her father's hand and shoved it into Michelle's face. "I call her Bradie cause she has lots of braids."

"Hello, Bradie." Michelle shook the doll's limp hand. "I'm Michelle, your new friend."

"Are you my friend, too?" Precious asked with a timid smile, apparently unsure if Michelle would forgive her earlier offenses.

"Of course, Sunshine." Michelle touched her cute button of a nose then tapped a finger to her chest. "That is if you have room for one more friend in that little heart of yours."

"I do." Her eyes sparkled with eagerness. "You know what?" She started chattering like a seven-year-old high on life. "I have two goldfish. One's named Charlie and one's named Sippy. Charlie is the big one. You wanna see them? You wanna see my room?" She tugged Michelle to her feet.

"Sure, I'd love to see your room and your fish." She looked at Erik. "If it's okay with your dad."

Erik pulled his gaze away from Michelle and walked over to his desk. She was crying, he thought in astonishment. She wasn't afraid to show her emotions. Tears didn't bother her. Cassie had hated tears. She never cried, at least not in front of him. He gave his wife's portrait a quick glance then cleared his throat before trusting his voice not to embarrass him. "Precious, go back to your room now, sweetheart. Ms. Carter—"

"Michelle," Michelle corrected him.

"Michelle will be along soon. I promise," he added at the reluctance in his daughter's eyes.

Precious glanced from Michelle to her father, then back to Michelle again.

Sensing her hesitance, Michelle pushed her hand into the front pocket of her jeans, pulled out a penny and held it out to

Precious. "This is my lucky penny. I don't go anywhere without it. So I can't leave without seeing you, right?"

Precious stared at the penny. "But it's old and rusty."

"That's exactly what I told my big brother when he gave it to me many years ago when I was just a little girl like you. But you know what he said?"

"What?"

"He said, 'Michelle, this penny may be old and rusty, but it's worth just as much as any brand new shiny one'. Do you know what that means?"

Precious shrugged. "A penny is a penny, no matter what it looks like?"

"You are so smart. What's important is what it means to you. So, is this a lucky penny or not?"

Precious snatched the penny from her hand. "It's a lucky penny."

"Good. Now the sooner you get upstairs, the sooner I can meet you there."

With one last big bright smile, Precious ran out of the room.

"Your big brother sounds like a very wise man," Erik said when they were alone.

"He is." Michelle smiled. "Precious is a sweet kid," she added.

"You have no idea what it did to hear her laugh. You almost made me laugh with that horrible pig face. Where did you learn to handle kids like that?"

"Babysitting and working at the youth center. Sometimes the kids walk in with such overwhelming problems that the only way to get them through the day is to make them laugh."

Erik perched on the edge of his desk, studying the lingering smile on her lips. He would love so much to reach out and grab a ray of that sunshine she'd just showered on his daughter. "Well, you seem to have what it takes to be a nanny," he said. "You are just what Precious needs. You have the job, Ms. Car—"

"Michelle."

"Michelle." He nodded on a smile.

Her black eyes sparkled with relief. "Thank you. I promise you Precious will be the happiest little girl in Amherst, soon. Just leave her to me."

"From what I just saw, I think she already is," he replied, fighting to disentangle himself from the invisible thread that seemed to be forming between them already. How was he going to maintain his sanity with this irresistible woman living under his roof? Erik wondered. It was too late to send her packing. She'd scored big with Precious. His baby had already fallen in love with her. He'd never seen her bond so quickly and eagerly with any other woman. And never had he, Erik realized as heat began generating in his loins again and his heart started to hammer in his chest.

He scooted off the desk and walked around to sit in his chair, but as he tried to escape the intense immediacy, Erik knew that putting physical distance between them was meaningless. He was so hard, he hurt.

His gaze shifted to the portrait of his wife as if she could help cool the fire in his veins. The fingers of his right hand mindlessly toyed with the gold wedding band on his left as he studied her classic pose. She was seated in a Victorian chair in front of the fireplace over which the painting was hung. She looked like a queen in a long flowing red dress—a red rose wedged between her fingers. Her flaming red hair completely covered her bare creamy shoulders. That was his Cassie. Elegant, sophisticated, and...

"She was very beautiful."

The mellow voice interrupted his musing. "Yes, she was." He met the million-dollar question in Michelle's eyes and to avoid it, he immediately asked, "Do you really only wear jeans and tank tops?" He groaned inwardly at how the question sounded, especially after he'd been admiring his wife's portrait.

"Why? Don't you like my style?"

"Well," he said, trying to choose his words carefully. "I was just hoping you had something a little less... How should I say this? Um—"

"Trashy?"

"I was thinking... provocative."

"Oh." She smiled tentatively. "The truth is, most of my clothes were stolen from a laundromat. Since I lost my job, I could only afford to splurge at thrift stores. They don't carry much for tall skinny girls, I'm afraid. Actually, I was at the laundromat when the agency called me. I hardly had time to finish my wash and get here. I was planning on wearing a jacket over the top, but when I got in the cab I realized I'd left it hanging on the doorknob. I didn't have time to go back."

So the explanation she'd given him earlier was payback for the lie he'd told Mrs. Hayes to relay, Erik thought with a smile.

He knew that Michelle's world, where people went out to do their laundry and had their clothes stolen, existed. He attended patients at the free clinic in Manchester who came from that world. He was just never part of it. He'd never lived in it.

Even though the circumstances surrounding his birth had raised a few eyebrows in the elite circle, he was born and raised in wealth. His late wife had also come from a wealthy family. Michelle Carter on the other hand had been born and raised in poverty.

As he gazed at her standing in front of him in clothes that someone else had worn and discarded, Erik felt a strong protectiveness toward her. He wanted to provide all the luxuries she'd been denied. Yes, he was physically attracted to the girl, but something about her touched a place deep inside him, a place no other woman—but Cassie—had ever been able to reach. Strange, since the two women were as different as pink diamonds and cubic zirconias. Nevertheless, he couldn't have her walking around the house or the neighborhood so distastefully dressed. "I'll give you some money for a new wardrobe," he said, reaching into his back pocket for his wallet.

Her shoulders stiffened and her eyes flashed with pride. "I don't take charity."

"Who said it was charity? Consider it an advance on your first paycheck."

Her lips relaxed into a smile. "That, I will accept."

Erik pulled out a stack of bills from his wallet and handed

them to her.

"Thank you." She tucked them into the pocket of her jeans without even looking at them.

Erik sensed her embarrassment for having to accept pay she hadn't yet earned, especially in cash. A check would have been the normal and appropriate form of payment, but she would have had to wait the usual two days for it to clear, and he needed her clothed in proper attire immediately. "I noticed you brought your suitcase," he said in an attempt to break the awkward silence between them. "Were you so sure you would get the job?"

She crossed her arms about her body. "I can be very persuasive when I want something."

Nothing kept her down for long, and she possessed an uninhibited streak he found absolutely enticing, Erik thought as he watched amusement sparkle in her eyes. His gaze roamed down her body as she tightened her arms across her chest, causing her breasts to push upward and her nipples to strain against the stretchy material of her top.

"Well, that's it for now," he said, eager to have her gone. "Your bedroom is next to Precious'. Up the stairs, third door on your left. I'll bring your suitcase up."

"Thanks for giving me this chance, and the advance on my salary, Dr. La—"

"Come on now," Erik cut her off with a grin. "If you insist I call you Michelle, you better start calling me Erik. Especially after subjecting me to that horrible pig face you made. It's the worst I've ever seen. Just promise me you'll never do it again."

They both burst out laughing.

Michelle's heart leaped at the sound of his deep chuckles. There was a humorous side to him under that grim exterior he'd initially exhibited. Michelle had no idea what had caused him to take an immediate dislike to her, but his attitude changed the moment she made his daughter laugh.

She could tell he loved his child more than anything else in his world and that he'd appreciate anyone who contributed to her happiness. Today, she was that *anyone*. She had a job. She had a place to sleep. She would have a home-cooked meal tonight. She wouldn't have to jump out of bed tomorrow morning and rush over to the corner store for a newspaper to check the want ads, or spend time on the Internet, sending off resume after resume into cyberspace. She could relax for the first time in almost two years.

Well, that is if she could bring herself not to fantasize about the dangerously sexy doctor. From the way he'd gazed at the painting of his wife while fiddling with the wedding band on his finger, Michelle sensed he was still in love with her. They were worlds apart—employer and employee, and the sooner she accepted that fact, the better off she'd be.

"I should check on Precious before she thinks I skipped out on her," she said, heading for the door on legs that felt like overcooked spaghetti.

"Michelle?"

She stopped, but didn't turn around. "Yes?" She licked her lips nervously.

"We'll go over Precious' schedule later. I have to return to the hospital, but I'll be back in time for dinner."

"Okay."

"And, Michelle."

"Yes."

"Thanks again for making my daughter laugh."

"You're welcome, Erik."

Erik watched her go, a fire kindling deep within him as he took in the delicate sway of her hips and buttocks.

Oh yes, she was trouble.

# CHAPTER THREE

"You know what, Daddy?" Precious beamed from the opposite side of the dining table.

Erik smiled at the enthusiasm in his daughter's eyes and voice. Since they sat down to eat, she'd been talking nonstop bringing him up to date on her exciting afternoon with her new nanny. "What, sweetheart?" he asked, wiping his mouth with his napkin and placing it on his lap.

"Michelle pushed me so high in the swing, I almost saw Grandpa Erik and Grandma Danielle all the way in Granite Falls."

"Wow, that's amazing. I didn't know Michelle was so strong. I guess we got us a super nanny, huh?" He winked at Michelle.

"Yeah, we have a super nanny. She's the bestest, funnest nanny ever."

The joy in his daughter's eyes filled Erik's soul with gratitude. He smiled at Michelle, hoping she understood what she'd done for him, for them.

"I think you should wait a while before you go handing me a diploma," she said.

"What's a diploma?" Precious asked.

As Michelle explained what a diploma was, Erik looked around the elaborately decorated room with its Waterford chandeliers and gold cabinets filled with priceless ornaments Cassie had collected over the years.

It had been a while since he'd taken a meal in here. He and Precious usually ate at the kitchen table, something Cassie would never have approved. She was all about prestige and appearances, the very lifestyle he'd been trying to escape when he left Granite Falls. The table had always been laden with gourmet dishes on Christmas, Easter, and Thanksgiving. They'd always had friends and family with whom to enjoy the elaborate meals. But since her death, he and Precious either went to his mother's on the other side of town, or up to Granite Falls, his hometown, a three-hour drive north of Manchester.

The dining room had become a passageway from the kitchen to the family room. This afternoon, for some inexplicable reason, Erik had called Mrs. Hayes from the hospital and asked her to set the table for dinner. A faint smile ruffled his lips as he recalled that conversation.

*"The formal dining room, Sir?"*

*"Yes, the formal dining room, Mrs. Hayes, where people sit down around a table and share a meal together."*

*"And how many people will be sharing a meal, Sir?"*

*"Three."*

*"Are you bringing a guest for dinner?"*

*"Tell Ms. Carter I expect her to dine with Precious and me tonight."*

As he gazed at Michelle talking so naturally and easily with his daughter, Erik wondered about his decision. Was he trying to impress her? And why? They were sitting around a dinner table like some normal happy family. He at the head, Michelle at the foot, and Precious across from him—the way it used to be when Cassie was alive. It was a good feeling. He couldn't remember the last time he felt this... well, content. He could say it's because Michelle had made Precious laugh. But Michelle had made him laugh, too. Really laugh.

He'd been closed and guarded for the past two years, and when he'd let his guard down this afternoon, he'd rediscovered something he lost the night Cassie died—his vulnerability. The thought of opening up himself and letting someone in both scared and thrilled him.

As the conversation about diplomas wound down, Erik caught Michelle's gaze. "Why aren't you eating?" he asked. She'd been twirling the stew around in the bowl since they sat down. He was on his second helping of the delicious stew and Precious was almost finished her first. Michelle had eaten two slices of sourdough bread, and two servings of the garden salad, but she hadn't taken one single bite of the stew. "Is it not to your liking?"

"I don't eat red meat," she said.

"Are you a vegetarian?"

"No, I just don't eat beef." She set the spoon down, seemingly relieved that she didn't have to pretend anymore.

"Is there a specific reason you don't eat beef?"

"Calvin."

A cold chill ran up and down Erik's spine. Was Calvin her boyfriend? He'd forgotten to ask her if she were currently involved with anyone. He'd asked for someone older to avoid a repeat of the nanny taking off when she decided to start her own family. He didn't want his daughter disappointed again. He took a quick glance at her and recalled the excitement with which she'd shared the stories of her afternoon with Michelle. She was already in deep.

He'd been so distracted by the effect Michelle had on him, he'd forgotten to ask her the most important question of the day. He couldn't very well ask her if she had a boyfriend in front of his daughter, so he asked, as placidly as he could, "Who's Calvin?"

A slow smile broke across her lips as if she knew the real question plaguing him. "A bull calf. Like in cattle."

*Calvin was a bull.* Erik let out his breath. "Where did you meet, uh—Calvin?"

"A few years ago, I stayed on a farm that my friend's family owned. I got very attached to this one bull that I named Calvin. He had the most pitiful eyes, like he knew what would happen to him. I used to wish I had a house with a big backyard so I could adopt him. I promised him that as long as I lived, I would never eat beef again. For a long time after I left the farm, every time I smelled burgers or steaks cooking, I would think of him."

"Yuck!" Precious dropped her spoon and spat a mouthful of stew back into her bowl.

"Precious, mind your manners," Erik said.

"But we could have just eaten Calvin, Daddy."

Michelle shook her head hastily. Her conviction was hers alone. She had no wish to convince Precious or anyone else to adopt her belief. "No baby," she said smiling at the little girl. "Calvin was rescued by a nice man who took him far away to another farm where he fell in love with a beautiful cow named Izzy."

"That's sweet," Precious said. "And they had lots and lots of baby cows and lived happily ever after, just like Cinderella and the Prince."

"Just like Cinderella," Michelle acquiesced, relieved at Precious' naivety. She really had to watch what she said around the child. She was hired to babysit her, not indoctrinate her.

"How many babies did they have?" Precious asked, biting into a slice of bread.

"Well, I'd say..."

Feeling quite uncomfortable with talk about love, babies, and happily ever after, Erik tried to tune out the exchange between his daughter and Michelle. Love, babies, and forever was what he'd hoped for when he married Cassie.

If it hadn't been for that drunk...

Well, he didn't know that exactly. They never had the opportunity to resolve their last fight that night. He had no idea what he would have done if Cassie had confirmed his suspicions about her.

He couldn't understand why people who claim to be in love lied, betrayed, and inflicted pain on each other. Love made you vulnerable. He'd been vulnerable to Cassie. He loved her more then he'd ever loved anyone, would ever love anyone again. Was that love strong enough to weather the storm of his suspicions, though? He would never know. All he knew was that he would never make himself that vulnerable to anyone, ever again.

Well, he was going to try not to, he reassured himself as his eyes rested on Michelle sitting where Cassie used to sit, her brown skin glowing under the richness of the russet cotton dress she'd changed into. Her obsidian eyes sparkled like black magic, daring him to reach out and taste the sweet essence of her soul. Erik tried to picture Cassie's chestnut-brown eyes, but all he saw were those fiery, black eyes of an irresistible woman gazing back at him, inviting him to explore and revel.

Shaking off the bewitching invitation, Erik pushed back his chair and smiled at his daughter. "Hey, little one. Daddy has a surprise for you," he said, deliberately interrupting their conversation about forever after. As far as he was concerned, fairytale endings were just that... fairytales that belonged in children's books.

Precious jumped out of her chair and ran to him. "A surprise for me? What is it, Daddy?"

Erik closed his eyes as he hugged his little girl. God, he loved her so much. She was all he had left of Cassie, and he cherished her with everything good in himself. He pried Precious' arms from around his neck and peered into her eyes—Cassie's eyes. He planted a quick kiss on her forehead. "Go wash up and meet me back here," he said, placing her on the floor.

She raced out of the room without so much as a backward glance, her long ponytails bouncing behind her like thick cords of rope.

Erik turned his attention to Michelle who'd left her chair and was now gazing out the bay window overlooking a rose garden. Habitually, his eyes swept the length of her. She had a good posture, he thought, and would carry a fetus well, but her slender form would make childbirth difficult, the astute physician in him noted with concern.

Since the moment he'd laid eyes on her, Erik could not stop thinking about Michelle's body, and how it would look naked, especially her full perky breasts and the shape and color of her nipples. He wondered about the haven of delight between her thighs. What were her waxing preferences? American, French, or Brazilian? He knew what he liked. Would Michelle deliver or disappoint him? As his eyes took in the gentle curve of her long graceful neck, he wondered how her silky skin would feel against his lips. He could easily kiss her nape without having to trek through a thick mass of hair as he used to do with Cassie. *Cassie.*

At the thought of his wife, Erik took a deep breath and forced the pleasing yet dangerous musings about his daughter's nanny out of his head. He took a moment to collect his thoughts then walked to the window to stand beside Michelle.

"They are beautiful," he said, gazing at the array of red, yellow, white, and pink roses, all in full bloom. Cassie had put her sweat into that garden and after she died, he'd employed a gardener to tend the thorny bushes. They added a magnificent view from the dining table. He remembered the numerous compliments the spectacular scenery had generated from their guests over the years.

"You don't look like the rosebush kind."

Michelle's voice interrupted his stroll down memory lane. She somehow had the uncanny ability to continually bring him back from his past. He chuckled softly. "They were Cassie's, my late wife's. She loved roses, especially the red ones, like her flaming hair. Red was her favorite color. You might have noticed that from the painting in my study."

"How did she die? Was she sick?"

Erik tensed with dread and perplexity. Did she really not know? The news of Cassie's death and the ongoing investigation to find her killer had made the headlines for months. He'd never met anyone who didn't associate the name LaCrosse with that tragedy. Well, not until now.

He didn't want to talk about it, but since Michelle was now an uninformed member of his household, the question would always be hanging over their heads. "She was killed by a drunk driver," he said, wishing to put it to rest.

"I hope they caught the bastard."

"Unfortunately, not yet." Erik frowned at her use of the word 'bastard' and the disdain with which she said it.

"How could they not have found him yet?" she asked as if she had a personal stake in his loss. "Drunks aren't that hard to find." She crossed her arms and stared straight ahead.

Feeling the tension building around them, Erik ran his fingers through his hair. He seldom talked about that night. And he definitely never spoke about it with a stranger. But something about Michelle Carter made him want to open up his heart to her, tell her the whole truth. Maybe it's because of the way she'd handled Precious earlier today. She seemed to have a gift to make people who were hurting feel better.

"It was a stolen car that was later abandoned. We knew it was a drunk because it was littered with empty liquor bottles. Cassie's blood, and fabric from her dress was wedged into the front bumper." He balled his fists at his sides. "*He* walked away without even a scratch while my wife bled to death in front of me."

"You were there? You saw it happen?"

How much should he tell this woman who was gently coaxing the most horrifying, most painful experience of his life out of him? "We'd gone to a birthday party at a friend's house in Manchester." He spoke slowly and cautiously. "On the way home, we got into an argument. It was late and Cassie begged me to wait until the morning and she would explain everything to me. She was like that, you know. She hated confrontations. If a fight began brewing between us, she would walk away to cool off and when she returned, we would resolve our difference more calmly."

He closed his eyes for an instant. "But that night, I wasn't having it. I wanted answers right then and there. So she insisted that I stop the car. We were passing a park, so I pulled over, thinking it would be a safe place for her to cool off for a few minutes. But just as she opened the door and stepped out, a car came whipping by."

"Didn't you see it coming?"

"It was dark. The driver didn't have his lights on. It happened so fast." Erik pressed his hands against his temples. His head was throbbing. At least, she was sensitive enough not to ask what they'd been arguing about. The only other person who knew about that argument was his ex-best friend, Clayton

Monroe. Nobody else. Not even his mother. As hurt and angry as he'd been at the time, he didn't want people speculating about his wife and what she may or may not have done. Most importantly, he didn't want anything to tarnish his daughter's image of her mother.

The authorities had questioned his action in stopping on the wrong side of the road and allowing his wife to exit into the street instead of the sidewalk. He'd been under suspicion for allegedly pushing his wife out of the car into oncoming traffic. But having no evidence that he wanted his wife dead, he'd been cleared.

He was an idiot, not a monster.

"I've never told anyone about that argument," he said, wondering if he'd made a mistake in telling Michelle so much. He didn't even know her, and yet he'd poured out the darkest secret of his soul to her.

Michelle gazed up at him with moist eyes filled with warmth, the kind of homespun warmth he longed to have wrapped around him.

"I won't repeat it to anyone," she said. "I'm sorry, Erik. I'm sorry you and your little girl had to go through such a terrible experience."

The sincerity in her voice seeped through his skin, into his blood. "You're remarkable," he said huskily. "Almost too good to be true."

His heart jolted when she unexpectedly took his hand and laced her fingers through his. Her touch was like quicksand, pulling him into a chasm of pure desire. He felt an avid quickening of his heartbeat as a violent passion pulsed through his veins, bringing his dormant body to life.

The moment she touched him, a hot flash swept through Michelle, and her heart began to hammer against her chest. It was as if she'd been struck by lightning. Instantly realizing it was a mistake to touch him, she dropped his hand. "I'm sorry. I didn't mean to do that." She cast her eyes downward to hide the boisterous storm raging inside her.

"Don't be. You acted on impulse." Erik put his hands under

her chin and raised her face to his. He wiped his thumb across the softness of her cheek, capturing a tear that had escaped from her captivating eyes. He rubbed the warm moisture between his fingers, relishing the feel of it against his skin.

Her lips parted slightly, and involuntarily, her pink tongue darted out to wet her dry lips. Erik groaned. Her compelling eyes spoke to him, offering him the intimate female delights he'd been deprived of for so long. His head started a lazy descent, and as he got closer, his predatory male senses were stimulated by the sensual fragrance exuding from her skin.

"What's that scent you're wearing?" he whispered.

"*Moonlight.* You like it?"

"Yes. I like it. I like it a lot."

Michelle closed her eyes as her heart jackknifed in her throat. She whimpered when his smooth, warm lips touched hers, and the heady scent of his masculinity attacked her. There was no spicy aftershave, no musky cologne, just his potent manliness. Her limbs turned to jelly when he pulled her to him and completely covered her mouth and swept his tongue inside, ravishing her hungrily. She clutched his shoulders and opened wider, giving him absolute permission to enjoy her.

Sweat beaded Erik's forehead as his body heat reached a record high. His breath came in gasps as he stroked his hands down her slender body. He pulled her closer, fitting his erection against the soft cradle of her feminine heat. He rocked against her gently as their tongues danced intimately around each other.

Michelle made a mewling sound, deep in her throat, like that from a cat being stroked by its master's hand. She wrapped her arms around Erik's neck and pressed herself into the hard curve of his body. She'd had boyfriends before, yet she had no idea that being in a man's arms could feel so gloriously wonderful. Somewhere in the dazed recess of her brain, she heard thunder rumble.

"I'm ready, Daddy!"

They jumped apart as Precious' voice yanked them back to reality.

Michelle gasped and swallowed hard, forcing her heart back

inside her chest. The rumbling she'd heard wasn't thunder, but Precious' footsteps clambering down the stairs. She turned toward the window and managed to straighten her dress just as Precious bolted into the room. She wondered how Erik was doing. She couldn't even look at him.

"You look beautiful, Precious," Erik said to his daughter, desperately needing any sound to break the steamy silence in the room. His voice shook so hard, he was afraid she would realize that something was wrong. She was too intuitive for her own good, and his. He dropped to the floor on one knee, placing his arms across his thighs in an effort to hide his arousal.

Precious had changed into a floral printed dress, but the two strips of cotton that would later become a bow in the back, hung down at her sides. She wore pink suede sandals, no socks.

"Daddy, your eyes are all red. Is something wrong? Were you crying?"

"No darling. Daddy's just excited about our date tonight."

Satisfied, she ran over to the window. "Can you please tie my bow, Michelle?"

Michelle took a deep breath before turning around. Her fingers trembled as she pushed the long braids aside and tried to make a perfect bow from the two strips of cotton. "There," she said, spinning Precious around. "Your daddy is right. You're as beautiful as a princess."

She gave her a bright smile. "Are you coming with us?"

"No. Not tonight. This is a father and daughter night out. I'll come next time. Okay?"

"Okay. Come on, Daddy, let's go."

Somewhat recovered, Erik stood up. "Go wait for me in the Mercedes."

"Bye, Michelle," Precious called as she ran out of the room.

"I'm sorry," they said in unison, then looked away from each other.

"Look," Erik said, "I was wrong to come on to you like that. I wouldn't blame you if you walked out the door right now. I hope you don't think I expect you to… well, I promise, it will not happen again."

"It was nothing." Michelle's lips trembled as she brought her gaze back to his. The passion still burned affluently within his eyes, as she was sure it did in hers.

"On the contrary, it was something." He watched her for a long, hard minute then said in a composed voice, "I should be home around ten. I'm taking Precious to see a production of *The Wind in the Willows*. I've had these tickets for a week, but lately, every time I suggested we do something together, she turned me down. Thanks to you, that has changed." He paused. "You sure you don't want to come along? I could get another ticket at the door."

"No," Michelle replied, thinking about what Precious had told her that afternoon about the day her mother died. She needed her father's undivided attention more than anything else right now.

"I have to clean up since Mrs. Hayes has left for the day. I also have to finish unpacking and make some phone calls. I need to let my brother know where I am before he puts out an Amber alert on me."

"Oh, yes, Mrs. Hayes mentioned you have a brother who's an orthodontist."

Michelle nodded, pride welling up inside her. Her big brother had made it. "We're really close."

"As family should be."

"Well, goodbye. Have a nice time." Michelle needed him gone so she could kick herself in the ass.

He lingered, looking around warily. "Are you going to be okay in this big house alone on your first night?"

What, was he afraid she was going to call her hoodlum friends to clean the place out the minute his car disappeared around the corner? Michelle smiled at the wicked thought. "I'll be fine, Erik."

"Okay, bye." He finally left.

"Stupid. Stupid. Stupid." Michelle slapped her palms against the sides of her head. How could she let this happen? She was hired to take care of the child, not seduce the father.

Her impulsive behavior could cause complications for all of

them, she realized as she began collecting the leftovers from the sideboard. She took the serving dishes to the kitchen that was as elaborately decorated as the rest of the house.

The alabaster marble island in the center of the kitchen was trimmed in red oak to match the cabinets with decorated glass doors and gold handles. His wife had definitely had good taste, which brought her back to her dilemma.

By now Erik was probably back to his initial impression of her—a cheap tramp from the wrong side of the river. If he did, she couldn't blame him. She had offered herself to him, and he was only a man—one with huge needs. Her skin tingled at the memory of his strong arms pulling her into him, his hot tongue ravishing her mouth, and the enormous bulge in his pants pressing into her heat.

*Whew.* She fanned her face with her hand and stood a little longer in front of the fridge before heading back into the dining room.

She was a half-day on the job and she was already giving her boss permission to do with her whatever he wanted. From now on, she had to be strong. Tough. His kind could hurt her. Real bad. She wasn't the kind of woman men like Dr. Erik LaCrosse considered as permanent additions to their lives. He went for the classy type. The *couth.* He would play with her like a little boy with a new toy on Christmas morning then he would toss her aside when he got bored.

Not that she was looking to settle down with anybody any time soon. She had to put her life back together. She had to write her book and build a new youth center for the kids in Manchester. Then if she was real lucky, she'd find the right man—one in her own league—settle down, have a few kids of her own, and live happily ever after like Cinderella and Prince Charming.

Michelle chortled. She should know better than to make plans and build castles in the sky. The plans she'd made so far had been foiled so badly she was now living in the house of the rich and famous and clearing their dinner table like a maid. Maybe she shouldn't even make plans. Maybe she should just take one day at a time and hope Fate eventually threw her a lifeline.

Michelle carried the last pile of fine china to the kitchen and was in the process of stacking the dishwasher when the phone rang. She glanced at the cordless extension on the counter, hoping it wasn't anyone looking for the doctor. He hadn't told her where he was going, just that he was taking his daughter to see a play. Worse, what if it was his couth lady friend? *Nah*, she was sure he would have told his woman where he was. She could be with him right now for all Michelle knew.

Or... it could be Erik, calling to see if she was still here, or if she'd called her friends to help her clean the place out and left. She smiled at the wicked thought. Maybe she should just let the answering machine pick it up. She was sure he had one somewhere in the house.

When the phone just kept ringing, she snatched up the extension. "Hello. The LaCrosse's residence."

"Hey, Mich."

Michelle let out a long sigh of relief at the sound of Yasmine's voice. She'd called her best friend earlier and left the house number since her cell phone didn't work in this area. Too many trees around. God, she was going to miss the buzz of Manchester.

"So did you get the job?" Yasmine asked.

"I got the job."

"Excellent!"

"Why, you happy to have your apartment back to yourself?"

"Come on, Mich. You know it's not about that. I'm glad you're getting your break."

Michelle chuckled. "I know. Hey," she added as she perched on a bar stool at the breakfast nook. "Speaking of breaks, you'd never guess who the housekeeper is."

"Okay, so tell me."

"Mrs. Hayes. You remember I told you I ran into her at Mama Lola's about a month ago?"

"Yeah. Did she get you the job?"

"She wouldn't admit it, but I'm sure she had something to do with it. She must have some clout with the owners at Ready Nanny Agency and asked them to cancel the other candidate and send me on the interview instead." Michelle didn't see the sense in telling Yasmine of the lie Erik had told Mrs. Hayes to tell her. "Anyway, she said I'm here because God wants me here."

"Well, maybe she's right. I'm glad you have somebody looking out for you over there."

"Yeah, I guess."

"So how is the kid? Not a rich spoiled brat, I hope," Yasmine said.

"She's sweet. I like her. I think we'll get along fine." She'd give Yasmine the facts about her and Precious' first meeting later.

"And her parents? What are they like?"

Michelle's lips ruffled into a smile. If Yasmine could see it, she'd probably slap the giddy out of her. "Well, her father is nice."

"Mich, you holding out on me."

Her smile deepened into a grin. Yasmine knew her too well. "Okay. He's handsome, sexy, and he's a brother."

"Really?"

"Well—half of him is. He's bi-racial. And he kissed me," Michelle added as her pulse raced with the sweet memories of being in Erik's arms.

A short silence rang on the other end then Yasmine shouted, "What kind of man kisses his child's nanny, especially on her first day at work? Mich, you need to get out of that house, fast. Just give me the address, and I'll come pick you up, right now."

"It's not like that, Yas," Michelle corrected her friend who had been looking out for her since they were in kindergarten. Yasmine had even offered to have her brothers beat the stupid out of her father for wrecking her life.

Michelle hadn't even told Robert what he'd done. It was for her brother's own good, because she knew he would find him and do something bad to him. She didn't want her brother spending the rest of his life in jail over their rotten good-for-nothing father.

Robert still thought she'd lost everything because she'd lost her job, and had been living beyond her means, which was partly true. But she'd been denied so much for so long, Michelle hadn't seen the harm in spoiling herself a little. In addition, she'd been buying clothes and other necessities for some of the kids at the center who had nothing. She wanted to bring some happiness to their lives, see them smile.

"And where was his wife while he was kissing you?" Yasmine continued. "Don't tell me they're a swinging couple who hire young girls to fulfill their sexual fantasies."

"Yasmine, his wife is dead. He's been a widower for two years."

Silence. "Oh, okay. Was she sick or something?"

"No. She was killed by a drunk driver," Michelle said quietly.

"Oh man, Mich. That's too close to home."

"You're telling me. The worse thing is they haven't found him, yet. As far as Dr. Erik LaCrosse is concerned, every drunk out there is a potential suspect, including my father."

"Did you tell him about your father?" Yasmine asked.

Michelle sighed and picked up a crystal saltshaker from the breakfast bar and twirled it between her fingers. "What am I supposed to say? By the way, Dr. LaCrosse, my father is a drunk. It's possible he's the one who killed your wife." He'd already formed an opinion about her the moment she stepped out of the cab. She'd had to prove herself fit to take care of his kid, and that still didn't mean he trusted her completely. He didn't know anything about her.

"I see what you mean," Yasmine said. "But what are you going to tell him when he does ask about your family? He will want to know. I'm surprised he hasn't already asked."

"I don't know what I'll tell him, Yas." Michelle set the saltshaker back on the counter.

"You know, I've said this before and I'll say it again. That man may not be your real father. Neither you nor Robert looks like him."

"Yas, give it up. Lots of kids don't look like their fathers or mothers for that matter. You don't look like your dad. And don't you think our mother would have said something to Robert if that were the case?"

"Maybe she wanted to, but couldn't. Maybe he threatened her. You know that temper of his."

"So if Dwight is not our father, where is our real father?" Michelle asked. "Why hasn't he been looking for us all these years?"

"I don't know, Mich. Maybe you should go find out."

"Yeah, right. You watch too much TV."

"It's not TV. It's the weird cases I come across since I've been studying criminal law. You wouldn't believe the things some people would do for no reason whatsoever. There are thousands of unsolved cases out there."

"Well, I'm sure there are a lot, but mine isn't one of them. Bye, Yas."

After she hung up, Michelle pondered over Yasmine's question about what she would tell Erik when he asked about her father. One thing she knew was that she could not tell him her father was a drunk, had been since she could remember. Erik would begin to second-guess her character, her ethics, because that's what people do when they learn you were raised in an unhealthy home environment. If Erik began to question her upbringing, he might be inclined to fire her.

As she slid off the stool and headed up a flight of stairs that led from the kitchen to the second floor, Michelle knew one thing: she would not let Dwight Carter take this job away from her. He had taken enough already.

As to the other matter about Dwight not being her real father, well that was just preposterous.

# CHAPTER FOUR

Erik poured himself a mug of coffee and sipped at it as he stared out the kitchen window at the mountain range in the distance. Usually after his daily seven-mile run, he'd enjoy his coffee over his edition of *The New York Times* while the house was as quiet as his thoughts. His thoughts were anything but quiet today. Images of a very beautiful young woman had been running about in his head since yesterday afternoon and he couldn't make them stop.

He hadn't even been able to enjoy the play with Precious last night. They had gotten home after midnight—not because the play had run late, but because he'd been too shaken up over that passionate kiss between him and his daughter's new nanny to come back to the house.

He'd gone to visit his mother, who was always happy to see her only child and grandchild. She was up late, packing for her annual three-week cruise to the Caribbean with her friends, and since she was leaving in two days, she'd assumed he'd come to say goodbye, and didn't question his late and impromptu visit.

His mother had put her life on hold to help out with Precious while he was searching for Holly's replacement, so it was no surprise that she'd thrown her hands in the air and exclaimed, "It's about time, Erik!" when he told her he'd hired a new nanny.

If she only knew the new nanny wasn't old, but an attractive, irresistible temptress, who'd already managed to wiggle her way under his thick skin, his mother would have brought out the champagne. After all, she'd been badgering him about remarrying and giving her more grandchildren before she was too old to spoil them.

He could tell her that since he had no intentions of marrying again, Precious was the only grandchild she'd ever have and that she should enjoy her all she could. But that would be cruel, so he indulged her and told her she would have all the grandchildren she wanted when he found the right woman, to which she always responded, "Fastidious as you are, that'll probably never happen. It's a miracle that Cassie managed to land you." The woman just could not be pleased, he thought, an affectionate smile spreading across his face.

Erik tensed as he heard footsteps coming down the hallway. It was too early for either Mrs. Hayes or Precious to be up, so he knew it was Michelle. She was an early riser, he thought, a bit disconcerted that he'd have to adjust his morning routine just when he'd finally gotten used to it.

He turned when the footsteps halted and a soft gasp echoed behind him. Michelle was standing under the arch separating the kitchen from the dining room. Thank goodness she was fully dressed in jeans and a far less revealing shirt than the one she showed up in yesterday. They looked clean, but a bit rumpled and faded. He hadn't suggested it, but he hoped she'd go shopping today for the new wardrobe she needed so badly. He'd given her quite a bit more than a month's salary, and he hoped her pride didn't get in the way of making herself presentable.

"Hi. Good morning," she said, her eyes darting around the room as if to confirm they were alone. "Um... I didn't mean to disturb you. I'll go back upstairs until you're gone." Her gaze flittered apprehensively over his damp shorts and T-shirt clad body.

What a picture he must make, he thought half amused, even as he marveled at the impeccable smoothness of her bare skin, and the black long lashes flanking those dark sensual eyes. She was one of those lucky women who didn't need makeup.

He set his empty mug on the table. "Michelle, it's okay. I was just having coffee. Besides, we need to talk about Precious' schedule and other things. What better time than when there's no one else around?"

"You run?"

"Seven to ten miles every day. And I lift weights three days a week at the country club." He chuckled. "Have to, or else I'll be as big as your pet bull Calvin. Mrs. Hayes is a wonderful cook, and I love to eat."

"I noticed that last night." A faint smile played at the corners of her voluptuous lips, but her eyes remained wary.

She was guarded, Erik thought with a frown. She wasn't the feisty spitfire that had burst into his study yesterday. Was it their kiss that was coming between them? Damn his blasted libido. "What about you, how do you stay in shape?"

She shrugged. "I walk. When I lost my job and had to give up my car, I learned to use the legs God gave me. But now—"

"Now you have a new job that comes with full medical and dental benefits and a membership to the Amherst Country Club. I take care of my employees, Michelle," he said with a smile.

"I noticed that. I visited Mrs. Hayes in the guesthouse last night. It's really nice."

"Well, she deserves it. Come, sit." He gestured toward the table. "Would you like a cup of coffee?"

"Please."

He took his empty mug to the coffee cart that Mrs. Hayes had been preparing every night for eight years. When Cassie was alive, after he returned from running, they would sit at the kitchen table and have coffee and read the newspaper together before he headed out to the hospital. Even after his wife's death, Mrs. Hayes continued to put out two mugs. This was the first time in two years that Erik would share his early morning cup of coffee with another person. Holly was a late riser—something he'd been thankful for.

Erik poured a mug for Michelle and refilled his. He opened the drawer of the cart, took out a spoon and set them on a tray.

"How do you like your coffee?" he asked.

"Just cream, thanks."

He got the cream from the fridge, added it to the tray, and took it to the table.

She gazed up with a half smile. "You sure I'm not disturbing you? Cause it looks to me like you had a private thing going here." She pointed to the unfolded copy of *The New York Times* on the table. "Some people need their solitude to get them going in the morning. Me, I just jump right into the day and tackle whatever it throws my way."

Erik grinned at her insightfulness. "It's a welcome change," he assured her, easing into the chair across from her. He watched as she picked up the jug and poured the cream into the coffee. He loved the way her slender brown fingers with the red painted nails enfolded the long white jug. Sexy fingers. He could just imagine them wrapped around his hard shaft.

"Did you sleep okay on your first night here?" He took a sip from his mug, grateful for the hot bitter sting to keep his thoughts from traveling down a salacious path. Everything about the woman made him think of sexual acts. He never realized he was this sexually deprived.

She shrugged. "I have to get used to sleeping in a strange house and bed, I suppose. You were out late," she added. "I turned in around midnight, and you still weren't home yet. That must be the longest running play in history." She took a careful sip of coffee, closing her eyes briefly as she swallowed the hot liquid.

"Actually, the play ended around nine then we went for ice cream, and finally ended up at my mother's."

"Does she live around here?"

"About fifteen minutes away. You'll probably meet her soon," he added with a hint of dread at that meeting. His mother wasn't one to hold her tongue. She spoke her mind, and if she thought he and Michelle were perfect for each other, she'd come right out and say it. Come to think of it, Michelle was a lot like her. She'd probably make Michelle her new best friend, just to annoy him.

"Precious will probably sleep late," he said. "You should wake her soon after I leave, or it would put a strain on her schedule today."

"Is she in boot camp? Will she be court-marshaled for skipping duty? Lighten up, Erik. She's only seven years old. It's summertime. She really shouldn't have a schedule. She'll survive sleeping in one day. I was a kid once. Trust me."

*Trust her.* He couldn't even trust himself. "You know, I know nothing about you," he said lightly. "Yesterday, I hired you to look after my daughter then I came on to you, for which, again, I deeply apologize. All I know is that you are good for my daughter." *And a damn good kisser.*

"Isn't the fact that I'm good for Precious enough?"

"I'm afraid not."

"What else do you want to know?"

"Just the necessary facts." Erik leaned back in his chair and folded his arms across his chest. His eyes assessed her softly. He wondered if she had a man in her life. Judging from the sexy sounds she made while he kissed her last night, he knew she could make a man forget everything but the softness of her delicate yielding body. Erik's jaws tightened at the image of Michelle's long legs wrapped around the waist of a nameless faceless man. Jealousy cruised through him.

"I am twenty-four," Michelle said. "You already know from my resume that I have a bachelor's degree, and you're aware of my past employment record. I've never been arrested. I love music, dancing, aerobics, and of course, children I adore."

"Any family besides your older brother?" He already knew her mother had passed away, but she didn't know that he knew.

"My mother died minutes after I was born. I never knew her. All I know about her is what Robert told me."

"I'm sorry about your losing your mother, but it does give you something in common with Precious. At least she had a chance to know hers, even if it was only for a very short time. I'm afraid that as she gets older, those memories will fade."

"Only if you let them. Even though I never knew my mother, I feel very close to her because of what Robert told me about her."

"What about your father?"

"He's dead, too." Michelle coughed, choking on the mouthful of coffee she'd taken before he popped the question. She reached for a napkin and pressed it to her mouth. She couldn't believe she'd just told the man a blatant lie. Up until this moment, she'd been an honest, truthful person. Of course, she'd told little harmless lies in jest before, but she'd never lied about anything so important.

She set the mug on the table and stared at Erik. She couldn't very well take it back now. Dwight Carter had been dead to her for years. But from this moment forward, he was also dead to the rest of the world.

"When did he die?" Erik asked.

"Some years ago," she answered simply, trying to avoid a specific date she would have to remember. *God, what had she done?* "And if you don't mind, I prefer not to talk about him."

Erik frowned at the bitterness in her voice and the hostility in her eyes. Yesterday, when Mrs. Hayes told him that Michelle's mother died when she was born, and how she used to look out for a little Michelle and Robert, he'd sensed that there was something else the old lady wasn't telling him. Did it have something to do with her father? Had the man abused her? What on earth could a father have done to his daughter to make her hate him so much, even beyond the grave?

He'd had a sheltered and happy childhood, and although his parents weren't married, they had both loved and cared for him. Something in Michelle's eyes told him she hadn't been that lucky.

"Is there anyone special in your life, Michelle?" He just had to know if there was someone out there she turned to when the sad memories of the past made her blue. Well, in all fairness these were the type of questions he would have asked yesterday before he hired her if he hadn't been sidetracked by her beauty, sassy mouth, and provocative attire.

She gave him a sidelong glance and asked rather cheekily, "You mean like a man?"

"Yes, like a man." *You wanted somebody older, someone unattached.*

*That's why you're asking,* he told himself.

She folded her arms across the tabletop and looked him squarely in the eye. "What do you think?"

"I don't know what to think. That's why I'm asking." Boy, his curiosity had gone way past the need-to-know interview stage. When had this line of questioning become so personal?

"Why is it important?" She licked her lips slowly as she held his gaze.

Erik rested his elbows on the table and laced his fingers under his chin as he studied her face. This cat and mouse game they were playing sent a hot tide of wanting through him. He'd never had to dance to this catch and release beat before. He'd known Cassie since they were teenagers. There had never been anyone else for either of them. This was all new to him.

Just who was the cat and who was the mouse here?

"It is important because the last nanny got married and resigned," he said with a patronizing edge to his voice. "That's the reason I wanted someone older. I don't care to put Precious through another loss anytime soon. I'm sorry if you think my question is too personal, but I'm just looking out for my daughter's best interest." *And the thought of another man kissing you, holding you the way I did last night is driving me out of my mind.*

Michelle let out a long slow breath and lowered her gaze to the coffee in her mug. Erik's grilling was getting a little too uncomfortable for her, especially the questions about her father. At least that boat had come to shore without capsizing.

After her talk with Yasmine, she'd gone down to the guesthouse to catch up on old times with Mrs. Hayes. During the conversation, Michelle had discovered that Cassandra Elizabeth LaCrosse had been killed months after Michelle's father had ruined her own life and disappeared from Manchester.

Since he was hundreds of miles away at the time, it wasn't even remotely possible that he could have committed the crime. Mrs. Hayes had also told her that the doctor and his wife were very much in love and that Cassie's death had changed Erik drastically from a happy, sociable family man to a grim workaholic who hardly spent any time at home. No wonder he'd been so aloof when she first met him, yesterday. Yet, she had to admit that something had changed in him by the end of the evening when he unexpectedly and passionately kissed the breath out of her. The man definitely had a volatile temperament, a trait she should pay careful attention to.

She'd heard him come in last night or more precisely, early this morning. As he'd put Precious to bed in the room next door, she'd fought the desire to get up and help since that was her job. But the memories of their hot kiss had kept her in bed. She wondered if it were the memories that had kept him from returning home last night.

It was a pretty embarrassing situation for both of them.

She wasn't ready to face him last night, nor this morning for that matter. She'd come downstairs to make a cup of coffee, hoping to escape back to her room without running into him. Yet, here they were in his kitchen—she in jeans and a T-shirt, mussed hair, and sleepy eyes, and he in a sleeveless jersey and running shorts, showing off his long strong limbs and muscular torso, and armed with a litany of questions about her personal life.

He had the right to probe her about her family background since he'd hired her to take care of his daughter. He had the right to know if she were psychologically and emotionally fit. And the one about her personal relationship with the opposite sex was quite legit, now that he'd explained his reason for asking.

She brought her gaze back to his. "If there was a man in my life, Erik LaCrosse, I would not have kissed you last night. I don't mess around. When I'm with a man, I'm with him only. I hope that answers your questions."

"Well, that's good to know since one of the requirements of this job is that you sign a five-year contract."

Michelle balked. "A five-year contract?"

"If that's a problem let me know now. As I said, I can't take the chance of another nanny walking out on my daughter. In five years, she'll be twelve and probably won't need a nanny anymore."

Michelle stared into her coffee mug again. She really had

nothing else planned for the next five years. So what the heck? "Okay, I'm yours for five years." By that time, she should have her own life back on track and ready to move on. It was a win-win situation.

Erik surveyed her quietly for a moment. The fact that she was unattached and available didn't make him feel any better. It just sealed his fate. He could have her if he wanted her. And he did want her, more than he cared to admit. He pushed back his chair and stood up. "Very well, then, if you'll come with me to the study, I'll give you Precious' itinerary. She's a busy little girl. I hope you can keep up with her."

"I better."

A slow smile crawled across his face. "You won your bet. The Jaguar is yours. Just be gentle with it, and make sure Precious is buckled up in the back seat at all times."

"Yes, sir," she said with a big grin and a soldier's salute.

Erik's heart did a somersault in his chest. That smile, those dark magnetic eyes, and those luscious lips were going to do him in.

***

"Can I have some Gummy Bears, Michelle?" Precious asked as the two walked down an aisle in the grocery store where Michelle had stopped to pick up her favorite treats.

"And some Oreos. They are my favorite."

"Anything you want." Michelle smiled down at the little girl's wind-blown hair and soiled clothes, evidence that she'd enjoyed her day.

Precious' schedule was filled with activities—ballet, music, swimming, theater, and horseback riding, not to mention two hours of reading every day. They were all noteworthy activities, mind you, but it was summertime, and a child ought to be able to relax and enjoy life for a couple months out of the year. And besides, Precious was scared of horses. But her father was too wrapped up in himself to notice.

Michelle believed Erik loved his daughter and wanted the

best for her, but knowing that some of the best things in life were free and spontaneous, she'd ignored the itinerary. Since she had to go to Manchester to get the rest of her stuff from Yasmine's apartment, she saw no harm in canceling Precious' classes and taking the little girl to her old neighborhood playground where she spent a couple hours playing with Yasmine's nephew, Peter, and some other kids.

Michelle knew she might catch hell from Erik for her impetuous behavior, but what was done was done. The important thing was that Precious had a great time, and she'd found a new friend in Peter.

"Grandma! Grandma!"

"Wait, Precious!" Michelle raced after the vanishing figure and turned a corner to see Precious enveloped in the arms of a woman who looked young enough to be her mother.

"How's my favorite granddaughter?" she said, grinning at Precious.

So this was Erik's mother?

"I'm your only granddaughter, Grandma." Precious giggled.

"Yes, you are. But you'd still be my favorite even if I had a hundred."

"Oh, Grandma."

The woman stared at Michelle. "Is this your new nanny?"

"Uh-huh. Her name is Michelle."

A subtle smile lit her face as she lowered Precious to the floor. She held a hand out to Michelle. "I'm Felicia, Erik's mother."

"Hello, Mrs. LaCrosse."

She chuckled. "No dear, I'm not Mrs. LaCrosse. It's Felicia Ryce, but you can call me Felicia."

Erik's mother was tall, with bouncy, black shoulder-length hair. She didn't look anything like a grandmother at all. She was classy and beautiful with a face that reminded Michelle of Diahann Carroll. Her smile was warm and genuine, as was her handshake. But why was her name Ryce and not LaCrosse like Erik's? Precious had told her about her two grandmas, Felicia and Danielle. She knew Erik's father was married to Danielle and living in the resort mountain town of Granite Falls. She'd assumed that Felicia had kept her married name after divorcing Erik's father—lots of women did that. Perhaps she'd remarried to somebody named Ryce... No, there was no ring on her finger, so...

"How do you like the job so far?" Felicia asked.

"I just started yesterday and I'm tired already," Michelle said, giving the woman a wide smile. "Your granddaughter has more energy that a fully grown thoroughbred."

Felicia grinned. "I know what you mean. You definitely have to take your vitamins to keep up with Precious." She frowned as she inspected her granddaughter. "Why is she so dirty? She looks like she needs a good scrubbing."

"I went to the park, Grandma. And it was so much fun, and I met Yasmine and Peter. He taught me how to spit, real far. You want me to show you?"

"Not in the store, baby. You only spit outdoors. Aren't you supposed to be at piano right now?" She directed her question to Precious, but her eyes were centered on Michelle.

"I canceled her lessons," Michelle said. "She was out late last night and I thought she needed a day off from her rigid schedule. Erik said they stopped by to visit you."

Felicia started laughing, almost doubling over with the humor.

Michelle frowned, wondering what on earth could be amusing the woman so.

"They did, and now I understand why he didn't want to go home," she said, sobering up a little. "Precious, baby, why don't you go to the end of this aisle and get your grandma two cans of tomato soup, and a can of lentils? Take your time."

She gave Michelle a whimsical grin when Precious was out of earshot. "I like you already. It's about time a woman stood up to that boy of mine. My son is a wonderful man; he was a great husband, but Lord he could be so bloody demanding, has been since the day he was born."

Michelle recalled the feel of Erik's firm lips on hers last night, and his strong arms pinning her to his hard lean body as he kissed her into submission. He was indeed demanding. A shiver ran up her spine as she pictured herself lying beneath him, naked and submissive, as he took her, hard and fast. God, she didn't even know she liked it that...

"When Cassie died, Erik didn't have a clue what to do with Precious."

She startled as Felicia's voice pulled her out of her licentious daydream.

"So he signed her up for every extracurricular activity that came across his path. I've spoken to him, but he thinks because he's her father, he knows what's best for Precious. He couldn't be further from the truth."

"I know," Michelle agreed, wondering what the woman would think of her if she knew what she'd been thinking about her son a moment ago. "Precious doesn't even like horses."

"Cassie loved them. She rode almost every day until she got pregnant with Precious, and never after she was born. She had a new second love."

Michelle guessed Erik must have been her first.

"I loved Cassie. She was a sweet soul, but too submissive. She never stood up to Erik. She wouldn't even give him a good argument."

Michelle's mind wandered back to the previous night and the story Erik had told her about the night his wife died. If Felicia was right, then the late Mrs. LaCrosse must have felt awfully trapped in that car with her husband pelting her with questions. No wonder she wanted to escape. Michelle felt a bit of sympathy for the dead woman.

"I'm afraid Precious is very much like Cassie," Felicia said. "She loves her daddy, and would do anything he asks. Holly used to complain about his high demands and expectations from her, but she was too scared to say anything to Erik, or do anything this drastic."

Michelle stiffened her back as the enormity of her actions finally hit her. "You think he'll fire me?"

Felicia gave her that once over again. "Fire you? I don't think so. Precious is the most important thing in the world to my son. He would cut off his right arm to see her smile. She's smiling again, thanks to you. He wouldn't mess with that."

"It's good to know I have an ace up my sleeve then."

Felicia patted her arm as Precious headed back down the aisle toward them. "He isn't going to like it, not one bit. He'll holler and beat his chest like the dominant male in an ape colony, but you stand up to him, you hear?" She smiled lovingly at her granddaughter then crouched down to kiss her forehead. "Grandma has to go, baby. But I'll be seeing you when I get back from my trip." She turned to Michelle. "Remember what I told you," she said and took off.

"Your soup, Grandma," Precious called, running after her.

"Take them home to your daddy. He might need something warm to settle his stomach tonight."

# CHAPTER FIVE

Michelle's heart jolted when she heard the front door open and close.

"Daddy's home." Precious jumped off her lap and bolted out of the family room. She hadn't seen her father all day, and even though she was worn out from her day at the park and shopping with Michelle, she'd been fighting sleep until he came home.

Michelle remained where she was, huddled in the corner of the sofa, too scared that her legs would refuse to bear her weight. *Stand your ground*, she told herself, remembering what Felicia had said. Ever since she'd met Erik's mother, she'd been rehearsing her explanation speech. Like Felicia and Yasmine had warned, it wasn't the fact that she'd canceled Precious' lessons that would upset him, but that she'd done it without consulting him.

She imagined he'd been too upset with her to even come home for dinner. Mrs. Hayes had been in the middle of setting the table when he'd called. He'd asked to speak with Precious, and judging from her responses, Michelle guessed he was asking her about her day's activities. What was to be a scrumptious meal of stuffed roast chicken and artichokes dipped in butter had felt like wood and sand in Michelle's mouth.

That was three hours ago. It was now past Precious' bedtime. Michelle looked up as father and daughter walked into the room. Erik's eyes impaled her from about twelve feet away. Michelle stared back with uncertainty, but innate tenacity as she closed the book she'd been reading to Precious and set it on the lamp table.

Dr. Erik LaCrosse was about to find out that she was nothing like his late wife. Cassie LaCrosse may have been afraid of confrontations. Michelle, on the other hand, had been tackling them all her life. She'd never backed down from a fight. You do that in her neighborhood, and people would be standing in line to stomp on you.

She watched as Erik crouched down to his daughter's eye level and brushed back some unruly curls from her face. "It's past your bedtime," he said. "Go to your room. I'll be up soon to tuck you in."

"Okay, Daddy." She yawned and turned to Michelle. "Good night, Michelle. I had a lot of fun today. Can we go to the park again, tomorrow?"

"We'll see. Sleep tight, honey. See you in the morning." Michelle prayed she wouldn't have to break that promise as she watched Precious leave. She pushed to her feet as Erik strode toward her.

"Do you have any idea how worried I was when I couldn't get a hold of you today? I called home several times and all Mrs. Hayes knew was that you'd taken my daughter to Manchester. Why didn't you answer your phone?"

Michelle swallowed. "I'm sorry you were worried, Erik, but I called the hospital and they told me you were in surgery. I left a message. As to my phone, I forgot to charge it last night and it died. I'm sorry," she reiterated.

"You're sorry. You're sorry." The muscles in his neck pulsed with barely contained anger. "Who do you think you are to be changing Precious' schedule on your first day here? You are her nanny, not her mother."

"Erik, I know I'm not Precious' mother and I'm not trying to replace her, either. But come on, you really think one missed piano lesson and two hours of reading for one day is going to have a lasting negative effect on her?"

"That's beside the point, Michelle. *You* don't make decisions for my daughter. You follow the ones I give you, not defy them. She's my child! Not yours!"

"It doesn't matter whose child she is, Erik. The important thing is that she is a child. One from whom you expect too much. You've overloaded her with swimming, dance, equestrian, and music lessons. The child doesn't even have a day off to relax and be a kid. And now you went and signed her up for the summer theater—acting lessons. She doesn't want to be an actress. She just wants to be a kid."

His hands balled into fists and his jaw muscles twitched. "Precious enjoys all those activities."

"She hates them. The only thing she likes is ballet, and maybe music. She's afraid of horses. Did you know that?"

He stiffened as though she'd struck him.

Michelle wanted to point out that Precious was not Cassie, but thought the sound of his beloved wife's name falling from her lips at a time like this would be a grave mistake. "You made up this itinerary to keep Precious out of your hair," she said. "She goes along to keep you happy."

"I don't want my daughter growing up without focus and discipline like you. And how dare you take her to that neighborhood of yours? You know what kind of..." His voice trailed off.

Michelle winced at the implications in the unspoken yet hurtful words, but decided to let it go. It was time for the doctor to face himself, deal with the real issue that was eating him up. She really didn't want to cause him more pain or guilt. God knows he had enough to last him a lifetime, but Precious was a powerless child and somebody had to fight for her. Holly, according to Felicia, was too chicken to do it.

Michelle realized that he might fire her when he heard what she had to say. If that was the case, then so be it, because she knew in her heart she could not do a good job at taking care of Precious if things remained the way they were.

Michelle wrapped her arms about her stomach to stop the panic rioting inside her. Her voice shook as she spoke. "Erik, I know you think that what you're doing is best for your daughter, but apart from last night, have you really spent any quality time with Precious since her mother died?"

"I have a demanding career. I don't have much time to spend with her. That's why I hired a nanny. I was just lucky my phone didn't ring during the play last night."

"That's exactly what I'm talking about. Precious lost her mother and she's scared she's losing you, too." Michelle knew how Precious felt. She and Robert had done everything to win their father's attention after their mother died. But it was never enough. If it weren't for good neighbors like Mrs. Hayes and Yasmine's parents, she probably wouldn't have even survived infancy.

"You don't understand." He grated out between clenched teeth. "Cassie was my life, and some drunk came along and took her away from me. I'm doing the best I can."

"Why don't you stop feeling sorry for yourself, Erik, and concentrate on your daughter? Yes, your wife is gone, but your daughter is alive, and she needs you. Stop wallowing in self-pity and guilt and show her how much you love her."

His chest rose and fell and his eyes glowed like a furnace. "Don't you dare tell me how to deal with my grief. You have no idea what I'm going through. This pain and this guilt... They are eating me up inside and there's no one I can talk to."

Michelle knew she'd struck a raw nerve—probably one that hadn't been touched for two years. She longed to tell him that he had her, that he could talk to her, but Precious was her primary concern. If she could just get Precious' straightened out, she would make time for Erik, she swore in her heart.

"Did you know?" she said in a strangled voice, "that the day your wife died, she was upset with Precious because she'd lost something dear to her."

His eyes clouded. "What are you talking about?"

Michelle paused, not wanting to go on, but knowing she had to. He needed to know how his daughter felt about him. It was the only way to bridge the distance between them. The truth hurt, but she knew it could also heal the pain inside them both.

She shoved her hand in the pocket of her shorts. "Here," she said pulling it out, and opening her palm.

He snatched the pink diamond bracelet from her hand. "Where did you get this?"

"From Precious. She has this little box where she keeps— things. I saw the bracelet when she opened the box to store my lucky penny."

He spread the bracelet in his palm and held it under the light of the table lamp. It shimmered, shooting rays of pink across the room. "I've been looking for this. It's the last Mother's Day gift I gave to Cassie." His eyes came back to her face. "Precious had it all this time?"

Michelle nodded. "That day, Precious took some of her mother's jewelry from her closet to play dress up with her dolls. Apparently, your wife wanted to wear the bracelet to the party that night, and when she realized that Precious had lost it, she told her she was grounded until she found it."

Michelle swallowed back a choke as he fisted his hand around the piece of jewelry and brought it against his chest. "Your wife left home that night very upset with your daughter, which is quite understandable under normal circumstances," Michelle continued in as tranquil a voice as possible. "But, Precious never saw her again, Erik. She thinks it's her fault that her mother left. She thinks she was a bad girl. That's why she does everything you ask. She thinks if she makes you angry, you'll leave, too. She tries so hard to please you, but you make it so difficult for her. She's just a little girl who needs her daddy's attention!"

The last statement was hurled from a place deep inside Michelle's heart. A place where she'd lived as a child, constantly trying to please her father, but getting nowhere. Tears pooled in her eyes for the desperate child upstairs and the half-broken man standing in front of her.

His fist dropped to his side. "How could I have not known? Why didn't she tell me?"

Michelle heard the anguish in his tortured voice. Her heart ached for him like it had never ached for another living soul. She took a step toward him, wanting to offer him comfort just as she'd done last night when he'd told her about the night his wife died in his arms. "Because she was afraid, Erik. She thought you'd be angry. If I can help you—"

"Help me? You can't help me." He stumbled backward, his huge body shaking uncontrollably. "Just... go. Leave me alone."

Michelle staggered blindly out of the room, not knowing whether or not she still had a job.

Erik closed his eyes and grabbed the back of the sofa to stop the trembling. His gut crunched painfully. He opened his mouth and took deep breaths into his constricted lungs, then fell to the floor, his head bowed in misery. He wept inside, but didn't shed a single tear. How could he have been so blind to his baby's pain?

Michelle was right for accusing him of being a neglectful father who was wallowing in self-pity and guilt.

*Damn her for being right.*

The truth hurt like hell. For two years he'd hidden behind his grief, afraid to face his loss because the future had seemed so bleak without his wife. He'd tried to imagine that it was just a long bad dream and that Cassie would come back to him. He'd told himself that she was on an extended vacation and that life would return to normal after she came home and they resolved that last stupid argument.

But she wasn't coming home. She was gone forever. He'd spent two years feeling sorry for himself, and denied his daughter the only other parent she had.

It had taken Michelle Carter, a girl from the wrong side of Manchester's tracks, to yank him out of his trance. *Damn her!* He slammed his elbows into the back of the sofa. Damn her for slapping him with the truth, for forcing him to face reality, to do what Cassie had asked as he'd held her bleeding mangled body in his arms on that dark horrible night.

*"Oh, Erik, you know how I hate tears. Don't cry, darling. Just live. Live, and take care of our baby. Love her, Erik. Love her for me. Tell her I'm sorry for—"*

Cassie's last unfinished request pierced him cruelly. All this time he thought Cassie had asked him to tell Precious she was sorry for leaving her, when in fact she'd been sorry for being angry at her. And all this time, Precious thought it was her fault her mother wasn't here.

God, it was nobody's fault but his. His alone.

Erik pushed off the floor and climbed the stairs two at a time, and headed in the direction of Precious' room. Her door was ajar and the light from the hall fell across her small form. Erik felt a tightening in his chest as he gazed at his child.

She was so beautiful and innocent. She shouldn't be saddled with the guilt of her mother's death. No child should. He'd spent two years wallowing in his own guilt when he should have been there for her, absorbing her pain, getting to know her the way her mother knew her. He was the only parent she had, and he'd let her down. Cassie must be so disappointed in him.

Erik moved closer to the bed where she lay with Bradie clutched in her arms. His jaws flinched when he saw the white streaks on her cheeks. She'd been crying. God, he hoped she hadn't heard his argument with Michelle. As angry as he'd been, he'd tried to keep his voice low so it wouldn't carry up the stairs.

Erik sat on the side of the bed and picked up her warm body. He laid her across his lap, cradling her head against his chest. Unbidden tears rolled down his cheeks and melted into her head of tangled curls. He just held her, and allowed the essence of her innocent childhood to seep under his skin, melt his pain.

"I'm sorry, Precious. I'm so sorry. I didn't know. It's not your fault, Muffin. Your mommy loved you very much. That was the last thing she said to me. She asked me to take care of you, and I haven't been doing that, have I? Baby, I promise I'll try from now on. I'll do my best to love you the way she did."

Precious stirred and clutched the front of his shirt. "Mommy."

Erik held his breath, his heart racing in his chest. "Precious," he whispered.

"Daddy."

"Yes, baby. It's daddy."

"I love you."

"I love you too, baby."

He gazed into her face. Her eyes were still closed. Was she dreaming or did she know he was actually holding her? Dreaming or not, her words sent a feeling of genuine filial warmth rushing through Erik's heart. Something he hadn't felt for a long, long time.

\*\*\*

The sounds of laughter caught Erik's attention as he came down the stairs. He followed it to the family room where he found Michelle and Precious on a couple of oversized pillows on the floor in front of the wall-mounted TV.

With mild interest, he noted the contrast of Michelle's short black hair to his daughter's long brown mane. They were both wearing white shorts and cotton tops. New clothes, he noted with a smile, glad that Michelle had something new, something of her own to wear.

Watching them brought back memories of coming home to find Cassie and Precious sprawled on the floor—sometimes reading, sometimes playing a board game, sometimes having tea with her dolls, and sometimes watching TV. And just as Michelle was enjoying Bugs Bunny—Precious' favorite cartoon—so had Cassie.

He wasn't sure what to make of his comparisons between his wife and his daughter's new nanny. He never had the same thoughts about Holly even though she'd participated in the same activities with Precious. Perhaps his feelings were derived from the fact that Precious had taken to Michelle like lightening to a rod when it had taken her weeks to warm up to Holly. His daughter had known Michelle for exactly one day and she'd already shared her heart's deepest fears and secrets with her— fears and secrets she couldn't share with him—her own father.

He, too, had succumbed to the magical spell of this beautiful woman when he'd told her about Cassie just hours after they'd met. Then last night, she'd made him face his own harrowing fears. There was no denying it: there was something special

THE DOCTOR'S SECRET BRIDE

about Michelle.

Was she an angel?

A wistful expression crowded his face as he wondered if Precious remembered him holding her last night. He dreaded their impending talk about the day her mother died, but he knew it had to be done today if their relationship was to improve. He couldn't have his daughter carrying the guilt of her mother's death or worrying about him leaving her any longer.

*Bang! Bang!* Michelle and Precious roared with laughter as Elmer Fudd fired his shotgun only to discover that the mischievous rabbit had bent the barrel backward so it went off in the hunter's face. Erik found himself grinning as well.

As his eyes fixated on Michelle's firm buttocks, slim hips, and a narrow waist he could easily span with his hands, his grin faded. Bolts of lightning shot through his veins as he imagined her sleek thighs and long smooth brown legs wrapped around his waist. The woman was temptation, personified. And she made him hard and hot and heavy. Erik knew his feelings went far beyond the physical when he found himself imagining a little boy with short black hair and black eyes lying beside Michelle and his daughter.

"Hey you two," he said, walking into the room. He needed something—anything—to derail those dangerous thoughts.

Precious jumped up and ran over to wrap her arms around his thighs. She gazed up at him with excitement. "We're watching Bugs Bunny. You wanna watch him with us, Daddy?"

"In a little while, dear. You and I need to have a talk, first."

Erik's eyes followed Michelle's movements as she uncurled from the pillow and rose to her feet. When her gaze locked with his, he saw the uncertainty in her eyes. After last night, the tension between them was understandably tenuous. It wouldn't take much to shatter it completely.

"I'll go... for a walk or something," she said heading toward the door.

It was Saturday, and Mrs. Hayes was off for the weekend. Holly used to have every other weekend off, depending on his schedule. She would have been free today, thus Michelle was free. But he wanted to keep her around. He told himself it was because it was her third day on the job, and she needed to get used to her new routine, but his heart knew better.

"Wait, Michelle. After my talk with Precious, I'd like to take us out to breakfast, that is if you have no other plans."

"You don't have to, Erik. I'm—"

"It's a peace offering after last night." He wanted to apologize for the insensitive words he'd said to her, but couldn't do so in front of Precious. She'd done him a wealth of good. He wondered how he could ever repay her.

She nodded her head in acknowledgment then left him alone with his daughter.

"I had a dream last night, Daddy." Precious jumped on his lap the minute he dropped onto the sofa.

"Was it good, or bad?"

"Good, Daddy. If it was bad then it would be a nightmare."

"You're so wise." He nudged her nose with his. "So what did you dream about? Me?"

She laughed. "No. I dreamt about Mommy. She was brushing her hair and I was putting on all her jewelry in her jewelry box. She said I looked pretty. And then she said she loved me."

Erik's heart stopped for a minute and he tightened his hold on her. She must have heard Michelle tell him about the lost bracelet then cried herself to sleep. Erik was not a superstitious man, but something told him that Cassie had seen her daughter's pain and had visited her dreams to comfort her. "And she does love you, honey," he said, his voice cracking a little.

"Even in heaven?"

"Even in heaven." He took a deep breath, and cradling her face in his hand, he gazed into her eyes. "Michelle told me what happened the day Mommy died. It wasn't your fault, Precious. You had nothing to do with what happened to her. You must always remember that she did love you, very much. You were the most important thing in the world to her. The last thing she said to me was how much she loved you."

"She did?"

"Yes. Would you like to have this?" He placed the bracelet in her hand. "It was your mother's favorite and I'm sure she would love for you to have it."

Tears gathered in her eyes as she stared at the bracelet glittering against her palm. "I'm sorry I took it, and made Mommy mad."

Erik pulled her close. "It's okay, baby. Mommy isn't mad anymore. And, Precious," he continued, "I am not going anywhere. I will always be here for you." Erik prayed in his heart that he wasn't making a promise he couldn't keep. But the child needed to be reassured that she had one parent she could count on. "If you ever think I'm being too hard on you, I want you to tell me. I won't get upset and I won't leave you. Okay?" He searched her face for an inkling of understanding.

"Okay, Daddy. You know what else?" she said after a brief pause.

Her brown eyes beamed with excitement, touching Erik in the deepest part of his soul. "What else?"

"Last night I dreamt you came into my room, and you were holding me, and you told me you loved me."

"I had that very same dream, Precious."

"Oh, Daddy. We were in each other's dreams." She pressed her lips against her father's cheek then wrapped her arms around his neck.

"We will always be in each other's dreams, my darling Precious. *Always*. Now, where would you like to go for breakfast?" he asked as he set her on the floor.

"McDonald's."

"Oh, Precious…"

"But, I love the pancakes."

Erik grimaced, getting to his feet. "Go get Michelle. She'll be delighted to know I'm taking her to McDonald's on our first date."

As Precious ran in search of Michelle, Erik pondered on his choice of words. *Date?* Did he actually say, *date?*

He went into the study, got his cell from his desk and slipped it into his shirt pocket. On his way out, he stopped at the door and gazed up at the picture of his wife. He instantly felt like a traitor for even thinking about taking another woman out for a simple breakfast.

"I'm just thanking her for bringing me to my senses about our little girl. You understand, right?" he said to the portrait.

He waited as if he expected a response. "I'm not breaking any rules," he continued as the two-year-old conversation between his wife and his best friend surfaced in his mind, reluctantly pulling him back into his friend's kitchen that awful night.

*"You have to tell Erik, Cassie. Tonight. I can't keep lying to him. He's my best friend."*

*"I can't, Clay. It will kill him. I can't hurt him like that. He loves me so much."*

*"Yes, he does love you. And it will break his heart, but he'll... he'll heal. He'll forgive you and move on. He'll still have Precious and—"*

*Unable to take any more, Erik barged into the kitchen. "What the hell is going on here? Are you two having an affair?"*

*Both Cassie and Clayton jumped at the sound of his voice. Cassie, being Cassie, just stood there, looking all sweet and innocent, staring at him with her big brown eyes and ringing her hands while Clayton immediately confronted him.*

*"Damn it, Erik. What the hell kind of question is that?"*

*He collared his best friend. "I heard you tell her that she has to tell me. I knew there was something going on between the two of you. All the secret stares when you think I'm not watching, the secret meetings of late—"*

*"Stop it, Erik," Cassie begged. "Just stop it, please."*

*And true to her character, Cassie ran out into the night through the back door.*

He'd found her standing beside their car, crying. It was the second time he'd seen his wife cry in all the years he'd known her. The first was when she'd held their newborn daughter in her arms for the first time.

After Cassie's death, he'd asked Clayton about the conversation he'd overheard. His friend had just looked at him and said, "What does it matter now? Cassie is dead. Let it go, Erik."

Then Clayton, whom he'd known since med school, pulled up his roots and left New Hampshire. Erik had no idea where he'd gone. It was just as well. He really didn't want answers to the questions in his head. He'd taken Clayton's advice and let it go, that is, until now. Could it be that he wanted the truth now that he'd met a woman to whom he was potently attracted? Was he looking for closure so he could move on?

Erik closed the door, shutting out the ghosts of his past. As he walked down the hall, he knew he would have to face them again. He wasn't looking forward to it. Not in the least.

# CHAPTER SIX

"Michelle, you know what?"

"What, Precious?" Michelle held her gaze in the dresser mirror as she brushed the little girl's hair.

"I want you to live with us forever."

"Forever is a long time, Precious, but I'll be here for as long as you need me." *Five years to be exact.* She put down the brush and led Precious to the pink canopy bed. She pulled back the ruffled comforter and helped her in.

The room was furnished with pink and white lacquered furniture and light pink wallpaper with an Arabian motif of princesses reclining on divans. Pictures of Precious and her parents were everywhere. They looked happy, Michelle thought, then wondered for the millionth time, what was it that Erik and his wife were arguing about the night she was killed.

Could it be that she was having an affair? Michelle found it hard to believe that a woman married to such a fine specimen of a man would cheat on him. He was everything a woman wanted in a husband. If she were married to him, she wouldn't even notice other men existed.

*But you aren't married to him,* a tiny voice whispered. *You're his daughter's nanny, not a replacement for his wife.* With that sober thought, she tucked Bradie under Precious' arms and pulled the covers up around them. "Prayers," she said, kneeling on the lambskin rug beside the bed.

Precious said her 'God Blesses' for all the people in her small world, then whispered something under her breath.

Michelle kissed each of her cheeks. "Your daddy will be in to read you a story."

"I asked God to let you live with us forever."

So that was the whispered request. Pain nipped Michelle's heart as she left the room. She'd become very attached to the child in a very short time, and she would love nothing more than to live with her forever, but the sensible woman in her knew that was not possible. She was the nanny, hired to take care of Precious, not fill the role of her mommy. After five years, she would have to leave, whether she wanted to or not.

In the meantime, everyone was benefiting from the situation. Precious had a nanny; she had a job and a place to live; and Erik, well, he had adult conversation during dinner, someone with whom to share his daily achievements.

She was sure there was nothing special about it. He probably had a similar relationship with Holly when she was the nanny. It was foolish to entertain the idea that she could ever be more than a live-in babysitter.

Michelle found Erik in the study leafing through a medical journal. "Precious is ready for you," she said, her heart fluttering at the sight of him reclined comfortably on the sofa.

He looked up and his eyes scanned down her body. "You're wet."

Michelle glanced down at the shirt she wore over a pair of old jeans. Sure enough, the front was damp from giving Precious a bath. It wasn't soaked, but it might as well have been, from the way it clung to her body.

She should have changed, she realized—too late—as she felt her nipples harden under his dark gaze. She'd taken off her bra because her breasts became excruciatingly tender when she was ovulating. She was ovulating tonight, and from the heat in her belly, she bet her optimistic eggs were on the lookout for a wandering sperm to make some magic happen.

Instinctively, her arms folded across her bosom. The pep talk she'd given herself just a minute ago meant nothing. Her traitorous body was crying out for this man like it had never cried for any other. She hadn't even felt this kind of excitement the night she gave her virginity to Ryan.

He was the only man she'd ever been with, but from the experiences, she'd long ago determined that sex was highly overrated. When Ryan brought up the subject of marriage, Michelle had fled from that relationship. No way was she going to suffer through a lifetime of boring sex and faked orgasms. She'd rather stay single.

Well, that was until she met this man who made her body throb from just thinking about him. "I'll go change my shirt." She would have to change her panties, too. They were soaked.

She noticed the muscles in Erik's jaws tighten as he got up from the sofa. He came and stood next to her, looking down with open desire in his gold-flecked eyes. She heard the long deep intake of air into his lungs before he strolled out of the room. He hadn't touched her, but he'd left his mark on her, nonetheless.

Michelle's body quivered as she watched Erik walk away from her. She could smell the desire in him. He wanted her just as much as she wanted him, but in his book, it was unethical to have a sexual liaison with his daughter's nanny.

Besides, the man was still in love with his dead wife. She wasn't competing with that.

Michelle was sitting on a lounge chair on the patio off the kitchen, gazing up at a starless sky and listening to crickets chirping in the woods behind the house, when Erik came out and eased into a chair next to her. He crossed one leg over the other, and leaned his head back.

There was no moon to light the night and the lights in the kitchen were turned down low. A slight breeze cooled the night air as they sat quietly. She was happy he couldn't see her because she hadn't changed her shirt. The coolness of the cloth against her skin reminded her of the charged, two-sentence conversation the wet shirt had sparked.

His breathing filled the air around her, causing tension to build. Michelle knew she should say something, anything to break the silence, yet she waited for him to start. She'd come out here to escape a run-in with him and collect her thoughts before going upstairs to work on her book.

She supposed he had sought her out because he had something to say. The only time they really talked was at the dinner table, or when they had to discuss Precious' schedule, including her activities, which had been cut to two—ballet and swimming.

Usually, after tucking Precious into bed, he'd escape to his study and she would open up her laptop. Writing had become a pleasurable escape for her to keep her mind off him. She was sure it was because she was writing about the kids at the youth center, kids she loved and could relate to. She missed them, and turning their experiences into a book made her feel closer to them, like Jo in *Little Women*, writing about her and her sisters' lives.

All the proceeds from her book, when and if she sold it, would go to the center. Since she'd left Manchester, she called the center every day, just to check in with Rose, one of the women who helped out. She wanted to make sure all the kids were okay, that none of them needed anything. She wanted so badly to go see them, but she couldn't leave Precious alone and she didn't dare take her back to 'that kind of neighborhood' again.

"What was it like growing up without a mother?"

His voice, and the surprising question, startled Michelle. She'd anticipated that when he finally said something, it would be about his daughter or the twins he delivered today. She didn't expect it would be personal. He hadn't asked her anything personal since her first morning on the job.

She wriggled around on the lounge chair and cleared her throat, giving herself time to think about her reply. At least he didn't ask about life with her father. He'd asked about life without her mother. *That* she could be truthful about. "Empty,

I guess, and a bit lonely and sad."

"What did you miss most? I'm asking so I'll know how to make up for Precious' loss. I hope you don't mind sharing that part of your life with me."

Michelle sighed deeply. "Well, she died when I was born, so I can't say I missed her, since I never had her. I think what I missed was the idea of having a mother. Knowing her touch, her voice, her smell, her laugh." Her voice cracked, and she sniffled, remembering the wonderful things Robert had told her about their mother. He'd tried to describe her laugh, her touch, her voice to her, and at those moments, Michelle would close her eyes and just imagine. "I never had those things," she continued, "but my brother tried to bring her to life for me by telling me about her. So, if I had suddenly lost my mother, like Precious lost hers, those are the things I would miss most."

"But you had your father. He must have compensated in some big way."

Michelle wanted to laugh even though her heart was heavy. Yeah, her father did compensate, but not in the way Erik thought. She turned to his huge shadow, silhouetted against the darkness. "My father wasn't there for me, Erik. He was too busy feeling sorry for himself after my mother died. He forgot about the two little children who needed him."

"That's why you got so angry with me for neglecting Precious."

"I know how she feels," Michelle stated softly. "The agony of losing one parent is bad enough, but when you have one who just ignores you—now, that's a killer. Soon you stop trusting or believing in anybody and you just lock yourself away inside you where it's safe."

"Is that what happened to you, Michelle? You stopped trusting?" His voice was gentle, probing.

Michelle uttered a dry laugh and wrapped her arms around her stomach. She wished she'd stopped trusting, believing. If she had, she would not be sitting on Erik LaCrosse's patio. She would be in Manchester, living the life she'd planned for herself, not the one someone else's destructive behavior had forced on her, but then again, she would not have met Erik.

"No." She shook her head. "I'm the anomaly, Erik. I'm always looking for the good in folks, hoping for the best, but I keep getting hurt. That's why I volunteer at the youth center. I know how those kids feel."

He leaned forward. Closer. "Who hurt you, Michelle?" His voice was low, husky.

Stirred by the tenderness in his voice, Michelle opened her mouth to lay her heart at his feet, but the fragile moment was broken by the sound of the phone ringing in the kitchen.

He swore softly as he got up to answer it. "Don't go anywhere. I'll be right back."

Michelle's heart hammered as she watched him walk into the kitchen and turn on the light. He left the sliders open, so she heard him say, "Hello," then chuckle at the response on the other line. But when he said, "Of course not, Bridget. I'm never too busy for you," a wave of jealousy ripped through Michelle.

*Who the heck was Bridget?* He had asked her if there was a man in her life—a legitimate question since the former nanny had married and left his daughter high and dry. It wasn't her place to question him about any relationship with a woman. Even though he came home for dinner every evening, and locked himself away in his study every night, she'd suspected he might have someone to turn to in his hour of masculine need. She'd assumed he kept them away from the house so as not to confuse his daughter who still wasn't over the death of her mother.

Men needed sex to survive. She'd heard that constantly from the few she'd dated over the years. She'd never felt compelled to give them any, so they'd quietly and solemnly faded away. She'd tried so hard not to think of Erik with another woman, especially since she knew what it was like to be in his arms, to kiss him, feel his hot hard body pressed up against hers. As long as she didn't see him with a woman, or hear him talk of one, she'd told herself that he didn't have one. There was no denying it anymore. *He had Bridget.*

Michelle got to her feet and studied the grin on his face as he leaned against the sink with the receiver clipped to his ear. She wished there was another way into the house without going past him, but since the other entrances were locked, she took a deep breath, walked briskly through the sliding doors, and tried to make a dash from the kitchen.

"Hold on a minute, Bridge," he said as she reached the island. "Michelle."

Michelle grabbed the cool marble and turned her head. His hand was over the mouthpiece. She stared at him, forcing a stiff smile. The last thing she wanted was for him to know she was jealous of some other female. "I'm tired. I'm going to bed, Erik," she said calmly.

"I said I wouldn't be long." He came over to her.

"You shouldn't keep Bridget waiting."

His eyebrows puckered. "She's just a friend. A colleague. We work together."

Now why did he think he had to explain himself? Erik wondered, as he gazed into Michelle's tantalizing black eyes. He'd been getting to know her a minute ago. He'd heard the ache hanging on the edge of her voice when she'd talked about her mother. He'd welcomed the sweet scent of *Moonlight* rising from her body.

As he'd sat quietly with her in the dark, he'd been thinking about that first night and the kiss they'd shared, and her hard nipples poking from beneath her wet T-shirt when she'd come down to get him earlier. He'd fought the urge to take her into his arms, kiss her again and again, feel her melt into him, tremble at his touch, moan with want for him.

After tucking Precious in, he'd gone back to his study, hoping to squelch his desires in the journal he'd been reading earlier. But after reading the same paragraph several times and having no idea what it said, he'd given up. He'd gone to the kitchen for a glass of water when he spotted her on the patio through the sliders. She looked lost in her own world, just sitting there staring into the dark night. His head had told him he should just leave her be and not play with fire. But his heart wanted to be close to her.

He'd been on the very verge of insanity when he'd joined her.

That's why he'd brought up the subject of her mother. He needed something far removed from the carnal need rampaging inside him. And now, here he was explaining a simple phone call.

"You don't have to explain anything to me, Erik. I'm just the babysitter. She walked stoically into the dining room.

Erik stared at her until she disappeared from sight. He didn't even know what the heck was going on in his house.

It was just one big bag of confusion. Maybe he should just bed the girl and get it over with. They were two consenting adults who wanted each other. That was as plain as daybreak. So why were they pussyfooting around the inevitable?

"Erik. Erik. Are you still there?"

He removed his hand from the mouthpiece. "Yes, Bridget. I'm still here."

"Goodness, I thought I lost you for a moment."

*You did.*

"As I was saying, have you given any more thought to my suggestion about the upcoming gala in Boston?"

"You mean the one where you want to be my date?"

She laughed. "Yes, that one. We're both unattached, so I don't see why we can't go as a couple. We can spend the night."

Erik ruffled his lips, ruefully. Now here was a woman in his own league and social class openly offering herself to him on a silver platter. One night of sex with Bridget would probably take care of his need—no strings attached, at least for him.

But he knew it wouldn't be enough. Sex for him was something special, only to be shared between two people who really cared about each other. He knew Bridget was in love with him, but he didn't think about her in that way. It would be wrong to toy with her heart.

It has been two plus years since he'd touched a woman's body for the purpose of pleasure. And the only one he wanted to pleasure was the woman upstairs in his guest bedroom.

"Precious has a new nanny now," Bridget argued her point. "So you can't use that as an excuse anymore."

He groaned. If she only knew that the new nanny wasn't an

older Bengay-scented matriarch, as he'd requested, but a young, alluring, *Moonlight*-scented temptress who was driving him out of his mind, she'd probably want to move into his house to fight the competition—when there wasn't really one. "Oh, Bridge, I might bore you to tears."

She found that amusing. "Like you could."

*It would bore him.* He rotated his neck, rubbing the back and sides to ease the tension in his muscles. "I have to go, Bridget," he said abruptly. *He needed an ice-cold shower to ease the tension in his groin.*

"Do you promise to think about staying the night in Boston?"

She was a brilliant doctor, and he enjoyed working with her. She was also a good friend who had helped him through the first few months after Cassie died, but that was as far as it went for him. He had to find a way to stop her shameless advances once and for all, but not right now. Michelle was the only woman on his mind tonight, and since he couldn't have her in reality, he'd have to take her in his fantasy.

"Okay, Bridget. I'll think about it," he said to get her off the phone.

"Excellent. Good night, Erik."

"Good night, Bridget."

Erik began unbuttoning his shirt as he climbed the stairs.

\*\*\*

Michelle parked the Jaguar on the far end of the lot, away from heavy traffic, and walked the short distance to the old building that currently served as a youth center in downtown Manchester. She'd seen the skepticism in Erik's eyes when he had handed her the keys, weeks ago. He was like all men. Their cars were their babies.

What she would really like to be driving was that red Porsche in his garage. But without having to be told, Michelle knew that car was off limits. That belonged to his dead wife.

"Michelle!" A mob of children flocked her the minute she hit the door. They'd been expecting her.

"Hi, guys." She dropped two shopping bags on a table near the door. "Uh-uh," she cautioned as they made a dash for the bags of goodies. "Those are for later."

"Oh…" they uttered in disappointment.

She smiled. It was so good to see them again after three weeks. She had some free time today because Erik and Precious were at an elite annual father-daughter function at the Conference Center across town. They would be dining at some fancy restaurant and would be out for the rest of the night, which would give her time to visit her brother in Cambridge once she left the center.

Precious had been so excited as Michelle had helped her into in a pretty little blue dress with ruffles and satin bows—a dress Michelle had helped her pick from the dozens that had been delivered from an exclusive children's store in Boston. It had cost hundreds of dollars. That was the LaCrosse's world.

As Michelle gazed at the children before her, she wondered when was the last time one of them saw a movie or ate out, or if they'd ever wear an outfit that somebody else hadn't worn before.

These kids were poverty-stricken and in need of a lot of things. Most of them hadn't seen their deadbeat fathers in years. Three hundred dollars would buy them a lot of necessities—like warm coats, shoes that fit, school supplies—things that people like Dr. LaCrosse took for granted. This was her world.

"I made you something, Michelle." A little ten year-old boy with new braces pushed ahead of the crowd and held up a yellow paper bracelet.

"Thanks, Malcolm." Michelle took the bracelet and read the inscription. *I'll love you forever. Malcolm.* It was decorated with little red hearts. She slipped it on her wrist and gave him a gentle hug.

"I made it in Sunday School yesterday. I told the teacher that it was for the most beautiful woman in the world, and she asked if that was her. I told her no way. This is for Michelle."

"Ha, ha, ha," the other children roared. "Malcolm has a

crush on Michelle," they sang in unison.

Michelle smiled at Malcolm, happy she'd talked Robert into giving him free braces. She wished she had the money to do a lot of things for all of them, for just like her, they had dreams. But right now, she was just as destitute as all of them. One day, she'd change their worlds.

Malcolm wanted to be a dentist like Robert. Twelve-year-old Angela wanted to be an astronaut. Nine year-old Clive, who was scarred from burns he suffered in a fire three years ago, wanted to be a firefighter like the brave one who saved his life.

There were about fifty kids who frequented the center on a regular, after-school basis while their parents and guardians worked. The center was also opened in the summer for parents who could not afford a sitter for the littler ones.

They all had their own little tales of hardship and neglect, and they had their dreams—dreams Michelle encouraged them to talk about so they wouldn't forget them. These were the stories she wanted the world to hear. These were *The Littlest Dreamers* she wrote about.

She clapped her hands to silence them. "Did you do your homework?" she asked of those who were in summer school.

"No. Yes. Almost."

"I need help with my apostrophe worksheet," Clive said.

"I came in just in time, didn't I?"

Michelle turned as a teenage girl burst through the door. "Hey, Amanda."

"Hey, Michelle. Sorry I'm late, but I had to stop at the bank and drop off a deposit for my boss."

Michelle smiled at the young girl. She was one of the volunteers who came into the center to help out the kids. As a matter of fact, she was a graduate of the center. Michelle had helped her out with her essays during her senior high school years. Amanda was giving back to the community. That's the way life should be—give and take.

Back when she did have a job, Michelle used her own money to pay for tutors when funds were low. She didn't mind spending her money as long as the kids were learning something.

Since their parents were too busy, too lazy, or too negligent to help develop their curious little minds, Michelle had assumed the responsibility.

"Okay, guys, Amanda is here, so get cracking. Later we'll have some snacks."

They scrambled around the long table in the room while Amanda began giving them instructions.

Michelle headed for the office where Rose, a seventh-grade science teacher and co-founder of the youth center, waited for her.

"It's about time you got here," Rose said, glancing up from her task of stuffing envelopes. "I thought we'd never see you again since you've living in a ritzy town, driving fancy cars—"

"It's nice to see you, too, Rose." Michelle winced as a wave of heat hit her in the face. The room was next to the boiler room and that made it as hot as a sauna. The air-conditioned car had kept her cool and comfortable, but now... She pulled a tissue from the box on the desk and mopped her forehead. When the sweat kept pouring she crouched down in front of the box fan and rotated her head to get the cool air on every inch of her skin.

"I guess you don't have that trouble anymore?" Rose declared, giving her that 'have you slept with him yet?' look.

"No, I don't. They have central air in those parts."

"Still sleeping naked?"

"Rose!"

"Just asking because..." Rose unlocked a drawer, pulled out an envelope and gave it to Michelle. "This was hand-delivered today."

Michelle opened the envelope and pulled out a check. "Whoa!" She exploded with disbelief at the generous amount made out to the center from Dr. Erik LaCrosse, Jr., OB/GYN.

"You had anything to do with that?" Rose asked.

Still in a sense of shock, she stared at Rose. "I mentioned that I volunteer here sometimes. Had to since it was on my resume. But I haven't spoken to him about the place since..." She did mention it last night on the patio.

"You didn't even ask him for money? You are campaigning,

aren't you? Everybody you come into contact with is a potential donor, Michelle."

"I know but, I just started working for the man. I don't want to be hitting him up for money already." Michelle handed the check back to Rose.

"Well," Rose said, returning the envelope with the check to the drawer. "He must be quite a man and have a lot of money at his disposal to have written a check this big."

*Apparently.* Michelle didn't want to discuss her relationship with Erik, especially with Rose, who was known as Gossip Girl. "Have you seen Jessica today?" she asked of an eight-year-old girl who frequented the center—her favorite little one—because she reminded her so much of herself as a child—skinny, feisty, and tough.

Rose nodded. "She's here. She wanted to be alone, so I sent her to the quiet room."

"She okay?" Michelle asked, frowning.

"Are any of these kids okay, Michelle? Every day brings a new challenge and a new set of trouble for them. You can relate."

Michelle walked to an adjoining door that opened up into the quiet room.

She knocked. When she got no response, she opened the door and peeped in. Jessica was sitting on a bench and staring out the window. The room was humid and stuffy, and she wondered how long she'd been in here. She went over and sat next to her. "Hi, Jess."

Jessica didn't move a muscle.

"Why the long face, honey?"

Sad, blue eyes stared back at Michelle, and the lower lip hung a little lower. "I can't go to summer camp."

"Why not? You told me your mom had been saving up all year to send you to camp."

"She was, but her car broke down. She has to get it fixed with my camp money. She says if she don't fix the car, she can't go to work, and if she can't go to work, she can't pay the rent, and if she can't pay the rent, we'll be on the streets." She swiped at the tears on her cheeks. "It's not fair."

Michelle sighed with exasperation. It never stopped. Just when you thought you were ahead, you step on a banana peel someone tossed carelessly in your path, and you find yourself flat on your ass. Again. "I'm sorry, Jessie. It isn't fair. You've been waiting for this all year."

"I feel so stupid. I already told everybody I was going to camp. They're gonna laugh at me." Her eyes flashed angrily. "My father is rich and he never gave me anything. He should give me my camp money. I hate rich people. They're all mean."

Michelle understood her anger, but not her logic. Jessica was the product of a brief affair her mother Gina had with a local businessman. He'd since married and started a family without ever acknowledging Jessica's existence. Too scared to fight, Gina let him get away with denying her child support and her daughter's rightful place in the family estate. If it were up to Michelle, she would have hauled his ass into court a long time ago. But it was not up to her.

Michelle pulled the girl into her arms. "Jessie, honey, you can't judge all rich people by the actions of one just as you can't judge people by the color of their skin or the clothes they wear. I work for some rich people and they are pretty nice to me."

"I don't care. I don't care about anything."

Michelle sighed. "Do you believe in miracles, Jessie?"

"My Sunday School teacher says they happen. But I've never seen one."

*Neither have I.* "Let's pray for one, anyway," Michelle said, even as she wondered how to go about bringing a miracle in the young girl's life.

# CHAPTER SEVEN

Michelle was on her way from ballet when her cell rang. She pressed the Bluetooth clipped to her ear. "Hello."

"Hi, Michelle."

She hesitated for a moment. "Hi, Erik."

"Where are you now?"

"On our way home from ballet."

"Just as I thought."

"Is that my daddy?" Precious yelled from the back seat. "I wanna talk to my daddy."

"Did you hear that?" she asked Erik.

"I heard that. But before you put her on, I called to ask you to bring her to the hospital."

"The hospital?"

"Yes, um... There's something I have to do tonight, and she'll probably be in bed by the time I get home. I can't let a day go by without seeing my daughter. You didn't have any other plans, did you?"

She had planned to leave Precious with Mrs. Hayes and go down to the club for some alone time, maybe go for a swim. But Erik spending time with Precious was far more important. He was making a big effort to bridge the gap between him and his daughter, and she wasn't going to stand in his way. "No plans.

We were just going to hang out at home."

"Is she dressed appropriately or do you need to go back to the house to change?"

"She's dressed."

"Good, then I'll see you in a little bit. Just come into the main entrance and ask for me. They'll point you in the right direction."

"Okay."

"You can put Precious on now."

No goodbye. Nothing. Michelle pulled into someone's driveway and made a U-turn. She parked the car on the side of the road, picked up the cell from the passenger's seat, set it to phone, and handed it to Precious.

"Hi, Daddy. You know what?"

As Precious brought her father up to date on her day, Michelle put the car into drive and started down the main road that led to Route 101 and Manchester.

Erik had left earlier than usual this morning, so she hadn't seen him since yesterday when he'd taken Precious to their father and daughter event. Last night, she would have thanked him for the money he'd given to the center, but by the time she'd gotten back from visiting Robert, both Erik and Precious were in bed.

Since that first morning when she interrupted him in the kitchen, she paced herself to come downstairs after he'd eaten breakfast, showered, and dressed.

She would lie in bed and listen to his footsteps past her bedroom door on his way to the master suite. She would imagine him stripping off his running clothes and standing naked under the shower. Her heart would race and her body would tingle from the vision of him soaping up a washcloth and rubbing the hard muscles of his chest and arms, moving lower to his washboard stomach, reaching around to his tight delectable buns, then sliding to the front of his strong thighs...

"Michelle! Daddy wants to talk to you again."

Michelle blew a puff of air out through her mouth. From Precious' tone, she imagined that the kid must have been trying to get her attention for a while. She licked her dry lips, took the phone from Precious, and pressed it to her ear. "Hi." Her voice cracked on that one syllable.

"Hi again. Um… I need you to do me a huge favor."

"What?"

"I haven't eaten since breakfast, and the food here isn't the best. I was wondering if you'd mind stopping at a deli on Elm and picking me up a sandwich. I'll call it in."

"Sure. No problem. Where is it?"

He gave her the name and location of the delicatessen.

"I know that place. They make the best sandwiches in town."

He chuckled. "You want anything? It's on me."

"No. I'm good."

"Thanks, Michelle. I'll see you soon." He ended the call.

Michelle tossed her cell on the seat. Her heart was beating with anxiety, but not just because she was going to see him. She wondered if she would meet Bridget, the 'friend' who interrupted them the other night. She was a colleague, a social match, and no doubt as couth as they came. The woman he'd told he was never too busy for, even though at the precise moment Bridget called, Erik had been asking her about her past life.

Maybe she should be glad Bridget had interrupted them since she had no idea how she would have answered Erik's question about the person who'd hurt her. She couldn't very well spill her guts about how her father had stolen her money then bailed. Instead of feeling jealousy toward Bridget, she should be thanking the woman for saving her hide, even if she was the woman Erik turned to for sexual gratification. Bridget was probably the 'something' he had to do late tonight.

Just as he'd promised, Erik hadn't touched her since that first night. He was probably just curious about her. And it wasn't as if she hadn't invited it. She'd made the first move by holding his hand, and he had responded.

It was never good to mix business and pleasure, anyway. Getting involved with her boss would only complicate both their lives. Things usually turned sour after a hot affair, and she was sure that's all it would be between them. The likes of Erik LaCrosse didn't get serious with women like her. And when the affair ended, she would have no choice but to leave her post, contract or not.

She was falling in love with Precious and really enjoyed taking care of her. She didn't want anything to mess up their relationship. And since sleeping with her father could definitely ruin that, it was out of the question.

\*\*\*

"I really appreciate all you're doing to help solve this case once and for all, Garret," Erik said to the detective on the other end of the line. "It's been on ice for too long. The fingerprints in that car belong to somebody and if I have to tear Manchester apart to find the man who owns them, then so be it."

"I understand your frustration, Erik, but you need to step back and let the experts handle it," the detective admonished. "I'll be briefing some of my best men later, and when we meet tonight, you can give them a first hand account of the accident. Until, then, stay away from inner city back alleys. They're the most dangerous places at nights. The people who frequent those spots are seriously unstable and they look out for each other. Your daughter has already lost one parent. Don't cause her to mourn for another."

"I won't do anything stupid. I just want this nightmare over once and for all. I have to go, Garret," he added when he heard a knock on the door.

"Alright. I'll see you tonight."

"Come in," Erik said as he hung up the phone.

The door opened and Bridget walked in, flipping her long blonde hair behind her shoulders. She threw him an easy smile. "My last appointment canceled," she said. "Since we're both free, I thought we could head down to the café and grab a bite. We still have to finish that conversation we started the other night."

Just what he needed—Bridget's unwarranted attention. Erik walked to a window overlooking an open field at the back of the hospital. It was a beautiful day and some employees were seated around picnic tables having lunch. A couple children played in the sandbox while others climbed a monkey bar. The sights took him back to the times when Cassie would bring Precious in to have lunch with him. He missed those days.

"I'm waiting for Precious, Bridget. Her nanny is bringing her in so I can spend some time with her. I didn't see her this morning and I have somewhere to be tonight. She'll be asleep by the time I get home."

"What, you have a date?"

Catching the anxiety in her voice, Erik pushed his hands into the pockets of his lab coat. Maybe if she thought he was dating someone else, she'd stop coming on to him. It was getting old and tiresome. A woman as intelligent, successful, and attractive as Bridget shouldn't be wasting her time trying to seduce him—a man who was clearly not interested. "I'm reopening Cassie's case, Bridge."

"Why, Erik? Haven't you put yourself through enough pain already?"

"Perhaps, but I'll never be able to move on until the bastard who killed Cassie is behind bars. I need closure."

A musing look cloaked her face. "Are you saying you're ready to move on?"

Erik gazed out the window again. Was he ready to move on? He didn't know. He just knew that his cravings for Michelle were growing by the day. He couldn't stop thinking about her. He had deep feelings for her. Feelings he hadn't had for a long, long time. Yet every time he looked at a picture of his wife, he knew he had to close that door completely before he dared open another. He didn't want that cloud hanging over his head any longer. He'd known the minute he saw Michelle walking up his driveway. She'd barged into his life and thrown open doors he'd closed two years ago, evoked feelings he'd buried with Cassie.

In addition to having Garret reopen the case, he'd also started his search for his old friend, Clayton Monroe. He hadn't really gone looking for an explanation about that night in Clay's kitchen because he'd been afraid of the answers. He was ready for the truth now, to unearth whatever secret Clay and his wife had been hiding.

Bridget's arms closed around him from behind, and her head fell against his shoulder. "Erik, if this is what you must do, just know that I'm with you. I'll help in any way I can."

"Um, Bridget—"

"Daddy."

Erik stiffened at the sound of his daughter's voice. He turned, with Bridget's hands still clasped around him. He wanted to die when he saw the stunned look on Michelle's face as she stood just outside the office, holding a brown paper bag in her hand. Why hadn't he closed the door when Bridget came in?

Untangling Bridget's arms from around him, he picked up his daughter and hugged her fiercely, raining kisses on her face. "How's my little muffin?"

"I'm a big muffin, Daddy. And it's gonna take a whole tub of butter to butter me up." She giggled and wriggled around in his arms as he tickled her tummy.

"Hello, Precious. How are you, little darling?" Bridget tried to ruffle her hair.

"Hi," Precious responded with minimal interest and turned her head to avoid Bridget's touch.

Erik smiled to himself as he analyzed Precious' relationship with the two women in the room. Precious had known Bridget for about five years, and she could barely tolerate her. She'd known Michelle for less than a month, and they'd already formed a solid bond.

"Who's that?" Bridget asked, jutting her chin in Michelle's direction. "I thought you said Precious' nanny was bringing her in, Erik."

"That's my nanny." Precious eagerly brought Bridget up to date as Erik walked to the door.

Erik heard Bridget gasp behind him. "Come in, Michelle," he said.

She shook her head. "I can wait downstairs 'till you're done visiting with Precious. Here's your sandwich." She held the bag out to him.

"Nonsense." He grabbed her arm and pulled her into the

office. He took the bag from her and set it on his desk. "Meet Bridget Ashley, my colleague," he said, putting extra emphasis on the word *colleague*. "Bridget, this is Michelle Carter, Precious' new nanny."

"Not what I expected," Bridget said, looking Michelle up and down. "What happened to the older, experienced nanny, Erik? She looks like a child herself, hardly a woman. You trust her with your daughter?" she asked silkily.

Her claws were definitely unsheathed, Erik thought in dismay. Was she going to start a catfight in his office, and in front of his child? He was about to say something when he saw Michelle's back straighten and her dark eyes glimmer with belligerence.

"I assure you, Dr. Ashley, I'm no child. I'm all woman, in every way that counts. I'm definitely not inexperienced. Your concern is touching, but just so you know, Precious and I have already bonded in a very special way. Our relationship is working out quite well, thank you." She finished with a smile Erik swore could melt the icecap on Mount Washington.

*Brava,* he wanted to shout at the top of his lungs. She could hold her own against snobs like Bridget. He'd been concerned about how she would react to his circle of friends and colleagues, but he should have known Michelle Carter could take care of herself, and with such class and composure. Hadn't she quite eloquently put him in his place the day he met her?

Erik glanced at Bridget's dumbfounded face. Served her right. "Bridget," he said, "can you take Precious out for a few minutes? I'd like to talk with Michelle."

"Sure, darling. Anything for you."

She smiled as if she thought he was going to scold Michelle for her insolence. He wanted to laugh. He set Precious on the floor. "I'll just be a minute, then you'll have me to yourself for one full hour. Okay, baby?"

"Okay, Daddy."

"I'm sorry about that," Michelle said the minute the door closed behind Bridget and Precious. "I didn't mean to—"

Erik did laugh out loud then. "Please don't apologize, Michelle. Bridget had it coming." He gestured for her to sit in the chair in front of his desk while he perched on the side of the desk. "She was rude."

"She felt threatened." She clasped her hands on her lap.

"And how would you know? Ah, I forgot you're all woman in every way that counts." He grinned down at her.

She pursed her lips and turned her eyes up at him. "That was just talk."

"Sure." He studied her beautiful flushed face, drinking in the sensuality of her delicate features. The only makeup she wore was lip-gloss. Her skin radiated like luscious caramel syrup. Definitely a woman in every way that counted. "Do *you* feel threatened by her, Michelle?" he asked softly.

"I was when she called the other night."

*Which meant she liked him, wanted him all to herself.* Her honesty was so refreshing. "And now?"

She shrugged, nonchalantly. "Now that I've met her, I can tell she's not your type."

Erik balked. "And just what is my type, Ms. Carter?"

She peered up at him. "You're a real man. You'd want a real woman. Not a superficial Barbie like Bridget Ashley. She's so obvious. You'd think a woman in her position would use a lot more decorum about what she wants, especially when she's trying to land a man."

A smile tugged at the corners of Erik's mouth. He wanted to ask her if she was being subtle about what she wanted. "You're very perceptive," he said instead.

She shrugged again. "When you grow up in an inner city neighborhood, you learn to read people, or they'll take you every chance they get."

Erik felt a certain sadness for the kind of life she'd lived. He wanted to fix that. Give her everything her beautiful heart desired. His eyes raked over her slender body, garbed in white slacks and an aqua top that exposed just a hint of cleavage.

He longed to brush his lips against every millimeter of her silky flesh, especially the sweet swell of her breasts, and bury his face in the valley between them. He still remembered the feel of her in his arms, the fresh scent of her honey skin. What was it about this woman that evoked an untamed passion in him? She generated feelings he'd never had before, feelings he never even knew were possible.

Even as he felt his loins stir under his coat, a surge of betrayal ran through him. He'd never felt this overpowering hunger with Cassie. Making love with her had been satisfying, he supposed. But what if there was a deeper level of passion to be achieved? He had no one to compare Cassie to because she was the only woman he'd ever been with.

"Um, Erik," Michelle interrupted his reverie. "I want to thank you for the money you gave to the youth center. We're hoping to build a new one with state of the art everything. Your contribution will go a long way. Thanks."

"You're quite welcome, Michelle." She was so altruistic, warm and sweet. Most women her age didn't do charitable deeds. They were too immersed in their own lives and careers to care about people less fortunate than themselves. If, and when they gave, it was usually money. Time was too precious.

Those inner city kids needed more than money. They needed someone to spend time with them, someone to show they cared. That's why Michelle had been so hard on him about spending time with Precious. He was grateful for her insightfulness, her concern for his child.

"I know there's a world outside the one I live in," Erik said, smiling at her. "A world in which you survived and became this incredible, loving woman whom I admire greatly. I just felt that if I could help in some small way to produce more like you, I would have done a great thing. The most amazing of all, is how wonderful you are with my daughter."

Her eyes brightened with warmth. "Precious is an exceptional kid, the kind I'd like to have one day when I meet the right man."

"How many do you want?"

"About seven or so, and I want a house with a white picket fence and a big backyard for them to play in."

Erik smiled. "Cassie and I wanted more children."

"Why didn't you have more?"

Erik sighed and rubbed his palms up and down his thighs. "God knows it wasn't for a lack of trying. She just never got pregnant again. I guess her body said one was enough." He chuckled. "When Precious was born, she took one look at her and said, 'Oh, Erik, she's precious.' That's how Precious got her name."

"It suits her. How did she get her nickname?"

He chuckled. "Cassie, again. When she was pregnant with Precious, she used to say she was baking a little muffin in the oven."

"Well, she is a precious little muffin. I hope all my little girls are just like her. But that won't happen for a long time. At least, five years. Remember, I signed a contract."

Erik nodded. "Yeah, that contract." Best thing he ever did. It gave him ample time to find his wife's killer and the truth behind their last argument. Which brought him to the reason he wanted to talk to Michelle. "I've reopened Cassie's case," he said.

Michelle held her breath. "Oh. Any particular reason?"

"I need closure. There were fingerprints in that car. I need to match them to their owner."

Michelle looked away then moved restlessly on the chair. "Didn't the police already try matching them with the ones in their data base?" She hoped her anxiety wasn't evident in her voice.

"Yes, but there was no match, obviously. New prints are added daily. Hopefully, the drunk was picked up for something else since we closed the case. But just in case the police still can't find a match from their pool, I'll be providing them new ones as often as possible."

Doubts and fears clouded Michelle's mind. She crossed her fingers. *God, please don't let those prints match my father's.* She couldn't bear the thought of her father causing such pain to two people she'd started to care so much about. Not to mention how Erik would feel about her. All the wonderful things he'd just said wouldn't mean squat if her biggest fears came to life.

Her gaze followed Erik as he moved over to the window and

gazed out with his back to her. She knew this must be hard for him. The investigation would take him back to that night and the months of pain that followed. She also knew that it couldn't have been her father who'd committed that ghastly crime. Cassie LaCrosse was killed months after her father disappeared. He wasn't in Manchester, maybe not even in New Hampshire at the time.

She'd already lost her job and moved to South Carolina with Ryan at the time of the tragedy. That's why she hadn't known about it until Erik told her. It was a cold case by the time she moved back home. Michelle wondered if she would have taken that interview if she'd known that a drunk driver who hadn't been caught yet had killed her potential employer's wife. "How are you going to provide finger prints?" she asked Erik.

He turned and leaned a shoulder against the pane. "I'll walk the streets of Manchester, myself. I'll talk to people and take the name of every crack head and drunk out there. I'll offer them coffee, sodas, food, whatever they want, and when I walk away, I will have the containers with their prints on them. Those I will turn over to the police."

"Is that why you'll be coming home late tonight?"

"Yes. I'm meeting with the city detective to recount the details of the case."

Michelle glanced around the barely furnished office. It was nothing compared to the elaborately decorated study in his home. There was a huge desk with a laptop on it, a couple chairs, a bookcase, and several diplomas and certifications from Harvard Medical School tacked to the wall. The man was a doctor, not a detective or a street thug, and he shouldn't be running about in the city alone at nights. She'd grown up in the place and she never went out at night if she didn't have to.

Michelle rose and strolled over to him. "The back alleys of Manchester are not places you should walk at night, Erik. You can be putting yourself in real danger."

"I'll be careful. I promise."

"Maybe I should come with you. I know the streets. I know the people."

"I've hired a P.I to work with me." He touched a finger to her cheek. "I won't think about putting you in danger. You stay home and take care of Precious. She needs you."

"She needs you, too." *And I need you.* Michelle's heart went out to him. She wanted to hold him and comfort him, tell him that everything would work out just fine. That he'd be able to put all this behind him soon.

But the last time she'd tried, they'd ended up locked in a passionate kiss. The last thing she wanted was to seem as desperate as Dr. Ashley. All she could do was pray for his safety. He had to be safe for Precious, and for her.

***

"Michelle! Michelle!"

The screams jarred Michelle from the depths of a deep, pain-free sleep. Immediately realizing that they were coming from Precious' bedroom, she bolted out of bed and ran next door. She rushed over to the sixty-gallon tank where Precious was standing with tears streaming down her face. Michelle dropped on her knees beside her. "Precious, what's wrong?"

"Charlie's choking on a rock."

Michelle's eyes followed her finger to the far side of the tank where the goldfish was struggling with a green rock fastened between its gills. Michelle had no idea what to do. Goldfish weren't her specialty. A bruised knee she could patch, a runny nose she could wipe. What do you do with a goldfish with a rock stuck in its throat?

"Do something, Michelle!" Precious was in hysterics.

"Precious, I don't know what to do." She felt sorry for the fish and anguish over the fear in Precious' eyes. The child loved her fish just as if they were her siblings.

"He's going to die..." Precious collapsed on the floor and broke into a storm of heart-rending sobs.

Michelle looked at the fish that was staring back through the glass with bulging eyes, as if begging her to save him. "Oh, Charlie," she groaned, pushing to her feet. She pulled the cover from the tank and stuck her hand into the cool water. She tried to grab the fish, having no idea what she would do if she caught it. But he kept avoiding her and whirled around the tank.

"Hurry, Michelle!" Precious was on her feet again.

"I'm trying." Michelle remembered hearing that fish could die from too much stress. She could see it happening. It wasn't just Charlie she had to worry about, either. Sippy had also started to swim about in an agitated state.

She pulled her hand out of the water to give them time to calm down. Charlie swam behind an artificial plant. Sippy took refuge in a log.

"Why aren't you helping?" Precious dropped to the floor again.

Michelle noticed the fishnet on the stand next to the tank. Why hadn't she thought of that before? She grabbed the net and plunged it into the water, this time hoping to capture the fish in the net and somehow squeeze the rock from its grasp. "Come on, little fellow."

Charlie swam up to the top and in his haste to avoid being caught in the net, catapulted through the water and bumped his head on the side of the tank. The rock dislodged from his gills and floated to the bottom of the tank. A frightened Charlie swam into the giant log alongside Sippy.

Michelle exhaled a sigh of relief. "He's fine, Precious. Come see." She picked the whimpering child up from the floor and held her so she could look into the aquarium.

Precious smiled when she saw both fish were okay. "He almost died."

"But he didn't. He's okay. Maybe now they'll stop munching on the stupid rocks."

"Daddy says they suck on the rocks to get algae because it's nutritious for them."

Michelle couldn't voice her thoughts about folks always trying to grab things they thought were good for them and choking in the process, but still grabbing anyway. Precious wouldn't understand. She set her down and added some stress-guard to the water.

Precious began calling at them, hoping to entice them from their hiding place. Michelle added a few flakes of food hoping to help lure them out. The fish stayed where they were.

"They're probably tired," she said, replacing the cover on the aquarium. "They'll be back to their old selves tomorrow." She went into the bathroom and closed the door.

When she came out, Precious was still at the tank. Michelle would have liked to give her all the time she wanted, but her cramps were coming back. She needed to lie down.

"Precious, it's time you get back to bed."

"I have to use the bathroom. That's why I woke up, and that's when I saw Charlie was choking."

"Okay. Hurry up."

Michelle slumped down on the window seat and rubbed her hand across her belly, willing the pills she'd just taken to work their wonderful magic. She looked up as Precious emerged from the bathroom, closed the door, and rushed back to the aquarium to check on her fish. Michelle struggled to her feet. "Bed, Precious."

Precious reluctantly said goodnight to her fish. Michelle got her settled in then sat on the edge of the bed, stroking her damp curls from her face.

"If Charlie had died, would he have gone to heaven with Mommy?"

Michelle briefly transferred her gaze to the photo of a very pregnant Cassie LaCrosse in the picture frame on the nightstand. She was standing on the porch of a summer cottage, and seemed one with the blue open ocean behind her. "I'm sure, honey," Michelle said, smiling at the little girl. "But he didn't die. He's fine now, and probably will be sucking on the rocks again tomorrow. We just have to keep an extra eye on him."

Precious giggled. "That's what Mommy used to say. But we don't have extra eyes."

*We do now*, Michelle thought to herself as she glanced at the picture of Cassie again. She was sure Cassie was watching over her daughter, just as she was sure her own mother had been keeping a watchful eye on her throughout her life. She'd often wondered where her mother was the night her father walked into her apartment and destroyed her life. She must have blinked.

"Night, Precious," Michelle said as another cramp ripped across her stomach. She started to rise from the bed.

Precious grabbed her hand. "Don't leave, Michelle. Please stay with me."

She didn't want to be kicked in the stomach tonight. And knowing that Erik always came in to check on his daughter when he came home late, she couldn't risk being caught asleep in his daughter's bed. He wasn't home, yet. "I can't, Precious."

"Pleeease…"

Michelle softened when she gazed at the pitiful face. "Okay, just until you fall asleep." She shooed Precious over, eased under the covers, and turned off the bedside lamp. Moonlight slivered in through the open window.

Precious fitted her body into the curve of Michelle's, and settled down.

Michelle wrapped her arms across the small body, welcoming the feel of the warm bundle in her arms. Actually, the warmth from Precious' body was a healing balm for her aching belly. She sighed deeply and closed her eyes.

"Michelle?"

"What?"

"I miss my mommy."

"I know."

"Do you have a mommy?"

"No. She died a long time ago."

"Is she in heaven with my mommy?"

"Yeah, I guess so. Go to sleep, Precious."

A tired sigh echoed in the darkness.

"Goodnight, Michelle."

"Goodnight, Precious."

"I love you."

# Chapter Eight

"Have you spoken with Dad since you returned from your cruise?" Erik asked his mother as they sat in the living room of her condo. The television hummed in the background, but neither paid it any attention.

"We spoke today. He took Danielle home a few days ago."

Erik leaned back in the recliner and eyed her through half-closed lids. He loved his parents, all three of them, but he would forever remain in a state of bafflement over their unorthodox relationship and the circumstances surrounding his birth. It had caused him much pain and ridicule throughout his childhood.

"When was the last time you saw her?" his mother asked.

"I drove up last week when she was hospitalized. I can't believe how much she'd deteriorated in such a short time. She used to be so vibrant."

"It's difficult for your father to watch her on a daily basis. He says there are days when she's lucid and others when she doesn't even know her own name. At least she's home, in a place that's familiar to her."

Erik pushed out of the chair, strolled across the room and stared thoughtfully at a picture of his and Cassie's wedding sitting on a grand piano. He pressed his fingertips into his temples as their last moments together surfaced in his mind. "I don't know which is worse, Mother, having someone you love die tragically in your arms, or watching them fade away slowly and painfully and not being able to do a darn thing about it."

"Cancer is a brutal disease, Erik," his mother said, coming to stand beside him. She placed a comforting hand on his shoulder. "Especially when it attacks the brain. But it doesn't matter how you lose someone you love, the pain is the same, I believe."

Erik knew his mother was still in love with his father. She'd never stopped loving him even after he chose Danielle over her. As far as he knew, she'd never become seriously involved with anyone else, which was a real pity, since she was such a beautiful, loving woman.

He placed a hand over hers. "Precious hasn't been to Granite Falls for a while. Do you think it's a bad idea for her to see Danielle in that condition?" he asked, recalling the last time he'd taken Precious to see Cassie's mother, who was institutionalized. It had been an upsetting experience for his little girl. Erik had never taken her back to that institution.

"Not at all," Felicia said. "It would be good for Precious to see Danielle one last time—say goodbye, especially since she didn't have the chance to say goodbye to Cassie."

"I guess you're right. I'll take her up to spend some time with Dad and Mom as soon as I get the chance."

"Don't wait too long. Danielle isn't going to last much longer. Are you taking Michelle?" she asked after a short pause.

Erik tensed. Michelle was the last person he wanted to discuss with his mother. He knew they would have to meet sooner or later, and later was working out just great for him. "Why do you ask?"

"Well, you used to take Holly with you."

"Then why ask the obvious?"

Felicia chuckled. "Oh, it's very obvious."

"What are you getting at, Mother?"

"Just that I've met Michelle and—"

"You met Michelle? When?"

"Just before I left for my cruise. I ran into her and Precious at the supermarket the day after you hired her. She's beautiful and spirited. She told me she'd ignored Precious' schedule that day and taken her to a park in Manchester, instead. I told her you'd be stone mad, but to stand up to you."

Erik chuckled, remembering the fire in Michelle's eyes as she stood up to him. "And she did. She accused me of being a neglectful parent," he said with a wry twist of his lips. "She told me to stop feeling sorry for myself and pay more attention to Precious. Best advice I've had in two years." A smile lit his face. "Precious adores her. Michelle had her giggling from the moment they met. I'm beginning to know my daughter in a way I never knew her before, not even when Cassie was alive." He sighed. "Cassie really hogged her. I've never admitted this to anyone, but I was jealous of their close relationship. I felt left out at times."

He saw no point in recounting the story Michelle had told him about Precious and Cassie's last day together. He was still wrestling with the painful knowledge that Cassie died, conscious of the fact that her child and her husband were both upset with her.

Erik watched as his mother picked up the photograph of him and Cassie. A frown marred her forehead as she stared at it. She set it back on the piano, looked up at him and said, "Cassie had her reasons for hogging Precious."

His eyes narrowed in question.

She walked back to the sofa. "Come sit down, son." She patted the seat next to her.

"What do you mean Cassie had her reasons for hogging Precious?" He sat beside her.

Felicia placed a hand on his arm. "Erik, just before the wedding, Cassie went to see a psychic?"

"A psychic? Whatever for?"

"I guess she was uncertain about the future, about the two of you."

"How could she doubt our love? We were together since high school. She's the only woman I've ever loved."

"She just wanted to make sure she was doing the right thing, I guess."

"Okay, so what did this psychic tell her, and what does it have to do with Precious?"

"She told her she would die young."

Erik scuffed. "You know I don't believe that garbage, Mom. Psychics are frauds who prey on the innocent and the insecure and take their money. I'm in the medical field. I believe in science, in the practical and the proven, not the phenomena of the spiritual world."

"You believe in God, in heaven, I hope."

"Yes, I do, Mother, but that's different. We're talking about someone who claims to have a heads-up on other people's futures."

Felicia sighed, probably in relief that he still retained the religious teachings she'd instilled in him. "Yes, there are some fakes out there, but there are some who do have the gift of foresight. And," she added quite pointedly, "Cassie did die young, Erik."

As the words registered in his brain, Erik dropped his head in his hands. Yes, Cassie did die young, but it wasn't a natural death. She didn't fall ill with some incurable disease. He raised his head in desperation. "Did this psychic tell her how she was going to die, that she would get run down by a drunk?"

"I don't know, son. She never shared that part with me."

"Why didn't she tell me about this… this premonition?"

"She didn't want you worrying every time she left the house or caught a cold. As you pointed out just a moment ago, you're a doctor, and you would have subjected her to every possible test out there to find out if she had some terminal disease. Even if she'd told you, what would you have done? You could not have stopped the inevitable."

A new anguish seared Erik's heart as he thought of his and Cassie's last moments together—the argument that began in Clayton's kitchen and continued in the car. God, if he'd only known. No wonder she never argued with him. She didn't want to waste precious time fighting over nonsense. Tears burned his eyes. "I could have been a better husband."

"Better in what way? You were the best husband this side of

heaven. You gave Cassie everything. You gave yourself, your love. You were committed and faithful. Tell me, what would you have done differently if you'd known?"

*I would have trusted her.* Erik pushed to his feet and peered out a window into the moonlit night as a host of unpleasant thoughts popped into his head.

Had Cassie told Clayton about the psychic? Was the conversation he thought to be about an affair, had really been about death? Had he hastened her death when he demanded the truth that night? If that were the case, he was just as guilty as that drunk driver who ran her down. It was his persistence that had driven her from the car. If he'd only left it alone, his wife might still be here with him now. To make matters worse, he'd insulted Clayton with his accusations, so much that his friend couldn't bear to be around him. He'd lost his best friend and his wife in the same night. He should have known Cassie well enough to know she would never break her marriage vows. *He should have known.*

"Cassie was happy, Erik," his mother said behind him. "She thanked me for giving life to you so that you could make her journey here on earth a joyful one. She also expressed her hope that you find someone else to love and marry again, someone who would love Precious as if she were her own child."

Erik blocked out his mother's voice as he fought the demons in his head. He didn't want to hear any more, didn't want to face the fact that he had found that someone. All he could think about was how unkind he'd been to Cassie in the last few moments of her life. Yet, as she'd bled to death, she'd told him how much she loved him. She'd pleaded with him to live for himself and for Precious.

*Precious.* He needed to go home—to hold his daughter in his arms.

She was all he had left of his beautiful, sweet Cassie.

\*\*\*

Half an hour later, Erik climbed the staircase in his home and walked down the hall in the direction of Precious' room. He opened the door and tiptoed toward her bed. But he stopped in his tracks when he saw Michelle, fast asleep in his daughter's bed. She was on her back, one arm above her head on the pillow and the other wrapped about Precious whose head rested on her bosom, her long brown hair spread out across Michelle's white nightshirt. The comforter lay in a pile at the foot of the bed.

As he stared at the moon-kissed faces, Erik fought to control the haze of feelings and desires swirling through him. He was reminded of the nights he'd come home late to find Cassie and Precious in this very position with the covers kicked to the foot of the bed. Sometimes he'd lie down next to them, throw his arms about them, and go right off to sleep. How he missed those intimate family moments.

His gaze wandered to the picture of Cassie on the nightstand, to Michelle, and back to Cassie again.

*She also expressed her hope that you find someone else to love and marry again, someone who would love Precious as if she were her own child.* His mother's words rang in his ears.

"I've found her, and I hope you approve," he whispered, as his gaze once again shifted to the live woman in the bed.

His heart thumped heavily against his chest as his eyes drank in the provocative sight of Michelle's dark lashes fanning her honey-colored cheeks, her slightly parted lips, awesomely amplified from sleep, and her toned thighs and long legs tangled with his daughter's shorter wiry limbs. The smell of *Moonlight* wafted up his nostrils, and images of Michelle chin-deep in a bubbly tub floated across his vision.

He swallowed the passion that rose to his throat as his gaze traveled along her slender form to where the shirt had ridden above her hips to expose her black panties beneath. How he longed to touch her in that most intimate part of her body, explore her moist heat, her soft delicacy.

He groaned inwardly with sweet longing as his gaze settled on Michelle's face again. Reaching out, he stroked her cheek with the back of his hand. Heat sizzled in his fingertips as he trailed them lower to the soft skin of her throat. He drew back when she stirred and stretched, arching her back like a lazy cat rising from a deep sleep. Her pink tongue darted out to lick at her fleshy lips before disappearing back into the warm cavern of her mouth. She sighed softly and settled down again. It was the most sensual act Erik had ever witnessed. He was so hard, he felt he might cause some serious damage to his manhood if he didn't immediately get out of his restrictive jeans.

He tiptoed back across the floor, closed the door quietly, and charged down the hall to the master suite. He slammed the door to his bedroom and clawed at his belt and zipper. He pulled his jeans and briefs off his hips and leaned back against the door trying desperately to catch his breath.

Some time later, Erik stood naked under the cold sharp sprays of the showerhead, and when he was numbed beyond all feelings, he turned off the water and gave his body a vigorous rubbing with an oversize towel. That should take care of his physical cravings, he thought, tossing the towel over a rack. Now, what should he do about his emotional dilemma?

\*\*\*

Just around dawn, Michelle opened her eyes and tried to stretch, but found she couldn't move. A warm bundle lay on her chest, and a pair of wiry legs was wrapped about her thighs. She blinked in confusion and reached out her hand to touch the bundle.

"Precious," she whispered as the past night's drama with the fish came back to her. She hadn't intended to stay the entire night. She was supposed to go back to her own bed after Precious fell asleep. Oh well.

As carefully as she could, Michelle eased her body from beneath the sleeping form and planted her feet on the rug. She picked up the cover from the floor and spread it over Precious, tucking the corners under her chin. Precious burrowed more deeply into the mattress, hugged her pillow, and went back to sleep.

Michelle rubbed her temples as she walked to the window.

The sun was trying to peek through layers of ominous clouds. The weatherman had forecasted rain and heavy humidity all day. Precious had swimming lessons and she had aerobics at the country club, but Mother Nature had her own plans, so it seemed they would probably be spending the day indoors.

She sighed. Thank God it was Friday, so Erik would be...

*Erik.* Michelle ran her fingers through her hair as she tried to connect the pieces of her fragmented dream. She had dreamt about Erik. It was true that she'd dreamt about him most nights since she'd met him, but last night had seemed significantly different. *Real.*

She had been lying naked on a bed somewhere and he'd been sitting on the edge, smiling at her with dreamy eyes. He'd told her how beautiful she was and how much he wanted her. Then he'd reached out and very slowly trailed his hand down her body. She'd spoken his name and raised her hips to his touch when he suddenly vanished into empty space.

Just more wishful dreaming. It seemed the only place she could have Erik LaCrosse was in her dreams. The sad news was that he didn't even want her there.

She turned her head and gazed at a picture of Cassie, Erik, and Precious that was on the bureau near the window. They were in a small yacht on a lake. It must have been taken shortly before she died because Precious looked around four years old.

"I'm really sorry about what happened to you," Michelle whispered, staring into Cassie's eyes. "But you had your time with Erik. He's alive and he needs a live woman. I love him, and I love your daughter, and I swear to you, I would never do anything to hurt them. I just want them to be happy. I know you want that, too. So please, just let him go. Let him live."

Certain that she was losing her mind for talking to the picture of a dead woman, Michelle headed for the bathroom between her and Precious' rooms. The door was locked. Darn it. She'd spoken to the kid about messing with the lock.

She walked to the door leading out into the hallway, and took the few steps to her bedroom. She was about to close her door, when she spied Erik, dressed in his running garb, coming from the direction of his bedroom.

Their eyes locked across the semi-darkened hallway. Time stood still for one breathtaking second as unspoken passion electrified the space between them.

Michelle knew she'd had no dream. Erik had been in Precious' room last night. He'd stood gazing down at Michelle as she slept. *And, he'd touched her.*

A smile of feminine power spread across her lips as she closed her door in his face.

\*\*\*

From his bedroom window, Erik watched Michelle bend her tall frame in order to get into Precious' dollhouse. It used to be a breeze for Cassie who'd been a mere five feet, two inches tall, he noted with mild amusement.

Judging from the chaos in the family room, he guessed Michelle and Precious had been cooped up in the house for most of the rainy day. His daughter could be a handful, and he was sure Michelle was relieved the sun had finally come out.

His house was starting to feel like a home again, he thought, loosening his tie and pulling it from around his neck. It felt good to have a family to come home to, even if it wasn't a real one. It was nice to have an adult to talk with at dinner, someone with whom to share his day, whether it was good or bad. And when it was bad, Michelle's tantalizing smile soothed away his cares. She was bringing him back to life, making him feel again, even if she didn't know it.

What he appreciated most though was what she was doing for his daughter. She loved Precious. He heard it in her voice and saw it in her eyes each time she interacted with her. What man wouldn't be drawn to a woman who was that devoted his child?

Erik turned from the window and walked into the direction of the bathroom. He knew full well that it was much more than Michelle's devotion to his daughter that endeared her to him.

Each time he delivered a baby, he imagined it was his child

he'd taken from Michelle's womb. He wanted to make lots of babies with her. He wanted to watch them suckle at her breasts and hear them call her Mommy. He wanted to see the love in her eyes as she tucked them into bed and kissed them good night. But he was a long way from bringing those fantasies to life.

He stared at his reflection in the bathroom mirror, last night's conversation with his mother fueling his thoughts. Cassie wanted him to fall in love and marry again. That knowledge should relieve his guilt, but sadly it produced the opposite affect. If he'd known Cassie believed some psychic's premonition that she would die young, he would not have fought with her so often, and especially not that night. He would have waited until morning as she'd asked.

But morning never came. He was stuck in that night, that moment when he heard the unforgettable thud of the car colliding with her body. He would give anything to take back the last unkind words he'd thrown at her, but he couldn't. *Ever.*

He would carry that load of guilt and stupidity for the rest of his life.

Knowing that, how could he ever expect to be happily in love again?

# CHAPTER NINE

Michelle was trying not to grin too widely as she descended the stairs. Anybody looking at her might think she'd hit the jackpot and was trying hard to keep it a secret. In her opinion, the joy that flooded her heart at the moment far outweighed the value of any million-dollar jackpot.

Last night, while she and Precious were watching *Ratatouille* in the family room, Erik had surprisingly walked in, plodded down on the sectional, planted his bare feet on the ottoman and dove into the bowl of popcorn she and Precious were sharing.

Except for the initial "Hi, Daddy," from Precious, who immediately snuggled up next to him, nobody said anything, yet it felt like a thousand conversations were going on around them. Michelle had never seen *Ratatouille* before and had honestly been enjoying the movie. After Erik joined them, she found her gaze wandering off to his masculine physique silhouetted against the sofa and wondering what it would feel like to snuggle up to his other side, lay her cheek against his chest, and listen to the beating of his heart beneath her ears.

It was at one of those precarious moments that he turned his head and gazed at her, sending a spark of eroticism bursting through the air. From then on, Michelle had kept her eyes on the television even though she'd lost her ability to follow the story line.

When the movie ended, they'd gone to the kitchen for lemonade and some homemade bread pudding. Afterwards, Precious had demanded that they both tuck her into bed. Michelle had gently declined as the situation had begun to feel too much like a family affair. Her love for the little girl and her strong feelings for her employer were getting way out of control. She had to pull back on her reins. But it was not easy saying no to Precious, and the little girl's persistence finally won out.

Except for one little glitch in the form of a phone call while they were putting away the dishes, she had to say that spending quality time with Erik and Precious last night was the most amazing experience she'd ever had. It was the kind of family she wanted one day.

By the time she and Erik left Precious' room, an intense sexual tension had developed between them. Neither said a word as they stood in the hallway outside her bedroom. She remembered the smoldering flame in Erik's eyes and the unsteady rise and fall of his chest as his gaze roved hungrily up and down her scantily clad body.

She'd never been more conscious of his virile appeal, and had hoped he'd drag her down the hall to his bed and make sweet, slow love to her all night long. But he didn't.

He'd groaned, raked his fingers through his brown curls and said, "Go to bed, Michelle. Just go to bed," before strolling down the hall in the direction of the master suite.

Their little arrangement had become complicated beyond reason, Michelle thought as she walked through the dining room. Something had to give. It was unrealistic to think that either one of them could resist this kind of temptation for five years while living under the same roof.

"Good morning, Mrs. Hayes," Michelle said as she sauntered into the kitchen. "Wait, a minute." She frowned as her eyes took in the slices of bread, turkey, cheese, tomatoes, and lettuce on the counter. "What are you doing here? This is your day off. Don't tell me you're getting senile in your old age," she added with a ripple of mirth.

"Senile? Me? That would be the day." Mrs. Hayes chuckled as she spread mayo and mustard on two slices of bread. "The doctor asked me to prepare a picnic basket."

"Picnic?" Michelle's happy bubble erupted. Erik hadn't mentioned a picnic last night. Her mind began to reel as she recalled the unwelcome phone call while she, Erik, and Precious were cleaning up after their snacks. She'd taken a quick glance at the LCD and felt a pang in her heart when she'd seen Dr. Ashley's name flashing in front of her. She'd been certain Erik would ignore it, but he'd picked it up, excused himself, and taken the call in his study.

Michelle wondered now if his chat with Dr. Ashley was the reason he'd sent her to bed instead of giving in to the desires that were so evident in his eyes. If that were the case, she was grateful for his remarkable power of restraint. She would have felt like a bigger fool if she'd allowed him to make love to her last night when he was clearly in a relationship with another woman. She could kick herself for opening up her heart, for allowing it to engage in silly hopeless fantasies.

Her mind flashed back to the day in his office when she'd told him that Dr. Ashley wasn't his type and that he needed a real woman. He'd neither confirmed nor denied it. Real woman or not, Michelle wasn't Erik's type either. He'd made that clear the first time he laid eyes on her. Even though he'd kissed her with a hunger and passion that superseded anything she'd ever experienced, she had to remember that men like Erik LaCrosse did not fall in love with women like her. They got curious about them, and depending on the level of interest, they either satisfied it or backed away from it. His level of his curiosity about her was obviously low.

She was the nanny, not the mother, the wife, nor the girlfriend, and she needed to remember her place in his house.

Michelle watched Mrs. Hayes wrap up the sandwiches and place them, along with three servings of homemade brownies, into a wicker basket. She got bottles of apple juice and lemonade from the refrigerator and put them in a small cooler. Fruit followed—grapes, apples, strawberries...

Feeling the tears about to burst, Michelle spun out of the kitchen. As she turned the corner from the dining room, she collided with the cause of her frustrations. "Excuse me," she said, earnestly avoiding his eyes as she shrugged his steadying hands from her shoulders.

"I was looking for you," Erik said, smiling down at her.

"You found me. What can I do for you, Dr. LaCrosse? Would you like me to get Precious up and dressed?"

Erik frowned at her wooden tone, confused at her cold behavior, especially after last night—the movie, the snack, the fun, putting Precious to bed—the way it used to be when Cassie was alive. The only difference was that he and Cassie would end the night making love before falling asleep in each other's arms. He'd been so close last night, so close to scooping skinny Michelle up and taking her to his bed. He'd had to call on everything decent inside him to resist the sweet temptation in her sexy black eyes, to control his ferocious craving for her.

"Did I do something to upset you, Michelle?" He tried to read her face, but she turned and hurried away from him. Lost in a sea of confusion, Erik threw his hands in the air and continued in the opposite direction.

"The basket's ready, Doctor," Mrs. Hayes said as he entered the kitchen.

Erik picked up the basket and cooler from the counter. A rueful smile tugged at the corners of his mouth. "Did you tell Michelle about the trip, Mrs. Hayes?"

"No, sir. But she seemed a little nettled when I mentioned the picnic. Guess you didn't tell her she was invited."

So that's what it was, Erik thought, grinning as he left the kitchen. She cared. She really did care for him. He placed the basket and cooler on the dining table and hurried after Michelle who was halfway up the stairs by now. "Wait, Michelle." He grabbed her upper arm and felt her tense under his palm.

She was livid. And he was hard.

"What do you want?" she muttered.

"To talk with you." He spun her around and felt an instant squeezing in his chest when he saw the tears shimmering in her eyes.

"So talk." She narrowed her eyes in the same way Precious did when she was angry with him.

*Females*, Erik thought with fascination. Just when a man thought he'd figured one out, she proved him a fool. And yes, he was on a one-way street to Fooldom for this particular female, so tough and streetwise on the outside, but a delicate little wildflower on the inside. He liked that about her. He liked it a lot. She needed protection, a large dose of TLC, and he felt honored to be the man to provide it, even if she was totally unaware of his self-appointed post to be her knight in shining armor. "What's the matter with you? You on your period or something?"

She shook her arm free. "Erik LaCrosse, I have a life outside this house, you know. If you intend to spend the day with some woman and your daughter, you could have at least told me in advance so I could make my own plans."

"So you're jealous."

"No."

"Then why the tears?"

She swiped at them with the back of her hand. "It's the onions."

A rich chortling sound escaped Erik's throat and his body shook with laughter.

His humor just seemed to incense her more, and she sent him a contemptuous glare before turning and charging up the stairs. He caught her again, around the waist this time. She tried to twist free. He lost his balance and slumped against the wall. She landed on top of him, their bodies meshing in perfect alignment.

Bold grey eyes met compelling black ones as heat ignited within and around them. Erik's arms slowly inched their way around Michelle's lithe body, drawing her closer to him. One hand clasped the back of her neck holding her still. He lowered his head, aiming for her inviting lips, but at the last moment, he groaned and buried his mouth into the scented hollow of her neck. He bit into her flesh until she moaned.

"Michelle... Michelle..." God, she smelled so good, felt so

perfect in his arms.

Michelle remained quite still, her arms locked around his neck. The warmth of his arms was so male, so bracing, it made her heart beat erratically and noisily in her ears. Or was it his heart? Her body quivered where their sexes were pressed together. She had no desire to back away. She wished he would hold her like this, forever.

Erik reluctantly untangled their limbs. Still weak from the fiery contact, he sat on the steps and pulled her down next to him. He searched her face and looked deep into her questioning eyes. There was so much passion there and he longed to liberate those desires, just so he could fill his soul with them.

The time wasn't right. He had no intentions of becoming involved with any woman until Cassie's killer was found and brought to justice. He was working overtime to bring that to fruition. Several nights, he'd walked the streets of Manchester with the private investigator he'd hired, asking questions to which no one knew the answers. But he'd missed being home with Michelle and Precious, and had finally left the case in the hands of the P.I. and the police. His decision had brought him home last night to find Michelle and Precious watching a movie. It had felt like old times when he'd joined them in the family room.

"Michelle, there's no need to be jealous of any other woman," Erik said. "I'm taking you and Precious away for the weekend."

"You could have told me. Asking would have been nicer. I could have had other plans, you know." She stuck her chin out at him.

"Yes, I know. I meant to mention it last night, but I got sidetracked. I'm telling you… I mean, asking now. Do you have other plans for the weekend?" Impatience edged his voice. He would like nothing more than to take her upstairs and spread her out on his big, lonely bed. Clear up all her doubts about his feelings for her once and for all.

"No," she answered grudgingly. "Where are we going?"

Erik rubbed his palms together then wiped them along his thighs. "To Granite Falls. My mother is ill."

"Your mother? Felicia?" She looked utterly dismayed.

"No, my other mother, Danielle. My father's wife."

She looked understandably confused since she knew nothing about his atypical family. Now was a good time to clue her in, he supposed. "My biological parents were never married, Michelle—not to each other, that is. Danielle and Felicia were best friends since childhood. They both, unfortunately, fell in love with the same man, my father. He apparently was in love with both of them, but he chose and married Danielle over my mother."

"But your mother was already pregnant with you?" Michelle asked.

"Nope. Danielle could not have children. So my mother volunteered to be a surrogate for them."

"You mean your mother maintained her friendship with them after your father left her?"

"Yep. She and Danielle had some kind of special bond, and they refused to let a man come between them."

"Wow, that's amazing. I don't think I could do that after a man jilted me."

"That's my mother. She conceived me through artificial insemination. Well, that's what they've told everyone."

"You don't believe it?"

He chuckled. "I don't know what to believe. Come on, they were in love. And I know my mother still loves my father. It's just twisted." He shook his head in frustration. "Anyway, the deal was that Felicia would let them adopt me, but she'd maintain a strong presence in my life. By the way," he added, after a short pause. "She told me you two have met."

Michelle grinned. "Yeah, the day I canceled Precious' lessons. She told me to stand up to you. I like her."

"She seems to like you, too."

"She must have a big heart to forgive your father for choosing another woman over her then giving them her own child to raise," Michelle said.

"When you truly love someone, you could probably forgive them just about anything." If Cassie had lived, he was almost certain he would've forgiven whatever secret she was hiding from him. He did love her, still did. And God, he missed her, even more now with Michelle's delightful presence in his home reminding him how much he enjoyed being a father, a husband, a lover.

"I hope I find someone to love me that much, one day," Michelle murmured, interrupting his nostalgic moment.

He smiled at her, his heart racing at the thought of loving her. "I'm sure you will."

"So what's wrong with your other mother, Danielle?" she asked quickly as if regretting she'd voiced her hopes.

"She has brain cancer."

"Oh, that's awful. I'm sorry."

"Thank you. That's why I'm taking Precious to see her before it's too late. She never got to say goodbye to her mother." Erik took Michelle's hand from her lap and curled his fingers around hers. "You still want to come along after I made you go ballistic?"

"I was acting like a jealous teenager. I thought you and Bridget had made plans."

"Why would you think that?"

"Well, you took her call in your study last night, and then when we left Precious' bedroom, I thought we would... Well, I just thought..." She dropped her gaze, seemingly embarrassed again to have vocalized her hopes.

Erik put his hand under her chin and raised her face. He brushed his thumb across her flawless cheek. "I have no interest in Bridget Ashley, and I'm not denying that I want you, Michelle Carter. I do, more than you can imagine. But making love with you would change everything. I'm not ready for that deep a commitment. Until then, I have to keep my desires in check. Do you understand?"

She nodded, her smile wrapping around him like warm honey. She leaned over and pressed her warm lips against his cheek then suddenly pulled her hand from his and jumped up.

The unexpected gesture sent Erik floating up on cloud nine. He pushed to his feet, grinning like a shot fox.

"When are we leaving?" she asked.

"In about an hour. I have to stop by the hospital to check on a patient then we'll head up from there. It's a three-hour drive. I thought we'd stop for a picnic on the way. Precious is already packing. I suggest you check to make sure she has the right clothes. She packed for our last Christmas visit and when we got there, all she had was a swimsuit, two pairs of shorts, a shirt, and no underwear. We were there for a week. She got a new wardrobe for Christmas. Maybe that was her plan all along."

Michelle laughed. "Then I'd better make sure she does it right this time." She glanced down at her attire—too short shorts and a spaghetti strap top. "I should change, huh?"

He gave her the once-over. "Yeah. I wouldn't want a line of horny truckers honking at us all the way to Granite Falls."

"Would that make you jealous, Dr. LaCrosse?" Her eyes challenged him to be truthful.

"Yes. Ms. Carter. It would make me extremely jealous." He turned and began descending the stairs. At the bottom, he stopped and looked up. She was still standing where he'd left her, and gazing at him with a warm smile on her face. "Michelle?"

"Yes, Erik?"

"Bring along a nice dress, nothing fancy. I'm taking you out tonight. I promise it won't be McDonald's this time."

Michelle bit into her lower lip, her smile spreading across her face as she watched him walk in the direction of his study. They were going on a real date. He'd said that lovemaking would change their relationship, but as far as she was concerned, it was already changed. They weren't just employer and employee any more, two people from two different worlds who'd come together for a common cause. They had crossed over into friendship and now maybe courtship. The knowledge sent a warm glow flowing through her.

\*\*\*

As the Mercedes sped along Interstate 93 North, Michelle

took a swift glance in the back seat. Satisfied that her charge was safely secured and still deeply engrossed in her latest *Dear America Series* book, Michelle donned her sunglasses, pulled the car visor down against the morning sun, and settled comfortably into the cool leather seat.

The sky was a deep-blue canopy with hardly any clouds overhead. The sunny summer day was predicted to be a hot one, soaring into the nineties, and she was dressed for it in a pair of white crop pants, a peach sleeveless cotton top, and sandals.

She'd brought along some pages from her manuscript, intending to edit on the road, but had found it difficult to concentrate with Erik this close to her. She peered at him from the corners of her eyes. He was dressed in linen knee-length shorts and a short sleeve shirt that showed off his muscular arms and legs. He was truly a beautiful man, and each time she saw him, was near him, her heart raced and her throat dried up.

"Had enough?"

Michelle startled at the gruff voice.

He turned his head and gazed at her through his Louis Vuitton sunglasses, his lips twisting into a subtle smile.

"No. But, it'll have to do for now."

His smile turned into a wide grin. He cast a cautious glance in the back. "How's everything back there, Muffin?"

"Good, Daddy. I want to finish this book before we get to Grandpa's. Ms. Clements is giving a prize to the person who reads the most books over the summer. I want to win."

"Okay then, baby. I'll leave you to your reading."

Michelle giggled. "She's such an avid reader. Two whole grades ahead."

Erik slowed down as he approached the tollbooth for the machine to read the speed pass on his windshield. When the light turned green, he fed the gas pedal. "She's been reading since she was two and a half," he said proudly.

"She has good genes, and big shoes to fit into. Her father *did* graduate head of his class from Harvard," she said.

"How do you know that?"

"I saw the diplomas and numerous certificates in your office

THE DOCTOR'S SECRET BRIDE

on the several occasions I've been to the hospital."

"You know quite a bit about me, Michelle, yet I know nothing about you." He paused. "That night on the patio, before Bridget interrupted us, I felt that you were about to open your past to me. For some reason, we never got back around to that conversation. Want to fill me in now?"

Since his eyes were sheltered behind the dark shades, Michelle couldn't read his expression. One thing she knew, she was not ready to talk about her past, specifically her father. Erik had no idea how grateful she was that Bridget had interrupted them. That was her one moment of weakness. She wasn't having a second. "I hardly think this is the time to bring up that subject," she said between clenched teeth as she thumbed toward the back seat.

"Yeah, I guess you're right. But we will finish. I do want to know you, Michelle Carter. All of you."

That's exactly what Michelle feared most. They rode in silence for a while, and when Michelle couldn't stand it anymore, she asked, "Do you mind if I turn on the radio?"

"Go ahead. It's on XM. Heart and Soul channel, I think."

She pressed a button on the dashboard then immediately pulled back when Jennifer Hudson's voice belting out 'Spotlight' filled the air. "Oh, I love that song."

"Me, too."

She chuckled. "I would never have guessed."

"What?"

"That you listen to this kind of music. I thought you'd have it set to classical or—"

"Something excruciatingly boring."

"I didn't say that."

"I'm eclectic. I enjoy a variety of music, depending on my mood."

She wasn't going to ask what his mood was with love songs floating around them. She laid her head against the headrest, stretched her legs out, and closed her eyes, as a sweet calmness settled in her heart. This feeling of happiness was so new to her. She liked it.

Close to one o'clock, Erik pulled off the highway and headed toward a picnic area. He was pleased that the only other people there were a middle-aged woman and a boy about ten years old.

Michelle and Precious helped unload the car and they spread a quilt on a patch of green grass under the shade of a willow tree, a good distance from the woman and child.

Precious dropped down next to her father on the quilt. "I'm so hungry, I could eat a whole horse and a pony, too."

"Thought you didn't like horses," Erik said playfully, as he leaned back, supporting his weight on one elbow.

"Daddy, I don't like riding them. It's just an expression." She spread her hands in impatience. "People don't eat horses."

*Well, not in this country.* "Sorry. My bad."

"You are bad," Michelle murmured, opening up the picnic basket.

"You have no idea." He sent her a sizzling smile over Precious' curly head.

She rolled her eyes and handed him and Precious a sandwich each.

He grinned as he opened his up. "So how many books have you read so far this summer?" he asked Precious as they began to eat.

She squinted her eyes and chewed on her upper lip, just as her mother used to do when she was in deep thought. His heart did a double take at the simple memory.

"Seven...no... eight... yeah... eight!" Precious said, beaming.

"So when you finish the one you're presently reading, it will be nine?"

"Uh-huh. Belinda's only read five, Daddy. She told me when we talked on the phone yesterday."

"Well, she's been on vacation in Maine visiting her grandparents. Belinda is Precious' best friend," he told Michelle. "She lives a couple streets over from us."

"Oh, I know all about Belinda," Michelle said.

"Just because you're on vacation doesn't mean you shouldn't read and do other productive stuff," Precious said around a bite of her sandwich.

Erik caught and held Michelle's gaze. Up until a month ago, he would have agreed with his daughter. After all, keeping the mind busy was the principle he'd been instilling in her for the past two years. But thanks to Michelle, he'd come to understand the value of relaxation and leisure time again. Like the way it used to be before...

He smiled at his daughter. "Well, Muffin, sometimes our minds need a break from reading and—uhh, productive stuff. Sometimes we need to put away the books, take out the ball, and play."

Play seemed to be the trigger word his daughter needed to hear, Erik thought as he watched her drop a half eaten apple on the quilt and reach for a plastic bag of crumbs from the picnic basket.

"Can I go feed the ducks, Daddy?"

"Okay, but don't get too close to the edge. I don't want to have to fish you from that filthy water," he said of the pond some fifty feet away where ducks were quacking away.

"I won't." She jumped up and took off.

"You're a good father," Michelle said, taking a sip of water from a bottle.

"Ha. That's not what you thought a month ago."

"I never thought you were bad, just a bit too demanding."

Erik studied her thoughtfully for a moment. "I'm glad you came along when you did. Precious had two other nannies and neither of them challenged me even though they must have known that I'd been asking too much of her. Why weren't you afraid of me?"

She shrugged and plucked a grape from a bunch. "I've had to fight for everything I've ever had in this life. Robert taught me to stand up for myself ever since I was a little girl. He told me that even when I'm afraid to never let it show, never let my enemy know I'm quivering inside. If I see someone I love being taken advantage of, especially if that someone can't speak for *herself*, I advocate."

"You do love my daughter, don't you?"

"Yes." She popped the grape into her mouth and glanced off

to the pond where the ducks quacked happily as Precious fed them the breadcrumbs.

Erik followed her gaze as he slowly sipped his iced tea. It was just like old times, he thought as he put the empty bottle in the basket. Feeling relaxed and very much at peace for the moment, he stretched out and closed his eyes.

With Precious gone, and Erik relaxing beside her, Michelle raised her face to the sky as a jet engine hummed high and far above them. A light breeze rustled through her short tresses and caressed her face. She smiled and pulled her legs up under her. Hugging her arms around them, she rested her chin on her knees as her thoughts filtered back to last night and the sweet tender moments she'd shared with Erik and his daughter in their home. Not once did he make her feel like a nanny, or an outsider.

Now that she thought about it, she was happy that he hadn't done the expected and made love to her, even though he'd admitted that he wanted to. It showed that he respected her, thought of her as more than a sexual object. She'd never had that from a man. She liked it.

Michelle glanced at Erik lying supine on the quilt next to her. His knees were bent and his hands were clasped behind his head. The steady rise and fall of his chest suggested that he might have fallen asleep. For the first time, she noted how thick and long his lashes were and how they curled against his cheekbones as he slept. A potent and magnificent man he was, Michelle thought, as her whole being seemed to fill with wanting.

She drew in a long, silent breath, pulled her eyes away and focused on Precious who was talking with the little boy who'd joined her at the pond. Michelle tried to keep her mind off of the irresistible man lying next to her, but as the moments slipped by, her desire to curl up next to him and throw her arms about him, grew more and more intense. She was about to push to her feet to go join Precious and the boy when she felt a firm grip on her arm.

"Running out on me, Sweet Brown Sugar?"

She looked back to see his sexy lips spread into a grin. Turning all the way around, she perched on her knees. "I thought you were sleeping."

He rose up on an elbow, gazing at her through hooded eyes. "It's kind of hard to relax with a drop-dead beauty sitting next to me and not be able to do what I want to do to her."

"What do you want to do to me?"

"I want to do a lot of things to you, Michelle Carter, and none of them are decent."

"Tell me," she whispered.

"I want to hold you, kiss you, and feel you melt under me like I know you would. I want to make love to you here, under the blue sky, with the warm breeze brushing our naked skin. I want to hear husky little moans coming from your belly as I caress and kiss my way down your soft body. I want to gaze deep into your fiery eyes as I enter you for the first time and feel your slick hot flesh grip my big hard—"

"Erik..." It was a tormented whisper, full of wanting and hoping.

"Excuse me."

# CHAPTER TEN

Michelle jerked around at the sound of the intrusive voice. She tried to catch her breath as she looked up into the freckled face of the woman they'd seen when they first arrived at the pond.

She had the worst timing. And God, she didn't know Erik could speak so…. so, uncouthly. It was so darn erotic. Her panties were soaked; her breasts ached with craving, and her nipples, hard now, tingled with anticipation. She was ready to explode.

"I couldn't help noticing you," the woman said in a friendly voice.

Michelle shook the sensuous thoughts from her head.

"You make such a beautiful couple and your daughter is gorgeous," she continued. "It's good to see young people so happily in love."

"Thanks for the lovely compliment, but we're—"

"Is that your grandson?" Erik climbed to his feet, holding his hand out to help Michelle up, giving her a silencing wink of the eye. He enveloped her left hand in his right.

"Yes. My one and only."

"He seems like a really nice kid," Erik said, following her gaze to the children as they tried to catch a mallard duck that kept eluding them.

The woman placed wrinkled, age-spotted hands on her hips. "Justin's parents are divorced and live three hundred miles apart. He lives with his mother, so I'm taking him to visit his father, my son, for a couple weeks. Divorce is so hard on children." She looked down at Erik and Michelle's entangled fingers. "Your little angel would never have to worry about losing either one of you. Watching the two of you together is like watching a summer sunset splattered across the horizon. The love you share is rich, deep and colorful, and long after the sun is gone, the iridescence remains. You will have a long and happy life together."

"You talk like a poetess," Erik commented, looping their joined hands around Michelle's waist as the woman's words permeated his brain. She'd confirmed what he'd felt in his bones, but hearing it from a stranger somehow brought the foggy images to a full circle of understanding. He kissed the top of Michelle's head, wishing he were free to make her truly his.

"Oh, I'm no poetess. I just know love when I see it." The woman gazed off over the pond. "I'd better be going. I have another two hours of driving, and you two lovebirds look like you want to be alone. Enjoy the great weather." She walked back to her picnic table, calling out to her grandson.

Michelle pulled away from Erik, crossed her arms, and sucked in a deep, shuddering breath. "Why did you let that woman think I'm your wife and the mother of your daughter?"

"It was simpler than giving a long explanation of the truth," he replied, bending down to gather the remains of their lunch and pack everything back into the basket and cooler. "I'm tired of people expressing their regret about my dead wife. Besides, you are like a mother to Precious. You do everything a mother does for her. More than some, actually. Furthermore, you just admitted to loving her."

"I'm not your wife, Erik. You shouldn't go around telling people that I am."

"No one got hurt and the old lady went away with a happy feeling in her heart. What's wrong with that?"

"You're giving me hope where there may not be any. This morning you admitted your physical attraction to me, but you also told me you weren't ready for a commitment. Then just now before we were interrupted… What was all that about? Don't set me up, okay? We don't know what lies ahead for either of us. I don't want to have my heart broken."

"I'm sorry," Erik said, picking up the cooler and basket off the quilt and placing them on the grass. "I didn't mean to upset you. And I definitely don't want to break your heart." He gazed at her, trying not to think of how utterly sexy she looked. He would love to pull her behind a tree and kiss her. "Forgive me?"

"Just don't do it again." She picked up the quilt, folded it with two swift twists of her wrists, and headed for the car.

"Yes, Ma'am," Erik said, following her.

"Is your father expecting me?" she asked as they put the items in the trunk.

"I told him I was bringing Precious' nanny along."

"He's probably expecting some old lady with grey hair, a couple of missing teeth, and a mole on her nose. That's the kind of nanny you were looking for, right?"

Erik laughed. "You're no Nanny McPhee, Michelle Carter."

She chuckled. "If he's anything like your mother, he'll probably take one look at me and draw his own conclusion, anyway."

"How do you know what Felicia thinks about us?" He hoped his mother hadn't told Michelle about Cassie's wish for him to fall in love and marry again. Wanting to make love to Michelle was one thing, but thinking about marrying her was entirely different. He didn't want Michelle harboring that kind of hope in her heart. Just moments ago, she'd expressed her wish not to have her heart broken. He could break it, quite easily.

"The day she met me and realized I was Precious' nanny, she couldn't stop laughing. I guess she thought you'd cornered yourself."

"She's a meddling old hag," he said, laughing with affection. "Don't let her get to you. My father is nothing like her. He minds his own business."

"Good," she said on a sigh of relief.

Erik was about to close the trunk when he saw the stuffed rabbit crammed into a side pocket of Precious' backpack. He glanced at Michelle, then back at the brown rabbit.

Michelle's eyes followed his gaze. It was the tag bunny Precious had told her about this morning. The little girl had pulled it from the back of her closet and explained how she and her parents used it to play tag. Michelle hadn't even realized Precious had brought it along.

"Oh, no, you're not," she said, backing away as he reached into the trunk.

He grabbed the rabbit and threw it at her. "Too late. You're *It*." He took off toward the pond and Precious, his laughter blending with the noise from the quacking ducks.

Michelle growled, picked up the rabbit, and chased behind him.

"Run, Precious," he bellowed. "The tag bunny is coming. Run!"

Precious squealed, abandoned the ducks, and took off.

Love filled Michelle's heart as she watched father and daughter running away from her. The carefree, playful family man Mrs. Hayes told her had disappeared after Cassie's death was back.

Had she done that for him? Had she healed him?

\*\*\*

As soon as Erik stopped the car Precious bolted out and ran toward the man descending a flight of stone cut steps leading up to a gorgeous three-story hillside mansion.

"You grew up in this house?" Michelle exclaimed, her eyes popping as she took in the surrounding courtyards, gardens, and fountains. The views of lakes and mountains in the distance provided a magnificent backdrop to the estate.

"Yes."

"Wow. I though your Amherst house was grand, but it looks like a woodshed compared to this."

"Well, thank you," he said.

"Oh, you know what I mean." She slapped him playfully on the arm.

Grinning, he got out of the car, and walked around to open her door.

Michelle felt suddenly uneasy as she watched Erik LaCrosse Sr. walking toward them, bouncing Precious in his arms. He was about an inch shorter than his son, with thin, firm lips and a high-bridged nose. His hair, the color of rich gold, was seasoned with silvery strands. His eyes were the same color of Erik's, just not as piercing. She noted the light of approval on his slightly wrinkled face as he took a good look at her.

He set Precious on the ground before gripping his son in a bear hug, and kissing both his cheeks. "It's good to see you, son."

"You too, Dad," Erik said, with a lot less enthusiasm than Michelle expected from him.

Erik Sr. turned to Michelle and gave her a wide smile. "You didn't tell me you were bringing a friend along, son."

Precious giggled. "Michelle's not Daddy's friend, Grandpa. She's my nanny."

The poor man was clearly taken aback. "This is Michelle?" he asked, blinking in confusion. "Michelle's the nanny? Felicia told me you'd met a beautiful young woman. She didn't tell me she was the nanny."

"Yes, Dad, this is Michelle Carter. Michelle, my father, Erik LaCrosse, Sr."

"It's nice to meet you, Mr. LaCrosse." Michelle offered him her hand.

"The pleasure is mine. You are very lovely, my dear. My son has always had exceptional taste," he said with a warm smile as he gave her hand a hearty shake.

"Thank you, Mr. LaCrosse."

"Please, it's Philippe. As a matter of fact, why don't you just start calling me Dad?" He gave his son a hearty slap on the shoulder. "Good job, my boy. Good job."

Erik growled beside her.

"Let's get inside where it's cool. It's a sauna out here." Philippe turned and followed Precious who was already racing back up the steps.

Michelle slammed the back of her hand into Erik's stomach, and knew it hurt her more than it hurt him. "Thought you said he wasn't anything like your mother. He's worse. He just told me to start calling him Dad."

Erik groaned. "I didn't want to scare you."

"Well, consider me scared." Michelle walked toward the trunk to get the bags.

"Michelle, the servants will take care of the bags," Erik said to her.

*Servants?* They had servants?

"Come on, let's go." Erik held his hand out to her.

Michelle took it, wondering how she was going to survive the weekend in a house filled with servants and Erik's father's speculating eyes watching her every move. And what the heck had Felicia told him about her and Erik? *Lady friend? Really.*

Philippe showed Michelle to her room, a spacious chamber on the west side of the house that overlooked tennis courts and a green wide meadow. The room was decorated with antique French furniture, like most of the other rooms she'd passed on the first floor.

Her room was separated from Precious' by a bathroom, just like in the Amherst house. Only this marble bathroom was three times as big and came with a Jacuzzi and sauna. Erik's bedroom was two doors away, with a library and a sitting area separating it from Michelle's. Yasmine wasn't going to believe it when she told her where she'd spent the weekend.

Michelle unlaced her sandals and dropped them on the Victorian rug at the side of the bed. She stretched out on the embroidered linen bedspread and stared up at the cathedral ceiling. Everyone was meeting in the family room in twenty minutes before going in to see Danielle who was presently napping.

She wondered about the bizarre love triangle between Philippe, Felicia, and Danielle. When Erik had mentioned his father this morning, Michelle had sensed a subtle recklessness in his voice. She had no doubt that the love between father and son was mutual, but seeing them together, she had to admit that there was a concealed aloofness in Erik's eyes when he looked at his father.

She supposed it stemmed from the circumstances surrounding his birth. She wondered if he resented his father for choosing Danielle over Felicia all those years ago. Or maybe it was the doubts about the method of his conception that bothered him. Since the situation was so 'twisted' as he'd called it, he had a right to question how he was conceived. But she was sure he would never ask his parents if they'd slept together, carried on a secret adulterous liaison with Danielle's permission, just so they could all share a child together. That was just… She shivered at the whole affair.

"Michelle."

Michelle turned her head to see Precious standing at her door hugging Bradie in her arms. She sat up in the center of the bed and folded her legs under her. She patted the mattress and Precious immediately ran across the floor and scurried up on the bed next to her.

"Do I have to see Grandma Danielle?"

"You came all this way. It would make her feel better to see you."

"How come I have three grandmas? Everybody else I know has two."

"Because you are a very special and lucky little girl. Some children have no grandmas at all, but you are blessed to have three who love you a lot."

Precious sighed, in the same way a confused adult would have done. Michelle's heart went out to her. She was still so young, so innocent. There was so much pandemonium in the grownup world that her childlike mind didn't understand. Heck, Michelle didn't even understand half of it herself.

"Where are your other grandparents?" she asked Precious. "Your mommy's parents?"

"Daddy says my grandpa died before I was born."

"What about your grandma?"

She shrugged her tiny shoulders. "I don't know."

"You never see her?"

She shook her head. "Daddy says she's sick and that's why I can't see her."

Oh damn it, Michelle thought, realizing her error. She shouldn't have asked.

"Can I stay with you until we have to go see Grandma Danielle?"

"Sure, kiddo."

"Cool. I had fun this afternoon by the pond," she said with a big smile.

"Me, too." Michelle smiled, as she tucked a long curl behind the little girl's ear.

"I liked playing tag bunny with you and Daddy. It was like when Mommy was alive."

"Oh, yeah? You like being tickled, too?" Before Precious could respond, Michelle pushed her onto her back on the mattress and tickled her tummy mercilessly until Precious screamed.

In the height of her elation, Michelle knew she loved this child as though she were her own.

Precious had stolen a big piece of her heart—a piece she knew she would never ever get back. Her heart was split right down the middle between Erik and his daughter.

How could she have set herself up for such a fall?

***

"What's the story with you and Michelle?" Philippe asked his son as they sat in a four-season sunroom overlooking the White Mountains.

"There's no story. She's Precious' nanny."

Philippe chuckled. "It's in your eyes, Erik. You can't hide it."

"What is?" His fists curled around the arms of his chair.

"The passion. You look at Michelle the same way I looked at

your mother thirty-eight years ago."

Erik held his father's watchful stare. "Your wife is dying and all you can do is talk of passion for another woman."

Philippe rubbed his palms together then ran them along his thighs.

Erik watched him, his eyes narrowing at the nervous gesture he also made when he felt cornered.

Philippe glanced at his son. "I was in love with your mother, Erik. I don't want you to ever doubt that. But I loved Danielle, too."

"So why did you choose Danielle over her?" There was a bitter edge to Erik's voice that he didn't even realize he'd been carrying all these years. Or perhaps, he'd just been in denial about the way his father had treated his mother. "Is it because of the race difference?"

"Erik, you really think I'm that narrow-minded?"

"Well—"

"*I* didn't choose, Erik. Your mother did. She told me to marry Danielle."

Erik's mind clouded with confusion. "Why would my mother tell you to marry Danielle when she was so in love with you? Still is, from what I can tell."

"I couldn't choose between them. I couldn't hurt either one, so I was prepared to walk away from both of them. They understood, but then Danielle got sick. They found a tumor on her brain and gave her three months to live."

"So my mother encouraged you to marry her."

"She wanted Danielle's last days on earth to be happy ones. She said it didn't make any sense that neither one of them could have me. It was decided that Felicia and I would marry after Danielle passed away."

"But she didn't die."

"No. They, um…" Philippe cleared his throat and ran his palms up and down his thighs again. "They went in and got the tumor. I didn't know what to do. As Danielle got stronger and healthier, I knew that your mother was *the one*. I really wanted to be with Felicia, but Danielle—"

"She was your wife. You couldn't abandon her."

"I had made my bed. I had to lie in it."

"But you didn't stay in it." Erik stared across the low marble table into the grey and amber eyes he'd inherited.

"What are you asking, Erik? Do you want to know if your mother and I were intimate after I married Danielle?"

"Well, were you?" Erik fired back, not knowing if he really wanted the truth.

His father pinned him with his eyes. "No. I would never do that to Danielle."

Erik let out the breath he was holding.

"When your mother found out that Danielle couldn't conceive, she offered her eggs."

"Why didn't you just adopt? Hadn't you put her through enough emotional trauma already? She had to watch you and her best friend live the life she should have had. You made her give up her child and leave her home to start over in a new place. I had to grow up without her. Spending an occasional weekend and a few weeks during the summer with her wasn't enough, Father. She's my mother. *She* carried me and gave birth to me. Not Danielle."

Philippe tossed his head defiantly. "Look, Erik, we all made what we thought were the best decisions at the time. I can never justify what I asked of your mother. There is just something about a man having his very own child that gives him a degree of pride he can't gain from raising someone else's. You should understand. When you look at Precious, you know that your seed created her. You made her happen. She is part of you, flesh of your flesh, blood of your blood, and nothing can ever change that."

*That,* Erik understood. Precious was his. A child created out of love. A child he would die for, and kill for. But still, if Cassie had been unable to give him Precious, he couldn't imagine making a baby with another woman then asking her to give up her child, especially not a woman he was in love with.

"Raising you brought Danielle so much joy, Erik. She and Felicia have always had a deep and lasting friendship that I still don't understand to this day." He paused. "Your mother is a remarkable woman for doing what she did. She has sacrificed her entire life for me. How can I not love her? I've always loved her and I always will."

Erik ran his fingers through his hair as he tried to absorb all his father just told him. As a child, he'd overheard whispers among the servants about his mother's frequent visits to this very house, and how sometimes Danielle would leave her husband and her best friend alone for long hours at a time. Those whispers had spread beyond the walls of his father's house and had caused his mother to move to Amherst after he was born. He'd carried the shame of the circumstance of his birth all through his childhood and dealt with the gossip within Granite Falls' elite circle. But according to his father, none of it was true. He'd really been conceived through artificial insemination. There was nothing to be ashamed of anymore. As he watched his father wipe a tear from his cheek, Erik felt his animosity slipping away.

Philippe looked over at his son. "Right after she found out the cancer was back, Danielle insisted that I follow through with our original plan and ask your mother to marry me after she's gone. She said I would be a fool if I didn't grasp the opportunity."

Erik left his seat and sat beside the man who was responsible for the confident individual and successful doctor he'd become. He rested his hand on his shoulder. "I'm glad we had this talk, Dad. It means a lot to me. I realize now that love isn't always about getting what you want. It's about allowing the person you love to be happy, even if it entails sacrificing your own happiness."

Philippe's brows arched upward. "You are in love with Michelle, aren't you?"

"I care deeply for her," Erik quietly admitted as he rose and shoved his hands into his pockets. "And you are right. If Cassie were still alive, I would probably feel the same way about her. But I doubt very much if I would have asked her to bear my child then take it away from her. In fact, I know I would not have put her through that kind of hurt."

Philippe sighed. "I'm sorry for the pain you suffered because of our decision, son. Looking back now, I realize that we should have thought about how it would affect you. We can't change the past. I regret not explaining the situation to you much earlier, but I don't regret having you. I would do it again just to have you and that precious granddaughter you gave me in my life. I love you that much, son."

"I love you, too, Dad."

Michelle and Precious joined them shortly afterwards for some light refreshments. Precious dominated the conversation as she sat on her grandfather's knee and brought him up to date with her little world. Finally, the nurse announced that Danielle was ready to receive visitors.

As they approached the bedroom, Michelle felt Precious' fingers tighten around hers. She gave the little girl a reassuring smile.

Philippe was first to arrive at the bedside. He leaned over and kissed his wife on the forehead. Precious was previously informed about the IV needles in Danielle's wrist, and that her face and body were swollen from the treatment she had been receiving for her disease. Philippe had also warned Erik and Michelle that this was not one of Danielle's better days.

"Danielle, honey. You have visitors." Philippe spoke in a gentle, patient voice.

He unfurled from the bed, and Michelle had her first glimpse of the pale woman propped up against the white pillows. There was no comparison between the skeletal form on the bed and the beautiful portraits Michelle had seen throughout the house. It was sad to look at her.

"Visitors? What?" came a frail response.

"It's our son, Erik, and our granddaughter, Precious?" Philippe motioned for them to get closer.

Michelle released Precious' hand, and the little girl walked cautiously but bravely up to the bed.

Precious stared at Danielle for a short moment then leaned over and hugged her, placing a wet kiss on her cheek. "Hi,

Grandma Danielle. I'm Precious."

"Precious." Danielle whispered. She struggled, unsuccessfully, to put an arm around Precious when Philippe leaned in to help.

Michelle pressed a hand to her mouth as she took in the heartrending scene, knowing it would be the last time Precious would hug her grandmother.

"I love you, Grandma Danielle. I hope you get better soon. My daddy is a doctor and he can make you better. Right, Daddy?" She gazed up at her father.

The panic in his daughter's voice and the hope in her eyes tossed Erik back a couple years to the day he buried her mother. He stepped forward and picked her up off the bed. Maybe it wasn't a good idea to bring Precious here, for her to see Danielle like this with the smell of death heavy in the air. "Take her out," he said, placing her in the arms of a maid lurking outside the door.

He took a swift glance at Michelle and noticed the tears in her eyes. He marveled that she could feel the pain and loss of a woman she didn't even know.

He sat on the side of the bed and held Danielle's frail hand—the hand that had soothed his brow, wiped his tears, and bandaged his bruises for so many years. She'd opened her heart to him, and raised and loved him as her own. Not once did he detect animosity or contempt in those beautiful hazel eyes that now stared vaguely back at him. Like his father said, what was done was done. He brushed back a few strands of wispy hair from her forehead. Her skin felt cool, puffy, and clammy—not warm and soft and plump as he remembered.

He managed to smile. "Hi, Mom. I want you to know that I love you very much. I thank you for opening up your heart and home to me. You were a wonderful mother—the best, and I shall miss you, dearly." He let the tears roll freely down his cheeks.

"You? Who?" The forehead wrinkled in confusion.

"This is Erik, darling. Felicia's son." Philippe stroked the thin layer of blonde hair matted to his wife's scalp. "You remember Felicia?"

Erik watched as Danielle's eyes moved beyond his shoulders.

"Fe...le...cia," he heard her say as her swollen face strained against the wide grin she tried to display.

Erik held his breath when he realized she was staring at Michelle. Felicia and Michelle both had black hair and similar body structure. They were both black. It was easy for a woman in Danielle's condition to get them confused.

He remembered what his father had told him about the special friendship between Felicia and Danielle. Would Michelle give his mother this last cup of happiness? He knew it was asking too much of her, especially after he'd pretended earlier today that she was his wife. If she didn't...

"Hello, Danielle. It's been a while. I hope you haven't missed me too much."

Erik let his breath out at the sound of her husky voice. Bless her sweet heart.

Danielle's eyes twinkled as she forced the words from her lips. "You... love... Erik?"

# CHAPTER ELEVEN

Michelle dropped her gaze to the floor, but she felt all eyes on her. She realized Danielle thought she was speaking to Felicia and the Erik she was referring to was her husband, not her son. Her first thought was to set her straight, but sympathy for the dying woman touched her deeply. Erik had already pretended she was his wife today, so why not pretend she was his mother, too? What could it hurt? Besides, she did love Erik. She could speak the words freely without him knowing the truth in her heart.

She smiled as she met Danielle's gaze. "Yes, Danielle. I love Erik very much," she said, a deep sense of longing brewing in her heart.

"You... marry... him."

"Yes, I'll marry him, and I'll try to make him as happy as you made him. I'll take great care of him, I promise."

Danielle heaved a weary sigh, slumped into the pillows and closed her eyes. "Tired," she whispered breathlessly.

Michelle rushed from the room and stumbled blindly toward the guest bedroom, but she hadn't gotten far before Erik's hand closed around her arm. He pulled her into a room and closed the door. She stood rigid as she fought to steady her ragged breathing.

"She isn't lucid, Michelle," he said in a heavy voice. "She thought she was talking to Felicia."

"I know."

Erik turned her around, placed a hand under her chin and searched her face. "Why are you crying?"

She sniffled, not answering.

"Tell me."

Michelle was sure he understood what had just happened in that room, yet he wanted her to say it again. "I can't."

"Tell me," he whispered in a tormented plea.

"Okay, it's true. I love you! I don't care if Danielle thought she was talking to Felicia. I was speaking from my heart. I meant every word. I love you, Erik. I love you, and I want to marry you and have your babies."

"Oh, Michelle, my sweet, sweet Michelle." Erik clasped her to him, his heart flipping erratically in his big chest. He felt her hot tears soaking into his shirt, scorching his flesh.

Michelle loved him, and she wanted to have his babies.

He groaned. God, how he wished he could tell her that he loved her, too. But he was not at liberty to do so. He was still battling with guilt, especially after what his mother had told him about Cassie. She had died so cruelly, cut down in the prime of her life. How could he love another woman before he avenged her death?

He was torn between loyalty for a dead woman's memory and the burning passion in his soul for one who was very much alive, and who was now crying in his arms because he couldn't tell her that he loved her.

Michelle pushed away from him. "I'm sorry." With trembling fingers, she tried to press the wrinkles from his tear-soaked shirt.

Erik captured her fingers in his hands and held them against his chest. "Michelle, I don't want you to be sorry. I appreciate your honesty, but you have to understand my predicament. I told you this morning that I'm not ready for this kind of commitment. Honestly, I don't know if I'll ever be ready to fully commit again. There are issues I have to resolve, questions I need answered before I can open my heart to another woman. I don't want to hurt you."

She gazed at him through teary eyes. "I understand. And I'm sorry. This is a difficult time for you. Your mother is dying. Your daughter is confused, and—"

"I'm the one who's sorry for pulling you into my topsy-turvy world. It's very selfish of me. I should have waited before I—"

She placed a finger to his lips and gave him a trembling smile. "I'm not afraid of topsy-turvy. I've lived it all my life. Your topsy-turvy world is a lot better than the one I came from. And you couldn't have pulled me in if I didn't want to be pulled in, Erik."

Erik threaded his fingers through her short silky hair, then trailed the back of his hand along her cheek. "You're too good. Too understanding."

"That's love."

"I just need time. That's all."

She uttered a shaky laugh. "You have four years and eleven months."

"God, I hope it doesn't take that long." He looked about him and his gaze settled on the bed in the center of the room. He suddenly felt exhausted, both physically and emotionally.

"Is this your bedroom?" Michelle asked with a 'need-to-know' look in her eyes.

"Yes. This is where I spent my childhood. Most of it." He reached behind her and locked the door. "Come lie down with me for a little bit."

"You think that's a good idea? I mean with the way we feel about each other?"

"Do you trust me?"

"Yes."

"Then trust that I will respect you. As much as I want to, I'm not going to make love to you, Michelle. I just want to hold you close to me."

"But Precious—"

"Dad and the staff will take care of her. We've been going all day. I just need a little quiet right now. No more conversation about anything, okay? Just let your mind relax and go wherever it wants to go, and let your heart feel whatever it wants to feel. But don't say a word." He put a finger to his lips. "Shh."

Michelle nodded and let him lead her over to the bed. She watched as he kicked his sandals off then knelt on the carpet and lifted her feet from hers with warm skillful hands. Except for Robert, no man had ever shown her such gentleness, such simple caring. Her heart swelled within her.

He stood up, pulled back the blue and white comforter and eased down on his side in the middle of the bed. He reached out his hand and pulled her gently down next to him, facing him. He smiled into her eyes then clasped his hand at the back of her head and pressed her face into the hollow of his neck.

He smelled wonderful, she thought, as his arms and legs wrapped around her and he tucked her into the strong warmth of his body, fitting them together perfectly. His arousal was evident, and even though her heart was beating out of control, the intense anxiety for sex wasn't there. Instead, she felt a deep satisfying peace wash over her. He was like a drug.

Maybe she was tired. She didn't know. But one thing she did know was that she'd never felt this safe, this secure with a man before. She'd never had this kind of intimacy. She never even knew it existed.

Ryan only held her when he wanted sex and right after he was done he'd pull away from her. At nights, he'd roll off of her, turn his back and begin snoring almost immediately while she laid in the dark looking up at the ceiling still waiting for something wonderful to happen. He never held her, never asked her if it was good for her. He just seemed not to care.

Michelle placed her open palm against Erik's chest and closed her eyes. She knew that when they did make love, Erik would hold her. He'd caress her. He'd make sure it was good for her.

Maybe that was it: Ryan had sex with her. Erik would make love to her.

Every nerve in Erik's body begged him to strip them both naked and make love to Michelle for the rest of the day, all night, into the early hours of dawn, until they were both too satiated to twitch a muscle, until Michelle couldn't tell her sweet juicy backside from her brown sugar nipples.

But years of practicing restraint gave him the strength to hold this lovely irresistible woman in his arms and not go the distance.

He had Cassie to thank for that. She'd been old-fashioned, so sex before marriage was not an option for them. As a young man, he had to learn to control his sexual desires when most of his friends were scoring on a regular basis. It's probably why he started running ten miles a day. He had to release that energy somewhere.

Cassie's choice to remain pure had taught him to respect her, and all women in general.

It was many intimate moments like this one that had strengthened the bond between them. Not giving in to their needs had taught them to trust themselves, and each other. They'd grown to know each other's bodies so well, and built so much tumescence during their courtship, he'd imagined their wedding night would be tantamount to a volcanic eruption.

Sadly, it was barely satisfying, probably because they were both virgins. It had gotten much better during their marriage, but he was still waiting for that big bang, the one he was sure he would experience with Michelle when the time was right.

Erik closed his eyes and embraced the sound of Michelle's heart beating next to his and the feel of her warm breath fanning his throat. He tightened his hold on her as slumber pulled him under.

\*\*\*

About an hour later, Michelle opened her eyes to find Erik leaning over her with a pleasant smile on his face. "We slept together," she said, noting the remnants of sleep in his eyes.

"That we did. How do you feel?"

How did she feel? She thought for a moment. "Respected and respectful."

Erik laughed so hard the bed shook. He ran a finger along her cheek, pausing to linger at a corner of her mouth. "Well, there's only so much respect I have and so much temptation I can resist, so…" He swung his legs over the opposite side of the bed and walked around to put on his sandals. "I'll go find Dad and Precious while you freshen up. The bathroom's through there." He pointed at a closed door.

"What do we tell them when they ask where we were, what we were doing?"

"We'll tell them the truth. We were napping. Don't be too long," he said, walking to the door, and unlocking, then closing it behind him.

Michelle turned on her back and stared at the ceiling. She couldn't believe they'd just been locked away in a bedroom, slept in each other's arms and he hadn't touched her.

"Well, that's not entirely true," she corrected herself as she abandoned the bed and walked into the bathroom. He had touched her, in the most intimate part of her being. He'd touched her heart and her soul, introduced her to a deeper, more meaningful experience to which no physical contact could compare.

He was the most extraordinary man—make that person— she'd ever met. No wonder Bridget Ashley and—she was certain—many other women she hadn't met were fighting for his attention.

He was worth fighting over. She smiled, feeling in her heart that she wouldn't have to fight for him. All the signs told her that if she played her cards well, he would choose her when he was ready.

As she emerged from the bathroom, Michelle scanned the bedroom with her eyes. Erik's presence was everywhere. Life size posters of famous athletes and banners of various sport teams were showcased on the blue-green walls—perhaps the way he'd left them before he went off to college, she thought.

She stood in front of a mahogany dresser laden with trophies and medals he'd won in cross-country and sprint races at Granite Falls School. He'd told her that he ran to keep the weight off, but now she realized that running was really a passion for him.

"Hey, are you coming out anytime soon?" she heard Erik ask

from outside the closed door.

"In a minute." Michelle picked up a brush from the dresser—Erik's brush—and fixed her hair. She slid a finger across her tongue and creased down her eyebrows. Satisfied that she looked decent again, she shoved her feet into her sandals and opened the door. "I was admiring your trophies," she said to Erik.

"Oh, those." He shrugged.

"Yes, those. You didn't tell me running was your passion."

He gave a seductive smile. "I have many passions, Michelle."

"I'm sure you do," Michelle said slyly.

"Where are you taking me tonight?" she asked as he took her hand and led her toward the back of the house.

"To a very special place. You'll like it.".

"Have you already asked your father to watch Precious?"

"Nope, but it wouldn't be a problem."

"Wouldn't he be surprised that you want to take your daughter's nanny out on the town for a romantic evening?"

He chuckled. "He'd be surprised if I didn't. Are you forgetting his reaction when he met you this afternoon? He's not stupid."

*But I am*, Michelle thought as her heart skipped a fast beat. What the heck was she doing?

*\*\*\**

"You look beautiful."

Michelle pulled her gaze from the window of the restaurant overlooking Crystal Lake to admire her date in a green silk sports-shirt and dark slacks. "Thanks. And thanks for bringing me to this lovely restaurant," she added, looking around the packed room. She wanted to add 'expensive,' but that would be too cheesy.

She'd almost choked at the prices on the menu. Even the appetizers they had decided to skip were in the double digits. This would definitely be the most expensive meal she ever had.

"Ristorante Andreas is the best in town—in food and venue.

This dining room is far less formal than the one upstairs. I'll take you upstairs on our next trip." He smiled. "Tables are booked months in advance with a non-refundable deposit."

"So, how did you get one at such short notice?"

"I know the owner, Adam Andreas. He was one of my three best friends growing up, and still is. This location is the first of what is now an exclusive international chain of hotels and restaurants." He paused. "I used to come here a lot with..."

"It's okay, Erik," Michelle said when his voice trailed off and a faraway look came into his eyes. "You can talk about Cassie." She reached across the table and laced her fingers with his. Yesterday, she probably would not have been so bold. But after the intimacies they'd shared today, she felt confident enough to initiate physical contact with him.

"I don't want to talk about Cassie tonight. Let's talk about you instead."

"Me?"

"You and your father. Is he the one who hurt you, Michelle?" His fingers tightened about hers.

Michelle's throat dried up. She took a sip of water. The absolute last person she wanted to talk about was her father. She tugged her hand from Erik's and folded her arms across the table. "There's nothing much to talk about."

"There might not be much, but there is something. Every time I bring him up, you get nervous or quiet. Can you not forgive him for turning his back on you after your mother died?"

Michelle dropped her gaze. There was only one way to end this constant barrage of questions about her father. After what they shared today, she felt she could tell him anything. He said he wanted her to trust him, and strangely enough, she did.

She swallowed the anxiety in her throat and raised her lids to find Erik watching her with tenderness and patience she'd seen only in one other man—her brother.

# CHAPTER TWELVE

"My father didn't just ignore Robert and me, Erik. He used to hit us."

His jaws tightened and the gold specks in his eyes that had beamed with patience just a moment ago, now glowed with fury.

"That was until Robert was old enough to fight back," she continued when he said nothing. "Even when I was older and Robert wasn't home to protect me, he'd let into me."

"He hit you. Your father hit you," he said through clenched teeth.

Michelle watched his hands ball into fists on the table. If her father was anywhere close by, Erik would kill him with his bare hands.

When she'd told Ryan about her abusive childhood, he'd rolled his eyes and said, "Lots a kids get beat up by their parents, Michelle. Mine knocked me around. You're not special, girl." Ryan had merely confirmed what she believed all her life—she wasn't special.

She'd never felt special until this afternoon when she'd fallen asleep in Erik LaCrosse's arms.

"If he wasn't already dead, I would kill him myself," Erik stated in a cold voice.

Ice spread through Michelle's stomach. How would he feel if

she told him her father was not really dead but a drunk who had stolen her debit card and wiped out her bank account? Last week, she'd finally told Robert what their father had done, and he wanted to find the man so he could beat the crap out of him.

She'd also relayed Yasmine's idea that he wasn't really their father. Like her, Robert had brushed it off as absurd since Dwight Carter was the only man he remembered being in his mother's life. He'd never had any other father.

Michelle took another sip of water. "Well, you don't have to kill him, Erik. Fate already took care of him."

"Good evening, Madam. Dr. LaCrosse, I'm your waiter for the evening."

"Good evening, Derek," Erik said to the young boy. "How are your parents and sister?"

"They're fine, thank you."

Erik turned to Michelle. "Derek's father is a local police officer. His baby sister was my first delivery."

"And she lived to tell about it," Michelle murmured, drawing chuckles from the men.

"Give them my regards," Erik said.

"I will."

"Is Mr. Andreas around?"

"He's in Italy visiting family."

"Perhaps I'll catch him next time."

"Would you care to order something from the bar before dinner?"

Erik turned querying eyes to Michelle.

"Just a club soda with a twist of lemon for me, please." She ignored the puzzled frown on Erik's face, frustrated that she couldn't explain. But after seeing what alcohol had done to her father and how it had caused him to almost completely destroy her life, Michelle had stopped drinking. Alcoholism was a disease that could be passed down through genes. She didn't want to be anything like him.

"I'll have the same," he said. "And we know what we want for dinner. You can take the order now."

Derek pulled a pad from his apron and wrote down the order.

"Excellent choices."

"I'd like to freshen up," Michelle said as soon as Derek left.

The look in her eyes told Erik that she felt uncomfortable about what she'd just told him about her father. He stood up and held her chair then motioned for a nearby attendant to escort her to the women's room.

As he watched her wind her way through the crowded room, the thought of a grown man beating up on her curdled his blood. He wondered where she got the strength to have survived and still be so emotionally and psychologically sound. He found himself comparing her to his fragile Cassie whom he knew would not have survived such horror. She probably would have curled up in a corner and died.

Michelle was a strong woman, no doubt about it. Yet, when he'd held her in his arms this afternoon, she'd felt like a vulnerable child in need of love and protection. He wanted to eradicate all the pain from her life, but he had to bury one woman before he awakened another.

He was almost sorry he'd brought up the subject of her father. It had really dampened the mood. For the rest of the night, he wanted happy thoughts. No more morbid discussions.

He rose again as she approached the table. She looked beautiful in a pale-pink slip-dress that buttoned down the front. It was simple, but he found it extremely elegant. She had good taste. She also looked more relaxed, he thought admiring the delicate features of her face as she blessed him with that sweet smile that took his breath away every time.

"It's a beautiful night. Maybe we'll go for a walk on the landing after dinner?" he said as he held her chair.

"I would like that."

Derek brought their drinks and told them their dinners would be right out.

"Erik? Erik, is that you?"

Erik looked up. "Bryce." He grinned when he saw his old friend.

"I didn't know you were in town," Bryce said as they embraced.

"I just got in today, actually. Brought Precious up to see her grandmother."

"I'm really sorry about your mom. I visited her when she was hospitalized."

"Yes, Dad told me. Thank you. She's home now."

"It's the best place for her." His eyes finally shifted to Michelle.

"Bryce," Erik said, reading the questions in his eyes. "This is Michelle Carter. Michelle, Bryce Fontaine, the man who owns half of Granite Falls. I'm sure you saw his name over every building as we drove through town today."

"He's exaggerating," Bryce said, taking the hand Michelle offered. "It's always nice to meet Erik's friends. And I must tell you, you're the most beautiful one so far." He kissed the back of hand.

"Thank you," Michelle said, placing her hands on her lap and smiling demurely at the compliment.

"How long will you be in town?" Bryce asked Erik.

"Until Sunday, hopefully. I didn't get a chance to call anyone yet, but I just learned that Adam is in Italy."

"Yes, and Mass is somewhere in South America, so it's just me. Give me a call tomorrow. We could putt a few balls at the country club for old time's sake. And I'm sure Jason would love to see Precious." He paused. "When are you moving back home, man? We all miss you."

Erik chuckled. "I'm seriously thinking about it, Bryce." He'd been thinking about it for about a year now. But he was happy he hadn't, or else he wouldn't have met Michelle.

"What's to think about? Just do it. I've taken up enough of your evening. Give my regards to your father, and Danielle." He turned to Michelle and bowed. "It was lovely meeting you, Michelle Carter," he said before turning and disappearing as quickly as he'd appeared.

"That's a very large man," Michelle said.

"Oh, but extremely harmless. He's also a widower. Lost his wife a few years ago. Unfortunately, he wasn't as lucky as me."

"What do you mean?"

"They weren't married long enough for her to give him a child. He still isn't over her."

"You're also still in love with Cassie," she said softly. "I see it in your eyes each time you talk about her."

"I will always love Cassie, but it doesn't mean I can never love another woman." He curled his fingers around his glass of club soda. He could really do with a stiff drink, but he didn't want to make Michelle uncomfortable. He knew why she didn't eat red meat. He wondered at her reasons for not drinking alcohol. Anyway, he liked that she didn't. It wouldn't be good for his babies when he eventually put them inside her. He held up his glass. "Let's make a toast."

"To what?"

"A newly discovered friendship—one I hope will deepen into something special and last for many, many years." He chinked his glass to hers.

"Here, here," Michelle said.

"You know, Precious will be going back to school in a few weeks, so you'll have a lot of time on your hands," he said placing his glass on the table.

"And you're wondering how I would spend all that free time, especially when you're paying me such an enormous salary." Amusement flickered in her eyes.

"I know where you'll be spending your free time. The same place you've been spending it whenever you get the chance. How's your book coming?"

"I'm almost done the first draft, but it's hard to write when I'm not with the kids. I get my inspiration from being around them, seeing them almost every day."

"Well, like I said, you'll have a lot more time once Precious returns to school." He paused. "I know you've been leaving Precious with Mrs. Hayes when you go to Manchester. You have my permission to take her with you if you want to. I know she'll be safe with you."

"Thanks, Erik. I'll take good care of her."

Their meals arrived and as they enjoyed the succulent lobster dishes, Erik lightened the conversation by telling Michelle all about growing up in Granite Falls, but especially about his best friends Bryce, Massimo, and Adam—very wealthy and powerful men in the area. He told her that they used to be known as the Billionaire Bachelors of Granite Falls until he broke the mold and married Cassie, then shortly after Bryce followed. The Italian cousins Massimo and Adam were never married. In fact, they were notorious playboys.

Michelle hadn't even realized that Erik's family was so wealthy until he mentioned private jets and mini yachts. Well, she should have known when they drove up to that mansion on the hill. As it turned out, his father's family owned a chain of Canadian banks. He came from old, old money, and yet he was so humble, so grounded. He must have inherited that quality from Felicia, although she had to admit, his father was very down to earth as well.

By the time he was finished telling her about Granite Falls, Michelle felt like she knew everybody in the town. It seemed like a lovely safe place to raise a family, and from the look in his eyes, Michelle could tell Erik missed living here.

They were lingering over coffee and dessert when Erik's phone began to vibrate.

He pulled it from his pocket and checked the Caller ID. "It's Russell, the doctor I told you is covering my patients for the weekend."

She nodded. "Go ahead."

"I'll be back soon," he said, dropping his napkin on the table. His face twisted into a regretful frown as he walked toward the foyer so not to disturb the other patrons. Russ would only call if it were urgent. He hoped he could fix the problem by phone. The evening was going well. He wanted to spend more time with Michelle. She made him feel good, alive. He hadn't had this much fun in years.

While Erik was gone, Derek returned with the busboy to clear the table. Realizing they might need to leave, Michelle asked him to bring the check. She was grateful that at least they had finished their meal before duty called.

She met Erik in the foyer. The worried look on his face

confirmed her suspicions.

"I have to go back to Manchester tonight," he said. "A high-risk patient went into early labor and it looks bad. Russ assured me he could handle it, but I'll feel better if I'm there. This woman has had two miscarriages already. If she should have another, I wouldn't forgive myself for not being there." Fatigue settled into the shallow pockets under his eyes.

"I can drive while you sleep," Michelle offered.

"It's a three-hour drive. We had a long day and it's late. I called Dad. His pilot is flying me back in the chopper. You and Precious can stay the night and drive back tomorrow, or you can stay until Sunday, or spend the week if you want."

*Of course*, Michelle thought, feeling stupid. The man had choppers and private jets at his disposal. Why drive when you can fly? "Okay, I'll see what Precious wants to do."

He looked at his watch. "Wait here while I pay the check."

"I took care of the bill."

He tilted his head. "You did?"

"I suspected we might have to leave in a hurry."

"That's what I like, a woman who takes care of her man," he said, guiding her out into the moonlit night and across the parking lot.

"Is that what you are, Erik, my man?" she asked as they reached the Mercedes.

His eyes glimmered in the moonlight. He groaned, and before she could move—not that she wanted to—he grabbed her around the waist, backed her against the side of the car and pressed his body into hers.

His lips were urgent, seeking, wild as they devoured her mouth. He tasted of lobster, raspberry tiramisu, and espresso. He kissed her so ardently, shivers of delight raced through her. His fingers found the buttons of her dress and undid them in a record hurry. The night air whispered briefly across her naked breast before he cupped them in his hands and squeezed them so closely together, her nipples almost touched.

"Michelle." He dragged his mouth from hers and trailed his lips down her throat and across her chest, leaving a blaze of fire in their wake. He licked at her hard nipples, one at a time, then closed his mouth over each of her firm mounds and sucked the common sense out of her. Excitement leaped through her veins.

With his mouth clamped to a breast, he dropped his hands to her legs and pulled up her dress. When she felt his eager fingers glide magically up her thighs across her taut buttocks then work their way toward her inner thighs, Michelle knew she should stop him, but she didn't have the strength or the desire to.

She gasped in both shock and pleasure when he caught the waist of her thong and edged it down her thighs. The pit of her stomach churned as he cupped her moistness then ran his fingers over the slick flesh of her womanhood.

Michelle moaned and grabbed his shoulders as her whole body began to quiver out of control. Her thighs involuntarily clamped together.

Pulling his mouth from her breasts, Erik slowly dragged his lips back up her body. "No. Spread your legs. Open up," he whispered against her mouth. "Yeah, that's good. You sweet Brazilian baby."

Erik parted her smooth outer lips, ran a finger from the hood of her clitoris down her inner folds and tried to slip it inside her. Wet as she was, he couldn't get in. She was so damn tight. Was she a virgin? He pulled back and pushed with a little more force this time. There was no hymen. He pushed deeper. She whimpered as the walls of her vagina gave way and her hot pulsing flesh clinched around him like a blood-sucking leech. Erik smiled and began working his finger back and forth inside her while the pad of his thumb strummed her swollen clitoris. His gaze dropped to her rosy, pebbled nipples, wet from his mouth. He reached up with his other hand and began kneading the swollen mounds of her breasts.

Her head fell back against the roof of the car and she gasped in absolute uninhibited pleasure. His eyes transfixed on her beautiful moonlit face. Her mouth was opened and her eyes were rolled so far back in their sockets only the whites were visible. She started bucking and thrashing about. He leaned in and pressed her against the car with his body, holding her down as he strummed her harder and faster with his finger.

"Erik…Erik… I'm… com…"

"Come, Michelle. Come to me, baby. Come…"

He covered her mouth with his to mute her shrill cry of ecstasy as she shattered in his arms like shooting stars and falling rain. She stiffened for an eternity then went limp. Erik could hear her heart thumping against her chest as if she'd just run a hundred meter race with everything she had. He buried her face in his chest and held her until she was quiet, until her muscles relaxed around his finger.

"You okay?"

"No. Yes. I don't know." She shuddered on an aftershock.

He pulled his finger from inside her, placed it under his nose for a second then slid it into his mouth. The smell of her, the taste of her made his hard shaft jump.

The headlight of a vehicle entering the parking lot blinded Erik. He hurried Michelle into the car and walked around to his side. He waited outside to give her time to fix her clothes, and for his arousal to dissolve before he climbed behind the wheel.

He had surely taken leave of his good senses to do what he just did in a public place. He had never been this reckless with Cassie. But then she'd never been this responsive to him either. Michelle, on the other hand, brought out something wild and savage in him, something he didn't even know he had. And he loved the way it made him feel. Potent. Virile. Unstoppable.

He opened the car door and climbed behind the wheel, knowing they had to talk about what just happened.

She turned to him, her eyes still misty with passion. "Erik, I've never done anything like that. I just want you to know. I'm not a—I'm not that kind of girl."

"I believe you, Michelle. I've never done anything like this before, either. But you have to admit, this day had been quite tantalizing. It had been leading to this. It was inevitable."

"So what do we do now?"

He sighed as he started the engine. "We go home."

"And pretend that it never happened?"

"I don't think either of us can pretend it never happened.

But I hope it answers your question."

She frowned. "What question?"

"Whether or not I'm your man."

A timid smile cracked her swollen lips. "After what we just did, you'd better be."

He hooked a finger under her chin and drew her face to his. Leaning over, he kissed her lightly, but persuasively. "And *you* are my woman. No matter how I behave toward you after we get back to Amherst, don't lose sight of that. Like I told you earlier today, I just need time."

# CHAPTER THIRTEEN

Michelle pulled the Jaguar into the driveway of 204 Jefferson Drive and shut off the engine. No need to put it in the garage since she would have to pick up Precious from her friend's birthday party in two hours.

She got out of the car and walked around the side of the house toward the kitchen. Life had returned to normal since their return from Granite Falls. She and Precious had stayed a few days with Philippe and she'd really grown to like him. He was the father she wished she had growing up, and he'd treated her like the daughter he never had. And thank goodness, everything had turned out well with Erik's patient.

Back in Amherst, her days were spent taking care of Precious while Erik spent his at the hospital. They had dinner together as often as he could, and his mother had joined them a few times. While he entertained Precious after dinner, Michelle would write. They'd gone to the movies a few times and picnicked at the local parks twice.

They were becoming very good friends, and she felt much more relaxed around him even though her heart hammered in her chest and her skin tingled every time she was near him or thought of the intimacies they'd shared in Granite Falls. Intimacies neither of them ever spoke about.

Sometimes, after Precious was in bed, they would sit around and talk. They talked about the kids at the center and her progress on raising funds to build the new one. They talked about the slumping economy, about the upcoming elections, and which party should lead the country. Their opposing views didn't matter. They talked about Cassie, his parents, and Robert and Yasmine. She'd told him about Ryan and how she'd followed him to South Carolina after she lost her job then returned to Manchester when they broke up. He never brought up the subject of her father again, and she was happy for it. That part was over and done with.

She was learning a great deal about Erik as a brilliant doctor, a devoted father, and a charming man who knew how to make a woman feel special by merely smiling at her.

She respected him. She trusted him. She loved him.

As she walked into the kitchen, Michelle eyed her laptop on the table. Before she left to drop Precious off at the party, she'd been in the middle of writing another fund-raising letter for the center. Rose had informed her that the one they'd been circulating wasn't doing the job. They were still very far from meeting their financial goal.

Some superb news had resulted from that old letter, though. The proprietor of one of the businesses they'd solicited owned a piece of land across the street from the projects where most of the kids who frequented the center lived. According to Rose, Mr. Mendes had himself climbed out of poverty into success and wanted to give something back to his community.

She would love nothing more than to plop down in front of her laptop and finish the letter, but she was driven instead to put away the bags of recently delivered groceries sitting on the island. Erik had made arrangements for the groceries to be delivered so that Mrs. Hayes didn't have to go to the store. Michelle had learned that before Cassie died, she was the one who did the weekly shopping.

She still couldn't believe the modest way they lived—well modest compared to the fully staffed mansion he grew up in— when Erik was worth millions, perhaps billions of dollars. He didn't have to work, didn't even have to be a doctor, but he'd told her that he loved helping people. She knew for a fact that most of the patients he saw at the free clinic didn't pay him. It was another outstanding quality that endeared her to him.

Michelle had emptied about half the number of bags when Mrs. Hayes shuffled into the kitchen.

"Michelle dear, you don't have to do that. That's my job." She walked over and tried to shoo Michelle away.

"Yeah, right." Michelle placed her hands on the older woman's shoulders and steered her toward the table, happy she could return a favor, however small, to the old lady who had been so kind to her and Robert when they were children. Many times, she had taken them into her little house that always smelled of cooking spices. She would feed them then wrap them in blankets she kept on her couch. She would turn on her TV and she and Robert would watch cartoons until they fell asleep in a warm, quiet room for a change. Then their father would come for them and take them home. Take them to hell was more like it. The same kind of hell children she cared about still lived in.

She helped Mrs. Hayes into a chair. "You sit yourself right down there and let me do this. She pulled out another chair and made the lady put her feet up. "Now there. Would you like something to drink?"

"A glass of water would be nice."

"Coming right up."

"Thank you, dear," Mrs. Hayes said, smiling as Michelle placed a crystal glass in her hand. "You remind me so much of Miss Cassie. It's the same way she used to fuss over me."

"Really?"

"She was a sweet woman." Mrs. Hayes took a long draft from the glass.

"How did you ever end up here… in this house, anyway?" Michelle asked, going back to the grocery bags.

Mrs. Hayes chuckled. "It's a long story."

"I have time." After all the time Mrs. Hayes had devoted to her childhood, she could spend a few moments listening to the old woman's life story. Besides, even though Mrs. Hayes still refused to admit pulling strings to get her hired, Michelle knew that if she hadn't run into the old woman that day at the diner, months ago, she never would have met Erik. She wouldn't be in this kitchen today.

"Well, my younger brother came down sick with leukemia. He didn't have medical insurance, so I started taking care of him. I sold everything I had and mortgaged my little house, but it wasn't enough. At the time, I was cleaning office buildings for a living. One of them was the free clinic on Bridge." She smiled as a far-away look came to her eyes. "Then this young doctor joined the staff."

"Erik?" Michelle asked.

She nodded. "Dr. Erik Philippe LaCrosse, Jr.—young, handsome, brilliant, and newly married. He'd be at the clinic at all ungodly hours of the night. Miss Cassie used to bring him lunch and sometimes dinner." She chuckled. "He used to complain that she was the worst cook and how he feared she would poison him one day. So I started bringing him little dishes here and there. You remember I like to dabble in the kitchen."

Michelle swallowed a lump that lodged itself in her throat as she filled the egg tray in the refrigerator door. "Yeah, I do." If it weren't for Mrs. Hayes, she and Robert would have died of starvation in their childhood.

Mrs. Hayes sighed and took another sip of water. "Eventually, my brother passed, but by then I'd lost my house to the bank. I didn't have anywhere to live, so I started sleeping at the clinic. The doctor figured out I was homeless and he and Miss Cassie insisted I come live in their guesthouse. All I had to do in return was cook. After she passed, I took over the housekeeping."

Michelle was rooted at the island, too choked to speak. Just the thought of this woman who'd been so kind to her and so many other kids in her neighborhood, not having a place to live was too much for her. Life was so damned unfair. Tears welled up in her eyes.

When she felt the comforting arms about her, Michelle let the tears flow.

"Michelle, darling," Mrs. Hayes said, guiding her over to the table and seating her, just as Michelle had done to her a short while ago. "The good Lord brought me here for a reason. All these years I didn't know what it was until I ran into you at Mama Lola's diner."

"So you did have the agency call me," Michelle said, smiling through her tears.

Mrs. Hayes smiled back, sheepishly. "Yes. I know the owners at Ready Nanny Agency. They used to be my clients. The doctor was getting desperate and Precious was growing more miserable with each potential that came through the door. I asked them to cancel the scheduled candidate and call you instead. I told them not to give you time to think about it."

Michelle smiled. "They didn't. Thank you. You are truly my guardian angel."

"The doctor is sweet on you, and I know you like him," Mrs. Hayes said softly.

She laughed. "Is it that obvious?"

"I may be old, but I'm not blind." She paused. "You need to tell the doctor the truth about your father. You shouldn't have lied to him."

"I didn't plan on it. It just kind of slipped out when he asked me about him." She crossed her arms to stop the quivering in her stomach.

"Your father is a drunk and a drunk killed Miss Cassie, but that doesn't have anything to do with you. Even if it was your father, the doctor wouldn't hold it against you. He's a fair man. I know that what he hates more than anything are lies and deception. Tell him the truth. All of it."

Michelle knew the old woman was right. She needed to tell Erik the truth, and she would. She just had to find the right time. "Mrs. Hayes, how well did you know my parents?"

"What do you mean, dear?" She dropped wearily down in the chair next to Michelle.

Michelle shrugged. "Well... I know they aren't from New Hampshire. All Robert and I know is that they moved here from the south when Robert was four years old, and my mother was already pregnant with me. They don't have any family. Not any we know about. They must have come from somewhere."

Mrs. Hayes placed her wrinkled hand over Michelle's. "Do you have a specific reason for asking these questions, Little Michelle?"

"It's just that one of my friends thinks that he may not be our real father. You know, because neither one of us looks like him. We don't act like him either."

"Hmm. I only knew your mother for a short time, Michelle, but we became close friends."

"So close that she asked you to be in the delivery room when I was born."

She nodded. "She was very sweet and shy and kept to herself a lot. Your father was very protective of her in public." She paused for a moment and her face twisted with concentration. "Now that you brought it up, I think he was more guarded that protective. If he saw Violet talking to me, he'd always find a way to stop the conversation and take her into the house."

"You think he was hiding something? You think he was afraid she'd say something he didn't want her to reveal?"

"I don't know, dear. I asked her if he physically abused her. She swore up and down that he didn't. I never saw any bruises on her, so I don't know."

Michelle clenched her teeth together. Her blood boiled at the possibility that her father had hit her mother.

"If you think he's not your father, then you should look into it," Mrs. Hayes said. "You should at least find out where you came from, or if you have any other family. There was just something about him that didn't quite fit." She paused for a while then added, "I should finish up the laundry and make up the doctor's bed. Thanks for putting away the groceries." As she straightened up, she swayed and grabbed the table.

Michelle was on her feet and holding her. "Are you all right, Mrs. Hayes?

"I just felt a little woozy there."

"Sit down."

"No child. I just probably need to take my medicine."

"Where is it? And what are you taking meds for?"

Mrs. Hayes placed a cool hand against Michelle's cheek. "I have all kinds of ailments. The doctor keeps me supplied with medicine. It's at the guesthouse. Perhaps if you could run down and get it for me."

"I have a better idea. Why don't you take the rest of the day off? And I'm not going to take *no* for an answer," she added, steering her across the kitchen and out the door. "If I could, I'd sling you over my shoulder and carry you, but since I'm so skinny, you have to walk. Just hold on to me for support."

Mrs. Hayes protested all the way to the guesthouse, but after making sure she took her medicine and propping her up on her sofa in front of her plasma TV, Michelle went back to the main house with a smile on her face.

But that smile slowly faded as she walked down the second floor hall toward the master suite. She'd promised Mrs. Hayes that she would make Erik's bed and put out fresh towels for him. An army of butterflies took flight in Michelle's stomach. She had been living in this house for almost two months and she'd never ventured into the master suite. On several occasions, curiosity had lured her in that direction, but each time she reached the door, she'd stopped. She always felt as if she were snooping, which in fact she would have been, seeing she had no reason to enter the private quarters that man shared with his late wife.

Now here was a legitimate chance to satisfy her curiosity. After work, Erik was flying up to Granite Falls to see Danielle and wouldn't be back until late tonight. She would be in and out before he came home and he would be none the wiser.

Taking a deep steadying breath, Michelle opened the door and stepped into a fully furnished cozy lime green and beige sitting area. A book lay on the table beside the sofa. Curious to know what he was reading, she went over for a closer look. *The Kite Runner.* She smiled. She'd read that book a while ago. She supposed he was a little behind in his reading.

Leaving the sitting area, she walked into another room where the only furniture was a double king-size unmade bed with an ivory marble headboard that extended into two nightstands on either side. The bed was situated in the middle of the room under a skylight. Michelle didn't even know they made them this big. She stepped inside and her bare feet sank with ease into the soft carpet as her nostrils picked up the heady scent of Erik's cologne.

She glanced around the softly painted room, noticing that the inside walls were mirrored, allowing a full view of the bed from several angles. Feeling an awakening blush come, she instantly flushed the images from her mind.

*You're here to make the bed.*

She walked toward an archway that opened into two separate walk-in dressing areas complete with built-in bureaus and drawers. She took a swift peek inside the *Hers* and her heart skipped a beat when she saw the rows and rows of clothes and shoes lined up against the walls. A purple silk robe was draped over a chair in front of a silver and white vanity, and a pair of black pumps lay on the carpet beside it—one overturned on its side. Michelle wondered if this was how Cassie left her dressing room the night she died.

*Poor Erik.* He was really living in the past.

Michelle continued down the corridor toward the bathroom—a spacious gold and ecru refuge of supreme tranquility. A large glass-encased shower stood in one corner next to a long slab of marble with two sinks. A sunken Jacuzzi with three steps leading up, then down into it, sat under a low window.

The tub in her bedroom was gigantic, but God, what she wouldn't give to be able to soak in this giant whirlpool covered to her neck in bubbles.

*You're here to make the bed, Michelle.*

She scanned the room then went over to what looked like a linen closet. She opened the door and stared at shelf after shelf of neatly folded towels and sheets in assorted colors.

She pulled out a set of navy blue towels and draped them over the towel rack next to the shower. She ran her palms slowly down the soft, fluffy fabric, knowing that later this evening Erik would use it to dry off the most intimate part of his anatomy. A wicked smile curled her lips at the thought, and feeling a sense of wantonness overtake her, like a kitty on catnip, Michelle picked up the towel and began rubbing it all over her face.

"Michelle, what on earth are you doing?"

Michelle clutched the towel to her chest and froze. A hand seemed to tighten around her throat, cutting off her breath. She couldn't move. She wanted to die, to melt into the marble under her feet, never to show her face again.

"Michelle." His voice got closer and her body got tighter.

He stood behind her, close enough for her to smell him. What was he doing here? He was supposed to be on his way to Granite Falls.

"What are you doing in here?" he asked again.

Michelle shuddered, released her grip on the towel, and with shaky fingers tried to straighten in on the rack. "I... I... um... Mrs. Hayes—"

A thrill of anticipation zapped up and down her spine when his hand closed around her shoulder. He turned her around then backed her into the glass wall of the shower. It was cold against her shoulders.

Afraid to look into his eyes, Michelle stared at the corded muscles of his chest straining against his blue shirt.

He put a finger under her chin and forced her to face him. Animal passion burned in his eyes and tightness settled into his sexy lips. "You trying to leave your scent for me, little kitty?" he drawled in a husky voice.

Michelle licked her lips then swallowed. Her body was on fire. She licked her lips again.

With his eyes glued to her face, he nudged a knee between her legs, urging them apart, then he bent down, looped his arms in the insides of her thighs and effortlessly picked her up.

Michelle grabbed his arms as he spread-eagled her then leaned in, curving his body into hers. She was wearing shorts and she looked over his shoulder to see her bare legs dangling in the air, her red-painted toes curling in expectation.

He thrust forward, slamming her against the shower wall. Hard. The glass shook so violently, she thought it would shatter.

"Is this what you want, Michelle?" he whispered in a ragged, tormented voice. "You want to feel me deep inside you?"

A gasp escaped her at the hard ridge of his penis pressing against her moist center. The inner walls of her vagina tightened into a painful ball of quivering flesh. Her legs trembled and blood pounded against her temples. She had hungered too much from the memory of his mouth on hers, the intense suckling of her aching beasts, the possessiveness of his touch, the perfect fit of his hard body against hers, and the shattering release he had brought her to in Granite Falls. But this time, she wanted more than his fingers. She wanted his...

"Yes, this is what I want, Erik. I want to feel you buried deep inside me."

He groaned, long and hard. "Okay, then. Let's give you want you want, right now." He gathered her close then stumbled out of the bathroom, through the dressing area and into the bedroom.

He placed her on the unmade bed then came down on top of her. His potent arousal pressed urgently against the softness between her thighs, causing a throbbing sensation deep within her core Michelle had never felt before. He captured her hands in one of his and pinned them to the mattress above her head. As his other hand reached under her shirt to cup and massage one breast then the other, he dipped his head and captured her mouth, forcing her lips apart with his tongue. Michelle tangled her legs about his and surrendered on a moan as he kissed her deeply and sweetly.

Somewhere, she heard a deep growl, followed by a mild swear, then he was off her, and sitting on the edge of the bed. Michelle's entire world crumbled as a truckload of rejection slammed into her chest. He didn't want her. Too stunned to speak, and too numb to move, she curled up in the bed and squeezed her lids, trying to stop the tears stinging her eyes.

Erik planted his elbows on his knees and buried his face in his hands. It was the house, this bedroom he'd shared with Cassie and her moral values. He felt like a caged tiger, wanting to break free and roam the jungle in search of a mate.

Since he'd returned from Granite Falls, he'd lain in this bed and imagined Michelle under him, on top of him, next to him, night after night. Her woman's scent had stained his brain. Her mewling sex sounds were stamped in his heart. He'd taken cold showers in the bathroom where she'd just been laying her scent like a cat in heat that wanted to make damned sure her male recognized and followed her smell. She was in his bed, and he couldn't take her, hard and ready as he was.

"I have to pick up Precious from that birthday party." Michelle said. "So it's just as well we didn't—"

Erik turned and looked at her. She was sitting up in the bed, staring at him. He saw the rejection, the disappointment in her black eyes. "It's not you," he said.

She snorted. "I'm the only one here."

"It's the bed." He threw her a crooked smile.

"What's the real reason you stopped?" she asked, her voice filled with frustration. "You keep leading me on. I can't take any more teasing, Erik. Is it really because of this bed you shared with Cassie?"

Erik chuckled. *Cassie.* He leaned back against the headboard. "Yes, it's Cassie, but not for the reasons you think." He sighed. "Cassie had these moral values. She didn't believe in premarital sex. I kind of adopted them."

She hissed. "So you're saying we have to be married to make love?"

That didn't sound too bad, he thought. The idea had crossed his mind, not only so he could have her without feeling he was doing something wrong, but because she had become a wonderful surrogate mother to his child.

Precious was happy, the happiest she'd been in two years. She loved Michelle and he knew without a shadow of a doubt that Michelle loved her. Michelle loved him, too, and she wanted to have his babies. So yes, marrying her would be a good thing, a sensible thing. And although he knew she would fill the hole in his heart, he wasn't ready to take it that far.

"No, we don't have to be married to make love, Michelle. We just can't do it here."

"We can go to my room. Mrs. Hayes is gone for the day and I don't really have to pick up Precious for another hour."

Erik chuckled again. "Michelle, darling, an hour is not enough time for me to make love to you properly and thoroughly." He raked his fingers through his hair. He couldn't believe he was having a conversation about *when* and *where* to make love to a woman. When he wanted Cassie, he used to just take her to bed. No discussions necessary. Marriage did have its perks.

He glanced at Michelle sitting in the middle of his bed. The cotton fabric of her shorts clung to her soft curves, accentuating the seductiveness of her swollen hips and long shapely legs. He wanted those brown legs wrapped around his waist and neck. His manhood stirred as he recalled the feel of her wonderful sable nipples in his mouth and her moist, tight woman's flesh pulsing around his fingers.

"So what should we do? Rent a hotel for a night?"

Erik stood up. "No. Well, yes."

"You're double-talking again, Erik."

"Okay. I'm supposed to attend this gala in Boston. It's an annual event for the doctors and their spouses in the tri-states to meet and socialize."

"I'm neither a doctor nor a doctor's spouse, Erik."

"But you can be my date. And if you would honor me with your lovely presence, Michelle Carter, by the end of the night, you will be a doctor's woman in every sense of the word. We can spend the night in Boston. What do you say?"

Her eyes lit up. "I say yes, yes."

Erik stared at her eagerness. He was going to make her purr, and she would no doubt make him growl. His big bang was coming, sooner than he anticipated.

"When is this event?" she asked, anxiously.

"Saturday."

"Saturday? That doesn't give me much time. I have to find the perfect dress and shoes, get my nails and hair done—"

Smiling, Erik grabbed her hands and pulled her off the bed to stand in front of him. "You have two days."

"I don't want to disappoint you."

Erik swallowed at the naked passion in her eyes. He brought her hands up to his chest. "You can never disappoint me, Michelle. I have faith in you."

She bit into her lower lip and smiled at him like a teenager on prom night. "We're really going to do it."

"Yes, Michelle, we're going to make love. Slow, sweet amazing love, all night long."

Her lips trembled. "I wasn't snooping, you know. Mrs. Hayes asked me to set out towels and make your bed. And that thing in the bathroom you walked in on, well I was just—"

A faint smile ruffled his lips. "Michelle, it doesn't matter. But if it would make you feel any better, to redeem yourself, you can help me make the bed. It's rather large."

She giggled. "You're telling me. I'll get the sheets. What color?" she asked on her way to the bathroom.

"Surprise me."

She stopped and curled her lips. "Speaking of surprises, what are you doing home? Aren't you supposed to be on your way to Granite Falls?"

"The chopper was delayed. The pilot is picking me up at a local airstrip later on."

"You could have called and warned me."

He laughed out loud. "And missed the scene I walked in on. No way."

She gave him a salacious smile that fired electricity through his blood. It was a feeling he wanted to experience over and over again for the rest of his life.

# CHAPTER FOURTEEN

Michelle stared at her reflection in the full-length mirror. She smiled, pleased with her appearance. She was lucky to have found this dress at such short notice. Felicia, her new best friend, had taken her on a shopping spree to some exclusive boutiques in Boston, none of which Michelle would have dreamed of visiting a few weeks ago, probably never. Felicia had pulled the dress from the rack and insisted that Michelle try it on. It fitted her perfectly.

Michelle had almost barfed when she saw the price tag, but she'd managed to swallow her reaction. It was a special occasion, probably the only one of this kind in her lifetime, and she wanted to shine. Most of all, she wanted Erik to be proud of her. Hair, shoes, nails, and a few sexy undergarments from Victoria's Secret had just about wiped out the money she'd earned in the time she'd been working for Erik. The rest of it had paid for Jessica's camp.

She twirled, feeling like Cinderella on her way to the ball. Only difference was, she'd already snagged Prince Charming. Oh, had she snagged him, she thought, remembering the conversation she had with Erik yesterday.

They'd been sitting on the patio off the kitchen watching Precious and her play date, Belinda, when Erik suddenly blurted out, "Marry me, Michelle."

Certain she was hallucinating and wondering what the heck Mrs. Hayes put in her lemonade, Michelle had just ignored him.

But he'd said it again. "Let's get married in secret. No one else has to know."

At that point, Michelle had eased her glass down on the tempered glass top table as carefully as she could. Under the right circumstances, she would have jumped up, wrapped her arms about his neck, locked her lips to his and screamed, "Yes! Yes! Yes!"

But it was not the right circumstance. That suggestion was born out of Cassie's moral beliefs about sex before marriage— the convictions he said had rubbed off on him. Michelle had looked at him sprawled out on the lounge chair, looking all potent and irresistible. "Why, just so you could have sex with me without feeling as if you're doing something wrong?"

"That's not the only reason."

"Do you love me?" she'd asked, simply and quietly.

"I have very strong feelings for you, and I'm certain that once I have the answers to Cassie's death squared away, I will allow myself to fall deeply and hopelessly in love with you, Michelle. You want to have my babies, and I would love nothing more than to put them inside you when the time is right. For now, I want to commit to you, show you I'm serious. We just have to keep it secret for the time being, especially for Precious. And," he'd added, a bit sheepishly, twirling his glass between his long fingers, "you're going to meet a lot of handsome doctors at the gala. I want you to remember who's taking you home at the end of the evening."

His insecurity had deepened her love for him. She'd smiled, feeling a bit of feminine power surge though her. "You're afraid another man would snatch me up."

"Yes," he'd admitted, giving her a heart-rending smile.

"You're the only man I've ever said *I love you* to, Erik, and if a secret marriage is the only way I can express just how deeply that love runs, then I'll be your wife."

And so this afternoon, on their way to Boston, they'd

stopped to exchange vows in the office of Anthony Paul, Erik's trusted friend and a Justice of the Peace. No rings were exchanged, just promises to love each other and be faithful to each other through sickness and in health, for better and for worse. In fact, Erik still wore the ring Cassie placed on his finger over twelve years ago, reminding Michelle that it wasn't a real marriage, just a license so he could make exculpatory love with her.

But as she'd pledged her life to Dr. Erik LaCrosse, Jr., Michelle realized that a secret marriage was the best thing for her, as well. News of her marriage into such an affluent family would spread like wildfire in her neighborhood, and beyond. She was certain that it would eventually reach her father and ultimately flush him out from whatever dark hole he'd crawled into over two years ago. She couldn't risk that happening—not until she had time to probe into his past—shake up her family tree, and see what fell out. That was the next item on her list of things to do.

So until then, she couldn't even share her happy news with her brother and her best friend. Robert and Yasmine would think she was out of her mind for sure. As far as Michelle knew, neither one of them had ever been serious about any of the people they dated, so she wouldn't expect them to understand how this kind of irrepressible love can cause one to do many stupid things.

People got married for all kinds of reasons, she'd told herself. At least she loved the man, and foolish or not, the ink was dried. She was Mrs. Secret Dr. Erik LaCrosse. And tonight after the gala, they would consummate their vows, just like a real honeymoon couple. She couldn't wait.

Michelle turned at the knock on the door that led to the living room that separated her and Erik's bedrooms. Even though they were husband and wife, Erik had booked a suite to keep up appearances, but he didn't need to knock, she thought, as she crossed the room and opened the door. She was his wife.

Michelle's heart fluttered at the sight of her husband in his black Brioni tuxedo with the snowy-white ruffled shirt and black silk bow tie. Her eyes appraised the hard shape of the athletic body she'd be cuddled up next to later tonight, and the olive, suave texture of his skin that her lips would be caressing. Seeing him triggered a supreme longing deep within her.

This was the world he was born into—sophistication and elegance, and he was sharing that part of his life with her tonight—a girl from the inner city, his secret wife.

"Erik," she said in a breathless whisper. "You look very handsome." She noted the sparkle of passion and admiration in his eyes. She smiled, happy that all her hard work had paid off. She felt equal to this man, her husband of three hours.

Erik trembled at the husky sound of his name. His breath caught in his throat as he gazed at his wife standing before him in a strapless elegant gold evening gown that hugged her slender body seductively. His temperature soared at the tempting hint of her swelling brown breasts left visible from the heart-shaped neckline, and the side slit that afforded tantalizing glimpses of her long sexy leg and delicate feet in a pair of gold stilettos. He couldn't wait to have those toned legs wrapped about him as he thrust hard and deep into her sweet tight body.

His heart raced as his gaze traveled slowly back up her body to her enchanting face. "You're stunning, Michelle." His voice was husky with tenderness.

"I'm glad you think so."

Erik took the delicate hands of his wife and gazed deep into her black hypnotic eyes. Tonight, she wore makeup, just enough to embellish the delicate features of her lovely face, especially her eyes. And he noticed that she was wearing a pair of gold and silver earrings he knew belonged to his mother. It made him happy that she and his mother were getting along so well.

"Any regrets?" he asked.

She shook her head. "I'm just a bit scared of what it all means. Where it's going. Where it will end."

"I am, too." He cleared his throat. "We'll take it slowly," he promised, bringing her hands to his lips and kissing the inside of her wrists. "One day at a time, okay?" His eyes shimmered in the low lights of the room. He wanted to kiss her, deeply and thoroughly, but knew if he dared just take a peck, they wouldn't make it downstairs.

They'd been married for three hours, and like any eager couple, they should have made love already, be making love at the moment. He cherished the fact that when he made love to Michelle, it would be as her husband and not just a man she loved, or one who simply desired her. He hoped his decision to wait would prove to Michelle that he didn't just marry her for sex.

"Ready?" he asked, smiling into her eyes.

"Yes." Michelle hooked her hand between his arm, but as they started for the door, she faltered as the sexy scent of his cologne gently fanned her nostrils. The wait was killing her. She just wanted to skip the party, strip him naked and show him what a sex vixen she could be in the bedroom.

But first, she had to prove she could be a lady in the ballroom. Holding her own while rubbing shoulders with some of the smartest people in New England was the greater challenge. If she could pull this off, she could do anything.

\*\*\*

Erik watched Michelle as she danced with yet another smitten man. She'd been in demand from the moment they'd been announced. He'd had one full dance with her before every eligible man at the function started lining up for a turn. He couldn't damn well protest since he'd introduced her as his daughter's nanny and not his wife. It's a good thing he'd married her this afternoon, put his brand on her, or he'd be sweating with worry and jealousy right about now.

"She's a real beauty, Erik. If I were you, I wouldn't take my eyes off her, either."

Erik glanced at Russell as they reclined on a couple of club chairs in a corner of the ballroom. Michelle was, by far, the most beautiful woman here tonight and he was happy that she was having a blast. But as the night dragged on, he could feel his patience begin to wane. He had a burning need to have her all to himself, upstairs and in his bed.

"Brings back memories," Russell continued, with a hint of nostalgia in his voice.

"Yes, I'm sure it does. Lisa was the belle of the night, five years ago when she accompanied her father to the ball."

Russell's face lit up on a grin. "Yep. I snagged her that night, and didn't let her out in public until I'd put my claim on her." Russell shifted in his seat to face Erik more fully. "The way you've been looking at Michelle tells me she's more than a nanny, Erik. My advice is that you refrain from flaunting her in front of other men until you make her yours. Make damned sure she knows she belongs to you."

"Am I that obvious?"

"It's all over your face, man." Russell took a sip from his wine glass then leaned in closer. "Look, I know what you went through when Cassie died. Your heart was ripped apart. Life as you knew it ended. There's a time for moaning and grieving. You've done it. Nobody would blame you for moving on, Erik. You deserve it. My goddaughter deserves a mother."

"There are still so many questions I need answered before I can make that move, Russ."

"And what if you never find them, Erik? Are you going to let that beautiful woman slip away from you? Just look at the attention she's been attracting from all the eligible doctors here tonight. I tell you man, if you don't make a move, one of them will. You can't play around with a woman like that."

Erik took a sip of the warm crimson liquid in his glass. He'd been nursing that drink all evening. It was his only one. He wanted to have a sober, level head when he went back to his room. He and Michelle had waited too long for this for him to spoil it with inebriation. He intended to make hard, slow love to her, all night long.

He smiled at Russ, wishing he could share his secret with him. When he'd proposed marriage to Michelle last night, he'd told himself that it was for guiltless sex. But deep in his heart, Erik knew it was more than that.

And until he could admit that to himself, he could not tell anyone else, not even his parents. He had to work this thing out by himself. He couldn't tell Russ that he'd already put his claim on Michelle, and that by the end of the night, she would be in his bed, and under him—his wife in every sense of the word.

"Excuse me, Gentlemen, but I believe one of you owes me a dance."

Erik went rigid at the sound of Bridget's voice behind him. He closed his eyes for a few tense seconds and inhaled deeply. When he opened them, she was standing in front of him, her blue eyes fixed on his face, her scarlet lips twisted into a smile, meant to enthrall him.

"You've been avoiding me," she said to him.

Russell cleared his throat. "I think I hear my wife calling." He gave Erik an 'I wouldn't trade places with you for the world, friend' look, rose to his feet and made his way through the throng of swaying black and white tuxedos and colorful floor-sweeping gowns.

Erik knew exactly what his friend was thinking. It wasn't too long ago that Russell had told him Bridget had commissioned him to put in a good word for her. Russell had thought the request humorous, since his opinion of Bridget matched Michelle's.

"It's just you and me now," Bridget said, holding out a hand while batting her eyelashes at him.

With an inward groan, Erik set his glass on a corner table and pushed to his feet. As he looked Bridget over, he finally realized the verity of Russell and Michelle's perception of her. Bridget was a phony—from her thin, carefully drawn eyebrows, her false eyelashes, to her scarlet Botox lips. He knew for a fact that she'd had breasts implants done. He thought of Michelle's breasts—real and perky—and the feel of her brown nipples against his tongue.

"I've been waiting to dance with you all night, Erik." Bridget placed her hands on his arms, indicating that she would not take *no* for an answer.

"Okay, Bridget," he conceded, to avoid a scene. He'd

succeeded in brushing off her advances in the past, but she was extremely aggressive tonight. He hadn't missed the shock on her face when he'd walked in with Michelle. She hadn't hidden her disappointment that he'd turned down her request to escort her to the party, and stay overnight. Bridget was an attractive catch, for a man who liked dolls. *He* wasn't that man. Michelle was the only woman he wanted, the only woman he burned for.

"One dance." Erik placed his hands on Bridget's waist and led her unto the floor. Although the room was cool, he was suddenly feeling very warm. He tried not to be too rigid as he forced himself into the rhythm of the band music.

"So, what's going on between you two?" Bridget asked.

"Who?"

"The golden princess you brought to the gala. Who else?"

"Careful, Bridget. Your claws are showing. There's no need for name-calling and jealousy." *Especially not at my wife.*

"Is that because there's nothing to be jealous about? She's just your daughter's nanny and nothing else, right? She's not even your type, Erik. You have nothing in common. You and I, on the other hand, are compatible in countless ways. I can't imagine you having an important conversation with her, unless it's about Precious, of course. Does she even have a college degree?"

*This dance was over.* Erik came to a screeching halt, and with his hand resting against her lower back, he practically shoved Bridget off the crowed floor and into an empty corner of the room. It was one thing when he was single, but he was a married man now, and even though Bridget didn't know of his change in marital status, her unwanted advances, and her diatribes about Michelle were grating heavily on his nerves. The time had come to end it.

He looked her squarely in the eyes. "There's no need to be jealous, Bridget, because, quite simply, there's nothing going on between you and me," he said as gently as he could. "We're friends. Great friends. That's all it ever was, would ever be. You have to stop chasing me. I don't want to be caught by you." He spread his hands and squared his shoulders. "I'm sorry, but

The Doctor's Secret Bride

that's the way it is, and if you can't accept that, then perhaps we shouldn't even be friends."

She looked up at him, disappointment and hurt in her eyes. "It doesn't have to be that way, Erik. I've never hidden the way I feel about you. If you'd only give us a chance, I can change your mind. I—"

"Erik."

Erik's heart missed a fast beat at the low sultry sound of his name. Only Michelle could say his name with such husky tenderness. He turned around and gave her a dashing grin. "Michelle, I was just about to come find you," he said, his ire dissipating at the enchanting sight of her. She stood confident and proud under the low lights of the overhead chandeliers, her brown skin glowing like amber against the soft material of her dress.

"Good, because we've only had two dances, and after all, I'm your date." Michelle eyed her blue-eyed rival with objectivity. She had noticed her flirting shamelessly with Erik all evening. And just a few minutes ago, she'd noticed the tension in Erik's body as he began to dance with Bridget, and then just a moment ago, when he'd brought it to a sudden stop, she knew something was wrong, so she'd cut her dance short and come to her husband's rescue.

No woman, no matter how alluring she looked, was taking Erik away from her, especially not tonight. She hadn't brought him back to life for Dr. Ashley to weasel him out from under her nose. Erik was hers, even if she couldn't shout it from the rooftop. And what was hers, she kept.

"Erik and I were in the middle of an important conversation about medical issues, Michelle," Bridget said. "Things you won't understand," she added with a hint of superiority in her voice. "So if you could spare him for a couple more minutes, I would be so grateful."

"Your medical issue will have to wait, Dr. Ashley. Erik's not here to talk medicine. He's here to have fun. And the look on his face says he isn't having any at the moment." She leaned possessively against Erik's arm, and her black eyes flashed mischievously and seductively at him. "I just made a request for us, Erik. I would love to dance with you."

"Sorry, Bridget. The lady does have a point. She *is* my… my… date, and I'm here to have fun."

Both amused and flattered by Michelle's blatant possessiveness, Erik bowed graciously to a pup-faced Bridget, took his wife by the waist, and waltzed her into the slow, seductive rhythm of 'We've Got Tonight'.

"I think Bridget's scared of you," he whispered as he drew Michelle into the circle of his arms.

"She should be," she threw back, lacing her arms around his neck. "I grew up in a tough neighborhood. I fight for what's mine. And you're mine."

"Sweet Lord." Erik chuckled. The *Moonlight* fragrance of her skin filtered through his nostrils, into his brain, until all he could feel, think, and smell was Michelle.

\*\*\*

The beating of her heart echoed loudly in Michelle's ears as she shed her clothes. The excitement and confidence she'd felt two days ago when Erik suggested this romantic evening had gone, and she was now a tight bundle of nerves.

This was the second man with whom she'd be intimate. She chuckled skittishly as she walked into the bathroom and began cleaning off her makeup. Her only sexual experiences had been awkward ones with an immature boy who'd caused her more frustration than pleasure.

Erik was a man, a very experienced one. He specialized in women's bodies, and for that specific reason she feared she would disappoint him.

She took a quick shower then applied a lightly scented *Moonlight* lotion to her damp body, then after donning one of the sexy lingerie sets she'd purchased from Victoria's Secret, she stared at her reflection in the mirror.

*Get a grip, girl. Everything will come naturally. Women have been doing this for ages. Just go with the flow.*

She brushed her damp palms across the ruffled stretch-lace teddy. The vertical slits in the cups revealed glimpses of her breasts and nipples. The bodice was tied in the front with three ribbons, and a pair of white panties topped off her seductive garb.

Was she too presumptuous for bringing along such a tempting garment? Would Erik find her sexy? Would she be woman enough to satisfy him? All these questions hammered through her head as she walked to the adjoining door and turned the handle to find an anxious Erik waiting on the other side.

A bolt of electricity coursed through Michelle as her eyes took in his lean, hard body rippling powerfully against the silky material of the black silk robe he wore. He groaned upon seeing her, and as she watched the flash of hunger in his amber eyes, and the rise and fall of his chest as he inhaled deeply and slowly, her heart began to hammer against her chest.

Without uttering a word, he took her hand and led her through the living area and into his bedroom. As he led her deeper and deeper into the candle-lit room, Michelle felt like a breathless girl of eighteen about to lose her innocence to a much older and experienced man.

"Are you scared, Michelle?" Erik asked as he came to a stop beside the bed. His heart ached at the tremors that shook her body, and at the uncertainly swimming in her dark eyes.

She nodded and licked her lips.

He stroked his hands gently down her bare arms, and felt her shiver from the caress. Her skin was soft, the softest he'd ever touched, and he'd touched thousands. It felt like warm butter, melting against his palms. "Don't be scared, baby. We've both wanted this for a long time." He ran his knuckles lightly against her cheek and felt her shivers intensify.

Michelle felt the eager affection coming from him, felt heat racing through her bloodstream, scattering her fears and doubts. She heard the urgency in his voice, felt it in his fingertips. "I've wanted to make love with you since I saw you, Erik, but now I'm afraid I won't be able to please you." Her voice was low and husky, and tears dampened her ebony lashes. "I love you so much."

He wished he could tell her that he loved her, but he didn't know; he wasn't sure. They were married now. She wasn't going anywhere. He had time to slowly and surely unravel his feelings. He wiped the tears from her cheeks with the pads of his thumbs then let his eyes sweep along her near-naked body.

"You look like an angel. My angel, in this sexy white lace." She was his, all his for the taking. He would claim her like man has been claiming woman since the beginning of time. They would become one in flesh, mind, and spirit tonight. *Man and wife.* His heart ached with wanting for her.

"Are you on the pill?" he asked, cupping her chin in his palm.

"No."

"Do you use any other form of birth control?" His breath was hot on her face as his mouth came closer to hers.

"No."

"Besides Ryan, have you made love with any other man?" His lips brushed lightly against the base of her pulsing neck, causing her breath to come out harsh and uneven.

"No." She couldn't call what she did with Ryan lovemaking. *This was lovemaking.* Her heart pounded heavily against her rib cage as the feathery touch from Erik's lips heightened her pleasure, deepened her need. She raised her arms and draped them around his shoulders, burying her fingers in his silky brown curls.

"Did you enjoy him? Did he make you come?"

His tongue teased one trembling corner of her mouth before moving upward along her cheek to kiss her damp eyelids.

"No. No." Her voice trembled, and so did her knees as he drew her into his powerful embrace.

# CHAPTER FIFTEEN

"I promise, you'll enjoy it this time. Just relax and let Dr. Erik take care of you, okay?" He held her head steady and gazed into her eyes. "One more question. Did you use protection, condoms with Ryan?"

"Yes. Every time." Michelle caressed the rigid muscles of his shoulders. He was a gynecologist, and confronted with STDs everyday. He'd be foolish to plunge headfirst into something he wasn't certain about.

The fact that he married her this afternoon proved that like Cassie, he still didn't believe in sex outside of marriage. But he was a man with needs. Could he have slipped up and been with someone since her death? Was that someone Bridget Ashley? Hey, it could happen. "What about you?" she asked in an unsteady voice. "Have you been with anyone since—"

"Cassie is the only woman I've ever been with, Michelle."

Michelle gasped as his hands closed on her buttocks and pulled her up against him. He was strong and solid under his robe. He rotated his hips, rubbing the outline of his erection against her belly. Bending his head, he swept his hot tongue inside her mouth. As his masterful tongue explored her sweetness, he released her buttocks and trailed his big warm hands slowly over her hips, up the arch of her back, around her sides to her stomach, and up along her chest, leaving a blaze of fire in their wake.

Michelle was panting and quivering by the time he slid his hands through the slit of the teddy and cupped her swollen aching breasts in his palms. He began to mold them, shape them, while his fingers tweaked at her pebbled, tingling nipples. Blood pounded against her temples and she was certain her heart would erupt from the sheer pleasure he inflicted on her. She never dreamed a man could make a woman feel this way.

"Undress me," he whispered against her mouth before releasing her and stepping back.

She gazed up into his face. His eyes glowed like two hot coals of fire. Still tingling from his touches and kisses, Michelle knew she'd do anything this man told her to do. With trembling fingers, she pushed the robe from his shoulders. It fell in a black pool around his waist where the belt held it secured.

Michelle swallowed as she stared at the beautiful stature of her husband. His chest was wide and powerful under a mat of curly black hair that extended upward from a corded washboard stomach. She licked her lips as she gazed at his tiny male nipples and wondered how they would feel against her tongue.

She stepped forward. He stood rigid. She placed her hands on his shoulders and dipped her head. His smell was intoxicating, his hair, silky against her lips, his skin smooth and salty under her tongue. She licked at one nipple then drew it gently into her mouth and sucked on it. He gasped and his body tensed under her hands, but he made no attempt to hold her or stop her. She smiled as she trailed her tongue across his chest and gave the other nipple an equal dose of attention.

He sucked air into his lungs. "Untie my robe," he rasped on a harsh breath.

Michelle's heart pounded heavily as she obeyed. The black robe slithered down his hairy thighs and legs and pooled at his feet. She stepped back and gasped in awe at his magnificent sex—a thick long column of flesh towering up against his tight hairy belly. In a daze, Michelle wondered how in everything sane would she be able to take him inside her. She swallowed from lust and fear.

"Don't be afraid," Erik whispered, pulling on the bows of her teddy. He pushed the thin straps off her shoulders and watched the material slither down to bunch in a silky pile around her hips. With ragged breath, he lowered his head to her chest.

Knowing they'd both soon be carried away on the waves of passion where neither of them would be able to think rationally, Michelle though she should speak up now. "Erik, what about protection?"

"I don't want to use a condom the first time with you, Michelle. I want to feel your slick tight flesh gripping me, not some foreign object."

"But, I could get pregnant. Yes, we're married, but I don't think either one of us wants a child right now, Erik."

"When was your last period?" His hands circled her hips.

"I... I... just finished a few days ago."

"Then we're safe, sweetheart." His breath was hot against her skin as his smooth tongue lashed across one mound of her breast.

Michelle trusted him. He was a woman's doctor and knew more about these things than she did. Women's bodies were his forte. In more ways than one she decided as his skillful hands and mouth made her flesh heat up under her skin.

Wild fire leaped in her veins as he knelt before her and trailed hot wet kisses across her belly, then back up to her heaving chest. She cried aloud when he finally took one swollen breast into his mouth and sucked it ravenously. The fire spewed from her core, sizzled up along her belly, into her breast, and passed through her nipple into his mouth. She collapsed against him, weak and dizzy. His arms locked against her back, supporting her. His mouth traveled across the deep valley to her other breast and he suckled with the same intense urgency while his hands caressed the curves of her body, seeking out her pleasure points before finally coming to rest between her quivering thighs. He'd saved the best for last.

He raised his head and gazed up at her, his eyes shimmering with enchantment in the candlelight. "Why, Michelle, no crotch?"

"Thought you'd like it." She managed a silky smile.

"Love it." Expert fingers made their way between the damp laces at her groin. "You're smooth and soaking wet." He gently caressed her slick folds then eased a finger inside her tightness.

Michelle whispered his name and her senses reeled as if short-circuited as he began to stroke her. All her fears, all her inhibitions left her at that instant. She was a woman—all woman needing her man.

With one hand, Erik pulled the bedspread off the bed and dropped it to the carpet behind them. He tugged Michelle down and spread her out on the soft covering. He positioned himself over her, supporting his weight on his knees and elbows on either side of her body.

His eyes took their fill of the sexy, slender woman under him, the white lace pooled about her narrow waist, her long legs and velvety thighs trembling with anticipation. He gazed at the black eyes burning like bright marble, the smooth lips—wet and swollen from his kisses.

As he admired his wife, Erik felt a great wrenching in his chest as something unlocked in his heart and soul, sending ripples of excitement flickering through his veins. This driving need, this powerful maddening emotion was new to him. He never dreamed he could need any woman as violently as he needed this one. Michelle's love for him was like a rich flowing river, sweet and full of enticement. He dropped his mouth to hers. "Feed me, wife. I'm hungry."

The torment in his voice uncapped a tidal wave of passion in Michelle. She knew at that instant that she could please him, give him the love he needed like no other woman could. She would love him with everything she was and everything she would ever be.

With hysterical delight rising inside her, Michelle ran her hands across his muscled chest and tangled her searching fingers in the soft hairs on his stomach. As he sucked the honey from her mouth and kneaded the tender flesh of her breasts in his palm, her hands caressed every inch of his powerful granite body.

She fondled his tight buns, molding and shaping them in her hands. She gently raked her fingers up his back and shoulders, then down his sides and back to his belly. Lower. He sucked desperate air into his lungs and shuddered above her when her fingers brushed across his erection. She curled her fingers around him, barely spanning him.

"So big," she whispered, pushing back the tight skin and touching her fingers to the tip where a pearly drop had escaped his body. She wiped the moisture along his rigid length, tenderly stroking him until his breathing came in a continuous flood of hard panting breaths.

Erik rose up, grabbed the lacy teddy in his hands and with one swipe of his wrists, he ripped it down the front and let it fall on either side of her hips. He gazed at the damp smooth area of her feminine delights, then lowering his head, he proceeded to act out a lascivious fantasy.

His hands slowly explored the softness of her inner thighs. Then he parted the slick folds of her womanhood and gazed in wonder at her. She was beautiful. He leaned in and placed his lips on her, kissing her tender flesh, stroking his tongue against her and inside her, lapping up her delicious juices that poured like warm honey into his mouth.

The pungent scent rising from her body, the thrusting of her hips against his face, and the moans of ecstasy coming from her throat, drove Erik over the edge. He'd always been a man who took great pride in his mastery of self-control. He wanted to prolong her pleasure before taking her, but she'd driven him crazy. He couldn't wait a minute more for her love. He rose up, spread her thighs, and knelt between them.

"It's time," he rasped, lowering his body to hers.

Heat rippled under Michelle's skin as flushes of lust and love inched through her veins. She was ready for her man—her husband. But as she glanced down to where his sex hovered just inches from hers, fear made her close her eyes and hold her breath. "It's not gonna fit, Erik," she squeaked.

"Look at me," he whispered, his mouth close to hers.

The scent of her woman's juices, musky and heady, lingered

on his warm breath. She obeyed his soft command and their eyes locked at the initial contact of naked flesh against naked flesh.

"We'll make it fit," he said. Rolling his hips from side to side, he rubbed his hard length against her little swollen knob of ecstasy until she began to writhe and pant with yearning. "Tell me you love me."

"I love you, Erik."

"Trust that love and know I won't hurt you. Now, reach down and guide me."

With trembling fingers, Michelle reached between them. He drew back his hips to give her room. He was so hard and hot in her palm. She'd never felt anything this splendid before. She guided the broad tip to her wet opening and gasped at the sharp pleasure it brought her. A wanton madness overtook her senses and needing to have the column of pulsing flesh inside her, Michelle threw her arms around her husband's shoulders and raised her hips to him.

Erik stilled. "Easy, baby. I know you want it, but if we rush it, neither one of us will have any pleasure tonight."

He pushed against her and moaned as her tight wet muscles resisted him. He pushed a little deeper. She clamped around his head. He pulled back slowly then gave her another inch, breathing hard and laboriously as the friction mounted. She quivered beneath him, trying to take him bravely. He gave her another inch, pulled back, and gave her another, over and over again, until she began to trust him, stretch for him, dance with him. He pulled all the way back, and somehow he knew she knew the time had come for him to possess her completely. She arched her back and raised her hips as he surged heavily into her with one strong thrust, burying as much as he dared inside her.

Michelle cried out in a moment's agony at the sharp unexpected pain. As her tender muscles strained and stretched, trying to accommodate his monstrous size, she clutched his shoulders in desperation, breathing her dewy breath into his mouth. Tears sprang to her eyes. She didn't expect it to hurt so much. She wasn't a virgin, but then he was an exceptionally large man.

Erik supported his weight on his knees and lay still, full and deep inside her. She could feel the heat of his body course down the entire length of hers. She tried to be brave, but her body quivered around him.

Erik placed his palms against Michelle's, twirled his fingers around hers and spread her arms wide across the coverlet. He planted light, tender kisses across her flushed face, calling on all his willpower not to move too quickly. She was so sweet, so delicious and hot. He sipped at the hot tears seeping from beneath her closed lids. She still didn't have it all, yet he'd hurt her. He knew she'd have difficulty taking him, slender as she was. What he didn't expect was that she would be as tight as a virgin.

"You okay, beautiful?"

She nodded, then her lids slowly opened and the hot passion coming from her eyes took a serious toll on Erik's restrain. Her flesh felt like hot velvet around him, making him forget everything but the need to satiate the fire in his soul, the burning she had ignited, and that only she could quench. He'd known it would be like this. "You're so hot and sexy. So tight, and you feel divinely wonderful sheathed around me," he said against her lips.

The strained smile that had started to form on Michelle's lips quickly vanished as he pulled back and started moving slowly inside her. The pain lessened with each masterful stroke and soon her body began to vibrate with the liquid fire he generated in her blood.

With their fingers still entangled, Erik raised their arms above her head and began to move with hard, steady thrusts, coming almost all the way out of her body, only to meet her halfway and slam her back into the floor again, each stroke bringing more power and fire and passion than the one before.

Michelle matched him, thrust for thrust as their passions rose to a high crescendo, overflowed and poured in torrents from their hearts. She pulled her hands from his and wrapped her arms about his shoulders, her legs around his waist. He was damp and sleek. She felt the powerful rippling of his magnificent muscles under her fingers as he took her hard and fast. Passion drove the blood through her head, chest, and stomach, down to her core, where it sizzled like a blazing furnace.

She gasped and writhed as a heavy fullness circulated low in her belly, dispersed throughout her thighs and legs, and rushed back to the sensitized spot where Erik pumped urgently into her. She tensed terribly, then erupted, shattering into a torrent of fiery sensations. She screamed his name over and over again as the thrilling shockwaves scorched through her veins.

Erik felt her legs tighten around his waist as she quivered from the force of her climax. He watched her exquisite, tear-streaked face, her tight trembling body. He didn't know a woman could come so hard, so passionately. He didn't know he could make a woman so violently wild with ecstasy that all her senses were shamelessly abandoned. He didn't know a woman could make him feel like this, so powerless, yet so in control.

He wanted to dominate her and be dominated by her. He wanted to shed all his fears and guilt and regrets inside her. He laid fully on her. Wet skin against wet skin. He passed his hands under her, clasped her buttocks and pulled her into his final, desperate thrusts.

His whole body cried out for release, and as a rough, hard sob escaped his lips, Erik buried his face in Michelle's neck. He thrust one last time, locked his hips to hers, and poured his love deep inside her.

Much, much later, Michelle felt a warm cloth pass gently between her sore thighs then she was lifted and placed on the mattress. She felt the weight of Erik's body as he climbed in and gathered her into his arms, pulling the covers up around them. Too exhausted to move, she laid her head on his warm chest and drifted off into sweet, fulfilled oblivion.

\*\*\*

On the fifth ring, Michelle realized she wasn't dreaming, and that the ringing wasn't in her head. Lugged from sleep, she untangled herself from the steel arms holding her prisoner against a hard wall of muscle, and reached for the receiver. "Hello."

"Michelle?" Felicia's voice drifted through the wires.

Michelle bolted upright. Oh, God. She was in Erik's room, in his bed, answering his phone at eight o'clock in the morning. Her mind swirled frantically at what his mother must be thinking.

She glanced back at Erik. He was fast asleep on his back— one arm above his head, the other across his stomach, and the bed sheets tangled at his feet. He looked as beautiful and tempting as a sun god. Her eyes inadvertently wandered to the junction of his muscular thighs where his ample sex—now semi-hard—lay nestled in a mat of curly black hair. Memories of his power scorched her mind. How did she ever take all of him? *Or did she?*

"Michelle?"

Michelle whipped back around at Felicia's voice. "Um—" She placed a hand against her thumping heart, and wet her dry lips with her tongue, trying to think of something to say. "Felicia, uh—is everything okay? Is Precious okay?" *Lame.*

"Precious is fine. We're having a great time. I'm sure she'll tell you all about it when you get home." She paused. "Michelle, you and my son are two mature consenting adults. I didn't call to check up on him or to pass judgment on you. Quite frankly, if what I think happened really did happen, I'm glad it's you he chose. Now, be a dear and get him for me."

Michelle colored at Felicia's easy acceptance of her. If she only knew she was speaking to her new daughter-in-law and not just some woman her son had taken to bed… "Well, he's—"

"Who's it?" Erik asked from behind her. His voice was husky from sleep.

Michelle shivered as she felt a finger trace down the outline of her spine, reminding her that she was butt naked. She turned to look at him, feeling uncertain about everything, until she saw him smile with warm memories of their night together. She covered the mouthpiece with her hand. "It's your mother. Felicia."

A scowl immediately replaced his smile. "What does she want?"

"I don't know. But she now knows that we slept together."

"I'll take care of it," he assured her as he propped himself up on his elbow and took the receiver from her. *Damn.* What did his mother want? Why did Michelle have to answer the phone? He wished now he hadn't turned off his cell last night. He leaned over and gave her a lingering kiss on her lips.

Michelle startled as his facial stubble grazed her face. She liked the feel.

His hand tightened on her arm as she started to get out of the bed. "Stay."

"I have to use the bathroom."

"Hurry back, baby. This won't take long." He put the phone to his ears. "Mother, you'd better have a very good reason for calling me so early."

In the bathroom, Michelle leaned against the door. Darn it! Their secret wasn't a secret anymore. And of all people, his mother had to be the one to find out. How could she face Felicia again, knowing that she knew what she knew?

She studied her naked body in the full mirror. There were tiny bite marks on her neck and chest and around her breasts. Erik was definitely a breast man, she thought as she ran her fingers carefully over her sore nipples. He'd suckled as if he were drawing nourishment from her. She wondered if he was unconsciously making up for the fact that he wasn't breastfed as an infant.

She let her fingers trail down her belly as memories of Erik's passion surfaced. Three more times during the night, he'd awakened her and taken her. It seemed as though she only had half-hour intervals of rest between each salacious session. Over and over, he had brought her to the brink of pleasure, and held her timelessly there until she had begged him to end her sweet misery.

The first time had been fierce and intense. She supposed it was because he'd been starved for two years. But later, the cadence changed, and their lovemaking had been slow, long, and drawn-out. Erik had been powerful and tender, hard and sweet, and she'd yielded shamelessly to the flames that had been held captive within her since Ryan, maybe even before.

Michelle took another step and gasped as the muscles between her legs screamed. Erik's stamina and endurance had taken her by a storm of surprise. Erik LaCrosse was an expert in the art of lovemaking. He knew exactly how to please a woman. Cassie had been the luckiest woman on earth, Michelle thought with a hint of jealousy toward the only other woman he'd made love to.

She hadn't wanted last night to end, but it did, and soon they would return to the home he'd shared with Cassie, the house where he couldn't make love to her. *Would he be able to now that they were married?*

Michelle was standing under the hot shower sprays when the door was slid back and Erik stepped into the tub behind her. Silently, he reached for her, drawing her slippery body against him. She felt the full force of his manhood pressing against her slick buttocks. His hands went to her breasts and he cupped them in his palms, and squeezed. Michelle gasped in pleasurable pain as her body turned as hot and liquid as the water falling off her skin. But something was terribly wrong. Something was eating him up inside. She felt a kind of wild fear in his touch, an acute possessiveness that went deeper than the desires of the flesh.

"Erik." She tried to turn her head to look into his eyes, but he pushed her against the wall and bent her forward, raising one of her legs and placing her foot on the edge of the tub. His knees bent slightly. She felt his fingers brush between her thighs as he fitted the head of his erection to her opening. He came up hard and strong, entering her swiftly and deeply from behind.

Michelle felt every straining muscle, every blood-filled vein in his shaft as he sliced through her. He didn't wait for her this time. He just started bucking and pumping wildly into her. His teeth sank into the back of her neck as he worked himself in and out, back and forth. His breathing labored, his grunts hard and rough.

But despite his roughness, the power from his thrusts sent spirals of ecstasy through Michelle. She gave herself up freely to the intense passion until she felt him stiffen and tremble.

Erik's hands tightened on Michelle's breasts, so swollen with passion, the nipples felt like rough pebbles. And as the hot water cascaded down their heaving bodies, he poured himself into her. She was his salvation, his hope.

"Tell me you'll never leave me."

"Erik." Michelle instinctively pushed backward to meet a hard delicious thrust.

"Tell me!"

"I'll never leave you, Erik. I'll never leave you."

"Good. Good. Michelle…"

Erik came. He came hard and long as cries erupted from his throat. He fell forward, crushing Michelle between him and the wet tiles. He clung to her as his sex pulsed inside her. He never wanted to let her go. He never wanted to lose her. He never wanted to have to live without her.

Finally, he pulled from inside her and turned her around. He could tell she had been crying. She had cried for him, for his pain, his loss, his grief.

He turned off the faucet then kissed her wet cheeks and puffy eyelids. He kissed her mouth, his tongue seeking hers. He brought her close to him and felt life return to his loins. God this, sexy, slender woman was going to be the death of him.

He lifted and placed her on his shaft again, wrapping her legs around his waist, and his hands around her body. Carefully, he stepped out of the shower and stumbled toward the bed, their wet bodies still joined together. He arranged her buttocks on the edge of the mattress and draped her legs over his shoulders. He cupped her breasts, leaned in, and sank deeper into her.

She bucked, and her mouth opened on a long scream.

It was pure madness. They weren't leaving this hotel room any time soon.

A deep growl erupted from his throat as he began to pump inside her.

***

Michelle gazed at Erik as they waited in the lobby for the valet to bring the Mercedes around. They had made love over and over again until their bodies literally shut down on them. They had no choice but to succumb to fatigue and had fallen into a long, deep sleep.

It was now early evening, and Michelle was dying to know what had driven him to take her so violently in the shower. She'd asked while they were getting dressed, but he hadn't responded. Had they found Cassie's killer? It was the only thing she knew that could unhinge him. "Are you ready to talk, Erik?" she asked gently. "I need to know what's eating you."

His eyes clouded over. "Danielle died early this morning."

Michelle's hand automatically flew to his arm. They'd been expecting it, but still… "Oh, Erik, I'm so sorry." She now understood why he'd made her promise not to leave him. The women in his life were dying around him. He needed to know he could count on one. She would be there for him for as long as he needed her. "I meant what I said. I'm here for you. I'll never leave. I'll help you get through this difficult time, however you want me to."

He placed his hand over hers resting on his arm. "Do me a favor."

"Anything."

"Can you start joining me for coffee in the morning? It'll brighten my day."

"I'd love to."

"I'm sorry I hurt you in the shower," he said with a tender hum in his voice.

She smiled. "I'm over it. Been over it. Couldn't you tell?"

He touched a finger to her cheek. "You have brought so much happiness back into my life and my home. Last night and today were the most magical and incredibly beautiful moments of my life. You were unbelievably amazing. It was never like that for me. Ever."

Michelle's heart leaped with happiness. She had something

on the late Mrs. LaCrosse, and he'd been honest enough to tell her. "Well, I can't take all the credit. I had an excellent teacher. I didn't know my body could do half the things it did in the last eighteen hours."

He chuckled. "There's a lot more I plan to teach you, Mrs. LaCrosse. You haven't seen anything yet."

Michelle smiled in euphoria. She was sure she hadn't.

# CHAPTER SIXTEEN

Back and forth, Michelle paced the length of the porch as her mind raced in anxiety. She was a desperate woman who had lied to her husband, and if her brother didn't go along with her, she could lose everything.

Robert had to corroborate her story. He just had to.

It was exactly a week since her secret marriage and one-night honeymoon in Boston. There hadn't been time to dwell on the memories since Erik had been preoccupied with Danielle's death. Last Sunday, they'd driven up to Granite Falls for the funeral that took place on Tuesday. It was during the ride back on Thursday that Erik told her he wanted to meet her brother and Yasmine, the two people who were closest to her. He wanted to invite them to dinner before he left for a medical conference in D.C. tomorrow.

When she'd asked him why he wanted to meet them so suddenly, he'd simply stated that they were married, albeit secretly, so it was time he met his in-laws.

Michelle couldn't argue with his logic without causing suspicion, and so had reluctantly made the phone calls, hoping that since it was short notice both Robert and Yasmine would have prior engagements. They didn't.

With Robert and Yasmine coming to dinner, the subject of

her father was bound to wind its way into the conversation. So while Precious and Erik were getting dressed, she'd decided to keep vigil on the porch for Robert. He'd always been there for her. He had to come through for her again tonight. Her entire future depended on him lying for her, just this once.

Michelle stopped her pacing when she spotted her brother's car coming up the long path to the house. She was down the stairs waiting anxiously in the driveway by the time he pulled to a stop in front of the three-car garage. She broke out into a wide grin as Robert pulled his tall, lean frame from his silver Lexus.

"Come here, little sister," he said.

Michelle threw herself into his arms. She hadn't seen him in weeks, and even though they spoke on the phone regularly, she still missed him.

Myriad memories assailed her. Noble ones of Robert as a young boy, working at the local supermarket after school, bagging groceries, sweeping floors, cleaning up, just so he could earn some money to buy them food. Robert shoveling snow, mowing lawns, delivering papers in sub-zero temperatures on an old bicycle he found at the dump and fixed up. Robert reading to her at nights, calming her, soothing her fears.

Then there were the unpleasant ones of Robert standing in front of her to shield her from their drunken father's rage. Robert taking a beating for her while she crouched in a corner, listening to the blows their father delivered to his young body. Tears sprang to her eyes at *those* memories.

Robert held her at arm's length so he could look into her eyes. "You still crying, Mich?"

She chuckled at the endearing nickname. He and Yasmine were the only people who called her Mich. She sniffled and poked him in the chest. "I'm just happy to see you, you big hunk."

Robert grinned and looked up at the house. "Some place. Big change from where we came from."

"Well, you live in a brownstone on Beacon Hill."

"True," he said with a whimsical smile.

"Did you ever imagine I'd end up in a place like this?"

"Well, I did teach you to dream high. But you just work here, Mich," he astutely added.

Michelle gave him an obscure look.

"Oh, it's more than that. See, I've been racking my brain, wondering why I got an impromptu invitation to meet your employer of barely two months. What's going on, Michelle?"

"We've become very close, and he wants to meet my family."

"Sounds serious."

She dropped her gaze.

He put his hand under her chin, raising her face. "So it is. Are you in love with him?"

She so wished she could tell Robert everything. But Erik was right. It was best they kept their marriage a secret, especially for Precious' sake. They had to consider the psychological and emotional impact it might have on her. "Yes, I love him." That much she could share.

"Then my only question is, does he deserve you?"

"You'll get your chance to judge him. See if he's good enough for your little sister."

"In my eyes, nobody would ever be good enough for you, Michelle. And if Dr. Erik LaCrosse can't see what a terrific woman you are, I would be very happy to tell him what a dumb turkey I think he is, right to his face."

Michelle laughed with a mixture of warm emotions. Robert used to warn the boys in their neighborhood to stay away from her, or else. Because of him, she'd managed to hold on to her virginity until she was old enough and ready to give it up. She wished she'd waited for Erik instead of wasting it on Ryan who couldn't even appreciate the priceless gift she'd given him.

But there wasn't one shred of comparison between Erik and the men in her old neighborhood, nor her father. Erik would never hurt her intentionally. She was the dishonest one here. If Erik found out about her father, he might want nothing more to do with her. She was certain of it. He might fire her—contract or not—annul their secret marriage, and worst, cut off her relationship with Precious.

That last reality brought her back to the reason she had been lying in wait for Robert. She wasn't a little girl anymore and Robert didn't need to protect her—except from herself—but she would ask him to do her one last favor.

Michelle took a deep breath of the warm, late-summer afternoon air. "Robert, before we go inside, I need to ask a favor of you."

"Anything for you, little sister."

"I told Erik that Daddy is dead."

Robert slumped against the car and let out a mild swear. "Why did you do a stupid thing like that, girl?"

"At the time, I thought it was the best thing to do. Now I'm not so sure. But I can't change my story. Not yet."

"Lying to him, Mich? How could that be for the best?"

Michelle saw the disillusionment in her brother's eyes. She had looked up to Robert her whole life. He had always been her hero. He'd taught her the good principles of life that had kept her honest and out of trouble. The last thing she wanted was to disappoint him. "Because it was a drunk who killed his wife," she said. "I'm ashamed of him. I hate him for what he did to us."

Robert wiped his hands down his face. "Oh, Michelle, I hate the bastard, too, especially for stealing from you and nearly destroying your life. But I don't go around telling people he's dead. I'm proud of the man I've become. It doesn't matter who or what my father is. He can't take my pride or my dignity away from me."

Michelle sighed. Robert was right, but she knew how passionately Erik felt about drunks. They were all suspects, and he would keep believing that until the one who ran his wife down was brought to justice. "I just know I can't tell him about our father."

Robert placed a hand on her shoulder. "What does Daddy have to do with it, Mich?" he asked in a big brotherly tone. "He didn't run down Erik's wife, and even if he did, Erik wouldn't hold it against you, I'm sure. You don't lie to people you love. You can't build a relationship on deception. What do you think will happen when he finds out you've been lying to him all this time?"

"He isn't going to find out," Michelle said adamantly. "Not as long as Daddy stays wherever he is. And if he does come back, I hope Erik would have grown to love me enough by then to understand why I lied to him."

Robert shrugged as he pushed off his car. "I don't know, Mich. Seems to me you are setting yourself up for a lot of grief. I don't think Erik would care if your father were Charles Manson as long as you were truthful with him. When he finds out that you deceived him, it will destroy any trust or faith he may have had in you. You're taking a big chance, little sister."

That was a chance Michelle was willing to take, because if she came clean now, she was sure the end results would be the same. She had already lied. "Well," she said, crossing her fingers behind her. "It's possible that I may not even be lying. Our father may really be dead."

Robert's face furrowed into a frown. "What are you talking about, Mich?"

"Remember I told you Yasmine thinks Dwight may not be our real father? Our real father could be dead, or out there looking for us."

Robert sighed and shook his head. "Michelle, you need to stop this foolishness. Horrible as he is, Dwight is our father. I would have remembered if—"

"But you were really little when we moved to New Hampshire, and Mom was already pregnant with me. You could have suppressed a terrible memory. And Mrs. Hayes says he used to act suspicious when he saw our mother talking to her, or anybody else. He practically kept her locked up in the house."

"You talked to Mrs. Hayes about this?"

Michelle shrugged. "Yeah. She was like a grandmother to us after Mom died."

"What did she say?"

"She said if I believe there's a secret to be uncovered, I should go uncover it."

Robert regarded her quizzically for a moment. "You really believe there's something out there, Mich?"

"Yes. I mean, look at the way he treated us. He hated us,

Robert. Especially me. He accused me of killing our mother. If I can prove he's an impostor, I wouldn't be so scared of telling Erik about him."

"This man… Erik means that much to you, Mich?"

"He means everything to me."

"Okay, little sister. Even though I think it's a futile cause, I'll give it some thought and perhaps hire an investigator, just to put your mind at ease. And speaking of Erik," Robert added, as he looked up at the house, "he's waiting for you."

Michelle's heart leaped at the sight of Erik standing on the porch. He looked appealing in an indigo short sleeve shirt and grey slacks. "Come on. You have to meet him." She threaded her arms through Robert's and started for the house. The smile in his eyes assured her he'd agreed to keep her little secret, even though he didn't approve of it.

When they reached the porch, Michelle did the introductions.

"I've heard a lot about you," Robert said as he shook Erik's hand. "Your excellent reputation as a doctor and as an employer precedes you."

"As does yours as a dentist and big brother," Erik remarked as he studied the man—Michelle's brown-eyed, black-haired brother, who almost matched him in height. He and Michelle would have tall children, some with gray gold-speckled eyes, some with brown, some with black…

His eyes wandered to Michelle, dressed in an ankle-length animal print dress with a knotted sarong at the front. She looked like a female leopard, strutting gracefully through the jungle, and he felt like the hunter, the predaceous male in hot pursuit.

He missed her terribly, and he wished…

"…surprised I was when Michelle called last night and invited me to dinner."

Robert's hearty laugh dragged Erik out of his daydreams. He chuckled, having no idea what he was chuckling about. "Come on in, Robert. Mrs. Hayes has set out some hors d'oeuvres. We could have a drink until our other guests arrive." He led the way into the house.

"Other guests? I thought I was the only family you had,"

Robert whispered to Michelle.

"Oh, I forgot to tell you, I also invited Yasmine and her nephew, Peter."

"Yasmine? How is she?"

"You can ask her when she gets here," Michelle said, wondering at the smile on his face.

"What would you like to drink, Robert?" Erik asked.

"A martini, please. Dry, if it's available."

"Coming right up." Erik made himself busy at the bar.

"Michelle, can you tie my bow in my hair, please?"

Michelle turned at the voice of her ward. "Sure, baby. Come on."

"You must be Precious." Robert smiled, crouching down to eye level with the little girl as Michelle fiddled with the long strip of ribbon.

"And you must be Robert." Precious returned his smile.

"Mr. Carter to you, young lady," her father said.

"Robert's fine with me."

"I think that's a bit too informal," Erik said.

"How about Uncle Robert? I never had an uncle before," Precious proposed.

"And I never had a niece," Robert responded with an animated smile. "Deal?" He held up his hand for a high-five.

"Deal, Uncle Robert." Precious slapped her palm to his.

"All done." Michelle almost choked on the words. She turned to the table, laden with goodies, picked up a chunk of cheese and stuffed it into her mouth. The very idea of Precious calling her brother 'Uncle' shattered her nerves. If Robert was Precious' uncle, that made her her mother. And she was her stepmother, so Precious was indeed Robert's niece—by law. But nobody knew that—nobody but her and Erik.

She cast a wary look at Erik who was keenly observing his daughter and her brother as they talked and laughed as if they'd know each other for years. He turned his head and his eyes caught and held hers. The warmth she saw spilling from him made her heart ache with need.

The doorbell chimed, breaking the intangible web of

memories spinning between them.

"Peter is here!" Precious deserted her new uncle and raced to the door.

"The real man of her dreams," Erik murmured. "Even I come in second to this Peter guy."

"So I figure you haven't met him yet?"

"Not yet."

Robert laughed as he took the martini glass from Erik.

Michelle left the men, but by the time she got to the foyer, Yasmine and Peter were already inside.

"I saw Robert's car outside, I hope we're not late," Yasmine said.

"You're fine." Michelle hugged her friend. "I asked Robert to come earlier. I had to talk to him about something. You look good, girl," she added, taking in the little black dress her friend was wearing. "I know you didn't wear that for Erik, so it must be for Robert."

"Robert? Please." Yasmine tossed the absurd statement aside with a swipe of her wrist.

Michelle laughed. Robert and Yasmine never mixed well. He used to call her a sassy-mouth little minx, and she'd called him a stiff-shirt prude—all in teenage jest of course. "Come on, the men are waiting," she said as Precious and Peter raced back to the formal living room.

"Smells great in here," Yasmine said.

"We're having roast quail for dinner."

Yasmine smacked her lips. "Lead me to the kitchen, now."

As they entered the room, Michelle saw Erik standing tall and imposing over poor little Peter, a devilish look on his face.

"So, you are the young man who's been courting my daughter? Keeping her out at all kinds of ungodly hours. Well, let me tell you, young man, I won't stand for it."

Peter literally trembled in his little sneakers. "I... I didn't *coat* her," he stammered, backing away from Erik. "I... I just play with her. I... I didn't keep her out late." He turned frightened eyes to Yasmine. "What's *coating*, Aunt Yasmine?"

The adults burst into laughter.

"Well, if you have to ask, I guess you're on the up and up."
Erik tried to keep a straight face. "Just remember, she's my
baby, so you better treat her right." He ruffled Peter's curly
black hair. "Now, run along. Precious is anxious to show you
her fish. And keep the noise down," he called, as they scrambled
up the stairs.

"Wow, talk about pressure." Yasmine fanned her flushed
face with her hands. "You almost made that little boy wet his
pants."

"He's practicing for the real thing when Precious is old
enough to date," Michelle said.

"That'll be about thirty years from now." Erik chuckled.

Michelle noticed Yasmine eyeing Erik up and down,
practically sizing him up. If it were any other woman, she would
wrap her hands around her hair and rip it from her scalp. But
she knew her best friend would never make a move on a man
she was interested in, much less her husband. Yasmine was just
trying to figure out if he was worth Michelle's trouble.

Michelle stepped forward and introduced them.

"Nice to finally meet you, Erik." Yasmine smiled sweetly.

"Yasmine," he said simply, shaking her hand.

"You have a very lovely home."

"Michelle will be delighted to give you a tour after dinner."
He gestured for them to sit.

"Michelle has told me a lot about you," Yasmine kept up the
conversation as she sat down next to Michelle on a burgundy
divan.

"Really?" Erik cast a questioning glance at Michelle.

"Just what a brilliant doctor, devoted father, and marvelous
employer you are," Michelle said. Was he being cool toward
Yasmine because he thought she'd told her about their marriage
and night of passion? Men assumed their women talked to each
other about such private matters. She hoped Erik knew her well
enough to know she'd keep their intimate relationship a secret.

"Would you care for a drink, Yasmine?" Erik asked.

"Yes, Chardonnay, please."

"I know what you want," he said, his eyes softening as he

gazed at Michelle.

*Yeah, I bet you do*, she thought at the loaded statement.

"Help yourselves to the hors d'oeuvres, ladies," Erik said on his way to the rolling bar cart.

"Where's Robert, Erik?" Michelle asked, as she and Yasmine reached for plates and began filling them with the delicacies on the long low table in front of the divan.

"He's visiting with Mrs. Hayes in the kitchen." He brought over Michelle's Perrier and Yasmine's glass of white wine, and then sat down in the chair on the other side of the table.

"So, Dr. Erik," Yasmine drawled in a silky tone, battering her eyelashes at him. "Are you receiving any new patients? I haven't had a thorough checkup for a while."

"It's recommended you have one every year." Erik was mildly amused with her audaciousness. No wonder she and Michelle were best friends.

His gaze wandered to Michelle. He wanted so badly to erase the memories of her abusive childhood, give her some new ones to muse on, like those they made in Boston a week ago. Because of Danielle's death, he hadn't had time to properly reminisce on that night. But now that life had somewhat resumed its normal pace, he'd begun craving the taste and smell of Michelle in his mouth again, the feel of her tight body gripping him like a glove.

He would have to wait another week since he was leaving for Washington, D.C. tomorrow for a medical conference. He'd thought of taking Precious and Michelle along with him, but there were more pressing matters to attend to.

He'd learned that Clayton had recently returned from a medical mission to Uganda, and would be attending the conference. This was his chance to learn the truth about the scene he'd walked in on between Clayton and his wife, over two years ago. The scene that had started the argument that ultimately led to Cassie's death. He was not leaving D.C. without answers.

"Yasmine," Michelle scoffed, "when we were kids you always said you would never go to a male doctor."

"The doctors we knew back then were old and bald. I'll

make an appointment anytime to see a hunk like Dr. Erik." She placed a stuffed clam in her mouth and slowly chewed on it.

"Yasmine Reynolds, you're still the impertinent fresh-mouthed girl I remember." Robert strode into the room.

"And you still have the most kissable lips I've ever seen on a man—stiff, but kissable." Yasmine set down her plate and hurried over to give Robert a hug.

Michelle smiled at the pair who as far back as she could remember fought like cats and dogs. But when the mist cleared, they were one happy little family.

Yasmine reclaimed her seat while Robert sat in the chair close to Erik. He picked up the martini he'd left on the table.

"You look yummy, Robert. Perhaps I should make an appointment to have my teeth cleaned," Yasmine said with a twinkle in her eyes.

"I'm sure you have very strong teeth, Yasmine Reynolds."

"I don't know, maybe if I bit you on those kiss—"

"You two need to stop," Michelle said, feeling herself flush at the heat her brother and her best friend were generating. Was something going on between them? She looked at Erik who was watching them with a purely enjoyable expression on his face. She was certain he was thinking of their time together in Boston and the sexual banter they'd exchanged while making love. He'd made it fun. She wanted to smack the stupid grin off his face.

"Just like old times?" Mrs. Hayes bustled into the room, grinning from ear to ear. "Never in a million years would I have thought I would be serving dinner to Robert and Michelle in the doctor's dining room."

"Mrs. Hayes, do you remember Yasmine Reynolds?" Michelle asked.

"Of course. Luke and Marie's little girl, right?"

"Right." Yasmine said. "I remember the delicious bread pudding you used to make and invite the neighborhood kids to sit on your porch and wash down with cool lemonade."

"Those were the good old days." The older woman's eyes lit up with joyful memories. "You've all grown up into such beautiful young people—Robert a dentist, Michelle advocating for the poor and needy, and Yasmine, Michelle tells me you're studying law. I wasn't blessed with children of my own, but I couldn't be prouder if you were mine."

"Oh that's very sweet." Michelle dabbed at her tears as she rose and walked over to her dear old friend.

"We think the world of you, too. You kept Michelle and me alive, gave us hope," Robert said as he and Yasmine joined Michelle in giving the kind old soul a group-hug.

A smiling Mrs. Hayes finally turned to Erik. "Dinner is about ready, Dr. Do you want me to call the children down?"

"Yes, please, Mrs. Hayes." Erik waited until the housekeeper had vacated the room and everyone had returned to their seats. "So, Yasmine, you grew up on the same street as Michelle and Robert? You must have been friends since..."

"First grade," Yasmine supplied. "We were dirt poor, but happy." She glanced at Michelle. "Well, sometimes we were."

"Michelle told me about the abuse she suffered from her father," he said to let her know she was not betraying her friend by telling him about her past. "I'm really impressed at how all of you have made such success of your lives. I was born with a silver spoon in my mouth, yet I feel like a failure compared to you who had to work hard for your achievements."

"To balance it out, Erik, lots of kids from your side of the fence end up on ours. The teenage daughter of one of my affluent clients got hooked on drugs. They tried everything to rehabilitate her, but eventually had to let her go for the sake of their other children. She's now living on the streets of Boston, doing any and everything to find her next fix. That's just one example," Robert added, dolefully. "We have no control over where we come from, only where we end up."

"A proven truism," Erik declared. "You're all survivors, and now you're helping others find their way out of the same situations you were in." He glanced at his darling Michelle, the sweetest, most altruistic soul he'd ever met. "The work Michelle is doing at the youth center is absolutely amazing. She gives of her time to make sure those kids have a chance to make it over the fence."

"Michelle has the biggest, kindest heart. I'm not surprised at the path she's taken." Robert smiled at his sister. "We had very little as kids, but Michelle still gave away what she had to her friends who had even less."

"You're very protective of her."

"Yes, I am."

Erik reached for an escargot. He heard the pride in Robert's voice. He'd done an excellent job of raising a beautiful, self-assured young lady who'd easily held her own in a room full of brilliant doctors. "I'm an only child. Often I wish I had the support of a sibling, like what you and Michelle had when your mother passed away, and more recently when your father died."

Yasmine coughed. Michelle glanced at her, and their eyes held for a few seconds before Yasmine looked away. Michelle could just imagine what was going on in her friend's mind.

"Sorry." Yasmine covered her surprise and took a long sip of wine. "The shrimp's a little too spicy for me."

Robert got up, walked to the back of the divan and placed his hands on his sister's shoulders. "I've been taking care of Michelle since the day she got home from the hospital, Erik. Our father was so busy feeling sorry for himself over the loss of our mother, he forgot about us. I was only five years old, but with the help of kind neighbors like Mrs. Hayes, I learned real fast how to feed, bathe, burp a baby, and change diapers. So, yes, Michelle and I have always had each other, and I will continue to protect her until another man steps up to the plate."

Michelle trembled with anxiety, but gathered strength from her brother's supportive touch. She was such a hypocrite for teaching the children at the center to always tell the truth, no matter what, when she, herself, was living a blatant lie.

She glanced at Erik. He stared back at her with tenderness and admiration brimming in his eyes. Michelle knew at that moment that she had to tell him the truth. He didn't deserve this kind of dishonesty. She could not continue with this lie. Not after what they had shared in Boston. Not after all the sweet things he'd just said about her. And not after dragging Yasmine and Robert into her dark dungeon of deceit. She hadn't had time to warn Yasmine, but her friend had come through for her, as well. Robert and Yasmine had proven their loyalty. It was time she proved hers.

Coming clean was the ethical thing to do. She didn't think Erik would fire her since she took such good care of his daughter. Precious' happiness was the most important thing to him. Although it may mean losing whatever it was he felt for her, at least she would regain her dignity. She had no idea what he would do, but she had to trust in what they shared.

So when Mrs. Hayes announced that dinner was ready, it was with a prayer in her soul and a strained smile on her face that Michelle took Erik's arm and allowed him to escort her into the dining room.

His eyes were warm as they stared into hers. His hands were strong as they guided her. He had shared his name and his body with her. It would make her confession so much easier if she only knew exactly what was in his heart.

That part of himself he kept locked away from her.

It still belonged to Cassie.

# CHAPTER SEVENTEEN

Michelle pulled to a stop in front of Amherst Preparatory School just as a noisy cluster of kids came rushing through the double-doors.

Just in time, she thought, stepping out of the car. Now that Precious was in school, she spent her mornings at the youth center buried in clerical work, sending thank you letters as the funds kept coming in, and getting things ready for the after-school kids. She'd taken on a lot more responsibilities now that Rose had returned to the classroom.

Since they'd been able to raise the funds they needed, she spent the early afternoons going over blueprints with Bill Wilson of Wilson's Construction. She was so excited that their plan for a new center was finally coming to fruition. She was happy her nanny position allowed her the space and time to devote to her cause. If she never did anything else worthwhile with her life, Michelle felt she would go to her grave contented that she'd done this good deed for the needy children in Manchester.

Maybe losing her job and hitting rock bottom was a blessing, for she could not have accomplished half as much for the kids if she was still in the corporate world.

"Hi, Michelle."

Michelle turned as Belinda's mother approached her. Maggie

was the closest friend Michelle had on Jefferson Drive, so far. Well she didn't have a choice, actually, since Belinda and Precious were best friends. She'd met some of the other parents when she and Erik had attended Open House at the school, but Maggie had remained her favorite.

"Hey, Maggie. What's up?"

"The weekend. We're leaving for Hampton Beach this afternoon to enjoy the fantastic weather. It might be the last before winter sets in. Are you guys going anywhere?"

Erik had told Michelle that he'd rented a cottage on Cape Cod, but it hadn't been used because of the many upheavals this summer. She would like to see what it was like on the Cape, how the folks on the other side of the tracks vacationed. "Erik just came back from a week-long conference in D.C. last night. He probably just wants to relax at home." She waved as she saw Precious and Belinda tumble down the steps of the school.

"Erik is one lucky man to have found you," Maggie said. "We were worried after Holly left, but you're great with Precious. I don't think I've seen her this happy since her mother died."

Precious came up and wrapped her arms around Michelle. "How was school?" she asked the little girl.

"Boring," Precious and Belinda said in unison.

Michelle and Maggie rolled their eyes, and laughed.

"Now that the girls are in school, we should plan some lunch and shopping dates," Maggie said.

A week ago, Michelle would not have been able to afford it. But since she'd become Erik's secret wife, he'd deposited a huge amount of money into her account. He wanted her to feel like his wife, at least in one other aspect other than the bedroom. She could walk away today and be good to start over anywhere in the world, but she won't trade Precious and Erik for anything. "Sounds great," she told Maggie.

"I'll call you." Maggie took her daughter's hand.

"Bye, Belinda," Precious called as Belinda and Maggie walked to their Volvo SUV, loaded with weekend luggage.

"Bye, Precious. Have a fun weekend."

Michelle helped Precious into the car. "So school was boring, huh?" she asked as she leaned over to buckle her seatbelt.

Precious grabbed her around the neck and planted a sound wet kiss on her cheek.

"Whoa, what was that for?"

"Cause you look like you could use a hug."

"Oh, I do, do I?" Michelle rubbed her nose against Precious'. She did need a hug to calm the quivering in her stomach. She was going to tell Erik about her father, tonight.

"So what's the problem? Want to talk about it?"

Michelle stared into her innocent, trusting eyes, marveling at her ability to pick up on her mood. It was true when you were close to people, you could read them like a book. When Erik didn't come down for coffee this morning, she knew something was wrong.

"I miss hanging out with you all day," she said closing the door, then quickly walking around the car to slide behind the wheel.

"I miss you, too. Maybe we can do something fun like go see Yasmine and Peter or Uncle Robert," Precious said with a hopeful lilt in her voice.

"We can, if your father doesn't have any plans for you," Michelle answered as she pulled out from the curb.

"Where's Daddy? He was supposed to pick me up."

Michelle had been wondering the same thing since Erik called and asked her to pick up Precious. He'd said he was in the middle of something important. "He's at home."

"Goody. It makes me sad when he goes away. Did your daddy go away when you were a little girl, Michelle?"

"Yes." *And I wish he'd stayed the hell away.*

"Did it make you sad?"

She slowed down as she approached a four-way stop. "No, I had Uncle Robert to play with me."

"I wish I had a little brother or a sister to play with me. Then I won't be so sad when Daddy goes away. But you play with me, and I'm not so sad anymore, but I still miss my daddy, and my mommy, too."

As Michelle eased up off the brakes and proceeded across the intersection, her heart ached for the child whose world had been turned upside down by the loss of her mother. Even though she was trying as hard as she could to fill the maternal void, no matter how close they got, Michelle knew she could never replace Cassie in Precious' life.

"I'm happy Daddy's home. Are you, Michelle?"

"Yes." She was both happy and nervous. Telling Erik about her father was not something she was looking forward to. All week long, she'd been rehearsing the speech she should have given last Saturday after their dinner guests left.

She was all prepped to confess that night, but while she was putting Precious to bed, Erik was called to the hospital. She was asleep when he got home and then he left early the next morning. She'd planned to tell him over coffee this morning, but he never came down, and had asked Mrs. Hayes to bring breakfast to his room for him and Precious. He was still there when she left to take Precious to school, and then go on to Manchester.

The only communication she'd had with him all day was when he interrupted her meeting to ask that she pick up Precious from school. He was unusually vague, seemingly cool with her. He was almost as aloof as the day they met.

Something had happened in D.C. She was certain of it. She'd been living with this man for more than two months. He had a routine. This was the first time it had changed. No running, no lingering over the paper and early morning coffee.

A lot had happened since Boston, she realized. Danielle's death and the conference had kept him preoccupied. But now that he had time to reflect, she wondered if he were having second thoughts about his impulsive behavior in marrying her, making love to her. Did he feel he'd betrayed Cassie's memory by remarrying before her case was solved? She had no idea what was going on in his head, and it was making her crazy.

"Why's Mommy's car out?" Precious asked as Michelle came up the driveway and parked behind the fire red Porsche that had been garaged for probably over two years.

As Precious bolted out of the car, Michelle watched Erik

deposit an armful of clothes into the trunk of the Porsche. He slammed it shut and turned around just as his daughter leaped into his arms.

"How's my baby girl?" he asked hugging her to his chest and planting kisses on her face.

Michelle wished his love for her could be as open and wholesome as it was for his daughter. Her mind burned with the memory of being held against that strong naked body, the thrill of his mouth on hers and on every other crevice of her body. Her blood soared as she recalled the raw passion that had consumed them. Her whole body ached for his touch again.

Over his daughter's shoulder, Erik met Michelle's gaze as she leaned against the hood of the Jaguar. The longing he saw in her beautiful black eyes stirred a primal need deep within his own soul. He'd missed her something fiercely while he was in D.C. He'd dreamed about her every night and thought about her all day, so much that he'd been unable to concentrate on the brilliant and informative lectures going on around him.

Then yesterday, he'd finally cornered Clayton and demanded answers. It wasn't even close to what he'd expected, but it had, nevertheless, left him wondering if he'd ever be able to trust, much less love another woman again. He even thought of annulling his secret marriage and letting Michelle go.

God, he still couldn't believe what Cassie had done. How she'd deceived him for five years, just because of something some psychic had told her. If she'd only trusted him. So full were his anger and sadness, he'd had no will, no energy to get out of bed this morning. He hadn't wanted to see Michelle. He hadn't wanted to see anyone. He'd just wanted his head and the world to stop spinning. He'd felt as lost and hopeless as the morning after Cassie's death.

But when Precious bounced into his bed, screaming with joy that he was home, Erik knew he had to go on for her, just as he'd done two years ago. When she began babbling about all the fun things she and Michelle did while he was away, hope rose in Erik's heart once again. She was the happy, spirited child she'd been when her mother was alive. He wanted to keep her that way.

And seeing Michelle now, his beautiful wife, with love in her glittering black eyes, Erik knew keeping her around was just as vital to him as it was to Precious. He needed her to banish the pain, the anger, and the sadness from his heart, as only she could do.

"I need to talk with Michelle, Muffin. Mrs. Hayes just took a fresh batch of chocolate-chip cookies out of the oven. Tell her I say it's okay if you have one with a glass of milk."

Erik set his daughter on the ground then like a man on a mission, he closed the short distance between him and the sweet little woman he had grown to depend on so much—too much. She smelled lovely. He wanted to drag her into his arms, hold her close to his heart and kiss her senseless, but he couldn't—not here. "Thanks for picking her up at the last minute," he said, smiling down at her.

"It was no problem. She's happy to see you."

Her eyes looked vague, worried. "And you? Are you happy to see me, Michelle?"

She shrugged. "I guess."

"You guess? You're supposed to be happy to see me. I'm your husband of just two weeks, Mrs. Michelle Juliet LaCrosse." He loved the sound of that name.

Her face took on a somber expression. "I'm happy to see you, Erik. The problem is I have to tell you something that could have a big impact on our relationship."

"Are you pregnant?"

She shook her head. "No, it's nothing like that."

A knot formed in the pit of Erik's stomach. He didn't know if it was from relief or regret. "So what else can you possibly tell me that could change our relationship, Michelle? Did you accidentally tell someone that you and I are married?"

She folded her hands across her stomach and dropped her gaze. As he watched her chest rise and fall with the effort of her ragged breathing, Erik knew it was big. Fear came tumbling down on him. He'd been gone a week. What the heck could have happened to make her so distraught? His hands went to her shoulders. "What is it, Michelle?" he whispered softly, urgently.

She lifted her head and stared at him through teary black eyes. "It's about my father."

"Is he back from the dead?"

"Oh, Erik." She looked away from him.

Now he was confused. "What about your father?"

"He's alive."

Erik dropped his hands from her shoulders as a cold chill swept over him. "What do you mean he's alive? You and your brother, *and* your best friend sat in my house just a week ago and swore your father was dead."

Her lips trembled. "I'm sorry, Erik. He isn't dead. I lied to you and I convinced them to corroborate my story."

*Not another lie from another woman he…* Erik balled his hands into fists and closed his eyes. "Why?"

"He's made my life so miserable. I told you how he used to hit me when I was a child."

*This better be good,* he thought, as he pinned her with his eyes.

"A couple years ago, he stole my debit card, figured out my PIN, which was my mother's birth date, and cleaned out my bank account—all in one night. I had a sizable amount of money saved—money I had plans for. I didn't know what he'd done until I stopped to put gas in my car two days later and couldn't find my card. When I called the bank and they told me I had seventy dollars and fifteen cents to my name, I almost died, Erik. Then shortly after, I lost my job, my car, and my apartment. I lost everything I'd worked so hard for—even my clothes were stolen from me. If it weren't for Yasmine and my brother, I probably would have ended up on the streets." The tears ran unrestrained down her face.

Erik's anger switched gear. "That bastard. I'm going to break his neck for what he did to you. Where is he, Michelle? Where is he?"

"I don't know. I haven't seen him since that night. As far as I'm concerned, he's dead. I never want to see him again. That's why it was so easy to tell you he was dead when you asked me about him. I'm sorry for lying to you. I didn't plan to lie. It just slipped out."

All of a sudden, Erik didn't care who was watching them. He pulled Michelle into his arms and buried her wet face in his chest. He threaded his fingers through her soft silky hair. "There's nothing to be sorry about. He should be dead for hurting you. I can't understand how a man could be so cruel to his own child. You're his little girl, no matter how old you get. He's supposed to protect you, not hurt you."

She raised her head and gazed up at him, love and wonder in her eyes. "You're not upset that I lied to you?"

"I am disappointed, but under the circumstances, I understand why you did. Just don't lie to me again." He paused. "Is there anything else you need to tell me, about him or anything in your past?" he asked with an urgency that surprised even him.

She shuddered and pushed out of his arms. "No."

Erik watched her closely for a moment then glanced at Cassie's car loaded with half her wardrobe, and wishing she had trusted him with the truth. He'd known Cassie for twenty-two years, Michelle for three months, and Michelle had just proved that she trusted him more easily than Cassie ever did, and with something far less significant. That was a powerful insight.

"Why is Cassie's car out?" Michelle asked, following his gaze. "And why is it filled with her clothes?"

"I'm giving it all away to charity. Someone's coming by to pick them up later."

She eyed him warily. "Why now?"

He couldn't tell her he'd been blind-sided by the woman he'd loved for most of his life. He held up his left hand. "See, the ring is gone. I tossed it into the Potomac River, and I dismissed the private investigator I'd hired to find the drunk who'd killed her. I'm done living in the past. I want my life back."

Michelle's heart danced with excitement. She couldn't believe what she was hearing. Erik was ready to move on. There was no need to tell him that her father was a drunk since he was long gone by the night Cassie was killed. Just like Erik, she was ready to let go of the baggage of her past. Well, that part of it. She was still certain that Dwight Carter was hiding something, especially since Robert had begun searching through the boxes of old papers and stuff they'd stored from their past in his brownstone, and so far, hadn't found anything that linked Dwight to a life before New Hampshire.

Strange. Very strange, indeed. Everybody kept links to their pasts. That is if they had nothing to hide. It was as if Dwight had fallen from the sky with a four-year-old son and a pregnant wife, right into the middle of Manchester.

"Hey, baby, where did you go?"

Michelle started at the sound of Erik's voice. She looked up at him. "When you said you were in the middle of something important, I never thought it was this big. Actually, when you didn't come down for coffee this morning, I was kind of scared that you were regretting what happened between us."

His chest heaved. "So much has happened in the past two weeks to keep us apart, but I've missed you every moment of every day. I need to be with you. I need my wife."

"I've missed you too, Erik. I'm going insane with my need for you." She glanced up at the house, hope dancing in her eyes. "Can we make love tonight after Precious is in bed?"

"We'll make love tonight, but not here," Erik stated brusquely. He didn't want any memories of Michelle tied to this house. As a matter of fact, he was thinking about selling it and moving back to Granite Falls. He missed his home, the place where he was born and raised. He'd only moved to Amherst to be close to his mother. She'd been denied the opportunity of raising her son, and he was hell-bent on giving her the chance to make it up with her grandchildren—well, her only grandchild, he thought with a sour twist of his lips. But recently, Felicia had been spending a great deal of time in Granite Falls, comforting his grieving father. Cassie was gone, and since it seemed the authorities would never find the man who killed her, there was nothing keeping him here.

Except, maybe Michelle. He still hadn't quite figured out what his true feelings for her were. Or maybe he knew and just didn't want to admit them—especially after just learning that his darling wife of twelve years had deceived him for five. The only thing he knew right now was that he needed Michelle. He was burning up with a hunger only she could satiate.

"So what are we going to do?" Michelle asked him. "Rent a hotel room for a few hours? It's not like we can spend the night together without creating suspicion. Our relationship, our marriage is still a secret to the rest of the world."

"I was thinking we could spend the weekend in Cape Cod."

Her eyes lit up. "Really?"

"Hmm. Plus, Sunday is your birthday and I want to do something special with you away from here." *In a place that has no memories of Cassie.*

"You remembered my birthday?"

He grinned at her enthusiasm. "Well, Precious reminded me this morning. I called the caretaker and the cottage is being prepared as we speak."

"Okay. I'd like that. I've never been to the Cape."

"Then it's settled. We'll leave ASAP." He started walking toward the house. "I thought about leaving Precious with Felicia just so I could have you to myself, but she and Dad have plans." A relaxed smile curved his lips as he spoke of his parents.

"Those two aren't wasting any time." Michelle giggled beside him.

"They've been in love for forty years. They've sacrificed their love to keep others from being hurt. They deserve some happiness together."

Michelle rested her hand on his arm. "As do you," she said, staring up at him as they stood at the front door.

"You make me happy." He cupped her chin, leaned down, and brushed his lips lightly over hers. Electricity sizzled between them. "Go pack. The sooner we get out of here, the sooner we can start enjoying each other." He slapped her playfully on her buttocks, opened the door, and pushed her inside.

"I love you," she said, the warmth of her smile echoing in her voice as she looked back at him.

Erik walked toward his study. He had to let the hospital

know where he would be in case of an emergency. He prayed to God there'd be none. He needed some time, one uninterrupted weekend with his family. As he opened the door of the study, Erik gasped as if he'd been slammed in the gut with a sledgehammer.

He'd just referred to himself, Michelle, and Precious as a family.

Involuntarily, his gaze wandered over the fireplace to meet his late wife's brown eyes. She wanted him to be happy, according to his mother. She wanted him to find someone new to love and care for him and their child.

Michelle's love for Precious and him was pure and strong. She had brought so much joy into his sad, pathetic life, so much inner peace to his soul. She had filled his world with so much light he couldn't remember it ever being dark. She made his heart sing with delight, his flesh dance with enthusiasm. And she trusted him.

Erik strolled to the fireplace and unhinged the painting of his late wife from its hook. He stared at her long and hard, awed that the bevy of emotions he usually felt when he gazed at her were gone.

He opened the closet door and placed the painting inside.

\*\*\*

"Alone at last." Erik eased down next to Michelle on the sofa.

She laid her head on his chest and wrapped her arms around his that circled her upper body. It felt so good, so natural cuddled up to him.

The night had turned a bit chilly, so Erik had lit a fire—the only light in the room—that now crackled softly in the fireplace behind them. They sat quietly for a while, just enjoying each other's presence, as they gazed out the sliders at the ocean, and listened to the mellow sounds of waves lapping at the stretch of white beach.

"Are you sure Precious is asleep?" Michelle asked as Erik

began massaging her arms in very slow motion, spurting excitement inside her. Even though they were away from Amherst, they had to be careful for Precious.

"The poor darling is worn out. Was snoring before I finished reading two pages of her book."

Michelle giggled. "Well, you did entice her play volleyball with those kids on the beach this afternoon, Erik, just to make sure she wouldn't protest when you sent her to bed."

He chuckled. "She enjoyed it. She told me she had fun. It was the last thing she said before she fell asleep."

"Sure, try to justify your actions, Dr. LaCrosse." Michelle's mouth twisted with humor as she turned her head and gazed up at him.

"Well, if I didn't come up with a master plan, Mrs. LaCrosse—" His hands moved inward from her arms toward her chest and he gently caressed her breasts through her blouse. "We wouldn't be able to do this until after midnight."

"Hmm, I see what you mean," Michelle murmured as her skin started to tingle under his touch. She dropped her hands to his thighs and massaged the hard muscles there. He felt like polished marble under her soft palm. "I definitely wouldn't want to wait until midnight for this."

"I knew you'd see it my way, darling." He chuckled, picked her up and placed her across his lap, facing him. He dragged his hands up her legs along her thighs and brought them to rest on her buttocks. "Feel that?" he asked in a husky voice as he moved her gently up and down, back and forth on his erection. "Feel what you do to me, Mrs. LaCrosse?"

Michelle licked her lips as fire swept through her veins. "Yes, I feel that, and I like what I do to you."

As he claimed her lips with his, Michelle clasped her arms around his neck and surrendered to the hunger. It had been two weeks, and they were both starving.

"I want you so much," Erik whispered against her mouth as his fingers tugged eagerly at the tail of her shirt, lifting it up along her belly and over her chest. He growled as her breasts sprang into his hands. Bless her dear heart for not wearing a bra. Her nipples were round and smooth and he massaged his palms over them in slow circular motions until they hardened in response to his touch. He dragged his mouth from hers and trailed his lips over her chin and down to the delicate skin of her neck. Her intoxicating smell and the sweet little whimpers coming from her throat made his groin throb with so much pain he though he would explode in his pants.

Eager to love her, Erik pressed Michelle back against the soft cushions and covered her body with his. He gazed at her face and the trust and love swimming in her eyes tugged on his heartstrings. "Michelle, I wish—"

"Shh. Don't wish. Just talk to me with your body. Show me what you can't tell me." She opened her legs and her arms to receive him.

With an ache in his belly, Erik settled between her thighs and hurriedly unbuttoned her blouse, swearing mildly at the precious time it wasted before he could feast on her beautiful breasts. "Oh, I've missed these," he moaned, gazing at them, totally mesmerized.

"You're a breast man, aren't you?" Michelle asked him.

He chuckled, softly. "You're just figuring that out, darling?" He held one between his thumb and forefinger and sucked it into his mouth, using the muscles of his jaws, his teeth and his tongue to spawn illicit pleasure inside her.

She arched her back, dug her nails into his arms and thrashed restlessly under him. God she was so damned sensuous. It made him wild. Wilder. He pulled his mouth from that delectable mount of swollen flesh and lavished his attention on the other until Michelle whispered his name. When he felt his hunger had been appeased, he pulled his mouth from her breast and trailed his lips slowly and tantalizingly over her chest and down the soft contours of her flat belly. One hand crawled up her legs and thighs as he kissed his way lower and lower. He loved the smell radiating from her hot heat.

"If I don't get inside you now, I'm going to explode," he whispered against her skin as his fingers curved around the waistband of her shorts.

Michelle fought her way through the haze of passion when she felt Erik tugging at her shorts. She grabbed his hand. "Erik, no. Not here," she said, her maternal instincts kicking into gear.

"Why not?"

Her lower body curled into his mouth as the tip of his tongue made shocking contact with the hollow of her belly button.

"Precious," she whispered in a tormented plea, even as she made seductive little motions with her hips.

"She's asleep." His voice was tight and hoarse with need. His loins hurt. He needed to be inside her. Right here. Right now. "Come on, let's be spontaneous."

As much as she longed to throw caution to the wind, common sense warned Michelle it would be a terrible mistake for them to make love on the sofa in the open living room with a precocious seven-year-old sleeping upstairs. What if she walked in on them?

The stakes were too high. The price of losing Precious' trust and respect was too great. Michelle couldn't afford to risk that, not even for Erik. He was a man after all, and when it came to sex, everybody knew they thought with their...

She pushed at his head with both hands. "Erik, we can't make love here. Stop. Stop."

He growled with impatience, the golden embers in his grey eyes glowing with deep dark desire. He scooped her up off the sofa and took the short flight of stairs to the master bedroom. He closed and locked the door then strode across the floor. He set her gently down on her back on the bed and switched on the table lamp. He bent over her and swiftly removed her shirt, shorts, and thong, and tossed them across the room.

A distinct light shimmered in his eyes as he admired the gentle curves of her body. She was smooth and perfect, his to enjoy to his fullest. His gaze moved to her dusky eyes, and the tender love he encountered caused a huge lump to lodge in his throat. No woman had ever moved him like this before, and suddenly, he wanted to take his time with her, worship every inch of her sweet body. Without taking his eyes from hers, he reached up and removed his shirt, dropping it on the floor before his fingers went to the waist of his slacks where he slowly released the button.

Michelle's emotions whirled and skidded into high gear at the metallic grate of Erik's fly being unzipped. He bent forward to remove his pants and briefs, and when he stood upright again, honoring her with a full view of his erection straining to the ceiling, heavy and thick against his tight belly, she swallowed the ache of love in her heart.

He was hers. Truly hers. She'd come clean about her father and he'd forgiven her, freeing her to love him uninhibitedly. There were no shadows over her heart tonight.

"Now, where were we?" His eyes impaled her as his magnificent body came closer to the bed.

"Right here." Michelle placed her hand on her quivering stomach.

# Chapter Eighteen

The mattress sagged as he lowered his weight next to her. Supporting his body on one elbow, he traced his fingers slowly down her body from the valley between her breasts to the apex of her quivering thighs. She moaned softly as his fingers slid across the Brazilian waxed area of her groin.

"Yes, this is exactly where we were." He pressed the heel of his palm into the smooth mound of her pleasure box, teasing the sensitive knob of her clitoris before parting the flesh and sliding a finger inside her moistness.

Michelle gasped as his finger began to slide magically back and forth inside her. She dug her nails into his arms and squeezed her thighs, afraid of the strength of her own passion. While his fingers wreaked havoc between her legs, he lowered his head and sucked on her breasts again, only much more gently this time as if he wanted to savor the taste and feel of her in his mouth. She groaned when his lips trailed down the hollow of her throat, drizzling feathery kisses on her skin as he continued to strum her with two fingers, now. Her insides clamped around him. "Please, Erik..."

"Please what?"

"Take me, now. I want to feel you pumping away inside me." She reached out to clasp his sex that was pressing urgently against her thigh.

He sprang out of her reach. "Not yet. I want to enjoy you, feel you fall apart in my mouth."

Michelle shuddered as his lips started down the slope of her body, leaving a fiery trail of desire everywhere he touched. He dipped his tongue into her bellybutton then dragged it south. When his mouth neared her garden of delight, he pulled his fingers from inside her, nuzzled her clitoris with his nose and inhaled deeply. "Sweet."

He spread her thighs, settled between them, and pinned them to the mattress with his arms. He grinned wickedly up at her as he used the pad of his thumbs to expose her completely to him. He blew his hot breath on her sensitized clit; he flicked her gently with the tip of his tongue, then grazed her ever so lightly with his wet lips. Over and over again, he repeated the agonizing foreplay until she began to writhe in uncontrollable ecstasy.

Michelle clasped her hands over her mouth to stifle the scream that erupted from her throat as firecrackers seemed to explode beneath every inch of her skin. "Erik," she cried as she burst into flames that consumed her for what seemed like an eternity. Eventually, she went limp on the mattress, her body jerking around like livewire.

But he wasn't done with her, yet. He dragged his tongue downward from her clit, probed the sensitive area just below it for agonizingly tense moments before he plunged it deep inside her. He covered her completely with his mouth, clamping his lips about her and explored the hot depth of her passion, pulling the copious liquid from the reservoir of her desire.

She cried out his name again as the passion lashed at her. He passed his hands under her and cupped her buttocks. Pulling her into his face, he rammed his tongue in and out of her and lapped up the molten lava coursing from her squirming body. The primal animal sounds coming from deep in his throat coaxed her onward and upward to another mind-blowing orgasm.

"Come again, wife. One last time for your husband."

Michelle moaned as her body began to vibrate, as desire pumped through her veins, hurling her beyond the point of sanity. She exploded into a million sensitized pieces.

Erik kept his mouth glued to her until she stopped shaking. Then and only then, did he withdraw his lips from her. The scented heat of her soft flesh was so intoxicating it made him lightheaded. He rose above her like a dark and powerful lord with a single purpose in mind—to enjoy his lubricious booty.

He retrieved a small packet from the lamp table and tried to rip it open. The damn thing wouldn't give. It was the first time in his life he would use a condom, and he hoped it fit and held. He didn't want to, but Michelle had warned him that she might be ovulating. Michelle wanted to have his babies and he would love nothing more than to see her little belly swollen with his child. She was already his wife, but it wasn't time for babies.

Coitus interruptus crossed his mind, but Erik knew when the time came, he would not have the strength or the desire to leave her.

"Let me help," Michelle murmured dreamily as she watched him fumble with foil. She took it from his unsteady hands and ripped it open with her teeth and fingers.

He chuckled. "You're an expert at this, huh, Mrs. LaCrosse?"

"I've had practice." She smiled as she held his turgid erection in her hand and somehow between them, they got the rubber on. She brushed his hand away and smoothed it down to the base. Instead of letting him go, she began to pump him in her palm, sending electrical shocks spinning through him.

"You're hot and hard as a rock, my husband," she said on a girlish giggle.

"And I'm going to rock you hard, my tight hot wife," he responded on a throaty laugh.

Damn, he didn't know sex could be this much fun, that he could speak uncouthly in the bedroom. Cassie had been extremely conservative, almost puritan, the very opposite of the current woman in his bed who'd turned him into a bad, bad boy who deserved a spanking, he thought with wild excitement as he came down over Michelle and spread her thighs wide apart.

He grunted when she eagerly wrapped her arms and legs around his shoulders, leaving her lower body open and vulnerable to him.

It was a sweet act of divine submission.

He loved it.

*He loved her.*

Erik held her eyes as he guided his shaft to her moist entrance. They both inhaled sharply at the contact, as if they were touching for the first time. He knew it would be like this every time they made love. His heart swelled with the knowledge.

He placed his hands on the pillow on either side of her head and drew closer, pressing his arms against her thighs. He wanted to take it slowly and savor every delicate thrill of her tight body encasing him. He wanted to hear every little sigh, every infinite sob, but the fervent heat in his manhood wouldn't let him. His mouth captured hers as he surged fluently into her, pushing ambitiously onward and upward until he felt the sensitive head of his cock lock tightly against her cervix. Another powerful thrust of ownership took him completely home. Finally, she had all of him.

It was a raw act of ultimate possession.

And he was making no apologies.

"Are you okay?" he asked, on a ragged breath.

"Yes," she whispered shakily, whimpering and trembling at the deep invasion. "I just have—hmm—have to get used to it—um—to you."

"Any pain?"

"No. No pain. Just a feeling of complete fullness."

"Good. Good. You're mine. Only mine," he groaned against her mouth.

He felt her insides tighten around him like smooth, wet velvet. She was so small, so hot and tight, he closed his eyes against the intense pleasure, his heart hammering as his breath caught in his throat.

He captured her face in his hands and his tongue swerved into her mouth as he began to move inside her. He rode her slowly, coming all the way out and then thrusting possessively back into her. Again and again he slammed into her, rotating his hips and flexing his buttocks, repeating the exquisite dance until their bodies were in glorious harmony with one another.

The sensual heat of ageless mating consumed them, body, mind, and soul, pushing them higher and higher until the precipice of delight was breached. Erik didn't want to leave her, ever. He wanted to remain like this, hard hot flesh sheathed securely inside silky hot flesh for all eternity. This was love, pure and explosive.

Time literally stopped moving as Erik and Michelle labored lethargically in the glory of their passion-filled lovemaking. Her world was filled with him. His was filled with her. Nothing else mattered. Nothing, but what they presently shared. Nothing, but what they gave to each other. Nothing, but what they received in return. This was what love was all about—giving and taking. And they each gave in turn, just as much, then more than they received.

Michelle gasped in a continuous flow of sweet agony as the powerful impact of Erik's masterful thrusts raced through the core of her body and spiraled through to her throbbing heart. She was acutely aware of every millimeter of his thick length, every muscle, every ripple, as he pumped in and out of her.

Her tender nipples pressed intimately into the damp hairs of his chest as electrical shocks scorched through her body. She stroked the strong tendons in the back of his neck and ran her fingers down the damp, slick muscles of his back and across his tight flexing buttocks, urging him on as he filled her with an amazing sense of heavy completeness.

Her moans were deep and guttural as she moved intimately and subtly beneath him. And as sweat poured from their bodies, she succumbed to the erotic pleasure he stirred in her soul.

"Erik... Erik... Don't stop. Don't ever stop..."

But all good things, Michelle knew too well, eventually came to an end. Her movements became wild and frenzied and she bucked with uncontainable ecstasy as the tremors of another climax began in the deepest parts of her being. The powerful vibrations spread to her toes and she curled them to capture the fiery sensation, not wanting to surrender to the explosions. It was too sweet. "Not yet.... Not yet..."

"Let it go, Michelle," Erik rasped against her mouth, his hot, racy breath mingling with hers, their lips and tongues intertwined like their limbs. He couldn't hold out any longer. He felt her tensing, tight as a bowstring as she pulled him along with her into the vortex of blissful splendor.

"Come with me. Let's ride the wave together, my sweet, beautiful Michelle."

"Yes... Oh, yes... Yes.... Ahhh... Ahhh... Hmmm...."

Her quivering body arched upward to meet his final, desperate thrusts. Her limbs locked about him, and she hung there, suspended as she felt the raging heat of passion rising in her like the hottest fire, washing over her, pulling her into an undertow so primitive and violent that it clouded her brain. She abandoned herself to the whirl of inebriating pleasures that rippled between her thighs and leaped through her system.

Erik shouted something in her ears, and as she quivered, teetering on the edge of the powerful eruption, she felt him tense within her, pouring his seed into the thin sheath of protection. Animal-like grunts rumbled from his throat as he collapsed on her, crushing her into the wet sheets, his huge body trembling with the shuddering release.

Michelle held him as her tender muscles milked him, relishing the pulsing tremors of his orgasm deep inside her body. His mouth was buried against her throat, and as she lay in the haven of his love, she began to sob.

Michelle wept, because Erik had told her that he loved her.

Her brain may have been numbed from the floodtide of passion, and he may have been engrossed in the throes of his earth-shattering orgasm, but the words had melted into her heart and soul, just as distinctly as his flesh had melted into her.

*"I love you, Michelle."*

Michelle thought it would be a long, long while before she heard those words from him. They rang in her ears, loud and clear. She dragged her legs from his shoulders and dropped them to the mattress.

He left her briefly and went into the bathroom. When he

returned, he spooned her against his hard warm body and spread the covers over them. He said not a word. With a deep, satisfying contentment, Michelle liberated her mind and soul to those four precious words and drifted off with Erik into blissful oblivion, their exhausted bodies so tightly intertwined, it was difficult to tell where one ended and the other began.

\*\*\*

"Daddy, are you and Michelle going to have a baby?"

Erik stopped dead in his tracks on the beach where he and Precious were taking an early morning jog. He tried to maintain his composure as he stared at her in dazed exasperation.

His chest heaved from the exertion of his run, and from his daughter's left-fielded question. He bent forward, resting his hands on his knees. "Where'd that come from?"

"I saw you kissing Michelle."

"When?"

"Last night in the living room."

Erik cursed inwardly, but he forced calm into his voice as he addressed his daughter's question. "Precious Rebecca LaCrosse, you were supposed to be in bed. Why were you sneaking around in the middle of the night spying on Michelle and me?"

"I wasn't spying, Daddy. I was thirsty and just wanted some water."

"What else did you see?"

"Nothing. I went back upstairs when I saw you. I'm sorry, Daddy."

Erik started an irritated walk toward the cottage, angry with himself for almost being caught in the act. He should have known better than to be carrying on like a horny teenager getting his first piece of tail on the living room sofa with a child in the house.

Hearing a sniffle behind him, Erik stopped and glanced over his shoulder. Precious was slowly following him, her head low, her shoulders drooped and tears running down her cheeks. His heart took a giant leap to his throat. It wasn't her fault that he was almost caught in the act. He was the adult here.

He knelt on the sand and held out his arms. She immediately ran to him, burying her wet face against his chest. He curled his fingers into her soft hair. "It's okay, baby. Daddy's not upset with you. You didn't do anything wrong." He held her until her sobs quieted then he took her small hand in his, gave her a wide grin, and continued on to the cottage.

A soft breeze off the ocean rustled through their hair as cool waves lapped playfully at their feet. The sky was a bright, deep blue with just a hint of wispy clouds scattered high and far away. Seagulls squawking overhead, flapping their wings noisily as they dove into the ocean to catch an early breakfast.

It was going to be a beautiful day. It had been a splendid night. He and Michelle had made sweet love until the wee hours of dawn before he sneaked back to the third bedroom to avoid Precious finding them in the same bed.

"So are you and Michelle going to have a baby, Daddy?"

"Precious, babies don't come from kissing."

"Yes, they do."

"Who told you that?"

"I asked Mommy where I came from and she said you were kissing, and I grew in her tummy, and then you took me out. Sam Martin at my school tries to kiss me, but I don't want a baby, Daddy. I wouldn't know what to do with it, and my tummy's way too small."

Erik stopped walking and closed his eyes, momentarily at a loss for words. It took all his effort to hide his humor. Precious was too young to understand the facts of life, but he could not have her believing babies came from kissing someone of the opposite sex. And he was definitely going to have a little chat with this Sam Martin. He spoke in as casual a tone as the delicate situation afforded. "Precious, babies don't come from kissing."

"Mommy lied to me?"

Caught in a pickled jam, Erik stooped down to her eye level. "No. She didn't," he said firmly, taking her hands in his. "It does start with kissing, though. When two people like each other, they enjoy touching, hugging, and kissing each other."

"You like Michelle?"

"Yes." *Love her.* His forehead wrinkled as a faint memory from last night flashed across his mind. *Did he say it?* "I enjoy kissing her and hugging her, but it takes a lot more than kissing to make a baby."

"Like what?" Her eyes were wide and questionable.

Erik stood up. Here he was, a gynecologist, and he was too embarrassed to discuss the facts of life with his daughter. *Damn.* He didn't ever want to explain sex to her. He wanted her to remain his sweet innocent baby, forever. "It's complicated. When you're older, I'll explain it." She needed a mother. He was more certain of that now than ever.

"How old?" she asked, skipping merrily along beside him.

"About fifty."

"Fifty? I'll be too old to have a baby then."

"That's the idea." He grinned down at her scowling face. "Okay. Maybe in a year or so."

"Okay. I'll remind you."

"I'm sure you will."

"Daddy?"

"What now?"

"If you and Michelle get married and have a baby, will she be my mommy, too?"

*She already is.* "I suppose so."

"I think she'd make a great mommy."

"You think so, huh?"

"Hmm." She threw back her head and smiled at him.

Erik squeezed her tiny fingers. "I smell banana pancakes and sausages all the way down here. You think those are Michelle's?"

She wrinkled her nose. "Yeah. We better hurry before she eats them all up. I'm really hungry," she said, rubbing her tummy.

"Me, too." He picked Precious up, and with one swift motion, tossed her over his shoulders. Her soft giggles blended harmoniously with his deep chuckles as he trotted in a happy gait back to the cottage and Michelle.

Erik couldn't remember ever being this happy. Life was smiling on him once more.

After breakfast, they took the ferry across Nantucket Sound to Nantucket Island and spent half the day touring the island and shopping exclusive stores.

Michelle couldn't believe how easily Erik dished out money on her and his child. Her protests were lost on him. Last night, she learned he was a man who always got what he wanted. He had ways to make her do things, try positions she didn't even know were possible.

When she'd asked how he became such a master at the art of love, he'd grinned and said, "The Kama Sutra, baby." Then he'd explained some of the Tantric and Taoist secrets of love to her. If every man on the planet would take the time to learn those secrets, all women would walk around with stupid grins on their faces all day, Michelle thought. She was blessed to be one of the grinning, lucky ones.

"Come in here for a minute." Erik edged Michelle into a small jewelry shop. "You have one more birthday gift coming."

"You just bought me three gorgeous dresses and a Prada purse, Erik. I think that's more than enough."

Ignoring her, he pulled her over to a middle-aged man behind a glass counter.

"Erik, you made it," the man said as he pulled a pair of thick spectacles from his face. He smiled at Precious. "She's getting more beautiful every time I see her. Wait until she starts dating. You'll be wearing a hole in your floor and tearing your hair out."

Erik chuckled. "So that's why you're bald, Joel?"

"Mock all you want, man. Your day will come."

"I know, and I'm not looking forward to it." He placed his hand in the small of Michelle's back. "This is Michelle. The birthday girl."

Michelle exchanged a smile with the kindly man who immediately reached behind the counter and handed Erik a small gift-wrapped box.

Erik handed the box to Precious.

Precious handed it to Michelle, a dazzling smile lighting up her perfect little face. "Happy birthday, Michelle."

"Come on, guys."

"You don't want my present?" Precious asked, pouting.

"Of course, honey." She glanced at Erik, knowing that he knew she would never say no to Precious. She reluctantly took the box.

"Open it," Precious chirped excitedly.

"Okay." She pulled off the wrapper and flipped the lid on the black velvet box. A pair of platinum, heart-shaped earrings, with two huge diamonds nestled in the base of the hearts, dazzled her. Michelle gasped. They must have cost a small fortune. "Erik, I can't accept these," she said adamantly, holding the box out to him. Wife or not, this was too much.

His eyes twinkled, mischievously. "You can't refuse a present from Precious."

"Please, Michelle. I picked them out myself on the computer," Precious said.

So that's what they were doing on the laptop while she was getting dressed after breakfast. She'd come downstairs just as they were putting it away. They looked like they'd been caught with their hands in the proverbial cookie jar.

"But these?" She eyed the jewelry skeptically.

"You don't like?" Joel asked.

Michelle glanced around to find that they were the main attention of the few other patrons in the small store. She was causing a scene. She gathered Precious to her. "Thank you. This is the best gift I've ever received. I'll wear them always, starting now." She pulled a pair of zirconias studs from her earlobes and dropped them in her purse.

"I'll help," Erik offered, moving closer to her. "You are a LaCrosse woman and you should be spoiled like one," he whispered for her ears only.

The warm touch of his hands made Michelle tremble. Even after making love with him all night, her body still craved to dance beneath his fingers. She couldn't wait for night to fall again.

They had a light seafood lunch then spend the other half of the day on the Children's Beach on Harbor View Way next to the Steamship Wharf. Precious met up with some of the kids from the beach yesterday and played softball and other games into the early afternoon.

They went back to the cottage to shower and dress for dinner at a local restaurant, not as posh as Andreas Ristorante, but elegant, nonetheless. Michelle wore one of the dresses Erik had bought her that day. Erik surprised her with a cake, and the staff and other patrons sang happy birthday to her. They were worn out and dragging by the time they returned to the cottage, and it didn't take long before an exhausted Precious fell soundly asleep.

Michelle was waiting in bed when Erik finally emerged from the bathroom with a towel hitched around his hips. Judging from the subtle tent in front of him, Michelle knew he was ready—ever ready—for her.

She pulled back the covers with a smile. Erik dropped the towel to the floor and climbed into bed next to her. He bent over and kissed her lips. Words were unnecessary between them. He kissed her deeply and thoroughly while his hands played with her breasts. The smooth length of his penis grazed her thighs, sending pleasure shocks through her. And just as she was about to melt with desire, he released her mouth and said, "Precious thinks we're having a baby."

Michelle's eyes flew open. "What? Why?"

"She saw us kissing last night."

"Oh, no." Michelle pounded her fist into the mattress. "Erik, suppose we'd made love on the sofa."

"It would have scarred her for sure. We have to be careful. I don't want her confused."

Michelle stiffened at his words. Well, she was the child's nanny, not her mother. It wasn't like she and Erik had made their marriage known to her, or anyone else. *This*, right here, was the reason he'd married her.

"I'm sorry. That came out wrong." He kissed the corners of her mouth.

Michelle shrugged. "I understand. It's okay."

"It's not okay." He rolled off of her and turned onto his back, staring up at the ceiling. "You're my wife. I shouldn't be worrying about our relationship confusing my daughter."

Michelle turned on her side, propped her elbow on the pillow and cradled her head in her hand. "Erik, you married me for this, and I went along with my mind, heart, and soul wide open. You're still confused about your feelings for me, so it's—"

"I'm not confused."

"Even so, I'm her nanny, still."

"She thinks you'd make a great mommy."

Michelle grinned. "She said that?"

"Her exact words." His eyes softened as he gazed into hers. "And I agree. It's just that—" He closed his eyes and sighed.

"What?"

"I learned something in D.C." He paused and took a deep slow breath. "You remember I told you Cassie and I were on our way home from a birthday party in Manchester the night she was killed?"

Michelle nodded, remembering too well the pain in his voice as he'd confided in her the first day on the job.

"Well, we were arguing about a conversation I overheard between her and Clayton—the birthday boy who used to be one of my best friends and colleague. He was telling her to tell me the truth because he couldn't lie to me anymore."

Michelle was not going to ask if they were having an affair. She didn't want to know. "You don't have to tell me, Erik."

"They weren't having an affair," he voiced her thoughts. "I accused them of it, though. I was badgering Cassie to either deny or admit the affair. I mean, what else was I to think?" He sighed again. "I should have known Cassie well enough to know she would never do something like that. But I was blinded by jealousy. After she died, I asked Clayton to tell me what the secret was, but he refused. Then he resigned from the hospital and went to Africa."

As it got real quiet in the room, Michelle watched him closely, wondering what else besides an affair his wife could have done.

He wiped his hands down his face. "Clayton was at the

convention in D.C. I was not leaving without answers. He finally told me that Cassie had a tubal ligation after Precious was born. He said he kept quiet after she died because he thought the truth would hurt me even more."

Michelle gasped in shock. No wonder he'd tossed his wedding band into the Potomac River. "You had no idea?"

He shook his head. "It was a laparoscopic procedure. Just a small puncture, so scarring was practically imperceptible. She had many freckles on her body, so..." He shrugged.

"Why would she do something like that?"

"A while ago, my mother told me that before we were married, Cassie saw a psychic who told her she'd die young."

"Oh my gosh, Erik."

"Apparently it was to happen in childbirth. Well, I'm assuming, from the course of her actions." He snickered sarcastically, and Michelle knew it was to cover his pain, his guilt. "I wanted to start a family immediately after we were married, but she wanted to wait. It took three years of begging before she agreed to have Precious." His chest heaved on another sigh. "She didn't trust me enough to confide in me, so she had her tubes tied. And for five more years, she laid in my bed and made love with me, listening to me go on and on about having more children, knowing she could not give them to me, and not saying a word." Anger and betrayal were evident in his voice and eyes.

"I can't imagine what it's like to have somebody you love lie to you like that," Michelle said in an attempt to comfort him. "My little fib about my father was eating me up inside. I'm so grateful you forgave me for lying to you."

Thinking about the irony of the matter, Erik shook his head. The thing is, if Cassie hadn't deceived him, there would've been no secret, no conversation between her and Clayton for him to overhear, no suspicions, no fight in the car, no hopping out into the road at the very moment that drunk came along. And there would have been no Michelle.

"I don't know if I would have forgiven Cassie if she'd told me the truth that night," he said, stroking his hand up and down Michelle's arm. "I don't know if I could have stayed with her, even if I'd forgiven her. Maybe our love would have survived it. *I don't know.* One thing I do know for certain is that I loved her and I did not want her dead." His voice shook with sorrow. "Precious should not have had to suffer the loss of her mother. She should not have to grow up without her. That's my biggest regret in all of this."

Michelle stretched out beside him and laid her head on his chest. His heart beat heavily beneath her ears. His pain became hers. He'd been deceived by the woman he'd shared his life with. It would be hard for him to trust another woman again— even a woman who brought him unimaginable pleasure.

So what if he didn't remember yelling out his love in the heat of passion last night? The knowledge was alive in her heart. And just a minute ago, if she dared be presumptuous, he'd spoken of his love for Cassie in the past tense.

Erik eased Michelle gently against the mattress, leaned over, and gazed intently into her beautiful, compelling eyes. Eyes through which he could see his future. Children. Grandchildren. The cautious side of him wanted to wait until he got to know her better before telling her how he felt. After all, he'd known her for only three months. He'd known Cassie since high school, and look how she'd deceived him. He still hadn't really *known* her. But his mother's words, when he told her what Cassie had done came back at him.

*"Erik, if it's one thing Cassie's sudden death should have taught you, it's that life is short. You must make every second count, dear. If you love Michelle, and I know you do, you should tell her, and start a future with her right away. What's the point in waiting when your heart knows what it wants?"*

His mother was practicing what she preached. She and his father were already engaged.

Erik smiled down at the lovely naked vixen in his bed. His heart knew what it knew. Michelle was the only woman for him. "Michelle," he said softly. "I remember yelling out that I love you last night while we were making love. The fact that I can't get enough of you should tell you how I feel. But to clear up any doubts in your beautiful mind," he continued, threading his fingers through the short silky strands of her hair, "I'm helplessly, hopelessly, head-over-heels in love with you. I think of you all the time when we're apart. When I'm with you, the world and all its pressures just melt away. Your smile gives me hope, courage, and strength. You make me feel like a man who can do anything.

"And this, right here—" He traced a finger down her throat, to her heaving chest, circled her breasts, then down her belly to the soft flesh of her Venus mound, "is the best this side of heaven. I do love you, with all my heart, soul, mind, and body, Michelle Juliet LaCrosse."

"Oh, Erik." Tears seeped from the corners of Michelle's eyes. He'd finally said exactly what she'd been longing to hear for three months. And she was too choked to respond to his poetic, romantic, heart-rending declaration of love.

Her heart beat heavily with requited love for him, but at the same time she feared what being in love meant. Especially since she hadn't been completely honest with him about her father. Yeah, she'd fessed up and told him that he wasn't dead, but she hadn't told him that he was a drunk, that he was no different from the man who'd killed Cassie. "Erik, I—"

Erik bent his head and kissed the tears from her eyes. "I know you love me. You've said it often enough."

Michelle cupped his chin and gazed into his soft grey eyes. Why spoil the mood with unpleasant talk of her father tonight? This was the moment for her to revel in the aftermath of Erik's declaration of love. There would be time to talk later.

"I know you want to tell everyone that we're married," he said, circling her mouth with his finger, "but I just want to keep you to myself a little while longer. The local press will have a field day with it. I don't want to share you, yet. Not even with my daughter. We'll make the announcements shortly after we get home."

"Okay, when we get home, we'll announce our marriage." *And I'll tell you the rest of the story about my father.* She had to since they were going public with their marriage. She just wished Robert would hurry up and find something on Dwight Carter.

Erik fell back against the pillow, pulling her on top of him. "No more talking. I need some loving. Can you handle that?"

"I can handle that." Michelle kissed him deeply and intimately, then feeling empowered by his love, she began kissing her way down his body. His fingers curled in her hair as she circled his nipples one by one with her tongue before tracing slowly down his chest to his belly. His stomach heaved on a groan when she dipped the tip of her tongue into his navel. His sex slapped against her thigh with anticipation, as she kissed the area around his groin.

Smiling seductively, Michelle kissed her way lower. She smelled his heat, his desire. It was poignant and it made her drool with the thought of taking him into her mouth. Just as her lips grazed the base of his turgid penis, he clasped the sides of her head and pulled her up.

Confusion swirled in her mind. Why wouldn't he let her go down on him?

Gazing at her intently, he positioned her knees so she flanked him at the sides like a stallion. His eyes blazed with passion as his shaft throbbed against the crease of her buttocks like an agitated snake. He took hold of her hips and raised her slightly upward.

"Erik. Why... Ahh..."

She curled her back as he began to penetrate her. God, he was so hot. She braced her hands against his chest, closed her eyes, threw her head back, and trembled with pleasure as he forced more of himself inside her.

He tightened his hold on her hips, pulling her down as he swerved upward, time and time again, forcing her to take him completely. And when she did, he held her by her buttocks, locked around him like hot, wet silk. He rocked slightly from side to side, hardly moving within her now.

Michelle loved this technique that he told her was a favorite of the Tantric and Taoists. This glorious feeling of naked pulsing flesh meshed in mating euphoria was an infallible way to engender love.

"You feel so good." He groaned.

Michelle's eyes flew open. She stared at the box of condoms on the nightstand. "Protection, Erik."

He pulled himself to a sitting position and wrapped her legs around his waist. "I'll pull out."

Michelle moaned as pleasure pulsed through her. "You won't be able to, and as much as I want to start a family with you, I want to wait until I'm finished with the center, and my book. Get one chapter of my life completed before starting another. Then I'll give you all the babies you can handle. Is that okay?"

Erik groaned again. "Fine. I get it. Just hurry."

Michelle reluctantly disengaged her body from his and reached for the box of condoms. She pulled one out, ripped it open and rolled the thin sheet of rubber over him. Task completed, she settled her hands on his shoulders and positioned herself over him again. He leaned forward and whispered something in her ear.

"Oh, you're so dirty, Dr. LaCrosse," she said on a shudder and a blush. "I didn't know the upper-class talked like that."

"Neither did I, until I met you." He laughed and guided himself back inside her. As she settled down on him, he sucked on her breasts, one at a time, making loud suckling sounds like a hungry infant. Michelle clenched her teeth and squeezed her eyes shut, trying to contain the quakes threatening to erupt inside her.

They remained in this position for an eternity, kissing, caressing, pleasuring each other with their hands and lips then Michelle decided it was time to grant the request he'd whispered in her ear. She pushed Erik back against the pillows then passing her hands behind his head she grabbed on to the iron headboard. Lifting her knees and placing her weight on her feet, she threw her head back, and began to ride her man, slowly at first, then harder and faster, moving up and down on his turgid shaft like a rodeo cowgirl on a bucking bronco.

"Yes, baby, yes... Work me..." Erik wrapped his hands around her waist, buried his head in the sweet valley between her bouncing breasts, and growled his sweet appreciation as his brain exploded.

Erik never knew love or passion of this kind existed.

# CHAPTER NINETEEN

Having seen his last patient and having made his last round of the day, Erik gathered some pamphlets from his desk and dropped them into his briefcase. A smile curled his lips as he shrugged out of his lab coat and hung it on a rack. He was anxious to get home. He'd booked a hotel room for the night where he planned to propose to Michelle—bended knees and all. Then tomorrow he was sharing their good news with his parents and Robert and Yasmine during a family dinner.

He could just imagine the awe on their faces when he announced that he and Michelle had been married for almost a month. Precious would be happiest of all, he thought, his smile breaking into a grin. She deserved to have a normal life. She needed to know that Michelle was there for her, not as a nanny who could someday leave her, but as a mother who loved her and would be there for her, always.

He and Precious had been to hell and back, and finally he could see the light at the end of their long dark tunnel of despair. Their lives were changing once again. This time for the better. And speaking of change, he'd contacted the Chief of Staff at Granite Falls Memorial Hospital about rejoining the staff there.

His heart was longing for home. He wanted his children to be born and raised in Granite Falls. He understood that Michelle had ties in Manchester—the youth center especially, but he hoped she loved him enough to follow him to the ends of the earth. He couldn't imagine moving without her, living without her in his life. But if she said no, he loved her enough to stay, with one slight change—they would have to buy a home right away. He wasn't spending any more time than he had to in a house in which he was psychologically incapable of making love with his wife.

When he'd called Michelle earlier to finalize their plans for tonight and tomorrow, she'd sounded a bit worried. She'd said that she wanted to talk with him about something important before they left for the hotel. He'd wondered if it were possible that she was pregnant. Even though they'd used condoms in Cape Cod, he knew those things were wont to break at times. He'd delivered many condom-breaking babies. That would be the happiest news she could give him.

Turning from the window, Erik walked back to his desk. He was reaching for his briefcase when the intercom on his desk buzzed. He stared at the blinking button, hoping it was not a patient. There was only one woman he wished to see tonight, and he didn't want anything keeping him from her. He pressed the answer button. "Yes."

"There's a detective here to see you, Dr. LaCrosse," the receptionist said.

"A detective?" His first thought was that something had happened to his daughter, his mother, or... "Did he say what it's about?"

"Erik, it's Garret," a masculine voice said. "It's old business."

*Garret.* A cold hand twisted inside Erik's gut. He really didn't want to deal with old news tonight. But he'd asked the detective to reopen the case, so it was only fair he heard him out. He would either tell him he'd found Cassie's killer or that he hadn't, and was closing the case permanently. He was moving on, either way.

He met the medium-built man at the door. "I didn't know you made house calls, Detective."

"Only for special friends on very special occasions." Garret threw him a wan smile as he stepped into the office.

Erik closed the door. On any other day, he would have loved to stay and chat with the man he'd come to know quite well two years ago, but not tonight. "So what's the news? Good or bad?"

"I'm afraid I have both."

That cold hand tightened around his gut again. "Good news would be that you found the bastard who killed my wife. Bad news would be that you're closing the case permanently because all leads have gone cold and since it can't be both—"

"Erik, I found him."

Erik took a deep ragged breath to combat the shaking in his bones. "What's bad about that? We've all been waiting for this day for a long time."

"It's the *who* that makes it bad."

Erik stared at the man, not understanding why he should care who the drunk was that had killed his wife. "Just give it to me."

"As you wish, but I think you should sit down," Garret warned.

"I don't want to sit."

"Okay then. A few days ago, some new prints showed up in the database. They were from a recent DUI in Trenton."

"New Jersey?"

Garret nodded.

"Did he kill someone else?" He couldn't imagine another family, a husband and child living through the same horror he had.

"Not this time," Garret answered. "He ran off the road and into the side of a cafeteria. Thank God it was after hours."

"And why wasn't I informed before now?"

"I didn't want to get your hopes up, unnecessarily. I wanted to talk to this man. Make sure he is our guy. Since he was still in the custody of the local police, I took a trip down to Trenton."

"And..." Erik spread his hands in impatience. He couldn't believe that after all this time, he could finally put this nightmare behind him. The timing was so perfect.

"That's the bad news."

Erik's heart beat hard and fast within his chest. "What's bad about that?"

Garret glanced away, his expression growing even more somber than when he walked into the office.

Erik felt the blood drain from his body. He didn't know what to expect. But somehow he knew he would not like whatever it was the detective would tell him next. "Garret."

"When I questioned him, he confessed everything. Erik, the man who killed your wife is—"

"Is what, Garret?" Erik took a step and towered over the detective. "Who killed my wife?"

"Dwight Carter. Your daughter's nanny's father."

Erik's heart dropped to his belly. He staggered backward against his desk. He took quick shallow breaths as bile rose in his throat. "No. It can't be. Not him," he mumbled, shaking his head in rejection. "It can't be him."

"I'm sorry, Erik. I wish I didn't have to give you this kind of news. He's already in custody. I could swing by your house and pick up the nanny tonight."

Erik raised his head. "Pick her up?"

"For questioning. She's an accomplice if she knew what her old man did and kept quiet all this time. I've contacted the Boston PD to take the son in for questioning, too. Come on, do you really think it's a big coincidence that she showed up at your house for a nanny position? I mean what are the odds? Nil to none, I'll tell you. It must have been guilt that sent her to you."

"Garret, I wish you'd never come here, today of all days. I wish you'd never told me who killed Cassie."

Garret tilted his head to one side. "I don't understand."

"I'm in love with her. I married her!" He pounded his fist on the desk.

"Oh boy, I didn't know."

The last thing Erik needed was the pity he heard in the detective's voice. He turned his back to him, trying desperately to hold back his rage. "Thanks for stopping by," he said as calmly as he could. "And please, leave his children alone. I know them, and I know they would never be mixed up in anything so horrible. If they'd know, they would have turned him in."

He couldn't even thank the man for cracking the two-year old case. This day that should have brought him joy beyond compare had brought him more turmoil than he'd had before.

"I'm sorry," Garret said again. "I'll keep you posted with the details."

When the door closed, Erik cleared his desk with one swipe of his hand.

"No! No! No!" Harsh sobs tore from his throat as he fell to his knees. Misery, far worse than the night Cassie died in his arms, tore away at his guts.

How could he have been so blind, so stupid, so trusting? How could he have entrusted his happiness and that of his child's—Cassie's child—to the very woman whose father had caused them so much grief?

Ice spread through Erik's stomach. Michelle had told him that her father was dead, then she told him she'd lied, and that she didn't know where he was. Was she slowly reeling him in, giving him a little bit here and there until she had him in her clutches? She knew it was a possibility her drunken father could have killed Cassie. That's why she never gave him the entire truth. When was she going to tell him? After the birth of their first child when it was too late to end their relationship?

His body trembled as nauseating despair buried itself in his chest. All the times she said she loved him, all the sweet words she'd poured like hot honey into his ears, now made him sick. He had believed her, trusted her with his love and his child.

That was the ultimate deception.

He closed his eyes as the harsh realities twisted inside him like a sharp knife. He'd given himself to her—heart, body, and soul. The passionate intimate memories that only minutes ago had brought him such joy, now tasted like bitter gall in his mouth. He'd loved her, enjoyed her much more than Cassie.

As night descended upon the town of Manchester, as the stars popped out, one by one, shining brilliantly across the dark canopy of open sky, Erik wept as the blackness that had cloaked his soul for two years returned, hardening his heart toward love and trust and forever. The swell of pain was so powerful, the anguish so acute, he could do nothing but surrender to the sorrow that shattered his soul, his hopes, his dreams.

\*\*\*

Where could Erik be? Michelle wondered for the millionth time as she paced back and forth in the family room. This morning he'd told her that he had something special planned for them tonight, and had even booked a room at a hotel in town. It had been three days since Cape Cod, three days since they made love. She'd been so filled with anxiety that she was barely able to get through the day. She'd dropped Precious off at Felicia's then hurried back home to pack and get ready for Erik.

It was during that time that her brother had called to let her know that he'd discovered something about their father—something that puzzled him. He'd promised to tell her all about it tomorrow night when he came for dinner.

After hanging up the phone, Michelle had decided that she wasn't going to wait. She was going to tell Erik everything about her father tonight, and had called to tell him that they needed to talk before leaving for the hotel. She could not let him publicize their marriage with that hanging over her head. She needed to be absolutely honest with him.

He should have been home five hours ago. It was almost midnight, now.

She'd called him several times but he never picked up. Filled with worry, she'd called Felicia a short while ago to see if she'd heard from him. She had, but he'd told her not to speak to Michelle.

At that point, Michelle knew for certain that something had gone dreadfully wrong. Erik would not ignore her for nothing, not after everything they'd shared. The only thing Michelle could think of was that he'd learned the truth about her father. That was the only secret she was hiding from him, the only bit of information that could destroy her.

She was scared, so scared of losing the best thing that ever happened to her. Erik was her life, the air she breathed. She loved him with everything in her that was sweet and good, and wholesome. Never in a million years did she imagine she would find a man who could love her so deeply and passionately. One who cherished and adored her. She was the happiest she'd ever been in her entire life. It was only natural to be scared of losing her husband and Precious, a child she loved as her own.

Sheer fright swept through her as a million possibilities flooded her mind. What if her father was back and found out she was working for Erik? What if he'd shown up at the hospital drunk, and demanded money from Erik to avoid the embarrassment of being associated with a drunk, or the family of one, when it was a drunk who'd killed his wife? He'd tried the same thing with Robert, years ago, by showing up and causing a scene in front of his friends and colleagues. Robert had threatened to kill him if he set foot at his practice, or at his home again. Erik was a different story. He was not accustomed to dealing with men like Dwight Carter. And she had brought this filth into his world, his life.

Michelle collapsed onto the sofa and wrapped her arms about her belly. She should have known it was too good to be true, too good to last. She'd forgotten who she was, where she'd come from in the space of four short months. She was a girl from the inner city, a nanny who'd secretly married the father of her charge, and who was stupid enough to fall in love with him.

The fact that he'd married her and told her he loved her brought her no solace. He was in love with a woman he didn't really know, a woman who'd lied to him. She'd seen the hurt and betrayal in his eyes, heard it in his voice that night in Cape Cod when he told her what Cassie had done. That's when she should have spoken up. God, she wanted to, but he was all talked out. He just wanted to make love. She should have been stronger. She should have insisted he hear her out.

As a feeling of utter defeat descended on her, Michelle got up and slowly walked up the stairs. When she got to her bedroom, she unzipped the dress she would have worn to dinner tonight and let it fall to the floor. She slipped on a nightshirt, crept into her bed and cried, for deep down in her gut, she knew it was over. She'd ruined Erik. There was no way he would trust another woman again. Not after Cassie.

And definitely not after her.

***

"Wake up, Michelle."

Michelle jumped awake at the rumbling voice. Her eyes popped wide open and her body went numb when she encountered the cold contempt in Erik's eyes.

He'd switched on the bedside lamp and was sitting on the side of her bed. Tension distorted his face. She'd never seen him like this, and it scared her that a man who she knew to be the gentlest creature on earth could be filled with so much rage.

"Erik—"

'Hush! Don't say a word!" He placed a finger against her lips. "You knew. You knew all along. You took me for a good ride, Mrs. Michelle Carter LaCrosse. Did you think I was so stupid I would never find out? Or did you think you were so good in bed that I wouldn't be able to resist you even when the truth came out?"

His hand crawled sedately down her chest and over the thin material of her nightshirt, but his eyes remained cold and deadly. He squeezed a breast, pinching the nipple until it hardened. With deliberate leisure, his hand trailed slowly down her body. He made a fist and pressed it into her stomach.

"Erik—"

"I said not to talk, Michelle. You had months to tell me everything. You are going to listen now. I am Cassie's husband," he said with deadly calm. "Precious is Cassie's daughter, and this is Cassie's house. You thought you could just waltz in here and claim it all?"

She read the sparks of ruthlessness in his eyes. This was definitely about more than her withholding information about her drunken father. "What did I do, Erik? Why are you looking at me with such disgust?"

THE DOCTOR'S SECRET BRIDE

"You knew where he was all this time, didn't you?"

"Who, Erik? Who?"

"Your father, Michelle. You knew where he was."

Michelle's mind whirled in a crazy mixture of confusion. "No. I don't know where my father is."

"Don't lie to me, Michelle! I've had it with deceitful women. I can't take anymore lies."

Trembling, Michelle tried to push his hand off her stomach and ease away from him. She was too vulnerable lying on her back in the middle of a bed with an angry man bending over her. She couldn't fight in that position.

Reading the intentions in her eyes, Erik grabbed her shoulders and pushed her back into the mattress. He fought the need in his body, the pain in his heart, the burning in his soul. He'd just spent the last two hours sitting on his wife's grave, begging her to forgive him for bringing the daughter of the man who'd killed her into her home, into their child's life, and most treacherously for loving her and for marrying her.

As he gazed at that woman now, all he wanted to do was make love to her. He wanted to bury his sorrow inside her, because as much as he despised her lies, his love for her was a thousand times stronger.

"You told me your father was dead," he said. "Then you told me you lied about that. You didn't give me the full story, Michelle. You withheld vital information."

The words stabbed at Michelle's heart. So he'd found out? How? And why did it make him this bitter? "No," Michelle blurted out. "I didn't give you the whole story because I was ashamed of him. He's a drunk. He's always been a drunk. And when I found out that it was a drunk who killed Cas—"

"Do not speak my wife's name, Michelle. You've lost that privilege."

"I'm your wife, Erik."

He uttered a contemptuous laugh. "Do not remind me of that. Is there anything else you'd like to tell me, Michelle?"

"No." Tears pooled in her eyes. She'd hurt him. She swallowed the bile that rose to the back of her throat. "I'm sorry." She placed a hand on his arm. "I was going to tell you the whole story tonight. I swear, Erik. I was going to tell you that my father is a drunk. That's what I wanted to talk about before we left for the hotel."

Erik wanted to believe her. He really did. Maybe Detective Garret had made a mistake. Maybe there was another drunk named Dwight Carter who just happened to have two children with the same names. It was a small world. Anything was possible. Damn, look at the situation he'd found himself in. Like Garret had said, it was a one in a million chances.

He glanced down at Michelle's slender hand on his arm and the heat they generated sent a surge of lust through him. His gaze shifted to her face, drenched with tears. He stared at her trembling lip. Lips that were sweeter than honey. Lips that aroused him at just the mere thought of them. He splayed his hand down her body, sliding it over the cotton material of her nightshirt.

He skimmed over the mound at the apex of her thighs where he'd come to know Nirvana again and again. He dragged his hand down her smooth thighs, then with unsteady fingers he caught the hem of her shirt and dragged it up along her body. He jerked it over her head in one fluid motion then discarded her sexy little red panties just as easily.

His eyes flinched as he gazed at her loveliness. How in God's name was he going to survive without her? He loved her. He needed her. Her pull on him was stronger than his loyalty to Cassie, stronger than the fight in his body.

# CHAPTER TWENTY

Michelle saw the raw need in Erik's eyes, felt it in his touch. He was hurting and he wanted her to make it stop. She'd had hungry sex, grief sex, regret sex, and worship sex with him. It was time for them to have angry sex.

Desire licked through her body as she watched Erik rise from the bed and unzipped his trousers, pushing them along with his boxers down to his knees. Her eyes immediately settled on his thick shaft, rising menacingly from the dark curls at his groin.

Her heart began to pound against her chest and the familiar moistness settled between her thighs. She'd been subjected time and time again to his strength, his power, and the unrelenting passion with which he loved. And she should be afraid. But she wasn't. She wanted him. She wanted him with every little neuron in her body. She was his wife and wives were supposed to ease their husbands' pain. She would ease his pain. She would make right whatever wrong he thought she had done him.

"Erik what did I do to cause you such pain, to make you so angry?" she asked.

He grabbed her by the ankles and pulled her toward him, positioning her buttocks on the edge of the mattress and throwing her legs over his shoulders. "You knew it was possible and yet you said nothing."

"What are you talking about?" Frustration inched through her.

He leaned into her, swung his hips and pierced through her, pushing his way completely to the hilt. Michelle cried out as her slick flesh parted to receive him. She clutched at his shirt, her fingers digging into the flexed muscles of his arms as he filled her.

Dropping his body on hers, Erik pinning her to the mattress and began to move with earnest strokes inside her. He curled his fingers through her hair and held her soft mouth prisoner with his own as he pumped deeply into her. Their grunts of lust filled the air. Their tears melded into a river of hopelessness.

Fire coursed through his veins at the velvety moistness of her clutching at him like a bloodthirsty parasite, sucking the very life out of him, pulling him toward the end of the universe. She wasn't supposed to feel this good. She wasn't supposed to be this delicious, this irresistible. His body had betrayed him, just as she had.

"How could you do this to me, to us?" His voice rang with pleasure and torture as he licked at her salty tears.

"Do what?" Michelle wrapped her arms around his neck, and sank her teeth into his shoulders as she was consumed with the conflicting agony of intense emotional pain and physical primal desire.

"Your father killed Cassie." He began to ride her harder.

Doom descended on Michelle. Her body tightened around him. He must be mistaken. Her father was a drunk, not a murderer. "Erik, it can't be true. He left Manchester before—"

"He came back. And he ran her down with his car that night." Rising upward, Erik thrust wildly into her.

The pleasure was so intensely passionate, they both became lost in the rhythm that melded their bodies together, even as their world fell apart around them.

With his groin locked securely to Michelle's, Erik's back arched upward, and when she saw his eyes close and his mouth convulse, Michelle knew he was near the edge. He wrapped his arms around her, and holding her tightly against his heart, he groaned then dropped his head into the softness of her throat. She felt the terrible trembling in his body as he growled then poured his ache, and his seed inside her. She cried out his name and exploded with him, their juices fusing in a cauldron of love and hurt.

The sound of Erik's sobs tore Michelle's heart to shreds. As her mind reeled with questions about the accusation he'd made about her father, she broke down and wept, for her pain for Erik was greater than any she'd ever felt from her father's hands.

After a long while, Erik got up and pulled his clothes back on. He stood at the side of the bed and gazed down at his wife, the woman he loved.

Yes, he loved her.

But the image of Cassie dying in his arms yanked him back to the fierce reality. Michelle had lied to him. She had deceived him.

Michelle sat up in the bed and pulled the sheet around her shattered body. What they had just shared was nothing short of a desperate need for survival. They were both drowning and they knew it.

"I know you would have come forward if you'd know it was your father who'd killed Cassie," Erik began in an unstable voice. "What I want to know, Michelle, is whether or not you suspected it could have been him. Is that why you didn't want me questioning the drunks in the back alleyways of Manchester? That day at the hospital when I told you I was reopening the case and that I would be combing the streets looking for him, you seemed scared. Were you scared that it might be him?"

Michelle hung her head. She couldn't bear the iciness in Erik's eyes. Gone was the lust, the desires that had just obsessed them. "Yes, it crossed my mind the first time you told me about the accident. But after I did some checking, I realized it couldn't be him because he'd already left town when it happened. I didn't know he'd come back. I'd already moved to South Carolina by then, Erik. I was gone for a year and a half. I didn't even know about Cass... what had happened until you told me about it."

Erik wiped his hands down his face. The smell of her

lingered on his fingers. "Why couldn't you have been totally honest with me? Why couldn't you have just trusted me?"

Michelle pulled the sheet tighter around her body. "I was afraid of losing you. Afraid you could never love the daughter of a drunk seeing it was one who killed Cass... your wife." She saw no need to tell him that the man who'd raised her, the man who'd killed his wife, may not even be her father after all. It didn't matter. She'd lied. "Who told you it was... my father? How do you know it's even true?"

He walked over to the window and turned his back to her. His voice was heavy with sadness as he told her what Detective Garret had told him.

Fresh tears sprang to Michelle's eyes. Dwight Carter had taken the life of another human being—Erik's wife, Precious' mother. He had hurt the two people who meant most to her in this world. Then he ran because he was a coward. He'd always been a coward. That was his yoke to bear. Hers was that she should have been truthful with Erik from the beginning.

She pulled her nightshirt back on and walked over to where Erik stood staring out into the night that was as black and brooding as the shadows hanging across their hearts.

She hugged her stomach and rubbed her hands slowly up and down her arms. "You know what my father did to me and Robert as kids, Erik. You know he stole my money and wrecked my life. But what he did to your family trumps it all. He robbed Precious of her mother, and you of the woman you loved. For that I hate him even more, and I'm sorry for not being totally honest with you."

Michelle gazed up at him. His lips were drawn into a thin line and his jaws were tight and hard. She wished he would say something. Anything. She swallowed. "I love you, Erik. I didn't lie about that. You have to believe me." She touched his arm. "How are we going to deal with this mess? How can we fix it?"

Her voice was a distant murmur. His misery a steel weight around his neck, hauling him into a sea of sheer despair. That bastard had hurt her, too. He so longed to make up for all the pain in her life, erase all her bad memories and give her the world. But the facts remained—her father killed Cassie, and Michelle had lied to him.

Erik pushed his hands into the pockets of his slacks. His fingers slid across the surface of the velvet box containing the ring he was going to give her tonight. Panic tugged at his heart, and anguish spread through his stomach as he gazed at her. She was an angel. His angel.

He remembered the day she stormed into his house, into his study, into his life, and into his heart. Instinct had warned him to send her marching back down his driveway. He had known she would change his life forever, but he never expected it would be like this. He hadn't wanted to be hurt again, to love again. But he did love. And he did get hurt.

And this was worse. This was so much worse than when he had stood in the cemetery, twenty-six months ago, and watched them lay Cassie's body into the ground. This was worse than watching his little daughter weep for the mother she could never have again.

He remembered Precious' tearful words as they left the cemetery to go back to their perfect house, on the perfect street, in the perfect neighborhood that wasn't so perfect anymore, because Cassie Rebecca LaCrosse wasn't there.

*"Daddy," Precious had cried as he wrapped her in his arms. "I miss Mommy so much. Why couldn't you make her better, Daddy? You always make people better when they're sick. I want my mommy, Daddy. I want her back."*

Erik remembered the pain in her wide brown eyes. He remembered the torture in her voice, and how she tried to be so brave throughout the memorial service because she knew her mother hated tears.

He remembered a whole lot of things, and he squeezed his eyes shut as tears of bitter regret seeped through his lids. This was the worst, because the woman he loved now had betrayed him. And by loving her, he had betrayed the memory of the woman he used to love. He was trapped in a cocoon of defeat with no way out.

There was no dealing with it. There was no fixing it. He could not build a life with Michelle knowing her father had killed Cassie.

"We can't fix this, Michelle," he said in a hollow voice. "It's too big. We can't go back, and we can't go forward. You deceived me. I can't ever trust you again. I can't be around you."

"Erik, we're husband and wife. We took vows for better and for worse. We love each other. You can't just toss us aside as if we never happened."

He turned and gazed down at her, the hurt in her eyes tearing at his heart. "I don't know who I married, Michelle, or with whom I fell in love. All I know is that you're not the woman I thought you were. It's a good thing no one else knows we're married, especially Precious. At least she'll be spared the pain of losing another mother." With that, he turned and walked out of the room.

The finality in his words was so debilitating that all Michelle could do was waddle back to the bed and lie down on it. She curled up into the fetal position as deep moans came from the darkest, deepest parts of her soul.

Dwight Carter had completely destroyed her life this time. There was no climbing out of this pit. There was no escaping the anguish that would plague her for the rest of her life. Her father had finally killed her last glimmer of hope, her one and only chance of happiness.

She dragged her body off the bed, across the floor, and into the bathroom. Her heart was as heavy as lead as she stood under the shower sprays and somehow managed to wash Erik's scent from her body.

It was almost dawn when she finally descended the stairs and roused a disgruntled Yasmine from sleep. Her dear friend asked no questions. She just held her while she cried, then helped her into the car. Michelle sat silently on the ride to Manchester, huddled against the door, feeling cold, shaken, and so alone.

\*\*\*

Three days later, Michelle finally mustered up enough courage, and borrowed Yasmine's car to go back to Erik's house for the rest of her clothes. For three days, she had been calling, and each time he picked up, he'd just remain silent, listening to her begging, pleading, and apologizing. At least he hadn't hung up on her, nor had he blocked her calls from his cell or the house. That alone told her that he still cared about her in some way. It gave her hope.

Dwight Carter was in jail waiting to face charges on first-degree manslaughter, fleeing the scene of a crime, theft, and for driving while under the influence. And she was left, once again, to salvage the life he'd ripped apart. Robert had stopped by yesterday to talk about what he'd discovered about Dwight, but she was in no mood to discuss him. The damage was done. Whether or not, Dwight was their biological father was not important at the moment. What mattered was that Dwight had killed Erik's wife, and she'd lied to Erik about him.

Her lies, not Dwight, had torn them apart.

Michelle felt a powerful throbbing in her head as she got out of the car and looked up at the house. Memories of the first day she set foot on this property assailed her.

She recalled, vividly, the first time she saw Erik, sitting behind his desk in the library, all virile, potent, and dangerously male. She remembered the sharp brilliance of his piercing eyes, and how her heart had lurched as her female hormones had soared to an all-time high. It was definitely love at first sight.

As she walked up the stairs to the porch and rang the doorbell, Michelle tried to control the shivers that ran through her. This was probably the last time she would set foot in this house. She hoped Precious was home from school. She longed to see her. She wondered how Erik had explained her absence, and the fact that she wouldn't be her nanny anymore.

Erik might not want her in his life, but at least she had Precious, and in spite of what might happen between her and Erik, Precious would always be a part of her life. She would not turn her back on her.

"Michelle, sweet child." Mrs. Hayes opened wide arms and Michelle fell into the motherly embrace.

"Hi, Mrs. Hayes. How are you?"

'Don't worry about me, honey. I want to know how you're holding up under this mountain of trouble. I pray day and night to the Good Lord to lay His mercies on you."

"Thanks. I need all the prayers I can get." She glanced warily around. "I came to get the rest of my stuff. Is Erik here? I didn't see his car in the driveway." She was actually surprised he hadn't packed them up and mailed them to her.

"He went to get Precious from her music lessons."

"How is Precious?" she asked, her heart aching with longing for the child.

"She misses you. She cries for you every day. I don't understand why the doctor is punishing you for what your father did. You had no part in it."

"He knows that," Michelle defended her secret husband. "He's just hurting. I should have told him that my father was a drunk and a possible suspect. I can't blame him for feeling betrayed. You, Robert, and Yasmine warned me that my lie would backfire. I have no one to blame but myself."

"Give him time," Mrs. Hayes said, touching a cool frail hand to Michelle's cheek. "I'm sure he'll come around and realize how important you are to him and Precious."

Michelle stared at the older woman who'd brought her into Erik's life, and wondered just how much she knew about Erik's and her relationship. She was certain she didn't know they were married, but did she know they'd been intimate? "Maybe he will," she said, "and if he doesn't, I'll have to live with it." Needing to escape the wise woman's scrutiny, she headed up the stairs.

Michelle packed hastily, trying not to think about the life she was leaving behind. As she opened the walk-in closet and gazed at the dress she had worn to the party in Boston, sweet memories of her one-night honeymoon echoed in the black stillness of her mind. Memories were all she had now. Nothing would ever erase those feelings of completeness, of oneness with Erik.

For once in her life, she had been truly happy. She would cherish those moments forever.

Leaving the dress where it was, she turned and gazed at the bed where they'd made love. Erik might try to make himself believe that he hated her, she thought, but deep, way down deep in her soul, she knew he cared for her. The way he had cradled her in his arms after the passionate storm was over was all the evidence she needed. She would cling to that thought.

Michelle was halfway to the door to load the suitcase into the car when she heard Erik's car come to a stop in the driveway. Her stomach clenched and her body broke out in a cold sweat.

The key rattled in the lock. The suitcase fell to the floor with a loud thud. The door opened, and his muscular, irresistible frame came walking through it.

Michelle froze as her eyes caught and held the piercing ones of her husband.

# CHAPTER TWENTY-ONE

Before Michelle could react to Erik, Precious pushed past him and raced into the house.

"Michelle!" She flung herself into Michelle's arms. "You're back. You came back!" Precious wrapped her arms about Michelle's neck, and showered her with kisses, hanging on like she never wanted to let go.

"Oh, Precious." Michelle squeezed the bundle of joy to her chest. She buried her face into the soft mass of brown curls and sobbed silently. "I missed you so much, so much."

Precious unraveled her arms from around Michelle's neck and looked into her face. "Why are you crying, Michelle? Aren't you happy to be back?"

"I'm not staying, sweetheart. I just came to get my things. I don't live here anymore."

"Did I do something wrong? I promise I'll be good. I promise."

"You didn't do anything wrong, Precious. You're the best little girl in the whole wide world."

"Did Daddy do something wrong?" She looked at her father. "Tell Michelle you're sorry Daddy. Tell her you're sorry and she'll stay."

Michelle glanced at Erik, still standing at the opened door, a watchful fixity on his face. "You're daddy didn't do anything wrong, Precious. In fact, he did everything right. He's a good man, and you're lucky to have him for a daddy."

"Then why don't you want to live with us anymore?"

"I do, honey, I do. It's just that..." She didn't know what to say. It felt like someone was holding her heart in a padlocked grip and was choking the life out of her. She fought the raw need to collapse right there on the floor. She felt so weak—physically, emotionally, and psychologically.

"Please stay, Michelle. I love you. Please live with us." Tears spilled down Precious' face.

Michelle choked at the pain in the child's heart and the sadness in her eyes as she placed her on the floor. She looked at Erik again, her unspoken requests rushing across the distance between them.

"Go on up to your room, Precious," he said.

"Please, Daddy. Don't let Michelle leave." Precious wrapped her arms around Michelle's waist and began to cry.

"Erik, please," Michelle begged in a broken whisper. "Can't you see she needs me?"

Erik swung away from the door and covered the distance in four long stealthy strides. He forced Precious' hands from around Michelle's waist. "She needs her mother. But her mother is dead, Michelle. Dead. And your—"

"Not in front of her, Erik," Michelle whispered. "Don't involve her in this." She knew that eventually Precious would be told the truth about the man who'd killed her mother, but now wasn't the time. Michelle was grateful that Erik had decided to keep the news of Dwight's capture private for the moment. And she knew that once it was made public, she might have to go into hiding. The media would be all over her. Erik's prudence, once again, demonstrated that he still cared about her.

Erik inhaled deeply then exhaled slowly. "You're right. Mrs. Hayes," he bellowed.

Mrs. Hayes immediately came rushing into the foyer with a wooden spoon in her hand. "Yes, Doctor."

"Would you kindly take my daughter to her room?"

"No, Daddy, no!" Precious threw herself on the floor and clung to Michelle's legs. It took all Mrs. Hayes' energies to pry her loose and escort her away.

"I'll come back to see you, Precious. That's a promise, sweetheart," Michelle called in a tear-choked voice.

Erik waited until Precious and Mrs. Hayes were out of eyesight and earshot. "You have to stay away from her. I don't want you calling or coming by here anymore."

"I wouldn't abandon her, Erik. I love her. I love her like my own child."

Her sadness ate away at his guts, but he had no choice. He was torn. He didn't know what else to do. "She's not your child, Michelle. She's Cassie's child."

"Erik, I'm sorry. I'm sorry for the pain my father caused you and Precious. But please don't punish me for what he did. Don't punish Precious. Please." She wiped at the tears blinding her.

He opened his jacket, pulled out an envelope, and handed it to her.

"What's this?"

"Annulment papers."

"Already? Erik, I love you."

"And I love you, Michelle. God knows I do. But love isn't enough this time."

"You once told me that when you truly loved someone, you could forgive them anything."

"Yes, I did. But a marriage also needs trust to survive. Cassie's failure to trust me is what really killed her. That day when you told me your father was still alive, I asked you if there was anything else you wanted to share about him. You lied. You didn't trust me enough to tell me the whole truth. Your not trusting me destroyed our love. Maybe in time, I'll get over your deception. But for now…" Erik's heart ached at the agony in her eyes. He took a deep breath and turned away from her. "You have to forget about us, what we shared."

Dear God, he didn't want to hurt her. But what her father had done was too appalling for him to forgive. And the fact that another woman he loved didn't trust his love, didn't believe in it enough to be truthful, was too much. All the raw wounds she had helped to heal had been ripped wide open and were bleeding profusely again. He had to forget her. He had to wash her completely out of his mind. And the only way he knew how to do it was to stop seeing her. Period. He couldn't be with a woman who didn't trust his love for her.

"Just sign the papers and mail them to the address on the envelope."

Michelle watched, broken and defeated, as Erik walked out of her life.

***

Michelle glanced at her ringing cell phone lying on the sofa table. Her heart jumped from fear, hope, and uncertainty when Erik's name flashed on the screen. It had been two days since she last saw him and Precious. Had he decided to forgive her? Did he want her back? Or…

"Are you going to answer that?" Yasmine asked, coming from the direction of her bedroom.

"It's Erik."

"Then answer it, girl. He might be calling to say he wants you back."

*Or maybe he wants to make sure I signed and returned the annulment papers.* Yasmine still didn't know they'd been married.

"You want me to talk to him? Cause I'm dying to give him a piece of my mind."

Michelle grabbed the phone. "No. I'll handle it." She walked into her bedroom and closed the door. She took a deep breath, pushed the answer button, and raised the phone to her ear. "Hello," she said in a shaky voice.

There was a long tense silence.

"Erik," she said.

She heard his sharp intake of air. "Hi, Michelle."

Michelle bit into her lower lip to stop the sharp cry of longing from bursting from inside her. Too weak to remain on her feet, she collapsed on the edge of her bed.

"I just called to warn you," he said.

"Warm me about what?"

"The news about your father has been leaked to the press."

"Oh, no. What—"

"I'm taking Precious out of the country for a few weeks until the commotion dies down."

"Where—"

"I suggest you... go somewhere... far... if you don't want to be eaten by the media vultures. They will be circling soon. They may be on their way as we speak. Use the money I deposited into your account when we got married."

"Erik—"

"Goodbye, Michelle."

Long after the phone went dead, Michelle kept it pressed against her ears while her other hand crushed into her chest in an attempt to quiet her thumping heart. Did Erik call to warn her about the impending mayhem because he was really concerned about her, or did he fear what she might divulge to the media vultures about their relationship? It would make him seem like a real jackass for marrying the daughter of the man who'd killed his first wife. She couldn't blame him for being cautious, concerned. But did he have to be so cold, so abrupt? They had been closer than any two human beings had the right to be, and yet he'd just spoken to her as if she were a mere acquaintance he felt obligated to warn about imminent doom.

*Time.* He needed time.

"So what did he want?" Yasmine asked from the opposite side of the closed door.

Michelle pulled herself together and went to open it. "I have to leave town."

Yasmine shook her head in confusion. "What? Why?"

"Somebody leaked the news of my father's arrest for killing Cassie to the press. Erik called to warn me. He and Precious are leaving the country, and he suggested I go into hiding." She glanced at her suitcase on the floor in a corner of the unkempt bedroom. "Good thing I didn't unpack yet."

"Where will you go?"

"I don't know. But I can't stay here. I have to leave Manchester. New Hampshire. Tonight."

"I don't think you should be alone in your present state of mind."

"I'm not going to hurt myself, Yas."

"I know. I'm just saying. I'd go with you if I could."

"Where am I supposed to go?"

"Why don't you call Ryan?" Yasmine suggested. "You guys are still friends, right?"

"Well, we haven't spoken in months. For all I know, he may have a girlfriend, be engaged or married, and want nothing to do with me. I mean I did reject him."

"Be realistic, Mich. Nobody gets married in that short a time."

*I did. And I'm about to be divorced.*

\*\*\*

As soon as he ended his call to Michelle, Erik fell to the floor on his knees and dropped his head on the bed where they'd last made love. While hot tears streamed down his face, he splayed his hands across the mattress and fisted the sheet into his palms, clenching his teeth to stop the screams that threatened to erupt from his throat.

The room still smelled of her. He saw her enchanting smile everywhere, in everything, and in everyone. He heard her husky voice calling out his name in the heat of passion, and her sexy laugh at his stupid jokes. Each time he closed his eyes, he felt the heat of her slender softness wrapping around him.

A week hadn't even gone by since the night she left, yet it felt like an eternity to him. How was he going to survive the rest of his life without her in it? Yes, he'd been angry that last night. Who wouldn't have been after receiving such horrible, and unimaginable news? He'd said some things he didn't mean, because his heart had been hurting, but he hadn't expected her to leave. When he'd come down the next morning to find her

ANA E ROSS

gone, it were as if someone had hacked open his chest and ripped out his heart. He'd been all set to apologize to her, tell her that they'd find a way to make it work, but she was gone.

He hadn't responded to her phone calls in the ensuing days, because he didn't know what to say to her, and the fact that she'd left had only sent him deeper into his tunnel of despair and distrust, so much so that he'd begun proceedings to have their marriage annulled. Hope had been renewed when he'd come home three days ago to find Yasmine's car in the driveway. But that hope had withered when he walked into the house to find Michelle standing there with her suitcase in her hand, even while she begged him to take her back.

Once again, she'd demonstrated that she didn't trust his love enough to stay and fight for them. She fought for everything and everyone else in her life. Why hadn't she fought for him, for them?

She'd quit on him, and on Precious, even after she'd promised never to leave them. How could he ever trust her to stick around when things got bad?

As much as he loved Michelle, he had to protect his heart, and his daughter from the possibility of future pain and abandonment.

\*\*\*

"I know I didn't give birth to an idiot," Felicia said, staring at her son across the coffee table.

"Darling, give the boy a break." Philippe squeezed her hand that lay on his thigh. "He's been through a rough patch. It's a terrible thing that happened between him and Michelle."

"I know he's been through hell and back, Philippe. But it's been two months since the media has left him alone and gone in search of fresher news. He should have been back with Michelle by now, but he continues to punish her, and my... our grandchild."

Erik looked from his mother to his father. They had summoned him to Granite Falls for an intervention, as they called it, but he'd been in no mood to discuss his relationship with Michelle. He had spoken to no one about her. He couldn't. It was just too damn painful.

"Erik," his mother said, turning her eyes on him, "Precious needs Michelle, and so do you. Why don't you go out and find her, bring her back to us?"

Erik pushed himself out of the recliner, shoved his hands into the pockets of his slacks and walked to a floor-to-ceiling window. He stood gazing out at Mount Washington, a massive, impenetrable symbol of the agony in his heart.

Of course he knew Precious needed Michelle. *He needed her, too.* But when he'd returned from Europe to learn that she'd gone running back to her ex, it had crushed him. He'd advised her to leave town, to go someplace far away to escape the frenzy of the press until the news about her father died down. He never for the life of him ever thought she would run right into Ryan's arms, and be so insensitive as to mail the annulment papers and a check for the money he'd given her from Ryan's address in South Carolina.

Even after she'd walked out on him, he'd been ready to forgive her, to ask her back into his life, and beg her to forgive his stupidity for hurting her. There were a lot of things he could forgive, but knowing she'd returned to her ex-lover wasn't one of them. The thought of her in another man's arms, in another man's bed, was nauseating.

Michelle had made her choice. She had moved on. It was time he accepted it and did the same.

"I'm inviting her to our wedding," his mother said behind him. "You'll have to talk to her then, Erik."

He turned and captured her gaze. "You do that, Mother, and I won't be there." He marched out of the room.

\*\*\*

The first few weeks of her two-month refuge in South Carolina had been the worst. Michelle hadn't been able to eat, sleep, or think, and when she'd finally let something down her throat, it had come back up within minutes. Her malady continued for about five weeks until she was so weak, had lost so much weight, and could hardly stand up that Ryan insisted she see a doctor, and had taken her to one himself.

As Michelle browsed a children's store in the Mall of New Hampshire, with Jessica, her self-appointed personal watchdog, trailing idly behind her, she reflected on that informative doctor's visit.

*"How long have you had these symptoms?"* Dr. Nixon asked.

*"About a month now."*

*"When was the last time you had your period, Michelle?"*

Her eyes narrowed. *"I—I don't remember."*

*"Is it possible that you could be pregnant?"*

*"Pregnant?"* she exclaimed in a stilted voice.

*"Well, all the signs are present—nausea, vomiting, appetite and weight loss, fatigue, and most significant of all, no period."*

Michelle uttered a strangled laugh. *"There has to be another explanation, Dr. Nixon. Erik... We used protection."*

*"Every single time, Michelle? Are you certain of that?"*

*"Well, except for that one time, but that—"*

*"It only takes one time, my dear. One daring energetic sperm and one ecstatic fertile egg and boom, you have a baby."*

Michelle had been speechless. Could she be pregnant with Erik's child? That last night when he had taken her in Cassie's house, could he have planted his seed inside her? Could his baby now be growing in her womb?

Trembling fingers had come slowly to caress her flat stomach as the shock of realization hit her full in the face. It was possible. The timing was right. She was going to have Erik's child. She would forever have a part of him with her. A part far more blessed than any memory.

And yet, four months later, she still hadn't told Erik that he was going to be a father again. She was certain that if he knew, he'd come back to her, but she didn't want him back out of obligation. He would have to come to her because he loved her, not merely because she was having his child.

In addition to her baby, she had a lot to live for. The

children at the center depended on her. Since her return to Manchester, they'd helped her heal one painful day at a time. They were no substitutes for the special love she had for Precious, but their daily devotion filled her days with contentment.

Her nights were a different story. Since the one hundred and twenty-three nights since she'd learned that the man who'd raised her killed Cassie LaCrosse, Michelle had cried herself to sleep.

She'd held on to the annulment papers for weeks, hoping that Erik would change his mind and realized they belonged together, but when she hadn't heard from him, she finally signed and mailed them from South Carolina. She'd also mailed him a check for the money he'd deposited into her account. Yasmine said she was foolish to send it back, and that she should keep it for his child who would definitely need it. Erik hadn't cashed the check, anyway. And she knew he never would. He was quick to take back his love, but not his money.

There was no denying it—that short sweet chapter of her life was over. There was no going back. She'd learned through Mrs. Hayes that Bridget Ashley was spending a lot of time at the house. Seemed they were becoming a couple. He was getting on with his life, with a woman who was his equal, both intellectually and socially.

His final words to her were forever etched in her heart: *You have to forget what we shared, Michelle.* And that is exactly what she was trying to do. Forget and move on.

A secretive smile softened her lips as she thought of the tiny life making roots inside her. She wondered about the gender of her baby, and whether it would have Erik's grey eyes and curly dark brown hair, or her black eyes and straight raven tresses. Would *he* be tall and muscular like his father, or would *she* be slender like her mother?

"Ain't that that little girl you used to watch? Ur—Cherish, Darling, Angel?"

"Precious!" Michelle's head whipped around at Jessica's question, her eyes wide and luminous.

"Yeah, that's it, Precious." Jessica snapped her fingers. "But if you ask me, she ain't look all that *precious*—"

"Where?" Michelle ignored the envy in Jessica's voice. She hadn't seen Precious for months, and just the mention of her name and the slight chance she could talk to her sent her heart racing.

"Over there." Jessica rolled her eyes and pointed.

It *was* Precious, standing next to a giant stuffed teddy bear. She must have been watching them for some time, Michelle speculated, because even from that distance, she could see the confusion and uncertainty in her eyes. She looked as sad as the day, seven months ago, when Michelle first saw her.

Michelle's heart throbbed loudly. It wasn't right. It just wasn't right. Erik had no right to make his child suffer this way. Her first instinct was to ignore Precious and obey her father's wishes, but the sadness in those brown eyes ripped a huge hole in Michelle's heart.

Before she knew what was happening, Michelle was standing in front of Precious, smiling down at her with gentle longing, fighting the need to clutch her in her arms. "Hi, Precious," she said softly.

"Hi." Precious hung her head and stared at her black kid leather boots.

She looked absolutely pretty in a pink cashmere sweater with pink lacy ribbons across the front, and black corduroy trousers with cuffs at the hems and pink bows at the sides. Her hair was loose and hung down to her waist with a pink ribbon on one side.

She was Erik LaCrosse's daughter—elegant and beautiful. She had the best of everything—food, clothes, toys, education... Michelle tried not to think of her own child, Erik's second child, and all the luxuries it would have to do without. "How are you, sweetheart?"

"Fine." Her voice was so low, Michelle could hardly hear her.

"Precious, who are you talking to? Get back here!"

Precious jumped. Her head flew up, fear glistening in her eyes.

Michelle did a right about turn. Who the heck thought they had the right to yell at her baby like that?

"Oh, it's you," Bridget Ashley said. Her eyes washed over Michelle with contempt as she came toward them, holding two little dresses in her hand.

Michelle remembered shopping with Precious. They used to have such fun trying on one pretty outfit after another. The kid didn't seem to be having any fun today. It was impossible to have fun around that woman, she thought, recalling the night in Boston when Bridget was shamelessly throwing herself at Erik— her then new, secret husband.

Bridget placed a possessive hand on Precious' shoulder. "Precious, you know you shouldn't talk to strangers."

"Oh, knock it off, Bridget." Michelle challenged the malice in the other woman's voice. "I'm no stranger to her." She was careful to place her wool coat in front of her stomach. She didn't need Bridget blabbing to Erik about her condition.

"Her father made it clear he doesn't want you near her. After what you did to Erik—"

"Don't even go there, woman. You know nothing about what I did or didn't do to Erik. You couldn't even begin to imagine what we had."

"*Had,* being the operative word. Well, as you can see, he's over it, over you."

"Stop it! Stop it!" Precious ran from them, tears streaming down her face.

"Look at what you've done." Bridget snapped in a condescending tone, casting a worried eye around at the attention they were attracting. "But what else should one expect from an ill-bred ghetto rat?"

*Oh God, that hurt.* Michelle ignored her insult and chased after Precious. She found her huddled on the floor in a corner of the store. Michelle dropped down beside her and pulled her into her arms. "Oh, Precious, baby."

"Michelle, I miss you so much, and Daddy says I can't talk to you. Why, Michelle? Don't you love me anymore?"

*Dear God, help me*, Michelle prayed silently as she rocked

Precious in her arms. "Yes baby, I love you. I will always love you, no matter what. You have to believe that. There isn't a day that goes by that I don't think of you. I wonder what you're wearing to school, if Sippy and Charlie are still sucking on those stupid rocks, if Sam Martin is still trying to kiss you." Michelle smiled as she arranged her on her lap. It felt so good to hold her, to smell her, breathe in her innocence.

Precious lifted limpid eyes and placed her arms across Michelle's shoulders. "You're wearing my earrings."

"I told you I would never take them out. Good thing they match all my outfits. Diamonds are forever, I guess."

Precious smiled then stated rather sadly, "You missed my birthday. I had a big party. I'm eight now. And look." She gave Michelle a wide grin. "I lost two teeth."

Michelle knew Precious was having a party and had wondered if Erik would have been upset if she sent her a gift. In the end, she'd decided not to. The man had asked her to stay away from his daughter and she was trying to adhere to his request. "I hear you have a new nanny," she said. "Is she nice to you?"

"She's old and she smells funny, and she doesn't put notes in my lunch box like you did."

"Well, we're going to fix that right now," Michelle said, as she searched her bag for a notepad and pen. When she was finished writing, she read the note out loud. *'Dear Precious, I love you today much more than I loved you yesterday, but still not as much as I'll love you tomorrow. Have a great lunch. Michelle.'* She drew a happy face, little hearts, and a half dozen x's and o's at the bottom of the note. "You keep this in your lunch box and read it every day. Okay?" she said, placing it into Precious' hand.

"Okay." Precious pressed the note against her heart then pushed her hand into the pocket of her slacks. "I have your lucky penny," she said, opening her palm. "I take it everywhere with me. Do you want it back?"

The light in those brown eyes widened the hole in Michelle's heart. It took all her energy not to break down in front of her. "No baby, you keep it. I have your earrings and you have my penny. Maybe one day you can pass it on to someone you love, someone who means a lot to you. Okay?"

Precious nodded. She folded the penny inside the note and shoved them into her pocket. "You know what else?" she asked smiling up at Michelle.

"What else?" Michelle managed a tentative smile.

"Grandpa Erik and Grandma Felicia got married. They went to Greece on their honeymoon. What's a honeymoon?"

'It's a special trip people take after they get married so they can get to know each other better." Felicia had sent her an invitation to the wedding, but she'd had to decline. Even though she wasn't showing much, one look at her, and Erik would have known she was pregnant. He'd told her once that he could tell a woman was pregnant even at two months. She was almost at the end of her first trimester at the time. He would have smelled his child growing in her womb from miles away.

Precious' eyebrows suddenly wrinkled as she pressed into Michelle's stomach. "You're getting fat, Michelle."

Michelle stiffened as a cold flush crawled up her spine. "Yeah, I'm—I'm putting on a little weight," she said, pushing Precious to her feet.

"I was just thinking the same thing." Bridget's eyes blazed down into Michelle's as she stood imposingly over her.

"Michelle isn't fat, silly," stated a defensive Jessica. "She's going to have a—"

"Jessica!" Michelle silenced the girl as she struggled to get up.

Jessica crossed her arms, pursed her lips, and rolled her eyes.

"Jessie, why don't you take Precious over to the toy section and help her pick out something. And you get something for you, too." Michelle pulled some bills from her wallet and thrust them into Jessica's hand.

Jessica snatched the folded bills, grabbed Precious' hand and practically hauled her away to the toy section.

"You're pregnant?" Bridget snapped.

"Yes."

"Is it Erik's?" Her tone grew more distasteful.

Michelle sighed. Nobody knew for certain, but there was a lot of speculation that she and Erik had been sleeping together.

She'd returned to New Hampshire, just as the news about her father was winding down. The press had hounded her for information, but when she simply ignored them, they finally left her alone. The man she'd called her father for twenty-five years had pleaded guilty to the charges, thank God, so there was no long drawn-out trial.

She could lie to Bridget about the father of her child. Ryan was back in town and was paying her attention. Their friendship had deepened while she'd been hiding out at his place in South Carolina. He'd taken good care of her when she was at the lowest point in her life, and since his return to Manchester, he'd started helping out at the center—which brought them even closer still. They'd gone out together a few times, as friends, but just in case Erik found out, she couldn't bear for him to think she had been intimate with another man so soon after their breakup.

Foolish rationale, considering she was speaking to the woman he was currently dating. "Yes, it's Erik's, but he doesn't know," she finally answered Bridget.

"My God," Bridget rasped, a cold, congested expression settling on her pale face. "He has a right to know. He would want to be involved in his child's life. You can't offer that baby anything, Michelle. Erik has every right to raise it. He could give it a good home, a good life. With you, it would just be another hopeless statistic."

The bottom dropped out of Michelle's heart, and fear, stark and vivid, pounded in her veins. Good Lord, she hadn't thought of that. What if Erik decided to fight for custody of his child? What if he won? And he could.

The odds were stacked highly against her. She didn't have a steady job. She was living in her best friend's apartment. The man who'd raised her and called himself her father was a convicted killer.

Erik was a respected doctor and upright citizen. He had money at his disposal. He could hire the best lawyers in the country. What he could do to her by taking her child away was snowflakes compared to what she had already been through. If she lost her child, Michelle knew she would literally crawl under a bridge and die. Her hands automatically clutched her stomach as her maternal instinct pumped the adrenaline through her veins.

"You listen, Bridget." Despite the terrible quaking in her bones, Michelle managed to keep calm on the outside. "If Erik knew I was carrying his child, he would come back to me. There is no doubt about it. So don't you start harboring any stupid ideas in your head, thinking you and Erik could take my child from me and raise it as your own. Cause it ain't gonna happen, sister. If you want to hold on to your man, I suggest you keep your scarlet mouth shut."

"But—"

Michelle wanted to be absolutely certain she got her point across as poignantly as possible, so she wasn't holding any punches. "Erik loves me. He has told me and shown me in ways far beyond your imagination or comprehension. His feelings for me are deep and strong. He shut me out of his life because of his loyalty to Cassie. If he finds out I'm carrying a part of him inside me, don't think for one minute that your little romantic farce with him won't be over. *I'm* the woman he loves. *I'm* going to be the mother of his child. Remember that before you go blabbing to him."

An open-mouthed Bridget was at a loss for words. She would have had to swallow them, anyway, because at that moment an excited Precious and an intensely serene Jessica returned, each carrying a shopping bag.

"Look, Michelle. I got a Snow White doll that dances." Precious held up the doll.

"Beautiful. Happy birthday, darling." Michelle pinched her cute nose, happy to see joy sparkled in her eyes again.

"Let me pay you for it." Bridget opened her Gucci handbag and extracted a matching wallet.

"I don't need your money," Michelle said with a slight smile of defiance. She turned an affectionate smile on Precious. "Every time you play with it, you think of me, for I'll be thinking of you."

"I love you, Michelle."

"I love you, too, baby. Always. You take care of yourself, and your daddy. Okay?"

She nodded as tears glistened in her eyes.

Michelle gathered her to her bosom one last time then quickly released her and turned away blindly. Her heart hurt so much, she thought she would buckle under the pain.

# CHAPTER TWENTY-TWO

The next day was Sunday. The sun came up high and bright against a clear blue sky, and as Michelle sat at the kitchen table in Yasmine's apartment, drinking a cup of hot chocolate and listening to the frigid February wind whistling sharply outside, she tried to analyze her feelings.

She'd gotten the call last night.

The man formerly known as her father was found dead in his cell. Apparently, he'd been suffering from cirrhosis, and last night his liver finally shut down on him. Well, he was a drunk, had been all her life, and even before that according to Robert and people who knew him back in Virginia.

Michelle was surprised he'd lasted that long, but grateful, nonetheless. If he'd died any sooner, she and Robert might never have found out that he wasn't their father, but a homeless impostor by the name of Timmy Gleason who'd killed and stolen their real father's identity.

While she'd been hiding out in South Carolina, Robert had found a note in the box of their mother's stuff stored in his home. The note was from a woman in Virginia addressed to Dwight Carter at the apartment on Pine Street where they used to live, but on the inside she'd called him Timmy. It was postmarked twenty-six years ago, shortly after her mother arrived in Manchester, and months before Michelle was born. The note merely stated that the man he'd stabbed had died and he shouldn't come back to Virginia.

Robert had straightway hired a private investigator to track the woman down, only to find that she'd been dead for years. After further digging, they'd discovered that Timmy Gleason had also been dead for twenty-six years. From there on, it was easy to solve the rest of the puzzle. Timmy Gleason had stabbed their father, for what reason, they'll never know. He'd stolen his identity, kidnapped her pregnant mother and Robert, and fled to New Hampshire. Michelle was sure he'd threatened to hurt her babies if she ever talked. It was the only way he could have kept her quiet.

Michelle couldn't even fathom the blanket of fear her mother must have lived under day after day and night after night. Her husband was dead—or did she even know that? And his killer was threatening the lives of her children. Her mother had to keep Timmy Gleason's secret to protect her and Robert. Michelle knew she would have done the same if she'd been in a similar situation. Yesterday, she'd felt she could strangle Bridget for even suggesting that she and Erik could take her child away from her.

She had no feelings about Timmy Gleason's death, but she was overwhelmed with questions, curiosity, and love for the father she would never know. Since Dwight Carter grew up in foster care, tracing their family line had become much more difficult than she and Robert initially anticipated. They weren't giving up, but she had to face the fact that Dwight Carter might forever remain a mystery to her. One more thing Timmy Gleason had robbed her of.

Michelle pushed herself out of the chair. She needed to get out of the house.

She walked the short distance to Yasmine's bedroom and knocked on the door. Yasmine grumbled something unintelligible. Michelle opened the door and walked over to the side of the bed. The shades were drawn, making it impossible for her to see much of anything. Michelle knew Yasmine was bone-tired from working overtime all week, and she felt terrible disturbing her sleep. But she was in need of some spiritual comfort for the turmoil in her soul.

"Yasmine?" she said to the long lump completely submerged from head to toe under the blankets.

"Hmm?"

"Can I borrow your car? Do you have any plans today?"

"I just want to sleep, if you let me."

"Thanks." Michelle bent down and kissed what she thought was Yasmine's forehead.

"You don't have to kiss my ass, Michelle. You're my girl. I'll do anything for you."

Stifling a giggle, Michelle tiptoed out of the room.

Pastor Dixon had just commenced his Sunday sermon when she got to the little church where she and her brother used to attend services, occasionally, when they were children. She slid quietly and unnoticed into the very last pew.

Michelle listened intently as Pastor Dixon talked about Faith, Hope, and Charity, the three spiritual gifts, and how Charity was the greatest and most blessed of the three. He called Charity *Love*, and explained how it conquered all, overcame any problem, moved mountains.

Michelle had never considered herself religious, but as she listened to the comforting words of wisdom, she thought of Erik and Precious, and how much she loved them. She wanted to be with them, especially now that she knew she had no blood ties to the man responsible for their pain. She wanted to tell Erik about his child growing inside her, that it was not related to the man who'd killed his wife. She wanted her family back.

Timmy Gleason had robbed her of her own father. She was not going to let him rob her child of his, or hers.

If what the minister said was true, that Love conquered all things, no matter how dismal the circumstances, she would just have to have faith, and hope that she and Erik find their way back to each other.

Michelle turned her head as someone sat down next to her. A smile brightened her face, and she reached out and clasped the large warm hand.

Her dear, sweet, big brother smiled back at her. He was hurting, too. Timmy Gleason had scarred her brother just as deeply as he had her. When Michelle hurt, Robert hurt, too. It had always been like that. It would always be like that.

They slid quietly outside before the benediction.

Robert put his arms around her without saying a word.

"Thanks for coming," Michelle mumbled against his chest. She'd called him this morning to let him know where she would be. They would spend the day together, comforting each other, asking questions neither one of them knew the answers to, yet, but which they hoped they'd find in time. "I lost Erik and Precious because of that homeless bastard. I may have lost my mother too because of him. I feel so alone."

"You're never alone, Mich, darling. You know I'll always be here for you. I asked you to come stay with me, but I understand you need to stay in Manchester for the kids at the center." He paused. "Do you want me to talk to Erik? Pound some sense into his thick head?"

"Oh, Robert." Michelle sighed and gazed into his face. "You're always picking up the broken pieces of my life and putting them back together. I'm not a little girl, anymore. I can't expect you to keep fighting my battles. I'm a woman now, and soon to be a mother. I destroyed my relationship with Erik, all by myself. I have to fix it, all by myself."

"You have grown up so much in the last few months, Little Sis. You've been broken, but you're a whole lot stronger than you were before. I hear it in your voice, see it in your eyes."

"I have to be strong for my child," Michelle said, as her brother walked her to the car. "As strong as our mother was for us."

\*\*\*

After pondering the words of the minister all day, Michelle decided to give it one last shot, and at midnight, she made her call.

"Hello." A woman's voice, groggy from sleep, drifted through the wires into Michelle's ears.

A sharp gasp escaped her as the shock of reality flew to her brain. She placed a trembling hand over her heart as anxiety spurted through her.

"Who's there? I know someone's there. I can hear you breathing."

With a slow unsteady motion, Michelle pushed the end button on the receiver. She fell onto the sofa and stuck her knuckles into her mouth so Yasmine wouldn't hear her gasping.

Then she felt it coming, hard and strong, like a whirling tornado rushing through her system. She barely made it to the bathroom in time. She fell to the floor and grabbed the sides of the toilet and emptied her stomach into the bowl.

\*\*\*

July finally dragged around again. And with it came sweltering heat and suffocating humidity.

It was a little over a year ago that Michelle walked up the driveway of 204 Jefferson Drive, and into Erik LaCrosse's life. One year ago, she had found love, and eight and a half months ago she had lost it, due to a terrible twist of fate.

She sat in the living room of her rented condo, arms folded over her enormous stomach, watching as rain formed puddles in the parking lot outside her window.

Her first book was sold, and would go to print within six months. In addition to that elated feeling of success, she had been fortunate to obtain a contract with the publishing house for a three-book series about 'The Littlest Dreamers'.

She was expecting a sizable advance any day now, which she would use to buy a decent car to replace the piece of junk that spent more time in the garage than it did on the road. She'd started freelancing in an effort to provide for her child. With Ryan photographing for her, she was doing pretty well. He loved to take pictures of her, too, she thought, glancing around at the many photographs in the room—some with her alone, some with the kids at the center, and an enlarged one of her and Ryan on the wall—his hand resting on her stomach as if he were the father of her child.

He'd given her that photo for Mother's Day, and had asked her to marry him again. Said he wanted to take care of her and her baby. And again, she'd turned him down. He deserved a woman who could love him for the wonderful caring man he'd morphed into. She couldn't. Not him. Not any other man. Ever. Perhaps if there was no Erik...

A slow smile twisted Michelle's lips as her baby kicked in her womb. She patted her stomach, love flooding her heart. She would have to love this child enough to make up for its father and sister—the family it would never meet.

Her eyes misted as she thought of Precious. She hadn't seen her since that day at the mall. Mrs. Hayes had told her that Erik had put the house on the market and was planning to return to Granite Falls. Felicia had already moved back there with Philippe. There was nothing keeping Erik in Amherst. She might never see him or Precious again.

Michelle's heart still ached with a raw pain for that child. She wondered if she remembered her, and if she still thought of her. She may as well face facts. Children forget quickly. Precious had Bridget to fill the void in her little life.

Her baby kicked again. "Just two more weeks," she said to it. Just two more weeks, then she would hold her baby, Erik's baby, in her arms. It was all she had left of the love they'd shared. And she would cherish, adore, and protect it with her life.

She thought about the upcoming opening for the new center. She should be there. She'd done most of the work to raise funds and find sponsors, but she didn't dare. Erik was the keynote guest speaker.

She couldn't risk Erik knowing about her child, not after what Bridget Ashley had said. She would lose any custody battle with him. And so to avoid running into him, or the local press, she'd moved out of Manchester, months ago when she really began showing, into a town close to the Massachusetts border where nobody knew her.

Trembling fingers stroked her stomach as she tried to connect to the child inside her. This was her only reason for living, her only hope for survival. Nobody was taking it away from her.

She was sorry it might never know its father. It would be just like many of the kids in her neighborhood—fatherless. Michelle was sorry, so very sorry for a whole lot of things. A permanent sorrow seemed to weigh her down.

*** 

"...And this, ladies and gentlemen, is the true meaning of neighborhood. When we pull together as a community and help our brothers and sisters less fortunate than us, there is no greater joy, no deeper pleasure or satisfaction than in knowing we have helped one small soul, made one tiny dream come true, kept hope alive in one tender, little heart."

Erik nodded and smiled at the resounding round of applause coming from the crowd of donors, sponsors, and grateful parents for the new Youth Neighborhood Center.

He cast an anxious glance once more toward the door before he stepped from the podium and took his seat with the other speakers on the makeshift stage. He listened halfheartedly to the vote of thanks and closing remarks by Rose Marlon the president of the organization.

Where was Michelle?

He couldn't understand why she wouldn't be here. It was her hard work that had made all this possible. Her love and devotion had moved people to give generously to these needy children.

"Great speech, Dr. LaCrosse." A petite woman who looked as if life had been hard on her came up to Erik and shook his hand. "Thanks for all the help you've given to our community and our children. My Jessica has benefited so much from hanging out at the center instead of idling on the streets after school. Michelle is a good influence on her, on all the kids."

Erik's heart danced as pleasant memories stirred deep inside him. He knew all those wonderful things about Michelle, and so much more than any of these people in this building realized. She was his sweet angel of mercy. He took a deep breath. "Speaking of Ms. Carter, why isn't she here tonight? Is she ill?"

"You mean you don't know?" The woman seemed deeply puzzled.

"Know what?"

"That she's—"

"I've been looking everywhere for you, darling."

Erik clenched his jaws as Bridget glided up to him and looped a possessive arm through his. He forced a bland smile.

"It was nice talking to you, Dr. LaCrosse. Thanks again for all your help. You should come by the center sometime. I'm sure Michelle would be happy to see you." The woman threw Bridget a cynical stare then took off as if she'd brought the plague with her.

"What was that about?" Bridget walked beside Erik as he moved over to a table laden with goodies.

He picked up a carrot stick and chewed on it, absentmindedly. "She was about to tell me something about Michelle, but you scared her off." He noticed that Bridget's false lashes came down to shade her eyes from him. "Do you know something I don't?" he asked.

"No." She shook her head vehemently. "Whatever she was going to say was probably insignificant. You know how these people like to make something out of nothing."

He didn't like her tone or the connotation in her words. Michelle was one of *these people* and he still loved her with all his heart. He needed to see her. He needed to talk with her one last time before he moved to Granite Falls. She hadn't responded to his letter, and he'd taken her silence to mean that it was really over. He couldn't leave it like that. He had to hear her tell him that she didn't love him to his face. That she couldn't forgive him for hurting her, and making her feel that she had no other choice but to leave.

"I asked her to forgive me," he said out loud. "I guess she can't."

A frown furrowed Bridget's brow. "What did you do to her, Erik? It was her father who killed Cassie. Why would you be asking her forgiveness?"

He averted his eyes and walked from the crowd, out the door, into the dark July night, around to the back of the building. He leaned against the wall. The smell of recently fallen rain on the lush grass beneath his feet was pleasant in the air.

It was a night, just like this one, hot and humid, with fever racing through his veins that he'd kissed Michelle for the first time. His lips still tingled from the memory of that first intimate touch, and all the sweet moments of loving that followed. She had yielded, so softly and deliciously in his arms. He wasn't aware that Bridget had followed him until she spoke.

"What did you do to her, Erik?"

His eyes burned with pain. His heart numbed with shame. He was grateful for the blanket of blackness. "I punished her. The night I found out that it was her father who'd killed Cassie, I went home, raging with a taste for revenge. Michelle was there. She was the perfect target. I wanted somebody to hurt as much as I was hurting. So I allowed my pain to blind me, and I unleashed it on the one person available, the one person I..."

"Love." Bridget quietly finished when he hung his head in silence. Michelle was right. He did love her. He had been grieving for her all this time. This was a suffering far worse than death. At least he knew he could never have Cassie back. But Michelle? As long as Michelle was alive, he would never be over her.

Bridget finally understood what Michelle had tried to tell her that day at the mall. As much as she wanted Erik, she could not settle to be second best to any woman. She deserved much more. What woman wanted to be with a man who could leave her some day? And she knew that *someday* would come when Erik discovered that Michelle had given birth to his child.

"Erik, Michelle is pregnant," she said before she gave herself time to renege from doing the right thing. "She may have already given birth—I don't know. I think that's what that woman wanted to tell you."

His head came up in slow motion, an acute pain in his chest. "What did you just say, Bridget?"

"I saw Michelle about five months ago. She was pregnant, Erik."

He gripped her by the shoulders, a tormented, haggard expression in his eyes. "And you never told me?"

"She forbade me to tell you. She had her reasons. I was jealous of what the two of you shared and I said some nasty things to her," Bridget added in a regretful tone.

"Like what?" He shook her. "What did you say to her?"

"I called her a ghetto rat, and told her she couldn't offer the child anything. That she should let you and me raise it." Bridget sighed with shame over her behavior. "She called the house the following night, but when she heard my voice, she hung up."

"How do you know it was her?"

"Her girlfriend, um... Yasmine's number showed up on Caller I.D."

"God!" Erik clutched at his face as though he were in excruciating pain. It must have happened on that horrible night. Michelle... *His* child... He'd turned his back on them. God, how Bridget's nasty words must have driven the cruel nails deeper into her coffin of despair.

He pushed away from the side of the building. "I have to find her." He sprinted across the parking lot toward his Mercedes.

"How am I to get home, Erik?"

"Whistle for a cab, Bridget."

"I'll give you a ride, doll," Erik heard a man's voice say behind him. He didn't care who it was. He didn't look back. His future was ahead of him.

\*\*\*

Within minutes, Erik was banging on Yasmine's door. He pushed past her when she opened it.

"Michelle! Michelle!" He raced through the apartment, flinging doors open and searching inside the rooms.

"Where is she?" He finally came back to the living room where Yasmine waited patiently with folded arms at the open door, right where he'd left her.

"If you'd asked me that before you barged in here like Shaka Zulu on the war path, I could have saved you the trouble."

"I don't have time for your smart mouth, Yasmine. Where's Michelle?"

"She isn't here," Yasmine said with a stiff face, jutting her chin at him.

"I can see that. Look, I know she's pregnant. That's my child she's carrying."

Yasmine raised a skeptical eyebrow. "Really now? And how do you know that, Dr.?"

"Are you going to tell me, or must I choke it out of you? And I will, Yasmine. Where... is... Michelle?" He spaced the last three words out evenly through clenched teeth as he leaned in toward her.

Yasmine backed away, her hands raised to ward him off. "Calm down, Erik. There's no need to resort to violence." She rattled off Michelle's address and gave him quick directions.

The minute the door closed, Yasmine jumped on the phone.

# CHAPTER TWENTY-THREE

Michelle jumped at the chime of the doorbell. "He's here," she said to Yasmine.

"That was fast," Yasmine said. "You can just ignore him, you know."

"You don't know Erik."

"Michelle, open the door!" Erik's voice bellowed from outside.

"I heard that," Yasmine said. "You want me to stay on the line, just in case?"

"No. I'm fine. I'll call you later. Bye." Michelle hung up the phone and stared at the door.

"Michelle, I know you're home."

Michelle bit into her bottom lip as it throbbed like her pulse. She didn't know if he'd come for his child or for her. All Yasmine had told her was that he knew she was pregnant, and that he was furious. Ice spread through her belly. "Go away, Erik."

"Not until we talk."

"I have nothing to say to you."

"If you don't open this door, I will break it down. I swear."

Michelle wobbled across the room and yanked the door open. Her black eyes met his grey, gold-flecked ones with a blaze of fury. "What do you want?"

Erik's eyes bulged when he saw her big fat stomach. "Oh, my God," he whispered as he stumbled into the condo and closed the door behind him. "You're on the brink of giving birth."

Michelle forced herself to hold his stare. It pained her to look at him, knowing he was now with someone else. He was dressed in a grey linen summer suit, pink shirt and striped pink and grey tie. He stood tall and proud—broad shoulders, straight back, with skin like suede, eyes like a tiger, and soft sexy lips she longed to kiss again.

"I see Dr. Ashley couldn't keep her big mouth shut," she said tersely as she watched him take a swift assessing glance around the room. She saw his nostrils flare and his lips tighten when his eyes landed on the photo of her and Ryan on the wall.

"You're wasting your time, Dr.," she said. "It's not yours."

His jaw muscles flinched and his eyes flashed flames of anger. He took a fuming step toward her. "Then whose is it? Who's that man with his hand on you stomach? Is that Ryan? I know you were staying with him in South Carolina. Is it his?"

"It's mine, Erik. Mine."

He assessed her quietly for a moment, then the muscles in his jaw relaxed. "I know you, and I know you wouldn't have been with anyone else, especially so soon after us. So it doesn't really matter who he is. I know he's not the father of that child you're carrying."

"Erik, just say what you came to say, and leave. You're not welcome here."

He shrugged out of his jacket and tossed it over the back of a chair, making himself comfortable as if he didn't hear her. "I hurt you. I hurt you deeply, and I'm sorry."

Michelle trembled where she stood beside the couch and forced herself into believing that she didn't care, that nothing he said would change the fact that he wasn't there when she needed him most. She fought the need to fall into his arms and tell him how much she still loved him and how empty her life was without him.

"Michelle, when I found out about your father, I needed somebody to blame," he said in a feeble attempt to apologize. "I needed someone to feel the same agony I was feeling. You were there with your sweet love for me so I lashed out at you. It was a mistake. The biggest mistake I've ever made, and I'm sorry, baby."

Michelle remembered the ease and speed with which he'd ended their marriage, severed their relationship. She remembered how she begged for his forgiveness, his trust, his love. He'd told her to forget him, and what they'd shared, and that's what she'd tried to do. She was trying to build a life for herself and her child. She never wanted to know hurt like that again, be abandoned again. For all she knew, he could just be here to verify the child was his, then take it away from her so he and Bridget could raise it. His moment of *déjà vu* wasn't happening.

"Okay, Erik," she said on the verge of fatigue. "I accept your apology. Now please go." She turned her back to him, afraid he'd see the truth in her eyes.

"Is that all you have to say?"

Michelle whipped around, months of suppressed hurt rushing to the surface of her soul. "What do you want me to say, Erik? You expect me to fall into your arms just because you said you're sorry? I told you I was sorry, and you still tossed me aside. I gave my heart to you, and you crushed it in your mighty strong hands. I needed you, Erik, but you abandoned me, just like my…"

The truth about Timmy Gleason was still not public knowledge. Knowing it would send the media into another frenzy over Cassie LaCrosse's death, she and Robert had opted to keep the news to themselves, at least for now.

People were already forgetting that she was tied to that case. She didn't want Erik and Precious to live through the horror of Cassie's death again. She just wanted to be left alone to live her life in peace. "I have just been through the loneliest, most difficult eight months of my life, and I'm really tired, okay? So, just go, Erik. Go, and leave me alone." She pointed toward the door.

Erik's eyes drank up Michelle's loveliness as she stood before him in a flowery cotton maternity shift. *Barefoot and pregnant.* She was even more beautiful than he remembered. She sparkled with an inner radiance, a soft glow of warmth and tenderness. She was so sweet and gentle, like the most precious rose, subtle and fragile in the wind. How could he have hurt her so? How could he have turned his back on this delicate creature? He had hurt her more than anyone else on this planet ever could—simply because she loved him. His shame choked him into silence.

"I lay in bed, night after night," Michelle said. "Needing you, crying myself to sleep while you were romancing Bridget Ashley, living your life as though I never existed." Scalding tears streamed down Michelle's face and she made no effort to stop them.

"That's not true, Michelle. I wrote—"

"You took Precious from me although you knew how much I love her. That hurt more than everything else you did to me. I thought you would have at least left me that relationship."

She was suddenly besieged with the memory of the night when she called Erik and Bridget answered the phone. He was sleeping with her, having sex with her in Cassie's bed, the bed he couldn't share with Michelle.

Michelle shuddered and ran her fingers through her hair. "Go home, Erik. I'm sure Bridget is waiting for you." She was so tired that her nerves throbbed. Her muscles screamed from the weight of the child in her womb and from arguing with its father. She just wanted to be left alone. She fell weakly to the couch and covered her face with her hands.

Erik fell on his knees in front of her. He pulled her hands from her face. His heart ripped at the raw hurt glittering in her dark eyes. "Okay, Michelle. I'll go home, but not before I tell you why I came here tonight. I listened to you, so now you will listen to me."

She stiffened and pulled her hands from his grasp. Her arms went around her stomach in a protective maternal gesture.

The bewildered look in her eyes sent a chill sweeping through

Erik's bones. Dear God, she thought he was here to take her baby away from her as Bridget had threatened to do. Had her opinion of him changed so much that she'd think he could be so cruel? Think that he would take a child from its mother? She knew how he felt about his own mother not being able to raise him.

"Michelle," he said softly, "I came here to tell you what a stupid fool, an absolute jackass, a class-A idiot, dull dimwit I am."

She put a hand to her mouth and started giggling.

*Now, that was his Michelle.*

"Yes, baby. You can laugh at me. Just hear me out," he said when her giggles finally faded and she stared at him with misty wistful eyes. "When Cassie lay dying in my arms, I swore I would find the bastard and make him pay. When I found out it was your father, I felt guilty. I had to punish myself, and in doing so, I punished you."

"Why did you need to be punished? What did you do?"

Erik cupped her face in his hands. His voice was rough and thick. "Don't you get it, angel? I've wanted you from the moment I saw you walking up my driveway hauling that suitcase behind you. I've loved you from the moment you made Precious laugh. You were a breath of fresh air, sunshine on a cloudy day. You were a better lover than Cassie. You awakened desires in me I never knew I had. You were awesome with Precious from the very first day. As I grew to know you, I realized how incompatible Cassie and I were. You are the one true love of my life. Then when the truth came out, I felt like a traitor for loving you more than I loved her."

"Oh, Erik, I knew you loved me, but I didn't know it was like that. I thought you came here to take my baby away from me."

Erik placed his hands over hers that were resting on her stomach. "Michelle, I would never do that to you."

"But you did. You knew I loved Precious like my own child, yet it didn't matter. You hurt her, just as much as you hurt me."

"Michelle, you left," he said as gently as he could. "I came downstairs the next morning to apologize to you, to tell you that we'd find a way to make *us* work, but you were gone. You left in the middle of the night without even saying goodbye to Precious, or to me."

"How could I have stayed knowing that my father had caused you so much grief, and after all the hurtful things you said to me? And I did call you Erik, for three days, and when I came by to get my things that day, I begged you to take me back. Why didn't you?"

Tears stung Erik's eyes. "Pride. Uncertainty. Fear of returning to that place of misery in the future. I didn't trust myself to trust you, but I never asked you to leave, Michelle."

"You never asked me to stay, either."

Erik's gut twisted with regrets. "I know, and I'm sorry, sweetheart. I promise that if you give me another chance, I will make it up to you, and our child. Just tell me that you still love me, Michelle. Please." Erik dropped his head onto her stomach and gave in to the turbulent storm that had been brewing inside him for eight long torturous months. He'd missed her so much. He'd missed her touch, her voice, her laugh, her smell. Her love.

Her fingers gently stroked his hair as her hot tears fell against his cheek. "I do love you, Erik," she said in a choked voice. "I never stopped. I can never stop."

Just then the baby in her womb kicked. Once. Twice. Three times.

Erik slowly raised his head and gazed deeply into the turbulent depth of Michelle's eyes. He held her hands in his. "That's my baby in there. Tell me it's my baby, Michelle. I want to hear you say it."

"Yes, Erik. It's your baby." Her eyes were dark and stormy, sparkling in the light from the lamp. All the love and hunger she had suppressed for months spilled from their warm depths.

"Our son seems happy that his parents are back together," he said with a wide grin.

She gave him a relaxed, happy smile. "You're so sure it's a boy."

"Of course. We already have a daughter."

The gentle motion of the pads of his thumbs stroking the

insides of her wrists caused Michelle to catch her breath. *We.* He'd said *we.* She put her hands around his neck and drew him close to her. "How's Precious?"

"Missing you, dreadfully. She hasn't forgotten you. I have to apologize to her for keeping you apart."

"Yes, you do."

"How are you, Michelle?" he asked, filial concern hanging on the edge of his husky voice. "Have you been eating right, taking care of yourself?"

"From the moment I found out I was pregnant, I've been doing all the right things to make sure I deliver a strong and healthy baby."

Erik smiled and stretched his arms around her as far as it would go. He caressed the curve of her back. He pressed his head into her chest, between her swollen breasts from which their child would be suckling soon. He inhaled deeply, drinking up her sweetness. "I almost forgot how good you smell," he whispered, raising his head. "I used to go into your bedroom and close my eyes, and let your *Moonlight* creep through my skin. I missed you so much. I need you. I want our son to feel me loving his mother. I want to show you how much I love you."

"What's stopping you?" she whispered, bending her head.

Their lips locked in a kiss that was as slow, drugging, and sedate as it was exciting. The strong smoothness of Erik's tongue flickered lightly, tantalizingly, across the softness of Michelle's lips. He teased the curved corners of her mouth, exploring the fleshy, velvety inside as if it were a luscious ripe fruit, bursting with warm honey and sweet nectar. He wanted to savor her, love her, cherish her, forever. Finally, his tongue slid into the warm, dark recesses of her mouth and he swirled it around, stroking the sensitive ceiling and inner cheeks of her sweet cavern, slowly, seductively.

Michelle moaned deeply and gave him full license to her sweetness. She tangled her tongue with his, twirling it around in a primitive, provocative dance before drawing back from him. Her eyes were laced with passion as they blazed into the murky depth of his. "Stand up," she commanded softly, pushing on his arms.

He pushed to his feet, frowning in confusion.

Slowly, Michelle's hands reached for his belt and unbuckled it. She unbuttoned his trousers then unzipped them carefully. As she pushed them off his hips, her lips came eagerly toward his groin. She kissed the rigid outline of his manhood through his black silk briefs.

Erik's breath caught in his throat at the intimate contact. He cupped her face in his hands. "Michelle, you don't have to do this."

Her smile was the epitome of eroticism. "I want to."

Michelle struggled off the couch and knelt on the floor in front of him. She drew his trousers very slowly down his thighs and legs, her lips pressing hot kisses against his hairy limbs as they became visible. She went as low as her fat stomach would allow her. She would have sucked each of his toes if she could. She unlaced his shoes and patiently held his legs, one at a time, as he stepped out of his shoes and trousers. She remembered the day in his bedroom in Granite Falls when he'd paid her the same service before lying down with her. She would lay down with him later. Right now, she wanted to give him something special. Something she knew Cassie had never given him.

Michelle's eyes scanned down his body, clad in nothing but a pink shirt, striped tie, black briefs, and brown knee-high socks. He looked beautiful, virile, and very masculine. She trailed her finger along the outline of his erection, starting from the solid base all the way to the throbbing head.

Erik quivered and closed his eyes.

Bringing her face close, Michelle placed her mouth to the throbbing head and gently and slowly nipped and licked her way down the outline of his brief-sheathed shaft, then back up again. She repeated the tantalizing acts of love until he groaned and shivered above her.

Erik opened his eyes and gazed down at a very pregnant Michelle on her knees in front of him, her face bathed in rapture. The sight of her beautiful lips moving back and forth over his shaft was so erotic it sent bolts of fire surging from his toes to his fingertips. He should stop her. He didn't want an embarrassing repeat of his honeymoon with Cassie. But Michelle had other ideas, he realized when she hooked her fingers in the waist of his briefs and pulled them down to his knees.

"Oh, Goodness. I don't believe this is happening," he exclaimed in a ragged voice as his erection jumped out and smacked her in the face.

Michelle gazed up at him, not believing it either. "You've never been loved this way?"

An embarrassed light flickered in his eyes. "Just once, on my honeymoon with Cassie. She gagged, bit me a couple times then threw up all over me. Doubtless to say, it's been a turn-off since then."

"Oh, baby." Michelle pouted. "No wonder you stopped me every time I tried to pleasure you this way. I've never done this before, either. But I promise not to bite you or throw up on you."

He gasped in pleasure as her fingers, warm and slender, closed around his flesh, pumping it lightly. His fingers tangled in her hair, pulling her closer. Michelle pushed the foreskin back and touched her tongue to the broad head. A drop of moisture, tangy and musky, washed over her tongue. She licked at it, enjoying the arousing masculine odor rising from his body.

How could Cassie, any woman not enjoy pleasuring the man she loved in such an intimate way? She'd never done it with Ryan because she was not in love with him. But Erik, she would pleasure him this way, any way, any time he wanted.

Erik bit into his lips and closed his eyes. "Michelle." He moved his hips suggestively as her tongue flicked sensually over him. A long moan erupted from his throat when her hot wet mouth closed completely around the head of his shaft, and she began sucking him with a delicious sensuous rhythm that erased all purpose, but the one of completeness.

She worked her mouth over him, trying to take as much of him as she possibly could. It was pure rapture to watch her. He held her head steady and thrust into her hot mouth as she worshiped and loved him like no other woman had ever done, or ever would. Back and forth, up and down, she teased and caressed and tortured with her mouth and hands.

Erik felt his lungs constrict, cutting off vital air to his brain. His body tensed as divine pleasure exploded through him. "Michelle... I'm com...ing..."

His breath came in hard cutting gasps. He tried to push her head away and disengage from her mouth, but Michelle held him by his tight buns and locked her jaws around him. She sucked him urgently and vigorously until the volcano inside him erupted in a violent explosion.

Erik expelled a long, rumbling, animal sound that started way down in his belly then he emptied himself into her mouth. She glued her lips to him, milking him for all he was worth.

Some moments later, when all was quiet again, Michelle looked up at him and licked her lips with the satisfaction of a cat that had just eaten the unsuspecting canary.

Erik pulled her to her feet. "You greedy little minx. If I'd known you were so good, I would have let you go down on me a long time ago."

Michelle smiled, kissed his lips, then her eyes opened in surprise when she felt him, still hard, pressing against her fat stomach. She had almost forgotten about his insatiable appetite. He was a multiple orgasmic man. One in a million. And he was all hers. She was the luckiest girl to ever walk the face of the earth. And to think she had almost lost him.

"Where's the bedroom?" he asked in a strained voice.

"But you just—"

"I've just begun, my love. I plan to make love to you all night, Michelle Carter. We have a lot of lost time to make up. He bent and picked her up.

"I'm too heavy, Erik."

"Never."

Giggling against his shoulders, Michelle pointed the way.

In the bedroom, he stripped off the rest of his clothes then slowly helped her out of her dress, bra, and panties. He stared at her naked body. "You're so beautiful." He reached out and palmed her swollen, tender breasts, kneading them gently, twirling the hard peaks between his fingers.

"I'm fat and ugly." She suddenly felt awkward and timid.

He placed a finger under her chin and raised her face to his. "You are more gorgeous than ever. And it's because you carry a new life inside you." His hand came down to caress her stomach. "This is the most precious gift a woman could give a man. To carry his seed inside her, to nourish it, love it, protect it with her life." He sighed. "I'm so sorry I missed out on—"

Michelle placed a finger on his lips. "All that matters is that you're here now, with me and our child. I have carried him, but you will bring him into the world. Yours will be the first face he sees. Yours will be the first hands that hold him. That will make up for anything you think you have missed out on."

"I love you so much." Gently, he lowered her to the bed and worshiped her body as she'd worshiped his. Only after he had taken her to the gates of paradise and back a few times, only after she clawed at him and begged him to take her, did Erik turn her on her side, position himself behind her, then slowly and carefully, entered her, one delicious, rigid inch at a time.

Their loving was slow, sweet, drawn-out, and intense. And when the waves of passion swelled beyond their control, they held each other tightly and rode the blissful currents to an awesome shuddering euphoric release.

A long time afterwards, while Michelle lay in Erik's arms, she felt the need to have some questions answered. "Erik?"

"Yes, baby." His voice was groggy, sleepy, his heart beating in a slow steady rhythm against the curve of her back.

"Were you sleeping with Bridget?"

"No. Never." His arms tightened possessively and reassuringly about her.

"Then what was she doing at your house—"

"At midnight, five and a half months ago?"

"You knew?"

"Bridget just told me tonight. She recognized Yasmine's number on Caller I.D."

"I still don't understand."

His chest rose and fell behind her. "Mrs. Smith had come

down with the flu. Mrs. Hayes was off visiting a friend in Florida. Mother was somewhere in the South of France. I had to go to Chicago for a conference. I was hard-pressed for someone to watch Precious. When Bridget offered to stay with her, I took her up on it."

"You could have called me."

"Michelle, I honestly thought of doing just that. It would have given me a reason to see you, talk with you, try to win you back."

"Why didn't you?" She rubbed her hands over his arms, loving the protection and security he offered her.

"Stupid pride and arrogance. Then when you didn't answer my letter—"

Michelle tensed. "What letter?"

"The one where I poured my heart out and begged your forgiveness. I told you how much I loved you and wanted you back. I didn't know if your feelings for me changed as time passed. So I wrote that if I didn't hear from you, I would assume you couldn't forgive me, that it was truly over between us."

Michelle took a quick sharp breath. "I never got that letter, Erik."

"You didn't? I know I mailed it, and it wasn't returned."

"When did you send it?"

"After Christmas. The holidays were so lonely. Plus my parents were on my case about letting you go. I just wanted you back in my life. When I didn't hear back, I just—"

"Jessica," Michelle grounded out after a long silence had passed.

"Who's Jessica?"

"Your rival. She lives next door to Yasmine and used to get my mail when I was still living there. She must have thrown it out when she saw the return address. She has a thing with rich people. Her wealthy father never acknowledged her. And she's jealous of my love for Precious."

Erik stroked his hands down her body, calming her. "Don't be too harsh on her. She was competing for your love just as I was. It's in the past now. We're back together. That's all that matters." He paused for a long moment then said, "I heard about your father's death. How are you handling that?"

Michelle took a deep unemotional breath. "That man wasn't my father."

"You're right. A father takes care of his children. I don't blame you for disowning him for treating you the way he did."

Michelle struggled to turn around to face Erik. She smiled as she placed her hand on his cheek. "He wasn't my father," she said again. "Robert and I are not related to him."

His forehead crinkled. "What do you mean?"

Michelle eagerly filled him in on the story about Timmy Gleason, and how he'd killed the real Dwight Carter, stolen his identity, and kidnapped her mother and Robert and brought them to New Hampshire.

"You mean to tell me that all this time your real father has been dead, and this man has been impersonating him?"

Michelle nodded.

"Why didn't your mother say something? Turn him in?"

"Come on, Erik, think."

"You're right. He must have threatened Robert an—" His eyes narrowed. "You said Robert was born in Virginia, but you were born in New Hampshire. How can you be sure you're not this terrible man's child?"

"Mrs. Hayes told me that my mother was already pregnant with me when she moved to Manchester. But when I began this investigation, I wasn't sure how long my mother had been his hostage, so when we found out that Timmy was an impostor, Robert went to see him in jail and came back with a couple strands of his hair."

"You did a DNA test."

"Yep. He's not the father of either of us."

Erik's lips spread into a relaxed smile as his hands reached for her stomach. "Thank God. I love you, and I love this baby— my baby, growing inside you, but the thought of that man's blood running through his veins was tearing me up inside."

"Well, you don't have to worry about it any more. I'm just happy he's dead, relieved that he can't hurt me or you and

Precious ever again."

"Why didn't you call to tell me?"

"I was going to that night when Bridget answered the phone."

"I'm sorry."

"It's okay. Robert and I kept it between us because we didn't want to stir up the news surrounding Cassie's death again. We just wanted to move on with our lives, and let you and Precious live yours. I've put it all behind me."

His warm palm gently caressed her naked stomach. "But what about your real father? Don't you want to know more about him, find out if you have family still living?"

"Robert is looking into that. It's another story I suppose." She sighed. "What about you, Erik? Have you put the tragedy of Cassie's death behind you?"

He kissed her forehead. "I have. There's nothing standing between us. No more doubts. No more anger. No more pain."

"No more lies."

"Just a bright and happy future with our daughter and our new baby."

Michelle settled more comfortably into his arms again. "I really thought I'd lost you that night when Bridget answered the phone. I knew you would make love to a woman only if you were in love with her."

"And that's the honest truth, my angel." Erik's lips gently brushed the bridge of her nose. "I never touched Bridget Ashley." He paused. "She told me what she said to you at the mall. I apologize for her unkind words."

"You can tell her I say there are no hard feelings there. Everybody was competing for somebody else's love. All's fair in love and war."

"Precious told me she had seen you that day at the mall. She showed me the doll you bought her. She also said you were getting fat, but I was too stupid to put two and two together. He smiled and pressed his palm against her as the baby leaped in her womb again. "He's an active little fellow, isn't he?"

Michelle chuckled and placed her fingers through his as she

marveled at the constant thumping of their child inside her. "He's happy to hear his father's voice."

"That must be it." Erik smiled. "He probably wants to know what my intentions are toward his mother, and I don't want to keep him waiting. We only have two weeks."

"For what?"

"To get married before he arrives. I should also tell you that I'm returning to Granite Falls," he said with a cautious tint to his voice.

"I know. Mrs. Hayes told me you put the Amherst house on the market."

"It hasn't sold yet. My parents want Precious and me to move into the LaCrosse estate with them, but I went ahead and made a deposit on a home in Granite Falls. I guess somewhere in the back of my mind, I was hoping we'd get back together eventually, and I wanted you to have your own home. Perhaps I should have waited since you'll have to give it your stamp of approval before we make any final decisions," he added.

"Tell me about it."

"It's three stories. The third floor is ours, and it's soundproof."

She chuckled. "We need soundproof. I don't know how I'm going to face my neighbors tomorrow. They've never heard these kinds of noises coming from this unit before. Well, not since I moved in here."

Erik laughed. "I'm sure they'll understand. Anyway, the house is on Crystal Lake. In addition to the master suite, it has seven bedrooms and six bathrooms, a white picket fence and a huge back yard for our seven children to play in."

"Sounds perfect."

"Would you go with me, then? I know you have the center and the kids."

"I'll go with you." Michelle brushed the pad of her thumb back and forth across his lips. "My work here is done. I got the kids a new center. I published my first book. My place is with you and our children. I love what I've already seen of Granite Falls. I want all our babies to be born and raised there. I'm ready for a fresh new start. Besides, their grandparents are there. I want Philippe and Felicia to play active roles in their lives."

Tears filled his eyes. He drew her close and kissed her. "I was hoping you'd say that."

"Erik, I need to tell you something, and I hope you won't get mad at me."

"Nothing could ever make me mad at you again."

"Well, when we were in Granite Falls, I asked Precious about her maternal grandparents. She told me that her grandpa died before she was born, but that she doesn't see her grandma because she's sick. What's going on?"

He was quiet for a long moment and when she thought he would never answer, he said in a gravelly voice, "Cassie's mother is in a mental institution in Connecticut."

Michelle closed her eyes and her mouth. Anything she said would sound trivial.

"She's been there for several years, long before Cassie died. She hears voices. After her father died, Cassie had to commit her to keep her from hurting herself. Anyway, shortly after Cassie's death, I took Precious to visit her. It was horrible. Being in that scary depressing place and seeing all those mentally ill people was too much for her. She had nightmares. I've never taken her back. But I still go down to see Sarah from time to time, even though she doesn't know I'm there. She has no other family. Cassie was her only child."

"I'm sorry."

"Life's a crapshoot and we have to play the hand fate deals us. I mean, you had a horrible childhood, but you survived to be here with me, give me a second shot at happiness."

"Erik, I know that a special part of your heart will always belong to Cassie. I'm not jealous of that. I just want to know that I have the best and the most of what's left."

"You do, baby. I love you with all the rest of me."

A warm satisfied smile spread across Michelle's face. She was blissfully happy, fully alive, wrapped in the silken cocoon of Erik's arms and his love. This time forever.

\*\*\*

*One week later...*

Dressed in her wedding gown, Michelle stood on the master suite balcony of her new home that overlooked Crystal Lake and the White Mountains in the distance. Her heart flooded with happiness as her ears were bathed in the soft music and lively chatter of the wedding guests waiting downstairs.

She'd had the choice of getting married in a church, but she'd chosen to exchange her vows in her new home—the place where her children would laugh and play and bring her joy beyond comprehension, the place where she would grow old with Erik by her side.

"You are an absolutely beautiful bride."

Michelle turned at the sound of her brother's voice. He looked dashing in his black and white tux, but she... "I'm big and fat," she said, resting her hand on her stomach.

"Looking at you from the back, nobody can tell you're pregnant."

"So should I walk backward down the aisle?"

Robert chuckled as he stepped out onto the balcony beside her. "Backward, forward, it doesn't matter. All that matters is that I walk you down the aisle. Pastor Dixon is here. Erik is getting anxious, and so are the members of your bridal party. They want to know if a wedding is really happening today."

Michelle smiled. It was a family wedding with Robert giving her away, Philippe serving as Erik's best man, Precious as her flower girl, Yasmine as her maid of honor, and Felicia insisting on being her bridesmaid. Their guest list was small, but it included the Rogers family who also lived on the lake, and of course Erik's childhood friends—the three remaining members of the Granite Falls Billionaire Bachelors Club—Bryce Fontaine, Massimo Andretti, and Adam Andreas. They had all readily accepted her as the newest member of their small circle.

"Let's get the wedding started," Michelle said, slipping her hand inside the crook of her brother's arm. "I don't want to be Michelle Carter any longer."

"Then let's go make you Michelle LaCrosse," Robert said, planting a soft kiss on her forehead.

Just the sound of that name made Michelle tingle inside and out. She was once Erik's secret bride. Today, she was his very public, happy, pregnant bride.

As she passed the huge bed where she and Erik would consummate their marriage later tonight, Michelle felt the familiar powerful throbbing in her body. They hadn't made love since the night they'd found their way back to each other. They both wanted to wait until they were remarried.

In just a few minutes, they'd have full blessings to enjoy each other again as man and wife. For some reason it seemed to her that when a man and a woman committed their lives to each other, their lovemaking became so much more satisfying.

# CHAPTER TWENTY-FOUR

Michelle bolted up in bed as a sharp pain ripped through her lower abdomen. She took deep steadying breaths like they'd taught her in the childbirth classes.

Erik sat up next to her. "What is it, baby?" He switched on the bedside lamp then searched her face in a flash of worry.

"I just had a contraction, I think."

"Is this your first one?" He caressed her back and shoulders with his big warm hands.

"I had a couple earlier, shortly after we made love."

He smiled. "Lovemaking does hasten labor. Why didn't you wake me?"

"Well, they weren't that bad, but this one cut deep and hard."

"How long ago did you have the last one?" He helped her lie back against the pillows.

She wrinkled her forehead. "About eight minutes."

"Eight minutes? We have to leave for the hospital right away, Michelle. They're too close for comfort."

"Okay, you're the expert here." Michelle allowed him to help her out of the bed and over to her dressing room where he helped her pick out a skirt and a shirt.

"You'd better wake Yasmine," she said. That should make her happy, she thought of her best friend and Lamaze coach who'd accompanied her to Granite Falls for the big day. She'd brought Peter along to keep Precious' company, only to find out that Jason Rogers, the little boy who lived nearby was fierce competition for her attention.

"And leave a note for Mrs. Hayes to make the kids banana pancakes, and to set up the tent in the backyard," she told Erik.

"You expect Mrs. Hayes to put up a tent?" Erik asked on a chuckle as he walked into his dressing room.

Michelle giggled. "I see what you mean. But I promised they could pretend they were camping in the woods." She wished she'd hired the servants Erik had suggested.

"They'll have to wait." Erik crossed the floor and pressed one of the buttons on a wall. "Yasmine, wake up, sleepyhead. It's time."

"Now?" a drowsy voice came through the intercom. "It's two o'clock in the morning. Why can't Michelle have the baby during the day like normal people?"

"I heard that," Michelle yelled. "You just wait—Aw..." she wailed as another contraction hit her.

Erik rushed to her side. He held her, and helped her breathe through it. He shook his head, his eyes dulled with worry. "They're less than five minutes apart. Come here." He led her over to the double king-size bed, laid her down, and pulled up her skirt.

"What are you doing?"

"Checking to see how much you're dilated."

"Right, you're a doctor." She smiled, leaned back against the pillows, and let him do his job. She knew he was worried about her delivery, because according to him, her pelvis was too narrow, and her uterus was tilted backward, which would make childbirth difficult. Even though he was quite capable of delivering his child by himself, he was more comfortable at the hospital in case there were any complications.

"Six centimeters," he said pulling down her skirt and helping her back on her feet.

"What does that mean?"

"That our baby is in a hurry to get here. Your water will

probably break soon." He looked around the room. "What do I do?"

Michelle rolled her eyes and shook her head. He'd just checked her, and now he was at a loss as to what to do next. "I can't believe how nervous you are. You do this everyday, for crying out loud."

"It's different when it's your own."

"Whatever," she murmured. "Just grab my bag."

"Push, darling, push. I can see his little head." Erik's voice hummed with excitement, but his hands were shaking. This was his baby. The child he had fantasized about taking from Michelle's body time and time again.

"I can't." Michelle squeezed one of Yasmine's hands while her friend dabbed at the beads of sweat on her forehead with the other. She was never going to do this again. There had to be an easier way to bring children into the world.

"You promised me a houseful of babies. So give me my child, Michelle. I want my son," Erik called from between her legs as he tried to clasp his hand around his child's slippery head.

"Come on, Michelle, just push, girl. It'll be over soon," Yasmine chimed in.

"Okay, Okay. Just one more." Michelle took a deep breath and pushed with all her strength. She felt a powerful relief between her thighs, as if she'd just pushed all her vital organs out with that bigheaded baby. She fell back weakly against the pillows.

Erik cupped his palms. Tears streamed down his cheeks as the tiny body slid into his hands. "It's a boy. It's a boy. I have a son." His heart swelled with emotion as he gazed into the little irritated face.

The attending nurse held the baby while Erik cleaned out his mouth. Once that task was completed, the baby let out a bloodcurdling scream.

"Sounds like a LaCrosse," Erik stated on a grin. He walked around to the head of the bed and placed his son into its mother's waiting arms. "Here's your firstborn, Michelle."

Completely exhausted and drenched in sweat, Michelle wept as she cradled her squirmy, red-faced little baby boy in her arms. "Oh, Erik, he's beautiful."

"No, Michelle. He is Erik Philippe LaCrosse, the third."

She chuckled, remembering how Precious had gotten her name.

Yasmine and the attending nurses left after the usual after-birth procedures were done, leaving the happy parents alone in the birthing room to bond with their child.

"You did well, Michelle," Erik said, as he gazed at his newborn, ten-pound son, cuddled snugly, and sucking hungrily at his mother's breast. He kissed her lips lingeringly as his hand caressed the soft coat of black hair on their son's head. His joy was so great, his emotions so overwhelming, tears streamed down his face. He climbed up on the bed and wrapped his arms around them, offering them his protection, his love.

"We both did well." Michelle gazed into Erik's eyes, filled with love and tenderness, so pure and sweet, it left her breathless. "And, you did say it was a boy." She stroked the baby's soft cheek. She counted his tiny toes and fingers again, and checked his ears to make sure they were both there.

"Want to take bets on the sex of the next one?" Erik asked with a warm twinkle in his gold-flecked eyes.

"I'm in no hurry to do this again any time soon. You're not coming near me for a long, long time. In fact, you'll be sleeping in one of the guest rooms on the second floor."

"Wanna bet on that one, too?" A devilish grin overtook his sexy face.

Michelle could only cut her eyes at him and smile. He was the horniest man on the planet, and she loved him.

Michelle watched Felicia and Philippe as they gazed at their sleeping grandson. She'd been moved from the birthing room to a private suite in the maternity ward of Granite Falls Memorial Hospital.

"So what have you two old love birds been up to?" she asked her in-laws.

Felicia turned. "Who're you calling old? Philippe and I could show you and Erik some moves that would make your heads spin."

"I'm sure you can," Michelle murmured, eyeing them up and down with an animated smile. She wondered from which one of them Erik had inherited his insatiable appetite for sex. Perhaps both.

"I knew what you were promising Danielle on her deathbed, last year, Michelle," Philippe said, with a tender smile. "And I knew that my son was in love with you then, too. This is a beautiful boy you've given him. He's so happy. He's already making plans for him."

Michelle smiled. She had plans for him, too.

Philippe bent over the side of the bassinet and kissed the baby's cheek. "Brings back memories?" he asked his wife.

"Many, my love, but also many regrets that we didn't raise him together."

"I know." Philippe touched his fingers to his wife's face.

Felicia sighed. "We'd better get going. Erik and Precious will be here soon. She is so excited to meet her new half-brother."

"Whole, Felicia," Michelle corrected her mother-in-law. "We are a whole family. I couldn't love Precious more if I'd given birth to her myself."

"You are a rare treasure," Philippe said. "I hope my son knows that."

"Oh, I think he does," Felicia said, giving her a goodbye kiss.

Precious and Erik arrived just moments after they left. Precious stood at the door, looking doubtful. But when Michelle beckoned to her, she flew into her arms.

"Take it easy, honey. Michelle is still a bit sore."

"It's okay, Erik." Michelle tried to camouflage her discomfort with a smile. "Love never hurt nobody. Are you okay, sweetie?" she asked Precious.

Precious nodded. "Mrs. Hayes couldn't get the tent up. But you know what?"

"What?"

"Uncle Robert came up this morning, and he put it up for us.

310

Then he took Peter and me down by the lake, and we caught a real live fish."

"That's great, honey. I'm glad Uncle Robert was there to help."

"I like him. He's wicked neat."

"Yeah. He's wicked neat," Michelle agreed with a knowing smile.

The baby started fussing.

"Is that my new brother?" Precious asked, staring at the tiny bundle in the bassinet beside the bed.

"Hmm," Michelle murmured, eyeing Erik with wary speculation. This was the moment she had been dreading, wondering if Precious would accept her new brother or if she would be jealous of him.

Precious left Michelle's embrace and edged slowly over to the bassinet. She stared at the baby for a long moment then she tilted her chin forward and said, "He looks funny, and all red and wrinkly."

Erik laughed out loud. "That's the way you looked right after you were born, Muffin. Funny, red, and wrinkly. But look at you now."

"Gross!" She gazed at the baby pensively then turned uncertain eyes to Michelle. "Michelle?"

"What, honey?" Michelle's heart pounded in her chest.

"Do you love him more than you love me?"

"No way," she replied without preamble. "I love him just as much as I love you."

Precious' eyes lit up with her smile. "I have something for him." She pushed her hands into her pocket and pulled out the lucky penny. "You're his mommy and I think he should have it."

"I think I'll hold on to that until he's old enough to appreciate it," Erik said, taking it from her. "As a matter of fact, I'll have it laminated. It's officially the LaCrosse Family Heirloom, to be passed down from one sibling to the next."

"I like that, Erik," Michelle said, smiling. That penny had brought her good luck, and Precious, too. She looked at Precious. "Would you like to hold your brother, Precious?"

"Can I?" Her cinnamon eyes widened.

"If you promise not to drop him," her father cautioned.

She shook her head. "I won't drop him. I promise."

Erik sat Precious on the side of the bed then picked up the baby and placed him cautiously on her lap. He crouched down in front of her, just in case.

"Oh, boy." Precious' eyes shone with excitement as she cradled her tiny brother. "Wait till I tell Peter."

Erik met Michelle's eyes. A warm light passed between them before they gazed lovingly at their two beautiful children.

"Michelle?" Precious had one last question.

"Yes, Precious."

"Can I call you *Mommy*?"

Michelle held her breath. She cast questioning eyes at Erik. He nodded his consent.

"Sure, baby. If that's what you want."

"Okay, Mommy."

Michelle cried happy tears. The family circle was complete. She had two wonderful children and a devoted husband to love.

"See, Daddy, I told you babies came from kissing," Precious said with a pulse-pounding certainty.

"What can I say, Muffin? You're a lot smarter than me."

Erik grinned with love and joy as he rose to his feet. He laced one arm around his wife, and the other around his children.

# EPILOGUE

Four pairs of curious eyes peered out the window as tiny snowflakes trickled lazily down from the blue skies, making a thin white blanket on the lawn.

"Here comes that rich girl and her father again." Angela was the first to break the silence as they watched the happy family emerge from the Mercedes and start up the walkway to the entrance of the center.

"The one who took our Michelle away," said a little disheartened Malcolm who still thought the sun rose and set on Michelle's brow.

"Yeah. Let's take her out back in the alley and beat her up, make her eat snow," said Clive who wanted so much to seem tough and strong, especially since the kids at his school teased him about his scarred face.

"Stop it, you fools. She ain't that bad."

Three pairs of disbelieving eyes turned to Jessica.

"You going soft on us, Jessie? You cuddling up to that rich girl now?" Malcolm asked her.

"No way, guys." Jessica thought fast and hard for a plausible explanation for her astute statement. She batted a combative eyelash. "I just learned how to use her to my advantage. That's all."

The truth was that Jessica had grown to really like Precious. She wanted to protect her like a big sister, but she didn't want the other kids to think she was soft. That was a 'no-no' around here.

"How?" asked Clive.

With an aura of supremacy, Jessica flashed the Barbie dolls she had gotten from Michelle when they had seen Precious at the mall. They still looked brand new. "Where do you think I got these? From cleaning-up-my-room money? All you have to do is be nice to Precious and Michelle will give you anything you want."

"Oh, yeah," chimed in Angela, with eager eyes. "I could use a new toy model space ship."

"Yeah." All the others murmured, neon dollar signs flashing brightly in their little, devilish eyes.

Just then the door opened and the LaCrosse family entered, bring with them a puff of the frigid New England winter air.

"Hi, Michelle. Hi, Precious. Hi, Dr. LaCrosse." The children sang in rehearsed chorus, facetious smiles on their faces.

Michelle set the baby carrier on a metal desk, and removed the blanket from his sleeping face. She stroked his black curls. Erik made himself busy unfolding the playpen. Precious stood next to her father and watched the children dubiously, Bradie clutched tightly in her arms.

Finally, Erik turned to Michelle and placed a warm kiss on her upturned lips. "See you at five o'clock. We have dinner reservations at that new Italian restaurant."

"We'll be ready." She smiled with sheer warmth and love. In a few days, they were taking the LaCrosse jet to the Seychelles Islands off the east coast of Africa where they would spend three warm weeks at the luxurious Hotel Andreas. It was their long overdue honeymoon. She would miss her children something awful, but she and Erik had never had time alone away from everyone and everything. The kids would be in good hands with Mrs. Hayes and their grandparents to take care of their every need.

Michelle's smile widened. She couldn't wait to tell Erik that he was going to be a father again. That shouldn't surprise him. Not at the rate they'd been going at each other. They made love every chance they got—even in Erik's office at the hospital, numerous times when he'd asked her to bring him lunch. After she'd returned home with the second picnic basket unopened, Mrs. Hayes had figured out that she wasn't going to the hospital to eat. Well, she was going to eat, but not the delicious sandwiches the old lady prepared.

They were still trying to make up for the nine months they'd lost while she had been carrying Little Erik. She would make certain that this time Erik experience all the joy and pains that came with impending fatherhood. She was also grateful that she wasn't experiencing any of the sickness she'd had in her first trimester with little Erik. She supposed it was because she wasn't under any stress this time. Only love, happiness, and contentment lived in her heart.

Erik turned to Precious, his arms wide. "A kiss for your old man, Muffin?"

"Daddy, not here. And stop calling me Muffin," Precious mumbled under her breath.

Erik stifled a laugh and turned to his seven-month-old son. His daughter was growing up. "Well, Slugger, you're in charge. Take good care of our women until I get back to pick them up." He brushed his knuckles against his son's smooth tawny cheek then kissed him on the forehead, his heart bursting with love and protection.

Little Erik raised dark lids, lined with long ebony lashes, and stared at his father through piercing grey eyes. He flashed him a two-teeth grin.

Erik grinned then turned to Michelle again. She looked damned sweet in jeans and a light blue sweater. Her hair was dark and short as ever. Her eyes shone like black marble, forever fiery. She was just as slender as the day he met her and just as wild. She still smelled of *Moonlight*. He loved her. He kissed her again, and she welcomed him. Well, at least one of the females in his harem wasn't ashamed to kiss him in public.

He knew she was pregnant again. Due to the chemical

changes in her body, she tasted differently lately, and her vaginal walls were softer and moister. He knew the feel of a pregnant woman. He smiled, wondering if she knew, yet. He hoped it was a daughter this time—a little girl who would look just like her beautiful mother. With that happy thought, Erik made a hasty exit.

The children circled Precious. "Hi, Precious, you wanna play with us?" Malcolm asked.

"Sure." Precious smiled as the little rascals led her away.

Michelle eyed Jessica with mild suspicion. The kids resented Precious because Michelle was now her mother. The house on Jefferson Drive had finally sold and they'd driven down from Granite Falls for the closing. Even though she had her own family now, Michelle visited the children as often as she could. She could never abandon them, no matter how busy her life had become. The children didn't know it yet, but she was planning to take her favorites up to Granite Falls for a weekend of skiing and fun when she returned from her honeymoon—that is if their parents granted permission.

She had seven bedrooms and six baths, an indoor swimming pool, a home theatre, and a humongous playroom stacked with all sorts of toys and games, and Mrs. Hayes to fuss over them. There was plenty to keep them occupied.

"Why are they so nice to Precious all of a sudden?" she asked Jessica.

Jessica shrugged. "I have no idea." They would all come to like Precious just as much as she did, she thought with a curt smile. The rich girl wasn't half bad after all. She was a decent human being despite the fact she had tons of money. Yeah, Precious would steal their hearts.

She was after all, *Precious*.

## The End

𝓡

# FROM THE DESK OF ANA E ROSS

Dear Reader,
I hope you enjoyed following Erik and Michelle on their journey to love and *Happily Ever After* in **The Doctor's Secret Bride**.

Reviews, comments, and 'likes' would be most appreciated.

www.AnaERoss.com
www.facebook.com/Ana-E-Ross
Twitter@anaeross

Until our paths cross again in Granite Falls, enjoy an excerpt from **The Mogul's Reluctant Bride – Book 2** in *The Billionaire Brides of Granite Falls* series.

Fondly,
Ana

# THE MOGUL'S RELUCTANT BRIDE
## BOOK TWO

## CHAPTER ONE

"There must be some mistake, Steven." Kaya Brehna's hands tightened around the arm of the chair.

"I really wish there was, Kaya."

"They— they left nothing?"

"Nothing," the man behind the mahogany desk reiterated with a shake of his head.

Kaya pressed an unsteady hand to her chest. Her heart raced with fear and her mind swam in a pool of confusion and uncertainty. Even though she'd never had a close relationship with Lauren, when Steven had called with the news of her sister and brother-in-law's deaths, and that they had named her guardian of their children, Kaya had dropped everything to be with her nephew and two nieces.

Up until a minute ago, she had every reason to believe that nine-year-old Jason, four-year-old Alyssa, and two-month-old Anastasia were financially secure. She hadn't met the children until yesterday, but the minute she saw them, Kaya knew she could never abandon them. She was all set to put her life on hold to nurse them through this most grievous time of their lives, but how on earth could she do that after what the executor of Michael and Lauren's will just told her?

*They died bankrupt.*

*Nothing made any sense.*

Forcing back the hysteria in her throat, Kaya struggled to her feet and braced her hands against the edge of the desk. "Steven, I've worked in the homes of some of the wealthiest people in Florida. I know money when I see it. That three-story, eight-bedroom mansion my sister lived in is worth millions, yet, you're telling me she died penniless?"

"I'm sorry to give you more bad news, Kaya, but, yes, those are the facts I'm afraid." His tone was apologetic as if he was the one who had caused her dilemma.

"Well, in light of that, Steven, I can't stay in Granite Falls now. I have no choice but to return to Palm Beach and take the children with me."

Steven rose and strolled around the desk. "I'm aware that you and your sister weren't very close, Kaya, and that there are events about her life you may not be aware of. But I was Michael and Lauren's friend as well as their attorney, and if there's one thing I do know, it's that they would not want you to take their children to Florida. Granite Falls is their home."

"*Was*, Steven. *Was*." Kaya threw her hands up in frustration. "Everything is changed now. I was willing to settle down in Granite Falls, put my life on hold for a while until they got used to me as their caregiver, but that option is off the table. My career in Palm Beach is the only fighting chance I have to provide a decent living for all of us."

"I understand the financial dilemma you're facing, but it wouldn't be wise to uproot the children so soon after the loss of their parents. They have ties in Granite Falls. Ties that shouldn't be severed at this precarious time of their lives."

"And their strongest tie is Bryce Fontaine, I suppose," she said rather grudgingly. Bryce was the children's godfather, and from what Kaya had learned from friends of the family who were gathered at the house when she arrived yesterday, he was a very present figure in the children's lives.

"Bryce is a big part of their lives," Steven voiced her thoughts out loud. "Despite the fact that you are their aunt and only living relative, they will need him to get them through this tragedy. He has been like a second father to them ever since they were born, and now that Michael is gone, they will need him more than ever."

Kaya tried to ignore the insinuations in Steven's words. She needed no reminders that the children didn't know her, that they'd never met her until yesterday. If only she'd been more congenial toward her sister, met her halfway. A few weeks ago, Lauren had invited her up to celebrate Michael's fiftieth birthday. She'd agreed to come, and they'd promised to take care of her travel arrangements. But unable to get past her juvenile sibling resentment, she'd reneged at the last minute. If she'd come up like she'd promised, she would have seen her sister and met Michael and the kids, but she hadn't.

"When is Bryce coming back?" she asked Steven. She was still to meet this Bryce who'd been on a skiing trip in Switzerland the day Michael and Lauren died.

"His jet could be landing anytime soon. You know what that means for Jason." His brows drew together and his blue eyes clouded with unease. "I can't force you to stay in Granite Falls, Kaya. I can only strongly advise that you consider sticking with your initial plans to remain here, at least for now."

Kaya walked over to the window and stared out across the parking lot. She felt as listless as the wind-blown snowflakes tumbling aimlessly to the ground. Steven was right about keeping the children in a familiar environment, around familiar faces. But what was she to do? They were destitute. Returning to Florida was her only option. Even there, with three children to support, she could still end up broke like Michael and Lauren.

Kaya never anticipated that her life could spiral out of control so quickly and unexpectedly. There was only one other time in her life when she'd been this scared—the day she saw her father for the last time.

She raised a hand to her chest and closed her fingers around the locket that her father had given her when she was five years old—the one with the code to a safety deposit box. Her father had instructed her not to go to the bank until she was eighteen, and now even after five years, Kaya was still awed at the contents of that safe.

She'd had the jewel appraised, and almost fainted when she learned how much it was worth. Her father had left a letter explaining how he'd come into possession of the gem. He'd written that he wanted her to know that it wasn't stolen. Unsure of what to do with it, Kaya had just left it alone. Had her father given Lauren a similar gem? Had Lauren sold her inheritance to purchase *L'etoile du Nord,* her multimillion-dollar estate? Had she squandered the rest on an extravagant lifestyle that she couldn't maintain?

Kaya sighed as the questions surged through her mind. Steven was right again. There was so much about her sister's life she didn't know. What she did know was that the contents in that safe was all she had of her father's memory, the only tangible bond she had to her ancestry. She couldn't bear the thought of parting with it, even though it would solve her newly acquired financial problems and set her and the children up for life. But that was asking too much. It wasn't fair that she should have to spend her inheritance on Lauren's children. She had preserved her heirloom while Lauren had wasted hers on a big...

Kaya turned from the window as the only other solution took root in her mind. "The estate," she said walking back over to Steven. "It's worth millions, hopefully more than Michael and Lauren owed their creditors. If I sell the estate, I can—"

"Um, Kaya, you can't sell that estate."

"Why not? Don't tell me there's a lien against it." That faint thread of hysteria was back in her voice. If their father had given Lauren the same kind of gem he had given her, Lauren could have paid cash for the estate. Did she mortgage it off to sustain her luxurious lifestyle?

"No. There's no lien against it," Steven said.

Kaya breathed a sigh of relief. "Well then, why can't I sell it?"

"Because it didn't belong to Michael and Lauren. It doesn't belong to the children."

Kaya's mouth dropped open. "What do you mean it didn't—doesn't belong to them? If it isn't their estate, then whose is it?"

"Mine. *L'etoile du Nord* belongs to me," came a rumbling voice behind her.

Kaya spun around, her heart flying to her throat when her eyes collided with the powerful bronze body of the man standing on a pair of legs that would make a Viking proud.

*Bryce Fontaine, New England's business mogul—CEO and president of Fontaine Enterprises—in the flesh.*

He was far more handsome than his pictures portrayed, she thought, staring in admiration as he bent his snow-dusted head to get his large frame through the door.

The ample shoulders, stretching beneath a dark-green sweater, the sharp chin, and generous mouth all spoke of power and resolute strength. The man possessed a captivating presence and an air of authority that made you stop and take note when he entered a room. She was taking note—a lot of notes.

If Kaya had to sum Bryce Fontaine up in one word, it would be *"intimidating"*.

A tingling sensation generated in Kaya's belly and traveled south to her thighs, and then to her knees, making them go weak. She slumped against the edge of the desk and tried to bring her escalated breathing under control.

Steven walked over and met him near the door. Even Steven—who was about six feet, two inches tall—had to roll his head back to face the giant as they talked in low voices.

Steven had called Bryce the night of the tragedy, but a blizzard in the Alps had delayed his return. He must have flown all night, Kaya thought, taking in his stubbled chin and disheveled appearance that made him seem even more imposing.

When Kaya had enquired about the hunk in her sister's family pictures, Libby—Steven's fiancée, and a close friend of the family—had given her a short version of his accomplishments.

Bryce Fontaine had started out in real estate—buying up a substantial amount of land in Granite Falls and the neighboring towns, then quickly expanded to the rest of the business world. He devoured companies from glass blowing to computer software programing, and as he'd just claimed, he also owned the estate on which her sister lived.

Seemed like the man owned the entire town, she thought, recalling driving by the Youth Performing Arts Center, Granite Falls Towers, and Country Club, to name a few buildings and skyscrapers that bore his name. His signature was everywhere in Granite Falls. He'd even built an airport with a runway long enough to accommodate his private jets and those of his friends,

Libby had told her.

As if sensing her scrutiny, he turned his head and pinned her with a calculating stare. Breathless seconds ticked by before he stepped around Steven and headed in her direction. A compelling energy seemed to coil within him at each step he took.

Forcing her legs to support her, Kaya pushed off the desk as he came to a stop and towered over her. His gaze was bold and penetrating. His eyes, enigmatic and unfathomable were like midnight's deepest black. As she gazed up at him, Kaya had the dizzying sensation of falling into blackness. She'd never felt so susceptible to a man in all her life. He could reach out and take a hold of her, do anything he wanted to her this very moment, and there was not a damn thing she'd be able to do about it. Vitality zinged through her bloodstream even as her body began to shiver from an unfamiliar awareness. How could she feel this vivacious and weak at the same time? Kaya wondered, as she once again leaned on the desk for support.

*If he could cause her to lose control of her motor skills by just looking at her, then God help her.*

"Bryce," Steven said, coming to stand next to the titan, "this is Lauren's sister, Kaya Brehna. Kaya, Bryce Fontaine."

# OTHER WORKS BY ANA E ROSS:

**Billionaire Brides of Granite Falls Series:**

The Mogul's Reluctant Bride – Book Two – May 2013
The Playboy's Fugitive Bride – Book Three – January 2014
The Tycoon's Temporary Bride – Book Four – November 2014

**Short Stories:**
Her Perfect Valentine Birthday Surprise
The Brit Who Loved Her
When Amber Got Her Groove Back

Visit Ana at:
www.AnaERoss.com